# THE SAINT

of

# WOLVES

and

# BUTCHERS

## ALSO BY ALEX GRECIAN

### SCOTLAND YARD'S MURDER SQUAD SERIES

NOVELS

*The Yard*

*The Black Country*

*The Devil's Workshop*

*The Harvest Man*

*Lost and Gone Forever*

NOVELLAS

*The Blue Girl*

# THE SAINT

of

# WOLVES

and

# BUTCHERS

ALEX GRECIAN

G. P. PUTNAM'S SONS
NEW YORK

G. P. PUTNAM'S SONS

*Publishers Since 1838*

An imprint of Penguin Random House LLC

375 Hudson Street

New York, New York 10014

Copyright © 2018 by Alexander Grecian

Penguin supports copyright. Copyright fuels creativity, encourages
diverse voices, promotes free speech, and creates a vibrant culture. Thank you
for buying an authorized edition of this book and for complying with copyright
laws by not reproducing, scanning, or distributing any part of it in any
form without permission. You are supporting writers and allowing
Penguin to continue to publish books for every reader.

Library of Congress Cataloging-in-Publication Data

Names: Grecian, Alex, author.
Title: The saint of wolves and butchers / Alex Grecian.
Description: New York : G. P. Putnam's Sons, [2018]
Identifiers: LCCN 2017012118 | ISBN 9780399176111 (hardcover) |
ISBN 9780698407275 (ebook)
Subjects: LCSH: War criminals—Fiction. | GSAFD: Suspense fiction.
Classification: LCC PS3607.R4292 S25 2018 | DDC 813/.6—dc23
LC record available at https://lccn.loc.gov/2017012118
p.      cm.

Printed in the United States of America
1   3   5   7   9   10   8   6   4   2

BOOK DESIGN BY MEIGHAN CAVANAUGH

*For Melanie and Kevin*

"The more I get to know people, the more I like dogs."

—HEINRICH HEINE

PART ONE

THE BEAST
of
BURDEN COUNTY

## AUGUST 1951

He came up from South America by bus. At the border between
Mexico and Arizona, he bought a train ticket and rode through
the night and well into the next day. A long arc through New
Mexico, across the southeast tip of Colorado, and most of the way up
through Kansas. He had nothing with him but his clothes and a small
overnight bag.

And a new name.

He had been born Rudolph Bormann, but the name on his passport
was Rudy Goodman. Rudy. A solid American name.

He kept to himself on the train, but the railroad employed a nurse,
and the conductor brought her to Rudy. He had a compartment to
himself, with a narrow bed that folded out of the wall. The nurse
arrived as the sun was setting and pushed her way in as soon as he
answered the knock at his door, overwhelming his objections with her
efficiency and her aggressively sympathetic manner. She was a big
woman, healthy and strong, with strawberry hair and a fetching over-
bite. She didn't tell him her name, and he didn't ask. She helped him
wash up and she stitched the cut above his temple, which had been
bleeding into his ear all the way north through Mexico. Six stitches

and a sticky bandage. When he thanked her in his pidgin English, she shook her head and smiled.

*"Sei still!"* she said. Her German was slightly better than his American.

He tried to pay her, took a roll of bills from his pocket, all the money he had with him, and peeled one off the outside. He held it out to her, but she shook her head again.

When she had left, he slid the window open an inch and breathed the soot-filled air. He undressed and lay on his back, listening to the rhythmic chug of the wheels. He allowed himself to relax then, his eyelids growing heavy as the locomotive swayed beneath him, bearing him to freedom.

Later that night the door creaked open and he woke. Yellow light from the passage spilled across him, then disappeared, and a moment later the nurse climbed on top of him in the dark. The bed's hinges creaked in protest. The scent of rubbing alcohol and cheap perfume filled his nostrils.

*"Wie?"*

*"Sei still,"* she said again, her lips brushing against his good ear.

When next he woke, a predawn glow filtered through the sheer curtains over the window, casting the compartment in flat shades of purple, and he was alone.

He disembarked in Phillipsburg, just south of the Nebraska border, and stood nervous by the tracks, which cut across a dirt road and disappeared around a curve behind a stand of stunted elm trees. The train chuffed away, taking with it the fragrant nurse and his roll of bills, which he did not miss until much later that day.

It was August, and there were no clouds in the sky, nothing between the sun and the scrubby brown grass but shimmering heat waves. Rudy's head hurt where the nurse had stitched it, a dull throbbing pain that was almost a noise. After ten minutes, a plume of dust and blue smoke appeared in the distance, coming from the direction the train had gone, and a truck lumbered into sight over a slight rise in the earth. It was the color of mustard, battered and rusty with peeling wooden sides. It stopped in front of him with a bang and a whimper, and Rudy saw that the tailgate was wooden, too, what was left of it. A slat was missing from one side, and yellow paint peeled away from the truck's hood.

The driver's-side door creaked open and a man jumped down, came around the front of the truck with his hand out.

"Jacob Meyer," the man said. He was smiling, short and wiry with thinning hair. Nearing forty but with the jittery energy of a teenager. Rudy liked him right away. They shook hands.

"I am Rudy Goodman." It was the first time he had said the name aloud, and he said it again, listening to the cadence of it. "Rudy Goodman." It still sounded authentically American to him.

"Sorry I'm late, Rudy," Jacob Meyer said. "This ol' girl picked a hell of a morning not to start. Had to change the plugs again already. I only just changed 'em in June."

Rudy nodded, but he didn't understand. He only wanted to be agreeable.

Jacob took Rudy's overnight bag from him and started for the pickup truck, but stopped and turned and looked at him for a long moment, his head cocked to one side like a dog listening to its master. "You're really him?"

"*Ja.*"

"I'll be damned." Jacob shook his head and whistled, then turned away again and dropped the bag in the bed of the truck. He hustled to the passenger-side door and held it open, slammed it shut when Rudy was safely in, then ran around to the other side and hopped up into the cab.

"Didn't turn it off this time, so don't have to worry about it stalling," Jacob said. "See, I can learn, can't I? You just see if I can't." He put the truck in gear and it lurched forward with a loud farting noise and another cloud of blue smoke. Jacob grinned at him, and Rudy smiled back. The dull throb in his temple had receded.

"Where are we . . . To where?" These weren't quite the right words, Rudy knew, but he hoped his meaning was clear enough.

"We got a place fixed up for you out in Paradise Flats," Jacob said. "You understand me good enough? I can talk German, but it's better if you use English now. You'll pick it up."

Rudy nodded.

"Good, good," Jacob said. "It ain't much, the house we got for you, but it's free and clear. Belongs to Don Veitch, but he moved into an apartment closer to the city when his wife died. Easier on his knees without all them stairs and havin' to go up and down all the time. Anyway, he don't live in it now, so it's yours long as you want it."

"How many?"

"What? I don't . . . Oh, how many of us are there? *Die Gemeinschaft*. Well . . ." Jacob fell silent and stared out the dirty windshield, drummed his hands on the wheel. "I wish it was more," he said. "Sad to say it's just seven of us in Paradise Flats, five others besides myself and Don. Used to be more, but folks kinda drifted away over the last couple years, you know? It's hard to keep 'em here."

Rudy understood all too well.

The truck picked up speed, bumping over ruts and clumps of hard dried mud. A grasshopper thumped against the glass and disappeared, leaving behind a messy white smear.

Watching out the window, Rudy saw a flash of gray fur among the vegetation.

"I think I saw a wolf," he said. "In English?"

"They're called wolves in English, too," Jacob said. "But there ain't a lot of those around here. You probably saw a coyote."

"I think it was a wolf."

"Fair enough."

Rudy waited again until Jacob glanced his way. "Jacob," he said. "This is a good start."

Rudy Goodman, formerly Rudolph Bormann, assistant administrator of the Mauthausen-Gusen concentration camp, looked out the window of the pickup truck. He looked out across infinite rolling fields and pastures, all the way to the thin black line of the horizon. He was twenty-seven years old that summer, and America stretched out all around him, a land of boundless opportunity.

# CHAPTER ONE

Trooper Skottie Foster refilled her coffee and gave the counter-
man a nod, headed back out to her vehicle. She snugged her
cup down into the well next to her and pulled her Explorer
around to the west side of the 24/7 Travel Store, where a bright green
Toyota pickup sat low on its back tires in the lot. She filled out a
tow report form on the computer mounted between the Explorer's
seats and pulled up OpenFox, the software used by the department to
run tag checks. She stepped out and approached the vehicle on the
driver's side.

Thanksgiving was three days away, and the sky was flat and gray.
Dizzy snowflakes eddied about, but there was no breeze, and she was
sweating under her heavy uniform jacket.

Skottie had been with the Kansas Highway Patrol for nearly six
months, transferred in from Illinois. She'd grown up in Kansas, had
left at the first opportunity, started her career and a family in Chicago. Now she was back, living in her mother's house and hoping for
a fresh start, for a stable environment for her daughter, for some distance from everything that had recently gone wrong in her life.

She had been required to go through twenty-two weeks of retraining after returning to Kansas, and she had used the time to adjust to her new circumstances. Back on active duty, she had been surprised to discover she was one of only a handful of female troopers in western Kansas, and one of three African Americans, but despite the usual stumbling blocks that came with any new position, she had encountered very little hostility or disrespect. She was tall, five feet nine inches, and slim, with skin the exact shade and color of her eyes. She kept her carefully braided hair pulled back low against her neck so that she could position her hat properly when regulations demanded that she appear in full uniform.

She had been watching the Toyota for two days as she made her rounds and had seen no one approach it. The wheel wells were crusted with rust and the paint had peeled off along one side, leaving a dappled surface like a bruise. There was a toolbox tucked up under the back window in the bed of the truck, big and heavy, long enough to hide a body inside.

She peered through the window to make sure the cab was empty. The driver's-side door was unlocked, and she pulled it open, releasing a heavy odor of must and disuse. The radio had been pulled from the dash, the mats had been taken from the floor, the glove box was open and empty. She wrote down the VIN from the inside of the door and closed it, then walked around to the back and flipped open the toolbox. An ancient ball-peen hammer, a length of bicycle chain, a cheap pair of rusty pliers, blue rubber crumbling away from the handles. She closed the box and went back to her vehicle.

She plugged the tag number into OpenFox and it spit out the VIN, which she checked against her notes, and the name of the truck's registered owner: Wes Weber. She unhooked her radio and called the information in to Sarah, the dispatcher in Norton.

A small stack of postcards was clipped to the back of the Explorer's sun visor. She pulled one off the top and filled it out with Wes Weber's address and a short note, letting him know his truck was being towed from the rest stop and where he could claim it. A moment later, Sarah called back.

"Norton to One-Eleven?"

"Here," Skottie said.

"Wrong case number on that."

Skottie frowned and checked her notes. "I see it."

"Go ahead with the last three."

She read off the corrected case number and hung the handset back up, set the postcard on the seat beside her, and put the Explorer in gear. Sarah would call the tow company and Skottie would drop the postcard in a mailbox at the end of her shift. She guessed Wes Weber would not show up to claim his property. The Toyota wouldn't bring much at auction and was undoubtedly destined for a scrap yard somewhere.

She headed toward the westbound ramp to the highway, but slowed when she saw a vehicle parked on the shoulder, its hazards blinking. She pulled in behind it and lit up the blue and red array atop her Explorer. A little boy waved at her from the back window as she put her hat on. She walked up to the driver's side, where a Hispanic woman was already rolling down the window, a sheepish grin on her face. A baby crawled across the back seat, clutching a french fry in one chubby fist, a stringer of drool dangling from its chin. The little boy was yelling at the baby in Spanish.

"Sorry, Officer," the woman said.

"What's the trouble?"

"Just need a second." The woman turned her head and yelled at the boy. "Hurry up and get her in her seat." She turned back to Skottie. "She got out. Wanted a fry."

Skottie nodded, watching the boy wrestle the baby girl up into the car seat behind the driver. The baby was oblivious, eyes only for the mangled french fry that circled her open mouth, waiting patiently for contact. Fast food as incitement for developing motor skills.

She leaned forward and caught the boy's eye. "What's your name?"

He looked up, his eyes wide, as if he'd been caught in a criminal act, and the french fry went up his nose. The baby started to laugh, and the boy looked at her and smiled. He looked back at Skottie, the fry still dangling. "My name is Miguel."

"You take care of your sister, Miguel." The fry dropped into his lap and the baby laughed again.

"She's not my sister. She's my niece."

Skottie looked at him.

"But I'll take good care of her, ma'am," Miguel said.

Skottie saluted him and turned back to his mother, or maybe she was his sister. "Don't proceed until the children are secured, okay?"

"I won't, Officer. Don't worry," the woman said. "It's why I'm pulled over in the first place."

Behind her, a black Jeep Wrangler zoomed down the ramp. She caught a brief glimpse of a man behind the wheel and someone in the passenger seat that she first thought was another big man wearing a fur coat. Staring at the license plate—it was a rental—she belatedly realized the passenger wasn't human.

Skottie focused her gaze on the woman in front of her and the two struggling children. Miguel had stuck the french fry back in his nose, but his niece was no longer amused.

"All right, ma'am," Skottie said. "Travel safe now."

She walked quickly back to her vehicle and turned off the array, pulled around the woman's idling car, and accelerated out onto I-70. She saw the Jeep again five minutes later, parked at a rest stop west of

Russell. A man in a gray peacoat was standing near the passenger side with the door open. Skottie pulled into the lot and coasted along the low wooden fence that bordered a tree-lined oasis with restrooms, a few vending machines, and a big grassy field for drivers to stroll and stretch their legs. There were no other vehicles in sight, but a dog was running back and forth at the far end of the field. It was hard to gauge the dog's size from a distance, but it had a bushy black mane and looked for all the world like a lion.

When he saw her, the man stepped back from the Jeep and smiled. He put his hands out at waist level and stood very still. He might have been a statue, something carved out of marble. He was very tall and very thin. His face was angular and unlined, and she would have guessed he was roughly thirty-five years old, except for his carefully tousled gray hair. He wore a light gray cardigan under his coat, charcoal slacks that matched his hair, and black shoes polished to a sheen.

Skottie flicked on the array and stopped behind the Jeep, blocking it from pulling out. She put on her wide-brimmed hat again and adjusted the strap under her chin, then opened her door and stepped down onto the pavement. "Move away from the vehicle please, sir."

The man took one more step backward. "There is a weapon in my vehicle, Officer, but I have a license for it." His voice was deep and guttural, barely more than a whisper.

She glanced through the open passenger door and saw a handgun lying on the seat, a semiautomatic pistol. She put her hand on the butt of her Taser.

The dog was approaching fast, and the man lowered his left hand, extending his index finger. The dog saw the signal and came to an abrupt halt. Up close, Skottie could see it was huge, easily a hundred and forty pounds of muscle and fur and long yellow teeth.

"Do you have a leash for that animal, sir?"

"I do, Officer. Inside the Jeep." The man kept his hands where Skottie could see them, but inclined his head in the direction of his rental car.

"Is your ID in the Jeep, too?"

"No," the man said. "That is in my wallet." He raised his eyebrows and held his hands farther out from his body, silently asking permission.

"Go ahead," Skottie said.

The man slowly took his wallet from the breast pocket of his coat and found three laminated cards, held them out for Skottie to take. "License for the firearm is there, too."

"Is that gun loaded?"

"It is, but it has a grip safety. I have two spare magazines for it in the back of the Jeep."

"Thank you, sir. State law requires you to have your dog on a leash at all times." She stood at the back of the Jeep where she could easily see the pistol on the seat. She kept one hand on the butt of the Taser on her belt.

"Bear is very well trained. The dog's name is Bear. He needed to run. Between the flight here and the car ride, he has been rather cooped up all day."

"I understand that, sir," Skottie said. She shifted from one foot to the other. "Good-looking animal. Pretty."

"He prefers to be thought of as handsome," the man said. He stole a glance over his shoulder at the dog, who had crept forward while they were talking. Skottie judged that Bear was now just outside the range of her Taser. There was no way she was fast enough to draw her weapon before the massive dog could reach her. The man made another small motion with his left hand and Bear stopped moving.

"Can you make him lie down?"

14

"Certainly," the man said. "Bear, *suben*."

Bear immediately dropped to his belly. He was panting hard, showing his fangs, but when he looked up at Skottie, she was impressed by the intelligence in his clear brown eyes.

"Trust me, you have nothing to fear from Bear. He respects the law."

"Then he ought to wear a leash," Skottie said. She glanced at the driver's license. "I'll be right back, Mr. Roan."

"It's Doctor." He smiled at her. "Technically I am Dr. Roan. But please call me Travis."

"Dr. Roan, go ahead and get your leash. But leave the weapon where it is on the seat." Skottie walked back to her vehicle with the cards.

Travis Roan walked around the front of the Jeep to the driver's side, where Skottie could still see him and where the gun was out of easy reach. Keeping things civilized, keeping her happy. She guessed he'd had plenty of experience with the police, and she wondered which side of the law he'd been on. While she watched, Roan reached behind the seat and came out with a tether, which he held up for her to see. He motioned to Bear, who trotted over and accepted the leash with grace. Roan leaned against the side of the Jeep and Bear settled down on the blacktop at his feet, and they waited while Skottie called in the rental's license plate and ran Travis Roan's ID on the dash-mounted computer.

After several long minutes she opened her door. Bear jumped up, but Travis put a hand out, palm down, and the dog sat again, his tongue lolling. Skottie watched Bear from the corner of her eye as she approached them.

"Everything looks in order, Dr. Roan," she said. "Can I ask what you're doing in Kansas?"

"Hunting."

"What're you after?"

Roan hesitated. "Deer," he said. "Maybe some pheasant, if it is in season."

"Sir, I don't know what it's like where you're from, but a handgun isn't the best weapon for hunting deer. Or birds, either."

"I do not like traveling with a rifle or a bow. It requires extra preparation and creates difficulty. I am hoping to purchase a proper weapon when I reach my destination."

"And where's that?"

"I have yet to decide. I thought I might see the sights while I am here."

"What sights are those, sir?"

Roan looked down at his dog as if Bear might remember something about the state they were visiting. "Dodge City?"

"Are you asking me, sir?"

"No," Roan said. "Dodge City, Kansas. Historic cowboy town, right? I am a fan of American Westerns. Dodge City is where *Gunsmoke* was set, is it not?"

"I wouldn't know," Skottie said. "Never saw it. But if you wanted to see Dodge City, you probably should've turned south on 156 a few miles back."

"I missed my turn?"

"If you were going to Dodge City." She fixed him with a hard stare.

Roan hesitated again, and his smile disappeared. "Very well then. May I get something from my bag? It might help matters here."

She was both amused and mildly alarmed by his formal way of speaking. "Your bag?"

"From the back of the Jeep." He inclined his head toward the rental. "Not a weapon. Nothing to alarm you. But it may be easier to explain what I am doing here if I show you some documentation."

"Sir, I'm not interested in anything except making sure you travel safe and don't present a danger to anyone else."

"Exactly," Travis said. "I can see that I have misjudged you, and now you think it possible that Bear and I present a danger. So long as I remain in your jurisdiction—"

"My zone."

"Yes, your zone. I am afraid that, even if you allow me to continue through your zone, you will alert the next man down the line and I will eventually have to explain myself to someone. More police will stop me. Am I wrong?"

"I can't speak for anybody else, sir." She rested her palm on the butt of her Taser again.

"I had planned to present myself to the authorities when I got where I am going, but I had hoped for more time to gather information. You have forced my hand."

"What kind of information?"

He shrugged.

"You can get your bag," Skottie said, "but move very slowly. Be careful here."

"Of course. I mean you no harm." He moved to the back of the Jeep and opened the hatch door. He looked back and raised his eyebrows at Skottie, then leaned slowly inside, unzipped his bag, and reached into it without taking his eyes off her. Skottie was watching the dog. Bear's reflexes would be faster than Roan's. She was ready to zap the dog first. But Bear licked his muzzle and grinned up at her, and Roan turned around and showed her a thick manila file folder.

"See?" he said. "Only paper."

Skottie withdrew her hand from the Taser and took the folder from him. She opened it and glanced at the top sheet, which was a letter of introduction from the Noah Roan Foundation in San Diego. There was an insignia embossed in silver foil at the top of the page: the letters *N*, *R*, and *F*, all intertwined in a cursive script. She looked back up at him.

"Same as your name," she said.

"My grandfather started the Foundation. I suppose you might call me a legacy." He smiled, but didn't get a smile from her in return. "Your name is Foster?"

She looked down at the name tag on her uniform: S. M. Foster. She indicated the folder. "What is this?"

"There is a woman—"

"The short version, please," Skottie said. She wasn't looking at the paperwork, but up at him. His smile didn't touch his eyes, but she didn't sense any malice. She hoped she was as good a judge of people as she thought she was.

"A few weeks ago, a woman saw someone here in Kansas, someone she had not seen in seventy years."

"Long time. People change."

"The circumstances . . . This woman—her name is Ruth Elder— she was in Germany during the Second World War. A camp there. The man she saw earlier this year was at the camp, too. But he was not a prisoner."

"A guard?"

"Something like that. Administration, she thinks. A paper-pusher."

"A Nazi," Skottie said.

"Yes. If it is indeed him, he was a Nazi."

"I guess I assumed they were all dead by now."

"He would be in his nineties now, at least, but it is possible he is still alive."

"And she's sure it was him. Like I said . . ."

"Yes. You are quite right. Often people are mistaken. They think they see a ghost from their past, but it is their memory playing tricks on them."

"And that's why you're here? To take a look and make sure it's really him?"

Travis held out his hand, his index finger and thumb an inch away from each other. "There is something more."

"You're here to kill him," Skottie said.

"Kill him? No."

"Wait. You said she saw him weeks ago."

"Approximately."

"And it took you this long to come out here to make sure?"

"That is the other thing. I am not the first person the Foundation has sent here. Another came before me. He has not communicated with anyone in more than a week."

"Something happened to him?"

"That is what worries me. Why I wanted more information before talking to the authorities."

"Have you filed a missing person report?"

"With whom would I do that? He is a grown man. If he wants to stop talking to us, that is his prerogative, is it not? Besides, I do not know what he was doing when he vanished, or where he was. Somewhere in Kansas, but where? Should I contact the police in Topeka? In Wichita? How would they help me? What could they do?"

"How long was he here before he disappeared?"

"Three days. Not longer than that."

"So it still took a long time before anyone came out here to see if we have a Nazi on our hands."

"It is a process. There are legalities and there is paperwork that must be filed. And there are not a lot of us left in the field, not a lot left who actually track these . . . these bad people. I was in Africa when Ruth Elder saw a Nazi here. It took me some time to extricate myself. Otherwise it might have been me who came first. Perhaps *I* would have vanished."

"You were hunting Nazis in Africa?"

"No," Travis said. "It is as you say. There are not many Nazis left alive. Not enough to make it a full-time job."

"So you hunt Nazis for a hobby?" Skottie raised one eyebrow.

"Not a hobby, no. But I must do other things, find other bad people when there are no Nazis to look for."

Skottie handed the file folder back to him without having looked past the topmost page. "Look," she said, "I can't let you run around playing Batman. You're not breaking any laws by being here, not yet, but—"

"I am not a vigilante," Travis said. He set the file folder down next to his bag in the back of the Jeep and raised his hands again in a placating gesture. "I am not here to hurt anyone, not even a Nazi. I must find my . . . my colleague. And I must talk to Ruth Elder. Hopefully she will lead me to both of the missing people."

Skottie took a deep breath and looked away, out at the highway. Cars and trucks zoomed past, some of them slowing noticeably when they saw the cruiser parked at the rest stop with its lights flashing. She didn't look at Roan when she finally spoke. "So I guess you're not headed to Dodge City. Where are you going?"

"Up near Phillipsburg. The place is called Paradise Flats. It is where my . . . where the first man from the Roan Foundation was going. I am planning to stay somewhere along the way tonight, and I ought to arrive there fairly early tomorrow."

"That's right on the Nebraska border," Skottie said. "I know the sheriff up there. He should be put in the loop on all this."

"You think he will give me any trouble?"

Now Skottie turned her head to look at him. "I'm not your friend," she said. "I'm not here to make things easier for you."

"I apologize," Travis said. "I did not mean to presume."

She shook her head. "But to answer your question, yeah, I do think he's gonna give you some trouble."

"All right."

"I'm not *his* friend, either. But you lied to me."

"Sometimes people are warned that I am coming before I am able to find them. They run. The more people who know what I am doing here, the greater the chance I will fail. And it is possible that my colleague was betrayed by someone here."

"Don't lie to the police anymore. You'll need to be on your best behavior when you meet Sheriff Goodman."

"Is he that bad?"

Skottie shook her head again and smiled. "Sheriff Goodman isn't going to like having a stranger running around in his backyard. Like I say, you'd better be straight with him and not surprise him in any way." She thought for a moment and then added, "Won't do you any good to drop my name with him, either, so don't bother."

"All right," Travis said. "I will get in touch with him as soon as I arrive tomorrow. Thank you. Is Hays a decent place to stay the night?"

"It's all right. I live there."

"Anywhere you would recommend for dinner?"

"The usual chains. Red Lobster, Applebee's, but there's a decent steakhouse that's local. The Roundup. If you eat red meat, it's probably the best spot."

"I do not, but Bear does."

"Good luck," Skottie said. "I hope you find your friend." She handed Roan's ID and license back to him. "Doctor, I'm gonna ask you to keep that handgun holstered or put away in the back of your vehicle while you're traveling."

"I will," Roan said.

Skottie tipped her hat and turned away. "Stay out of trouble, Dr. Roan." She walked back to her Explorer, pulled out, and rolled away. She parked on the ramp and watched the lot behind her in the mirror.

Bear got back to his feet and shook himself all over, his loose skin rippling up across the solid muscle beneath, his mane bristling. Roan reached down and unclipped the leash, threw it on the back seat. Bear jumped up into the Jeep and Roan followed. He waved in the general direction of the cruiser and accelerated past her, back onto I-70.

Skottie didn't wait until he was out of sight. She set her hat on the seat beside her and picked up the handset, keeping her eye on the dwindling black Jeep as she pressed the send button.

"One-Eleven Norton."

A moment later, Sarah's voice crackled over the radio's speaker. "Norton here."

"Hey, is Paradise Flats in Phillips County?"

"Nope. It's over in Burden."

"Do me a favor then—put me through to Burden County. I wanna talk to the sheriff."

"Will anyone do?"

"That'd be Goodman up there, right?"

*"Him?"*

"I know. Just do it, would you, please?"

"Got it," Sarah said. "Give me a minute."

Skottie hung up the handset and pulled the cruiser around. She waited for a break in traffic, then nosed out onto the highway and followed along in Travis Roan's wake.

Her cell phone rang and Sarah's name appeared on the screen. She wasn't using the radio, which meant she was calling back with a personal matter.

Skottie hit the green button. "You get through to Goodman?"

"Not yet," Sarah said. "Maddy's school just called."

"She okay?"

"I think so. She got in a fight."

Skottie sighed. Another fight. "They want me there?"

"The principal's got her in the office. Wants a word with you when you pick her up."

"Tell him I'm on my way."

"You still want me to raise Goodman?"

Skottie hesitated. "Can you get him a message? Tell him to be on the lookout for a rented black Jeep?"

"I can try."

"He'll figure it out from there. Thanks, Sarah."

"No problem. And don't worry. Maddy'll calm down after a while. It's an adjustment's all it is."

Skottie ended the call and tossed her phone onto the passenger seat. Since they had moved to Kansas, there had been some new kind of trouble every day. Maddy's grades were suffering and she wouldn't speak to her mother anymore, responding only in grunts and prolonged silences whenever Skottie attempted a conversation.

Skottie found a turnaround in the median and headed back toward Hays. Someone else would have to deal with the mysterious Dr. Roan. As serious as she felt about her job, her first priority would always be her daughter.

## AUGUST 1951

The clapboard house was small but solid, and it had recently been painted. Its outside walls were blinding white with red shutters, and there was a garden in the front where someone had planted *Taglilien* and *Glockenblumen*. He did not know the English words for the flowers. The red roof rose at a steep angle and flattened out at the side to form a carport, where Jacob Meyer parked the truck. Meyer gave Rudy a key to the front door and fetched his bags from the back of the truck. Inside, the walls were smooth plaster and the hardwood floor was tightly joined.

Rudy took his bags from Jacob and thanked him. "*Danke*, Jacob."

"*Bitte*," Jacob said. "You are most welcome, Mr. Goodman."

When Jacob had gone, the truck farting away down the street, Rudy walked through the house and took stock. The kitchen was little more than a wide corridor at the back of the house, but it had been fitted with a new stove and an icebox. There was a cellar with a dirt floor and shelves along one long wall. Someone had left a dozen jars of stewed tomatoes. Rudy remembered that there were tornadoes in Kansas and a cellar was an essential safety feature. He wondered what tornadoes looked like and how much warning they gave before striking.

Upstairs there were two bedrooms, and Rudy set his bags down on the floor in the smaller one. Sleeping did not require much space. The bigger room would be his office, as soon as he relocated the bed that was in there. He found a pencil and a tablet of yellow paper in his smaller bag and began a list of the things he would need for the house. At the top he wrote the word *desk*. After a moment's thought, he skipped down a line and wrote *map*. He used the English words, sounding them out as he wrote and repeating them to himself, mimicking Jacob's flat Midwestern dialect.

There was a comfortable old sofa in the living room, and he moved it so he would have a good view of the street through the front window. He walked through the kitchen and out the back door. Three steps led down to a stone path that petered out twenty feet behind the house at the edge of the tall grass. Someone—Jacob, perhaps?—had recently mowed, stopping at Rudy's property line. He breathed in the fresh green smell of the lawn and then sneezed, wiped his nose on his sleeve. Beyond the grass was a dense tree line, and Rudy knew from the drive in along winding country lanes that there was nothing beyond the trees but mile after rolling mile of farmland.

Only a week before, Argentina had loomed over him: tall pale buildings that hid thick jungle behind them in every direction, a multitude of brown people who had smiled at him for no reason, birds of every color that squawked at him from parapets and lampposts. Even the air had pushed him down, made him feel small, smothered him under a steaming blanket of perfume.

Kansas—at least this part of Kansas on this particular afternoon— was flat and gray. The people—judging by Jacob Meyer—were solid and white. He straightened his shoulders. Gray and solid were good qualities. They were the qualities of clay, unformed and malleable. Rudy Goodman felt a certain kind of power as he looked out across his newly acquired land at the shadows of trees. He felt free.

From somewhere nearby, he heard a dog bark and an answering whistle, high and sharp. He held himself motionless and watched the treetops as they swayed back and forth in some light breeze that Rudy couldn't feel. The scraggly bushes that marked the tree line rustled and a head popped up over the top of the grass. A child of perhaps ten or twelve stared at Rudy from several yards away. Dark hair and a round pink face under a sunburnt forehead.

"Hello," Rudy said. "You look very pretty."

"Who are you?"

"My name is Rudy. What is your name?"

"Nobody lives here," the child said. Rudy could barely make out her voice. "That house is empty."

"I live here now. Come closer so I can hear you."

The child disappeared, her head sinking beneath the shimmering brown surface of the field.

"I think I saw a wolf," he said. "Not far from here."

He watched for signs of motion in the grass, but saw nothing.

"Where did you go? Come back. I won't hurt you."

"Where are you from?" The faint sound of the child's voice was carried by the breeze in every direction so that Rudy couldn't pinpoint her location.

"I am from a place very far away. To the south of here, and the east. Do you know your directions on a map?"

"No."

"Where are you from?"

"Over there."

"I can't see you, little girl. I don't know where you are talking."

There was no answer. Rudy stood there, waiting, for another quarter of an hour, but the grass didn't move and the child made no sound. He considered wading out and looking for her, but she was probably long gone, and he was tired. He wondered if the dog he had heard was a companion to the child, and he wondered whether it would attack him if he managed to find its young mistress out there in the trees. He licked his lips and smiled.

He turned and went back inside, closed the door on the late afternoon sunshine. The child would come again. He knew that. She was curious about him.

And Rudy was a very patient man.

This isolated place would be a suitable home for him. He decided it was time to begin moving his money northward.

# CHAPTER TWO

## 1

Skottie glanced at her daughter in the rearview mirror. "You wanna tell me your version of what happened?"

"What do you mean?" Maddy was ten and still carried a little baby fat, her lips pushed into a bow by her full cheeks. When she wanted to appear innocent, her eyes opened wide and she looked like a toddler again.

"Why did I have to pick you up early?"

"Oh, that." The innocent expression went away and was replaced by irritation. Maddy looked down at her lap and Skottie could no longer see her eyes. "It was stupid."

The light changed and Skottie eased up on the brake, turned her attention to the traffic around her. She waited, sure that Maddy would say more when she was ready.

"Chloe wouldn't tell me a joke, is all."

"A joke?"

"Olivia told Chloe and Chloe wouldn't tell me," Maddy said, "and I thought they were laughing at me."

"You thought the joke was about you?"

"They weren't really laughing at me, but I didn't know."

"So you—"

"I cupcaked her."

"You did what?"

"I cupcaked her. It was red velvet. I should've used a vanilla one, but I already picked a red velvet one."

"A cupcake."

"They had cupcakes for the birthday party. There was juice, too, but I didn't have any. It had chunks."

"I don't understand. What does that mean, you cupcaked her?"

"You know, like I mashed a cupcake on her. In her face. Like at weddings and stuff."

"You were mad at Chloe so you . . ."

"Cupcaked her, yeah. Only it turned out she wasn't laughing at me, so it's okay now. Except the frosting might've messed up her shirt. Anyway, the red didn't come all the way out when we wiped it. There's a pink blob."

Skottie slowed down and turned onto their street, the street where Skottie had grown up. She pulled into the driveway, switched off the car, and swiveled so she could see Maddy over the back of the seat. "And that was the whole fight? That's what happened?"

"I guess."

"Well, you need to apologize to Chloe."

"It's okay. I'm not mad anymore."

"No, I said *you* need to apologize to *her*."

"But she's not mad, either. She said so."

"I want you to apologize to her anyway. Do it first thing tomorrow."

"Mom, that's gonna make it worse. It'll make her, like, remember I did that and she'll be mad at me again."

"Do it anyway." Skottie opened the car door, but turned back and grimaced at Maddy. "And find out if we need to buy her a new shirt."

Skottie sorted the mail and put a load of laundry in the machine while Maddy started her homework. At six o'clock, Skottie's mother, Emmaline, came home from a book club meeting at the church, and Skottie took her into the kitchen. In hushed tones, she related the story of Maddy's fight.

"Cupcaking?" Emmaline shook her head. "That's new. You never did that."

"Of course I never did that," Skottie said. "I've never even heard of that." She craned her neck around the corner to make sure Maddy was still concentrating on her math worksheet. "I'm worried about her."

Emmaline smiled and waved her hand in a dismissive gesture. "She's just testing her boundaries now her dad's not around. As I recall, you got in more than one fight at that age. Usually over something silly. Kid's gotta blow off steam just like everybody else."

"If you say so." But Skottie still felt anxious for her daughter. She wished she could be with Maddy everywhere she went, keep her from getting hurt. Keep her from cupcaking other kids.

Maddy wanted a baked potato for dinner, but their ancient gas oven would take an hour and a half to heat up a potato, so Skottie decided to pick something up. She left Maddy with Emmaline, with the understanding that the TV was to stay off until the girl finished her math problems, and drove two miles to the Roundup.

The restaurant was nearly empty, and she saw Travis Roan at the bar as soon as she entered. He was drinking from a rocks glass filled with clear liquid and ice. He had changed his clothes and now wore a white mock turtleneck with wide gray stripes.

He looked up as she approached. "Officer Foster," he said in his low whisper. He lifted his glass in a salute.

She nodded back at him. She was wearing a leather jacket, an unbuttoned white Henley shirt tucked into faded jeans, and an old pair of scuffed boots. "Dr. Roan," she said. "I guess you took my advice about this place."

"I told you, you should call me Travis. And when it comes to food, I always take the advice of locals. May I buy you a drink? I have vodka."

"I'm not staying. Just getting carryout."

"As am I. Bear gets steak tonight."

"Right. The dog. Where is he?"

"Back at the hotel."

She was curious, despite herself, and pulled out the stool next to him. "You found a place allows pets?"

"We usually stay at a Best Western. It is a good chain. They like pets."

Skottie nodded. Then there was a silence as she studied the menu the bartender put in front of her. She ordered a potato with everything on it for Maddy and a quarter of a roasted rosemary chicken for Emmaline. For herself, Skottie chose a Kansas City strip steak and french fries and wondered whether she would be eating the same thing as the dog. After the bartender wrote down her order and walked away, Skottie turned back to Travis.

"Does he sleep on the floor or in the bed with you?"

"Bear gets his own bed whenever there is a double available," Travis said. "Otherwise, he sleeps on the floor. He would probably smother me in my sleep."

"He's big enough," Skottie said. "What kind is he?"

"Tibetan mastiff."

"Did you get him in Tibet?"

"Kenya. He was being used by poachers to track rhinos."

"You're kidding." She turned on her bar stool to face him.

"I wish I were," Travis said. "They cut his vocal cords so he would not bark and scare the rhinos away. When Bear would find a herd for his masters, they would shoot two or three, cut off their horns, then leave the injured animals to die slowly and rot. Bad people."

"So Bear can't bark?"

"No. And he has stopped trying to bark. It confused him when he did, and it made me sad. Those men attempted to pass him off as part dingo, but I do not think there is any trace of dingo blood in him."

"But you got him away from them. From the poachers."

"I did. I did not know what to do with Bear after I dealt with them, so I took him with me." He shrugged. "He has been with me ever since."

"That's nice of you."

"Perhaps. Or maybe I identify with him." Travis pulled down on the collar of his sweater. A three-inch-long scar, jagged and bright pink, ran across his throat under his Adam's apple.

"What happened?"

He let go of his collar and picked up his glass. "In my business it is sometimes hard to know whom to trust."

"So you hunt Nazis *and* poachers," Skottie said.

"All manner of bad people," Travis said. He took a sip of his vodka.

"I say 'bad people.' It is a subjective term, I know, but I have found it useful. Most people I talk to can agree on certain moral standards of behavior, and a simple binary label, good or bad, often suffices."

"I guess Nazis are as bad as they come."

"Indeed. But I have had to branch out. In my father's day, there were still many Nazis to root out, but now? Not so many. Still, there are always bad people."

"What did you do with the poachers? The ones you took Bear away from?"

Travis stared at the ice in his glass, then set the glass down on the bar without drinking from it. "They will not poach again."

She sensed that he wasn't going to expand on his answer, and she wondered how dangerous he really was. "Before, earlier this afternoon, you said you weren't going to kill anybody here in Kansas. Was that the truth?"

"Would I tell you if I were lying? You are, after all, an officer of the law."

"I'm off duty right now."

"If I am able to determine that my witness is correct, that this man she saw is a Nazi, I will alert the local authorities and the Roan Foundation will file a civil suit against him on behalf of the survivors of his camp. All aboveboard, everything perfectly legal. I promise you."

"Is it ever tempting?"

"To kill?"

"I mean, nobody would miss a Nazi."

"Sometimes we must sacrifice our ideas regarding expediency and even practicality in order to uphold our core principles," he said. "Don't you agree?"

Skottie took a second to think, then nodded.

"My principles are quite important to me," Travis said. "So, no, I have never chosen to kill anyone when there was another option available to me."

"You never said what kind of doctor you are. Medical?"

Before he could answer, the bartender arrived with a takeout bag. Travis paid his bill in cash and stood, drained the rest of his drink, and set the empty glass back down on the bar.

"Perhaps I will see you again," he said.

"You okay to drive?" She tapped a fingernail on the bar.

"I walked. The hotel is right over there." He pointed to the east. "Or, wait . . . Over there." He turned and pointed in the opposite direction. "It is somewhere within this same parking lot."

"Good," Skottie said. "And good luck."

Travis smiled and tipped an imaginary hat to her. She watched him walk out and then pass by the big window at the side of the restaurant on his way to the hotel. He didn't look up at her. She caught the bartender's eye and motioned him over.

"Do I have time for a quick drink?"

"Kitchen's moving slow tonight."

"Bring me a vodka, then," she said. "No ice."

"Your friend had a double," the bartender said.

"Just a single for me."

"Tito's?"

"Is that what he had?"

"Yeah, Texas brand. Pretty good for a domestic."

"Texas, huh? Yeah, I'll have that." She turned on her stool to face the big window and waited, wondering if Maddy had made up the term *cupcaking* and whether cupcaking people might be a halfway decent way to deal with some situations. It was violent, a little, but it didn't do permanent damage. The thought of Travis Roan, the weird uptight cowboy, cupcaking a Nazi made her chuckle.

"Nazis," she said.

"What's that?" The bartender wiped the bar in front of her and set down a glass.

"Nothing," Skottie said. "It's just . . . some days are weirder than others."

# 2

They got an early start the next morning. Travis took US-183 north out of Hays and set the cruise control for seventy miles an hour. The highway cut straight through the Smoky Hills, exposing high limestone walls along both sides of the blacktop. Bear alternated between short naps and watching the scenery roll past, but Travis kept the passenger window up. He planned to hit Phillipsburg by nine o'clock, possible if he stopped only once to let Bear relieve himself.

They passed a town named Plainville and another called Stockton, eating up the miles faster than Travis had thought they would. They had the highway to themselves, no traffic moving in either direction at this time of day, and he had begun to consider taking a detour to someplace called Kirwin National Wildlife Refuge, thinking Bear would enjoy running free for a bit, when he saw orange cones in the highway ahead.

A Burden County sheriff's car was pulled off on the shoulder, and a deputy wearing dark pants and a light blue uniform shirt under a gray jacket was out in the road, putting down cones. Travis steered the car onto the shoulder, Bear watching the deputy out the window. There was a turnoff ahead, and Travis took it. He supposed there had been an accident somewhere between Stockton and Phillipsburg, and he reached for his phone in the cup holder between the seats. He'd have to find an alternate route north.

He glanced in the rearview mirror and saw that the deputy was still at work behind him, but hustling now, running back and forth, moving the cones two at a time from the road, blocking the ramp Travis had just taken.

Travis frowned and tapped the brake, slowing the Jeep to ten miles an hour on the dusty side road. He realized he had been herded off the highway and then efficiently isolated. He reached for the glove box and popped it open, pulled out his Kimber Eclipse Custom II. Bear immediately perked up, his black mane bristling as if charged with static electricity.

There was a stop sign ahead of them, and two silver sheriff's cruisers were pulled sideways, blocking the intersection, their blue and red lights swirling. A big man in a faded blue uniform was leaning against one of the cars, his thumbs stuck in his belt loops. He wore dark glasses, a cowboy hat low on his head, and a heavy jacket with a star pinned to it. He was maybe forty-five years old, by Travis's estimation, with a heavily lined face that had seen too much sun. The sheriff pushed himself away from the car, turned his head, and spat a brown gob into the grass. There was a deputy behind him who moved out a bit, keeping Travis in full view, a shotgun held loose at waist level.

Travis put his own gun back in the glove box and closed it. Whatever was happening, the pistol would cause more trouble than it would solve. Travis rolled down his window, put his hands on the steering wheel at ten and two, and sat waiting. The sheriff took his time walking over to the Jeep. Up close, Travis could see that the man was both older and larger than he'd thought, maybe sixty years old, maybe two hundred and fifty pounds, but spread over a six-foot-four frame. The sheriff put one hand on top of Travis's Jeep and leaned in the window.

"Step out the car, please, sir." He grinned, a bulge of tobacco in his lower lip, a brown dewdrop caught in the stubble on his chin.

Travis moved his hands off the wheel and pulled on the door handle, at the same time hitting the button that rolled up the window. He removed the key from the ignition and palmed it. He didn't even glance at Bear. He knew the big dog would not move until there was a clear signal to do so.

The sheriff took a step back as the Jeep's door swung open. His boots had steel toes. "Take it nice and easy. No surprises. We know you're armed."

"Was I speeding, Officer?" As he stood, Travis dropped the key on the asphalt and kicked it under the vehicle with his heel.

"Put your hands on the roof there, Dr. Roan."

Travis locked his door manually and closed it, then placed his hands in front of him, spread his feet, and braced himself for a pat-down.

The deputy ambled over—probably to make sure Travis saw the shotgun—and peered through the passenger window at Bear. "There's a dog in here," he said. "Big sucker, too." Bear sat still, watching the deputy, and Travis breathed a small sigh of relief that he had remembered to roll the window back up.

The sheriff checked Travis's chest, waist, and ankles, clumsily, without appearing to care whether he found anything. "The dog can stay there, out of trouble. What's his name, Dr. Roan? Or is it a bitch?"

"How do you know my name?"

"Done my homework."

"May I ask what this is about?"

"You can turn around now," the sheriff said. "Where's your pistola?"

"In the glove box."

"Good. Christian, you run and turn off the arrays. And check in with Ed up there. Make sure them cones got moved."

"But what if he—" The sheriff interrupted his deputy with a wave of his hand and Christian obeyed.

"Let's you and me talk, Dr. Roan," the sheriff said.

"Why did you send your deputy away?"

"He's a good kid, Christian is, but he flaps his gums too damn much. Figured we might want some privacy here."

"Your name is Goodman, am I right?"

"You been doing your homework, too."

"Someone mentioned you in passing yesterday. This is your county?"

"Next one up's mine. You keep going along that road there, headed north, you'll end up in my county about an hour from now, depending you stop and walk your bitch or not."

"The dog is male," Travis said. "You saved me having to find you."

"You lookin' for me, then?"

"I had planned to stop in to see you, probably later today or tomorrow. I will want to talk to the local police in Paradise Flats, too. And maybe in Phillipsburg."

"What kinda accent is that? Where you from?"

"All over. I suppose I must have picked up bits and pieces of a half dozen dialects."

"Well, I guess where you're from don't matter so much as where you are now."

"I have always thought so. Sheriff, I did not come here to make trouble for you."

"That so?"

"I am pursuing a fugitive who may be hiding in your jurisdiction," Travis said. "I intend to cooperate fully with law enforcement officers while I am here in Kansas. Surely you do not want a criminal in your county any more than I do. I promise I am no threat to you."

Sheriff Goodman scratched his chin and spat another mouthful of brown juice into the gravel beside the road. "I never said you was a threat to me. And I don't think you are. But I want you gone from here anyway, Dr. Roan."

"Are you going to arrest me?"

"I could. But if I do that, I imagine a lawyer'll pop up and raise a fuss. He'll probably have a real nice suit like yours and maybe some black-rimmed glasses, too, just to show how smart he is. Carry a briefcase fulla writs and habeas whatnots. And then I'll get more fancy dudes like you showin' up here. So no, I don't think I'm gonna arrest you just now. But I do hold out the possibility for the future, y'know, should things between us turn out not so friendly."

"Then we are at an impasse."

"Maybe. I see three possibilities here. Just three, so think careful on your choices." Goodman held up one finger. "I could arrest you, but I already said I ain't gonna do that right now. Which leaves us with the other two possibilities." He put the first finger down and held up a second finger, making an obscene gesture. "I ask nice and you disappear. Maybe I don't ask so nice. That part's up to you, but you go away from here either way. And later, if any more like you show up, I deal with them the same." He held up his pinkie and ring fingers now, his index finger still held down, so that he had three fingers extended. "Last option, as I see it, you musta come out here, but nobody seen you around." He grinned and put his hands out in a questioning pose, looking back and forth as if searching for something. "Maybe you went back home? I don't know. But when your people call me up, I tell 'em I'll have my people look for you. Can't make no promises, though. People do disappear from time to time. It's possible you got accidentally hit by a stray bullet somewheres. Maybe a deer hunter up in them woods didn't see you. There's a whole lotta woods around here, and I don't got that many deputies. Your own mama would understand if I can't find you."

"I see," Travis said. He pushed himself away from the Jeep. "But I do not think I like any of those options, Mr. Goodman."

Goodman leaned forward and cocked his head to the side. His smile revealed only the teeth in the left side of his mouth. "Didn't really think you would. But maybe I oughta sweeten the pot for you. What if I kill your dog?"

"You could try, but I do not think he will let you."

Goodman pulled on the driver's-side door handle, already reaching for his gun with the other hand. Bear immediately pressed up against the other side of the window, and Travis was pleased to see the sheriff take an involuntary step back from the Jeep.

"He moves quick, don't he? Where'd you put the key, I wonder?"

"Oh no, have I locked myself out of my car?"

Goodman shrugged. "Well, I guess that leaves us with option three."

Travis braced himself and was ready when Goodman pivoted and aimed a fist at his stomach. Goodman was big, but he was used to fighting drunks and weekend warriors. Travis deflected the punch, letting Goodman's momentum turn him around. He hit Goodman in the temple with the heel of his hand, but not too hard; he didn't want to kill him. The sheriff staggered sideways, and Travis grabbed Goodman's head in both hands and rammed his knee into the sheriff's solar plexus. Goodman hit the asphalt. Travis watched until he was sure the sheriff was breathing regularly.

"Hey!"

Travis turned to see the deputy charging at him. Goodman had called the boy Christian, and Travis could see that he was barely old enough to order a drink in a bar. Christian had his shotgun up, so Travis jumped forward, fell into a breakfall, and came up under the deputy's chin with all his weight, smacking the shotgun out of his hands and knocking Christian on his ass. The boy stayed down.

Travis brushed off his clothing, distressed to see that he had a long smudge of dirt down his right trouser leg. The palm of his hand ached a little where it had met with the sheriff's skull, but otherwise Travis was unharmed. He bent and fished the car keys out of Christian's pocket and threw them far into the November grass at the side of the road. Then he went to the two police cruisers and locked them. It occurred to him that it might have been wise to turn off the arrays before locking the doors, but he assumed their batteries would eventually run out of juice and shut down.

He went back to the Jeep and got down on his hands and knees and retrieved the key. Bear was on him as soon as he opened the door, licking his face. Travis chuckled and scratched the dog's ears through his thick mane. Bear jumped out and circled the intersection, checking each of the unconscious men, then returned to Travis.

"Nothing to worry about from these two," Travis said. "Shall we go?"

Bear bounded back up into the Jeep and settled down. Travis got in after him, but before he closed the door he leaned out and clucked his tongue at Goodman's limp body.

"There is always an option you have not considered, Sheriff. Watch out for that."

He closed the door and turned the Jeep around, drove back up the road, and peeled out onto the highway, racking the steering wheel to make the sharp turn. As he passed the second deputy, who was still holding an orange cone, he honked the horn and waved.

# 3

Skottie's day off started with an argument. Maddy couldn't find her shoes, and when Skottie gave her a short lecture on responsibility—the same lecture she had given almost daily since they had arrived in Kansas—Maddy barricaded herself in her bedroom. By the time Skottie talked her out, fed her breakfast, and found her shoes, Maddy had missed the bus and Skottie had to drive her to school. She was late and had to get a tardy slip from the office.

Skottie watched her daughter walk away down the empty hall, the other students and teachers already in class, her heavy book bag dangling from one shoulder, the tardy slip held loose in her hand. She was a good kid, Skottie told herself. This was just a phase. Once Maddy finally adjusted to the move and the new school, once she stopped hating her parents for the divorce, things would return to normal.

When Maddy had passed out of sight, Skottie smiled at the school secretary and went out to her car. She sat there for a long moment, summoning the energy to start the car and begin her day. It was a relief when her phone rang.

"Hello?"

"Skottie? This is Sarah." The dispatcher. "Sorry to bother you on your day off, but we got a call from someone who's insisting we put him in touch with you. Name's Travis Roan. You know him?"

"Roan? Yeah, I gave him a warning yesterday."

"Oh, crap. He said he was a friend of yours. I shoulda known better."

"No, it's okay. Um, yeah, go ahead and put him through, I guess."

"You sure?"

"Yeah, I'll talk to him. Thanks, Sarah."

"Sorry if I ruined your day," Sarah said.

There was a click and Sarah was gone. A second later, a raspy male voice came on the line. "Hello?" He sounded younger than he had in real life, his voice pitched slightly higher by electronics.

"This is Officer Foster. Can I help you, Doctor?"

"I cannot be sure yet, Officer. But I do hope so."

"Listen, I'm not on duty today."

"Sarah told me. She sounds lovely, by the way."

"Um, yeah, she's nice." She made a face. She didn't like the way he seemed to take over every conversation. Roan was strange, and although he was charming, she had no reason to trust him.

"I do hope you are not upset that I reached out to you this way," he said. As if he were reading her mind. "But I have not made a lot of friends here yet and I thought perhaps you would allow me to impose upon you."

"What do you need?"

"How far north of Hays did you say your zone extends?" The previous day he had referred to her "jurisdiction" and she had corrected him. Now he mentioned her "zone" without hesitation. He listened when people talked and he remembered things. She would have to be careful what she said to him.

"All the way to the border," she said. "I've got all these counties going north and west."

"That sounds like a lot of territory. Is there anyone else up here?"

"Where are you?"

"Approaching Phillipsburg. Actually entering Phillipsburg right now."

"Yeah. Ryan Kufahl's on duty."

"Am I likely to run into him? I mean, how would I find him if I wished to?"

"Tough to say. I can ask my dispatcher to have him call in his location, but the area up there is huge, lots of empty space and smaller roads to patrol. He could be pretty far away from Phillipsburg right now."

"Would it be possible for you to find out for me? As I say, I hate to impose."

"Something going on?"

"I would say there is. But I would rather not go into detail yet. You might not approve."

"Wait, what happened?"

"I will tell you when you call me back with Officer Kufahl's whereabouts. Are you able to get my number from Sarah?"

"Yeah. I'll get right back to you. But you'd better give me an explanation."

"I will."

And he was gone.

Skottie stared out the windshield and then frowned down at her phone. She put her car in reverse and backed out of the parking space, while at the same time hitting the dispatch number stored in the "favorites" list of her phone. By the time Sarah picked up, Skottie was turning out of the lot, her car pointed in the opposite direction from her home.

"Skottie?"

"Hi, Sarah. Hey, would you do me a quick favor?"

# 4

Travis slowed down as he entered Phillipsburg and coasted past a cemetery, which was followed by several blocks of squat homes and small businesses. A billboard at the edge of town advertised a local church with the slogan CREATED EQUAL = A LIE. Travis pulled in at the first gas station he saw.

It was time for him to make a call to the Roan Foundation, but he didn't want to. Something strange was happening in Kansas, but Travis didn't feel like anything had spun out of his control yet. Whatever was going on, Travis wanted more information before making a report. Sheriff Goodman might be acting on his own, not representing any sort of consensus of the area's law enforcement. Goodman would be angry now, and dangerous, but Travis didn't think the sheriff would call in reinforcements. At least nothing official.

There was a two-story motel next to the station, and Travis walked over with Bear. He put him on his leash for show. To his surprise, the Cottonwood Inn allowed pets. The woman at the front desk smiled at Bear as she explained that they preferred not to have cats in the rooms, but dogs were fine.

They walked back to the gas station and Travis took Bear off the leash. Clouds were rolling in, but the day was still bright and crisp, warm enough that Travis couldn't see his breath. When the Jeep's tank was full, he pulled out onto US-36, which turned into State Street through Phillipsburg, and headed west, consulting his phone for directions. Ruth Elder lived north of the highway on a charming redbrick road, lined with mailboxes at the curb. Tidy postwar houses stood in a queue behind brown front lawns that had been mowed within an inch of their lives, then put out of mind for the winter.

He had just pulled up in front of the house when his phone rang. "Yes?"

"Is this Dr. Roan?"

"Yes, Officer Foster, it is me."

"Where are you now?"

Travis gave her the address. "I am about to talk to my witness, if she is at home. I suppose I should have called ahead, but in my experience, these people sometimes change their minds if they are given too much warning. They become afraid, or decide they cannot stand to dredge up the old memories. Better to drop by unannounced."

"Will you still be there in forty-five minutes?"

"I hope so."

"Good. I'm on my way there."

"You are? Why?"

There was a silence before Skottie replied. "It might be a good idea for me to check out your situation up there. Let me know if you move on. I'm headed that way now."

"If she is not at home, I will stay where I am until you arrive." He hung up without saying good-bye.

When he opened his car door, Bear squeezed past him and bounded out onto the street. Travis looked away while the dog relieved himself against Ruth Elder's mailbox, then he clicked his tongue and Bear took his place at Travis's side, trotted beside him up the narrow path to the front door.

A moment after he knocked, Travis heard noises from the other side of the door. He took a step back and composed his face so that he would look solemn but unthreatening, his hands folded in front of him, his gray suit freshly steamed, his close-cropped hair carefully mussed. A delegate, not a salesman. Beside him, Bear sat silently panting, unable to appear benign, but doing his best. The inner door swung open and a woman squinted out at Travis before her gaze settled on Bear. She didn't reach to unlock the screen door.

She looked back up at Travis when he cleared his throat. "Excuse me, ma'am," he said. "I apologize for arriving unannounced, but I believe you might have been expecting me at some point. This"—he waved his hand extravagantly over his companion's head—"is my friend and partner. He is very obedient and will not harm you, but I will put him on a leash if that would make you more comfortable."

"Who are you?" She was in her late forties, dressed casually in a dark red drop-neck sweater and a khaki skirt. She wasn't wearing shoes. Her long hair was pulled up on her head, and the skin around her eyes was puffy, as if she hadn't slept well or had been recently crying. She was holding a cut-crystal bowl in her hand, and diffuse sunlight through the screen door was projected upon her through a thousand prisms, making her look blotchy or blurred, only partially there.

"My name is Dr. Travis Roan, of the Noah Roan Foundation in San Diego. I have my credentials with me if you would like to review them. And of course you may wish to call the Foundation to verify that they did indeed send me. Ruth Elder requested my presence."

The woman shook her head, but reached out and unlocked the screen door. She swung it open toward Travis, and when he reached for the handle she took a step back, allowing them to walk past her into a tiny vestibule that contained a bench and a row of hooks. A staircase along the left wall led to a second floor.

Travis remained quiet while the woman wandered away into the living room, holding the bowl out in front of her. At last she set it down on an end table and turned around.

She attempted a smile. "I'm sorry. What did you say your name was?"

"Roan."

"Rhone, like the river?"

"More like a horse, I suppose."

"Oh, of course. I wasn't thinking. I forgot. I saw your name on the website, didn't I?"

"Yes, I am sure you did. Please call me Travis. And this is Bear." Bear ducked his head at her and raised one paw.

"He's beautiful. Is he dangerous?"

"You have nothing to fear from Bear. He is exceedingly well-mannered."

"We expected you a long time ago. That man . . . I can't say whether he's still there anymore."

"Yes," Travis said. "I apologize for my tardiness. Was it your mother who called the Foundation?"

"No. It was me. She asked me to call. She was afraid she would lose her nerve."

"Yes, that sometimes happens."

"I'm sorry. My name is Rachel Bloom. Bloom's my married name. I'm her daughter." She laughed, a short, soft sound that failed to convey amusement. "I suppose you already know that."

"A lucky guess."

She smiled. "Can I offer you something? I have a half pot of coffee left. I can heat it up. Or I think there's tea, if you prefer."

"What sort of tea?"

"Let me look." Having a task to perform seemed to energize her. She hurried out of the room, her bare feet making no sound on the heavy carpeting. Travis looked around at the wallpaper and furnishings. They were as outdated as the carpet, left over from the late seventies. He followed Rachel to the kitchen and watched as she opened the cabinets above the counter, searching for the promised tea.

"May I ask you, Mrs. Bloom . . . has anyone else from the Foundation paid you a visit recently? An older man by the name of Ransom?"

"Ransom? That's a strange name."

"I take it you—"

"No offense, but you people were supposed to come back ages ago. You really left my mother hanging, and I know she was anxious."

"Then you—"

"Here it is!" She turned and held out a box of Bedtime Story tea. It was caffeine-free, and on the front of the box was a printed claim that it was "made with real chamomile flowers."

Travis smiled politely and nodded. "Yes, splendid."

Rachel turned and busied herself with making tea, filling a mug with water and putting it in the microwave to warm. "I'm sorry. I interrupted you."

"No, it is quite all right."

"Would, um . . . I'm sorry, what's your dog's name again?"

"Bear."

"Right. Would Bear like something? Water?"

"Thank you very much. I am sure he would appreciate that."

She looked through the cupboards again until she found a bowl, which she took to the sink and filled. She set it down in front of Bear and he snorted, then lowered his head and lapped, sloshing water up over the rim and onto the floor. Rachel didn't seem to mind.

"I used to have a dog," she said.

"Oh? What breed?"

"She died."

"I am so sorry."

"It was a long time ago. Her name was Niki, like Nikita. It's Russian, you know, after the Elton John song."

Travis nodded as if he understood the reference.

The microwave dinged and Rachel took out the mug, unwrapped a tea bag and dropped it in the hot water, then handed it to Travis.

"You said we were supposed to come back here," he said. "Does that mean you did receive a visit from the Foundation?"

"My mother did. I wasn't here anymore. I used all my leave on that last visit. It's why it's taken me so long to get back out here." Tears had begun to puddle on her lower lashes. "The man from the Foundation told her to write down everything she could remember and he would come back in a day or two, but he never did. If she told me his name, I don't remember. I just know she waited and waited and she was getting so worried."

He took a sip of tea. It tasted like swamp water. "You were with your mother when she saw the fugitive?"

"Yes, it was right here in town. What are the odds? I mean, really? He was as close as you are now. Mother went white as a sheet and grabbed my arm. I thought she was having a heart attack, but that man never even looked at us. Even when she reacted like that. Like, an ordinary person would have been concerned, but he didn't seem to notice. Maybe he's blind, I don't know."

"Will she be home soon? Your mother?"

"No. I'm sorry, Travis. I thought you knew. My mother died last week."

## JULY 1956

She arrived on the hottest day of the year, and on the same train that had brought Rudy. Her name was Magdalene, although she preferred to be called Magda. It was the first thing she said to him. She was of good stock, with sturdy legs and light brown hair that glowed gold in the afternoon sun. She was not pretty in any conventional way, but her posture was good and Rudy thought he detected something regal in the line of her jaw. She carried one small bag, and it apparently held all that she owned in the world because she did not ask him to wait for any luggage.

She was a cousin to Jacob, and although Jacob had never met her, he had assured Rudy that she carried no mixed blood and would be a good wife for him.

Rudy drove her home in his Volkswagen, which was only two years old, almost new, and chatted with her in German along the way. He told her about production at the ranch, how he and Jacob now had one hundred head of cattle—*Rinder*—and two hundred head of goats—*Ziegen*—and that they planned to expand when the purchase of some nearby farmland had been finalized.

"I talk English," she said to him. "Not good now, but one little bit."

Rudy smiled and switched to English, thinking that it might be good for her to listen to the way it should be spoken. It would help her adjust to her new home.

He was no longer living in Don Veitch's old house. He had built a new home for Magda and had finished it only the week before her arrival, so it felt nearly as alien to him as he thought it must to her. He had provided the house with a large kitchen, including appliances that he did not know how to use. He doubted Magda knew, either, but he anticipated that they would have many good years together and she would have time to learn. There was a den for him on the first floor at the back of the house, big enough that he planned to hold meetings there in the future, and three bedrooms upstairs for when they had children. There was a small fireplace, and Rudy had framed the picture Magda had sent him of herself and placed it on the mantel, where she would see it when she entered the front room.

She did not smile when she saw the house. He opened the car door for her, and she stepped out and looked all around her at the wide brown space full of neatly combed furrows and squat silos full of grain and herd animals on the distant horizon.

Nearly hidden in the shadows of a line of sycamores to the east of the house was an outbuilding, a tin shed that he had filled with gardening equipment. In the floor of the shed was a trapdoor that led to a small room with a steel table and a drain in the floor. Manacles were bolted to the table, and a rolling cart held the various instruments that Rudy used in his work. There was electricity and water in the room, and its thick concrete walls were soundproof. Rudy hoped Magda would never be curious enough to lift the trapdoor. That room was not meant for her.

She turned and looked again at the house and spoke without looking at her new husband.

"I wish that I . . . I am not old for you," she said.

"*Too* old, you mean," Rudy said. He wanted to teach her the proper way.

"Yes. Am I?"

"How old are you?"

"*Zweiunddreißig.* I am . . . I mean, I am thirty-two years of age."

"That is older than I thought you would be," he said. "But it is not too old."

She looked at him then, her eyes narrow, as if trying to ascertain his truthfulness. He stared back at her without smiling, his hands held straight down at his sides, not influencing her in any way. At last, she seemed satisfied that he was not lying, and she picked up her bag. He thought about lifting her and carrying her over the threshold, but was not sure he could manage it. Instead, he took her by the hand and led her into their new home.

# CHAPTER THREE

## 1

It was almost ten o'clock by the time Skottie pulled up behind Travis Roan's vehicle. She got out and walked around the Jeep, peered in through the tinted windows. There was no sign of the dog. The path to the front door was neatly edged, and there was evidence that the two trees in the yard had been trimmed back and cared for, but there was something about the house that felt abandoned. It sat quiet, watching the street like a pet waiting for its owner to return.

Skottie knocked on the screen door, and a moment later a woman opened the inner door and offered her a tentative smile.

"Yes?"

"I'm sorry, ma'am. I'm looking for someone. He's—"

"Oh, you must be with Travis?"

"Um, yes."

"Please come in." The woman stepped aside, and Skottie pulled the screen door open and walked in.

Travis Roan was standing in front of a plush sofa, holding a steaming mug and groomed like a mannequin, neatly pressed, gelled, and poised. He seemed to favor the color gray, and Skottie wondered whether it was an eccentricity or a practicality. Dog hair would be nearly invisible on a gray suit. Travis nodded at her in greeting and held the mug out. "There is a fresh pot of tea in the kitchen," he said. "I found some Earl Grey back behind the coffee."

"Thanks," Skottie said. "So there's coffee?"

"Yes," the woman said. "My name's Rachel, by the way. Rachel Bloom."

"Oh, sorry, I'm Officer Foster." She fished out her badge and showed it to Rachel, who barely gave it a look. "But it's my day off. Please call me Skottie."

"Okay. Coffee then? Or we have some decaf tea. It's got chamomile."

Rachel had her back to Travis and didn't see him shake his head, warning Skottie off the chamomile tea.

"Coffee would be great, thank you. Can I help?"

"Not at all." Rachel disappeared into the kitchen. "I think it's probably cold, but I'll heat it up." Her voice faded and was replaced with the sounds of cabinets opening and closing, microwave buttons beeping.

There was a glass-topped table in front of the sofa, piled with boxes and papers. Skottie guessed she had interrupted a historical search. Travis's dog sat on the floor beside the sofa. He looked up at Skottie as she entered, then laid his head back down on his paws. Skottie stepped over to the table and looked at the open boxes. In addition to the papers spilling out of them, the boxes held a jumble of photographs and costume jewelry.

"This isn't the woman you came here to see? The one who saw your Nazi?"

"No, this is her daughter," Travis said. "The mother is dead. I will not be able to talk to her."

"What happened to you this morning?"

"I promise to tell you later. But you really did not need to come. I feel I am monopolizing all your free time since I arrived."

"It's my time," Skottie said. "And I think I ought to keep an eye on things here. Unofficially, of course."

"We can talk later," Travis said as Rachel entered the room carrying a white mug with a *Mutts* cartoon printed on one side.

Skottie thanked her and took the mug, walked around the end of the table, and sat on the sofa near the dog. She looked down at him and he opened one eye, thumped his tail, and went back to sleep.

"I'm surprised you didn't leave your dog in the car," Skottie said. "Or at the hotel."

"I rarely leave Bear anywhere, if I can help it."

"But doesn't he intimidate people?" She smiled at Rachel.

"I think he's adorable," Rachel said. She sat on a straight-backed wooden chair across from them.

"He does intimidate some," Travis said. "But in other cases, people seem to like him better than they like me."

Skottie believed him. She took a sip of the coffee and swallowed. It was stale but hot, and it warmed her all the way down. She waved her hand at the table. "What's all this?"

"Travis caught me in the middle of going through my mother's things."

"I'm sorry to hear about your loss."

"It was kind of sudden, but she was over ninety years old." Rachel shook her head. "I guess that's not very sudden after all, is it? It's sort of expected."

"What was her name?"

"Ruth. Ruth Madeline Elder."

"My daughter's name is Madeline," Skottie said.

Rachel's eyes lit up. "It's a pretty name. I've been boxing all this up, getting ready to put most of it in storage until I can go through it. We'll probably have to auction it, but I need to put this house on the market as soon as I can. There's just no time. I have to get back to . . . back to everything, I guess. They need me at work and . . ." Rachel broke off and looked around the room helplessly.

"I'm sorry," Skottie said again. She was afraid Rachel Bloom might cry, so she changed the subject. "What are you looking for exactly?"

"We didn't think anyone was coming back," Rachel said. She looked at Travis and then quickly away. "After the first man came from the Foundation, nothing else happened, so we thought they'd forgotten about us. Mother wouldn't let me call again, no matter what I said. She wouldn't make the call herself. And I couldn't really call on my own. I didn't know what to say if someone asked me questions, you know? She told me about her past, I mean after we saw him. I never knew she was at a camp. She never told me before, never mentioned it at all."

"She was a prisoner there?"

Rachel looked down at her empty hands. When she spoke, it was in a whisper and Skottie had to lean forward to hear her. "She was a guard. But she wasn't a Nazi. She told me she was never a Nazi." Rachel looked up and raised her voice. "She was a good woman, all her life, a good mother. She cared for my father through the cancer and never once complained. Everyone loved her. Everyone. She couldn't have been a Nazi. Not in a million years."

"It is all right," Travis said. "I believe you. We both do." He looked at Skottie, including her in the statement, then back at Rachel. "Not everyone in Germany was a Nazi."

"No," Rachel said. She looked gratefully at Travis. "But you know, I never knew she lived in Germany. She didn't have an accent or anything. Not like you."

"My accent is not German," Travis said.

"No, but I mean she sounded American."

"She lived here a long time."

"Yes."

"So . . . this?" Skottie pointed at the table, trying to get the conversation back on track.

"After that first man came, before she died, Mother said that she wrote everything down. Or maybe not everything, but the important details. In case anyone ever did come back. She didn't want to tell me if there wasn't any use in it, but she didn't want him to get away with it, either. She wanted there to be something, some record of what he did." Rachel's fingers twined together and writhed in her lap. "I don't know. She can't have thought there would be any justice. Not after so long."

"There will be," Travis said. "At least, I will try. Justice is still possible, no matter how long it has been."

"How could she have been a guard at a camp, Travis, if she wasn't a Nazi?"

"It is possible. Hopefully she has left her story behind for us to discover. Somewhere in this." He glanced at Skottie and indicated the papers. "Will you help look?"

Skottie hesitated before setting her mug down and pulling one of the boxes toward her. It had been taped shut, and the words *papers* and *bedroom* were written in thick black marker on one of the flaps. She looked up again at Rachel. "Are there more boxes?"

"Some still in the bedroom," Rachel said. "That's where I was working this morning when Travis came to the door. She kept her old things in a closet. And there are other boxes around the house."

"I have checked the kitchen," Travis said. "When I was looking for tea."

"So no more boxes in the kitchen, then," Skottie said.

"None," Travis said.

Rachel excused herself and retreated down a hallway, where Skottie assumed the bedroom was located. There was a tiny pocketknife on Skottie's key ring, and she opened it. Bear was immediately there between Skottie and Travis, pressing against her knee, the black fur of his mane standing on end. She had thought the dog was asleep, hadn't even seen him move.

"Bear," Travis said, *"trankvilo."*

Bear sat back on his haunches and yawned, then thumped down onto his side and seemed to fall instantly to sleep.

"I apologize," Travis said. "He is very protective."

"What was that word you used?"

"It means *calm* in Esperanto. Not many people speak it. A semi-secret code between us that no one else will think to use with him."

"How do you tell him I'm . . . How do you say *friend*?"

*"Amiko.* That means *friend."*

"Does he know that word?"

"He does."

*"Amiko,"* Skottie said. "And that's in . . ."

"Esperanto."

"How many languages do you know?"

"A few." He smiled and picked up a sheaf of loose photographs, ending the conversation.

Skottie took a deep breath. She slit the tape holding the box shut and returned the knife to her pocket. Bear didn't move. Skottie opened the flaps of the box, removed a manila file folder, and set it on her knees. She reached for the mug of coffee and turned pages, not really sure what she was looking for, but hoping she would know it when she saw it. The folder was full of receipts for gas and groceries and small items of clothing: a scarf from a boutique in the Wichita mall, a pair of shoes from a local Payless, a blouse from Target. Ruth Elder had not thrown her money away. Skottie wondered whether Rachel was due to inherit everything or if she had siblings. Surely they would have come to help out if they existed, but it was possible, if there were siblings, that they lived far away or had cut ties with their mother. Maybe they had known about their mother's past, even if Rachel had not. Skottie set the first folder aside and got up, went to the kitchen, and filled the mug again from a Mr. Coffee on the counter.

Travis was holding a small black book and he didn't look up when she came back into the living room.

"Did you find something?"

"Hmm? No," he said. "She has a diary here, but it is just a record of the books she has read in the past few years. I thought there might be something here. Sometimes people read things or see things in movies and they think those things happened to them. They get confused between fantasy and reality. Ruth Elder was not a young woman, and perhaps her mind . . ." He broke off and made a fluttering gesture next to his temple.

Skottie nodded, but couldn't think of anything to say, so she lifted out the next item in the box, a black notebook like the one Travis was holding, and opened it. It was another diary, but this one was more personal. The first entry was written in a confident hand, with bold loops and straight lines, but Skottie flipped to the back and saw that in the last few pages the handwriting had degenerated into a pinched and shaky scrawl.

*May 8—Went to the fair in Hutch. R very pleased with all. H won a stuffed yellow bird and gave it to R. R ate a funnel cake and enjoyed, but later sick.*

Skottie assumed *R* was Rachel. And *H* might be Rachel's father.

*July 12—Back from SD. R went to zoo with H, but I stayed at the hotel. Did not feel well until almost time to leave. What a shame!*

Maybe *SD* stood for South Dakota. Or San Diego. A family vacation?

*November 2—H in his usual mood today. Took R for ice cream to get out of house.*

The diary skipped whole months, maybe even years, at a time. Apparently Ruth Elder had only recorded the most significant or troubling episodes of her long life and had left out the mundane details of her everyday routine in a small Kansas town. Skimming through the diary, Skottie found very little that might indicate whether Ruth had been happy. There was almost nothing about her feelings or thoughts, even as the person she referred to as *H* seemed to slide downhill, becoming more withdrawn or maybe abusive. It was impossible to tell. The entries were like notations on a calendar: just the facts, none of the color. Skottie found herself wondering what kind of woman the diary had belonged to. Had she felt suffocated, or had she loved her husband and child? Had she lived with guilt her entire life, unable to escape the shadow of wartime Europe, or had she buried her memories and never thought about her previous life again until she had spotted a Nazi across a crowded room?

"I think I found something!" Rachel scurried into the room holding a third black book. She looked at the notebooks they were holding and a sad smile flitted across her face. "Mother liked to buy everything in bulk." She handed the notebook to Travis. Skottie moved so she could see it over his shoulder.

There was a notation on the inside cover that read *For Rachel.*

*Please think kindly of me.* The opposite page, the first page of the note-book, was filled from top to bottom with odd symbols, all written in the same scratchy hand as the final few entries of Ruth's diary. Travis turned the page, then riffled through the entire book and made a short sharp noise that wasn't a gasp and wasn't quite a sigh. The symbols marched across every page, filling the entire book from top to bottom and into the margins on either side. It was a code of some sort, Skottie thought.

"Unreadable," Travis said.

"It's shorthand," Rachel said.

"This isn't like any shorthand I've seen," Skottie said.

"Because it's in German," Rachel said. "Mother taught it to me when I was little. We would pass notes to each other."

"So you can read it? What does it say?"

Rachel took the book from Travis and turned back to the first page.

"It says . . . She says, 'Please forgive me, Rachel . . .'" Rachel broke off and looked up at them. Her eyes were watery. "I don't know what I'm going to be reading here," she said. "Maybe . . ."

Travis produced a dazzling white handkerchief and handed it across the table to Rachel. "It will be all right," he said. "I am here for only one reason, and it does not involve judging you or your mother. If you would like us to, my associate . . ." He looked at Skottie and pursed his lips as if he had just told a mild joke. "My associate and I will leave you for a time so that you may read this privately."

Skottie sat still and waited as Rachel looked from Travis to her, then again at Travis. "But you'd come back?"

"I need information," he said. The low murmur of his voice was gentle and soothing. "The things your mother says in that journal, the things that are meant for you to read alone, those are not things I need to hear. But if there is anything in this book that can help me . . ."

Rachel nodded. "It's okay," she said. "Mother left this for me to find. She knew I would be the one to read it."

"Why use a code like this?"

"Maybe she was afraid of the Nazi. If your people could find her, he might find her, too. I'm the only person who could read it. The only person around here, but I really think she wrote it for you. For someone like you. She wanted this person, this horrible old man, she wanted you to catch him. I don't mean *you* specifically, you know?"

"I know." Travis took out his phone, and Skottie could see over his shoulder that he pulled up a voice memo app. He turned the phone toward Rachel, who nodded her assent, and Travis hit the record button.

"Okay. Here goes." Rachel shifted in her chair and put her head down and started reading again. "'I saw Rudolph Bormann today,' it says, 'and I know that it was him. Even though he has changed, I know him. I know him as if the war ended yesterday. It is Rudolph Bormann and he is alive.'"

Rachel went on, reading to them in a soft halting voice while Skottie watched the timer on Travis's phone and sipped her lukewarm coffee. After fifteen minutes, Rachel stopped and closed the book. She stood up, the journal held tight in her clasped hands, and Travis stood up, too. Skottie stepped around the table and gave Rachel a short and awkward embrace. But Rachel did not appear to want comfort or company and pulled away from Skottie after a few seconds.

"I'm sorry," Rachel said. "This is . . . I never imagined any of this had ever . . ."

"It is quite understandable," Travis said. He picked up his phone and switched it off, slipped it into his breast pocket. "Your mother was very good to leave this behind for us."

"Can you give me . . . I think I'd like to read the rest of this by myself, if that's okay."

"Of course," Travis said. "I apologize. I should not have rushed you today."

"That man, that monster she saw, he's not getting any younger, is he?" Rachel tried to smile, but suddenly burst into tears. This time she accepted Skottie's hug.

Travis waited until Rachel had composed herself, then thanked her and promised to look in on her the next morning. Bear followed him to the door and out. Skottie left with them, grabbing her purse off the floor, abandoning her coffee cup on the table.

Travis stopped on the sidewalk outside. "Perhaps we might talk later about this," he said. "I would not mind hearing your impressions. I have the facts." He tapped his pocket. "But there are things about this I find puzzling."

"Like what?"

"Small things."

"What kind of 'small things'? We need to start looking for this guy."

"I need to gather my thoughts first. Will I see you again?"

"Definitely. I'm not just walking away from this, and you need help. I don't start my next shift for another day and a half." She looked away and ran a hand over her hair. "I'm not sure any of this is in my job description."

"Yes. That is how I usually feel." He nodded as if they had just agreed to something and led Bear away to the Jeep at the curb.

Skottie was left standing on an empty street in Phillipsburg, with no real idea why she was there.

If there was really a Nazi somewhere nearby, Skottie knew she had to help find him. She had told Travis that this wasn't her job, but she knew she could not pass this along to another department until she absolutely had to. Kansas was her home, and her responsibility.

# 2

After she had collected Maddy from school and helped her with homework, after she had made dinner and cleaned up and tucked her daughter in and turned out the lights, Skottie poured herself a glass of white wine, checked her phone, and found that Travis Roan had sent her a file: the recording he had made of Rachel Bloom.

Skottie stared at the icon on her phone, wondering why Roan was including her in his hunt, why he had referred to her as his "associate." Was he as open and cooperative as he seemed or was he playing some sort of game with her? Either way, she needed to keep herself involved until the investigation became official and she could turn it over to someone in authority.

She topped off her wineglass, sat at the desk in the kitchen where she normally paid bills, and played back Ruth Elder's wartime account.

Rachel Bloom's voice was halting and her emotions were audible. Skottie had seen the tension in Rachel's face as she had read her mother's diary, and she could almost imagine how Ruth Elder must have felt while writing it. Skottie was touched by the bravery both women had shown.

Rachel paused frequently as she read, searching for the right words. Skottie knew that Rachel was not representing her mother perfectly, but was pulling from her own vocabulary. Shorthand, whether English or German, was not an exact science.

When she had finished listening to the recording, Skottie played it back again, this time transcribing it to her laptop, easing over the pauses and some of the awkward phrasing in Rachel's interpretation. It took her more than an hour, stopping occasionally to play certain passages back again and to add a handful of her own notes and questions. When she was done she took her personal translation of Ruth Elder's story to bed with her and read it until she fell asleep.

# 3

A Personal Account

By Ruth Elder

Translated from (German) shorthand by Rachel Bloom and recorded by Dr. Travis Roan

Transcribed by Officer Skottie Foster (KHP)

*Please forgive me, Rachel.*

*I saw Rudolph Bormann today and I know that it was him. Even though he has changed, I know him. I know him as if the war ended yesterday. It is Rudolph Bormann, and he is alive. You will remember that you and I were at the café* [query Mrs. Bloom for specific café] *last Friday with Peggy* [Peggy who?]. *Bormann entered and passed by our table without noticing or recognizing me. He sat down four tables away from us where a younger man was eating. He was facing me and sitting very close, and I knew right away that it was him. I remembered everything then. Things I had not thought of since before you were born. Things from a different life that I once lived. And I had to leave the café. I know that you were confused, Rachel, and maybe you were frightened when you followed me outside. You seemed even more frightened when I told you what I had seen and what it meant. And now you will know after you read this that I have not always been a very good person. I do not know whether we will talk about this or even if I will be able to talk about it, so I am writing it down in our secret language from when you were a child. I hope that you remember how to read this shorthand. Do you remember how we used to pass notes to each other? Notes that your father could not read? I hope that you do.*

*Rachel, I was never a Nazi. I promise you that.*

*I had a husband, a long time before I came to America and met your father, and of course long before you were born. I was young and in love. His name was Dierk and he died in the war. When we met, he was a clerk in a bank and I was a nurse. When he was taken from me, we had been married only three months. I had left the hospital and we had taken a loan from the government that was available to all newlyweds at that time. It was called the Law for the Encouragement of Marriage, and it was one of Herr Hitler's ideas for making new soldiers. He had many ideas. Dierk and I were able to borrow enough money to start a good life together. The plan was that for each child we produced, the government would consider a quarter of our loan to be paid. If we had four children, our loan would be forgiven completely. It was a way to ensure more citizens, more soldiers, more Nazis. But Dierk and I were going to have twenty children. A hundred children. So we did not care about owing money. It made life easier, and we did not think we would ever need to pay it back.*

*But we had no children after all, and Dierk was dead before I ever really knew him. I think that now. We didn't have enough time.*

*I was a widow and I owed the government a great deal of money.*

*I am getting to the time I met Rudolph Bormann.*

*In that time and that place, it was no shame to have a child out of wedlock. If a single woman got pregnant by a good Aryan soldier, it was considered a boon to the state. We were encouraged to associate with the soldiers when they were on leave. One evening I was invited to dinner by a friend. I thought she was a friend. But there was a young man there on a three-day furlough from the Wehrmacht, and it became clear during dinner what was expected of me. I was even shown a room with a bed at the back of my friend's apartment. It had all been planned for me without my knowledge or consent.*

*I fled.*

*Things were not easy for me after that.*

*In retrospect, I think I should have taken that young soldier to the bedroom and then got on with my life. I might have avoided many painful things that came after. But I loved Dierk still. I was young.*

*I was visited one day shortly after that evening by a man who represented the party. Women were being taught shorthand so they could take notes for generals. These women were expected to perform certain easy tasks for the Wehrmacht and to assist in the war effort. My loan would be forgiven if I went with them and did these things. If I did not, my debt would come due immediately and, since I was unable to pay it, I would be imprisoned.*

*And so I did what they asked. But I did not join the party. I was always a civilian and was able to prove it later, after the war. It's why I was allowed to come to America.*

*But before that, long before America and long before you, I learned shorthand, which is how I am writing this now. And, much later, when you came into my life and were old enough to learn, I taught this to you, dear Rachel. How I hope you remember it.*

*I did not tell the men I worked for that I was a trained nurse. I could not bear anymore to see men who were wounded and dying. I feared I would see Dierk when I looked at an injured soldier. But I did well in my secretarial duties and was put into the guard training program at Ravensbrück, in the north of Germany. I did not know what that place was when I was assigned there, but I soon discovered what kind of camp it was.*

*The prisoners were almost all women, and so the guards were women, too. The administrators were all men, of course, but interactions with prisoners were mostly left to us. There were female guards at other camps, but all of us went first to Ravensbrück. We were shown how to subjugate and terrify. We were given dogs and taught the commands that would make our dogs attack prisoners.*

*We were not taught any command to make the dogs stop attacking.*

*Many of the women who entered training with me went on to other camps. I never knew what happened to them. A few of us remained at Ravensbrück. It was very hard work, which I would rather not write about. The conditions were not good for us, but they were much worse for the prisoners, so I never complained. I did what I could to get extra food and privileges for the women in my charge, but there was little I could do and there were many injustices.*

*That is all I will say on that subject.*

*I had been at Ravensbrück for nearly a year when it was decided that brothels were to be opened at some of the other camps. The men in charge of those camps thought it would boost morale. They sent for women from Ravensbrück, for prisoners, for these new facilities.*

*I was ordered to accompany four women by train to one of these facilities at Mauthausen-Gusen in Austria. I was to hand the women over to the staff there and then return to Ravensbrück by the same train.*

*But there was much snow* [A blizzard? Worth checking weather reports for that region? What year would it have been?] *and the train was unable to return that night. I was shown to my quarters within the camp, a small shack that I was told to share with two other women, new guards assigned to Mauthausen-Gusen to supervise the new workers. Our dogs were caged behind our quarters, outside in the snow. At dinner, a man came for me. One of the camp administrators was curious to meet a woman guard. I had not brought with me any clothes that would be proper for dinner, but one of my new roommates lent me a dress. She would not look at me. I understood what was to happen and understood, too, that I was not the first to have it happen in that camp. But I had experienced much in my months at Ravensbrück, and now my time with Dierk seemed like a life that had been led by someone else.*

*I was escorted to the main building and that is where I met Rudolph Bormann. He was called "the Wolf" because of the way he looked at the women and girls who arrived on the train.*

*I was surprised to see that a meal had been laid out on the table in a long dining room that was lined with tapestries and framed photographs of party officials. Candles were lit and the curtains were drawn so that it seemed almost civilized, and I think I even relaxed, but only a little bit. Herr Bormann was polite. He was not old or ugly, and this surprised me, too.*

*Herr Bormann welcomed me and pulled out a chair for me. He opened a bottle of wine and poured a glass for me before going to the other side of the table and sitting. I remember all these details, even though it has been a very long time. I wish that I did not remember them.*

*A chef entered the room and set a large plate on the table, then removed the cover* [Mrs. Bloom asks for the proper word here and Dr. Roan tells her it's called a cloche], *and I saw and smelled a roast pig, which was better than anything I had seen or smelled since before Dierk died. The chef carved the pig and put some meat on my plate, along with small potatoes and greens, then left the room so that Herr Bormann and I were alone. This is when he revealed to me that he knew I was a nurse. How he discovered this, I do not know. He told me that he was studying to be a doctor before the war began and he had continued his education there at the camp. He had a laboratory in one of the outbuildings, where the guards were not allowed to go and where he could carry out his anatomical studies. He wanted me to assist him. All the nurses, you see, were with the medical units and the hospitals. They were helping real doctors. There was no one left to help Herr Bormann. He was very charming, but I was not fooled. Such a man in such a place? I knew the kind of research he must be doing, and I understood where he must have gotten his subjects.*

*I should have been careful about my response to him. I should have agreed in the moment and then made my escape the next day when the train returned. But I was tired and frightened and I thoughtlessly refused to cooperate with him. He first tried to persuade me, but I could see that he had no regard for human beings.*

*People were commodities to be bought, sold, and butchered at his whim.*

*When I told him what I thought of his "studies," he grew impatient with me.*

*He rang a bell and two other men in uniforms entered the room. They stood beside my chair, and Herr Bormann asked me again to assist him. When I again refused, he ordered me to remove my dress. And when I did not, the two men took my arms and raised me from my chair.*

[At this point, Rachel Bloom stops reading and the recording ends.]

## 1

It was not supposed to rain. *The Old Farmer's Almanac* had predicted cloudy but clear conditions. And yet Rudy was awakened by a clap of thunder, his bedroom still lit up by a lingering flicker of lightning. He sat up and swung his legs around, found his slippers, and staggered into the kitchen. He brushed his teeth over the sink while the coffeepot chugged. He filled his portable mug to the brim and went out the back door in jeans and a rain slicker over his homemade pajama shirt with the snaps up the front. The horses were nervous, and he chose his favorite, an old swaybacked mare who had seen her share of storms. She was less likely to buck under him or suddenly take off. He saddled her and rode out, his coffee balanced behind the saddle horn, the reins wrapped in his right hand.

The goats were huddled in their shed, the walls open, raindrops pelting the tin roof. He could hear the new kids bleating as if from far away and underwater, the billy goats and nannies standing at the rails, watching the wet gray air.

He let the mare ride easy out to the fence, kicking up mud. Water streamed off the edge of Rudy's hood, around and down the collar of his shirt. The fence was holding up well and he moved along it, watching for breaks or for calves that had been left behind if the herd had panicked. There was a big tree that grew along the western perimeter, and he thought the herd would have taken shelter beneath it. He urged the mare along, picking up speed as the rain grew heavier, not wanting to be out any longer than he had to.

Sure enough, he could spot the tree through the low-lying mist and there was an undulating earth-colored mass at its base. As he grew closer, he could hear them lowing.

## 2

Twenty miles away, lightning struck the church spire in Paradise Flats. It arced up and around and doubled over on itself, burning an eight-inch gash in the ceiling and a perfectly round hole in the floor below. The only person in the church at the time was a custodian, who took shelter between two pews at the back. But the fire burned itself out almost instantly, leaving the altar and the custodian untouched.

Back on the Third R Ranch, the cattle huddled closer together, raising their noses and lowing. A second later, the sky boomed and the rippling flood of beef moved away from the tree. Rudy unlimbered his shotgun from its holster and pointed it upward, firing into empty air, hoping to frighten the cows farther from the tree. But they didn't hear the shot and they didn't move. Rudy couldn't hear it, either, over the sound of the next thunder clap.

He slowed the mare and rode directly into the herd, nudging them aside, putting himself between them and the tree. He raised his rifle to fire again and the world disappeared in a flash of white. There was a sound, too, that was unlike thunder and unlike a gunshot, and he tried to place it, tried to figure out what it might be as he fell from his horse.

He didn't feel the ground as he hit it, but he felt the mud all around him, sucking at him, drawing him down.

He looked up when he heard a voice calling his name, and he peered into the blinding brightness all around him. He saw a pale horse galloping toward him, and a weight seemed to press down on him, as if he were sinking into a hot bath, a slight pressure on his skin and a comfortable warmth in his groin. He reached up, but he was moving too slowly and the horse was already passing him. He called to it, but it kept moving until he could no longer see it.

He lay in the mud and listened for the sound of returning hoofbeats.

# 3

When he woke in the hospital in Hays, Magda was there by the bed, her belly swollen, her eyes puffy. Jacob was there, too, with Gretel and their three boys. They did not realize he was awake until he spoke.

"How bad is it?"

Jacob sent the women and children out of the room. Magda touched Rudy's hand before she left and she smiled at him. He knew they would be returning to the hospital soon to bear their child in comfort and safety.

When they were gone and the door was closed, Jacob sat on the edge of the bed. "You got yourself hit by some lightning," he said.

"I figured that out," Rudy said. His voice was a guttural whisper. "Looks like I still got my hands and feet, though. Not burned too bad."

"They shaved your head. Most of the hair was already burned off."

"I thought I was dead."

"Almost, I guess. Pretty close to it."

"I felt something," Rudy said. "When I was dying, or when I thought I was. There was another presence."

"A presence?"

"It was good. It made me feel good. I was at peace. I was welcomed. It told me . . ."

"It talked to you?"

"No, there were no words. But it felt like it was telling me that I was forgiven, that I would always be forgiven, that I'm safe in this world. Chosen."

"Chosen for what?"

"Oh, hell, Jacob, I can't describe it. Not really."

"You feel okay now?"

"I can talk, I can see. But I can barely hear you, Jacob."

"It's good you can hear at all," Jacob said. "Doctor said you might not. You ruptured your eardrums."

"My chest hurts."

"Take a look."

He helped Rudy pull aside the thin hospital sheet. Rudy was not wearing a gown, and there was a thick bandage taped all the way down his chest. Rudy's hands were numb, so Jacob peeled back the tape along one side of the gauze. Underneath, the skin of Rudy's chest was decorated with ugly splotches, black and red, evenly spaced every two inches from his collar down to his groin.

"The damn *Schlafanzug* snaps," Rudy said. "My pajamas."

"Yup." Jacob laid the bandage back over Rudy's chest and smoothed the tape down. "That lightning jumped right down the length of you from snap to snap and burned most of your shirt off you. I think that plastic poncho protected you some or I guess it mighta been worse."

"I'll heal."

"Yeah, you will." Jacob looked away.

"The herd?"

"We lost near fifty beeves, Rudy. The next bolt hit that tree, that big one over by the fence, split it down the middle, and jumped away into the herd. Sizzled right on through 'em. Hell of a mess. Some of the guys are helping haul 'em off and get 'em buried. Started yesterday, but it's a big job."

"*Scheisse.*"

"Yup."

"What about my horse?"

"That old girl? Found her back in the barn, pretty as a picture. Came back all by herself. It's how we knew to go lookin' for you."

Rudy chuckled, but stopped when the pressure of his burns against the bandage sent pain lancing through him, like being hit by lightning all over again. "Can't rattle that old girl," he said.

"Lotta money down the drain, losing them cows, Rudy."

"We'll be all right. Got 'em insured, don't we?"

Jacob smiled and stood. "You bet. Long term it's gonna work out. Least you ain't dead. Can't come back from that. It'll take us a while to recover, I guess, but we woulda lost them beeves whether you was out there in the rain or not. How 'bout next time you stay inside where it's nice and dry and you just peek out the window and think about the beef, steada goin' out in it."

"Lesson learned." Rudy reached up to scratch his head, but then remembered he had been shaved and pulled his hand away as if his bare scalp might burn him. "Listen, Jacob . . ."

"Don't worry. I took care of the other thing. The *Untermensch*." He glanced at the door, making sure they were alone. "The girl?"

"In the lake with the others?"

"No." Jacob chuckled. "I couldn't resist."

"What?"

"The boys had that big ol' hole dug and I thought, what could be better? She's buried under a few tons of bad steak. They're still out there pilin' dead cows on top of her."

Rudy was silent for a moment, thinking. "Did she . . . ?"

"She was in a bad way. Took a while for me to get down there. Completely forgot about her for a while, I was so worried about you. Anyway, she was just about starved to death while you were in here."

"Starved."

"Nobody bringin' her food. I went ahead on and finished her."

"Good. Shame, though. Such a waste."

"Get yourself strong and we'll go huntin' again." Jacob winked. "Plenty more fish in the sea."

"Fish in the sea."

"Right. Well, I'll send Magda back in here, if you think you're up for it."

"Magda. Jacob, I almost died. What would have happened to my wife?"

"I'd'a took care of her, Rudy."

"I know that. I know you would have. But you have your own family. I have to provide, I have to do more. Jacob, we must make a great deal more money."

"We'll get more beeves. Maybe more goats, but they're—"

"No, not that. Not any of that. Something different. I have an idea, maybe more of a feeling. Struck into me by the lightning."

"Yeah?"

"Not yet. Let me think on it for a bit."

"Okay." Jacob patted Rudy's arm. "I'll go fetch Magda now."

"Please. But, Jacob, give me a minute, would you?"

"You bet, partner."

Jacob stepped out and closed the door behind him. Rudy looked around at the hospital room. There had been a time when he could envision himself working in a place like this, a time when becoming a doctor was the most important thing in his life. But that time had passed. The desire to help and heal people had changed during the war. He had become a more complicated creature.

He lay still and stared up at the ceiling, feeling his chest rise and fall with each breath he took. He was lucky to be alive. He knew that. But he also knew that there must be a reason he was alive, a reason he had escaped the mud and the endless bright void. He still had work to do in the world beyond raising cows and goats. Important work.

Magda would bear him a child, and he knew it would be a boy. That would be the first step. Raising a boy would be good. He knew he could teach a boy everything he would need to learn in order to grow up strong and right. Educating an entire community, shaping and nurturing Paradise Flats, would be the more difficult task, but it was the reason he had been spared while fifty head of cattle had been sacrificed.

He nodded at the ceiling, the vision he had experienced already changing in his mind, then reached down and covered himself again with the sheet, smoothed it across his body as well as he was able. He made himself presentable for Magda and waited for the door to open.

# CHAPTER FOUR

## 1

There was a building just off the main road with glass doors that faced a gravel parking lot. The outer doors were unlocked and they opened onto a dim vestibule with a corkboard on one wall above a rack of pamphlets detailing the many features of the Kirwin National Wildlife Refuge. The inner door was locked, and a hand-written sign was posted: *CLOSED UNTIL MONDAY. HAVE A HAPPY THANKSGIVING.*

Travis checked the calendar on his phone. There was still one day left before Thanksgiving.

"Inconvenient," he said.

Bear wagged his tail in response.

Travis took a brochure that described the local wildlife and they went back outside, where the cool air tightened Travis's chest. He lifted his gaze up past the tall brown grass to the distant sparkle of blue water.

"*Kuru,*" Travis said. "Go ahead."

Bear bounded away, the grass silently closing in behind him. Travis smiled and strolled toward a covered lookout point at the far end of the parking lot. The sun was an inch above the horizon, and geese honked across the early morning sky. There was a rusty telescope bracketed to the railing, and Travis swiveled it around, squinted through it, and saw a blurry kaleidoscope of colors. He let the telescope swivel back to its original position and he leaned on the railing, looking out at the lake, the submerged trees, the white tips of their nude branches barely breaking the surface of the water.

According to the brochure, the refuge had once been home to bison and elk, who had grazed along the Solomon River. Two hundred years ago, prairie chickens and prairie dogs had shared the wooded streams and rivers of north-central Kansas with wolves and bears and mountain lions.

A clatter of claws across the wooden deck alerted him to Bear's presence and Travis turned around, surprised that his companion had finished his morning run so soon. Bear padded up to him, circled twice, and ran a few feet away along the dirt trail that led from the observation post to the lake. He stopped and came back and sat, water dripping from his fur onto the dark wood of the deck.

"What did you find?"

Bear sprang back up, shook himself off and trotted away once more, stopped and looked back at Travis.

Travis held up a finger. "One minute." He ran to the Jeep and fetched his Eclipse from the glove box, checked to be sure it was loaded, then followed after the dog as fast as he could.

It was hard going. Bear had ventured well off the trail into thick grass. It might have been a wheat field for all Travis knew. It scratched at his bare hands and was so tall that it occasionally brushed against his neck as he ran, raising red welts on his skin. Bear stopped every few yards and waited for his master to catch up, then sprinted ahead again.

The grass thinned as it neared the water, and Travis burst through a thicket to find Bear waiting for him on a broad muddy bank. Travis held his pistol down at his side and approached cautiously.

Bear stood over a wet mass of duckweed and hair, and Travis thought at first that the dog had injured a big animal. As Travis drew closer, Bear lay down next to the shape, rested his head on his paws, and turned his big brown eyes up to Travis. When Travis realized what he was looking at, he turned his head away for a minute. He had seen dead bodies before, but it was never an easy thing. He stuck the Eclipse in his coat pocket and knelt, put one hand on the dog's head to reassure him.

"Where did you find her? In the water?"

Bear thumped his tail once and Travis gazed out at the lake. He could see a wide impression in the mud where the woman's body had been dragged up the bank, and Bear's paw prints weaved through the center of the swath. The dog had walked backward up the bank, pulling the dead weight behind him, before running to get help.

Travis looked all around them but saw no signs that they were being observed. He reached out with his free hand and wiped dirt and vegetation off the woman's cheeks and out of her open eyes. Her body was bloated and bruised, pale white skin crisscrossed by thick blue veins, and she was nude except for a leather collar around her neck that had sunk itself deep into her swollen flesh. The hair on the left side of her head had been shaved, and there was a livid half-moon-shaped incision above her temple, laced together with crude stitches that looked like a parade of black ants. Travis guessed she might have been in her early sixties.

He stood again and took out his cell phone. He only had one bar, so he walked away along the bank, trying to find a decent signal.

"Middle of nowhere," he said.

He dialed 911 and gave the dispatcher his location and a brief run-down of the situation, then hung up and dialed a second number. After it rang three times, a woman picked up.

"Noah Roan Foundation."

"Arletta?"

"Tell me you found him."

"Not yet," Travis said. "I am afraid the situation has become complicated. *More* complicated, I should say. Bear has discovered a body."

"Not Ransom?" Her voice quavered.

"No," he said. "A woman."

"Who?"

"I have an idea, but I cannot be sure yet. I am currently at the scene awaiting the authorities."

"Natural causes?"

"I would guess not," Travis said. "There is quite a bit of lividity, but some of the bruising might be older. It looks to me as if she was beaten to death. And more than that. I will have to wait until an autopsy is done to be sure, but she has untreated open wounds that look man-made. I think she was tortured."

"Judah is free. I'll send him out there today."

"No, let me gather more information before we bring anyone else in. Something strange is going on here, and I want to tread lightly."

"Well, obviously something strange is going on. You've found a body."

"Bear found her."

"It could be unrelated," Arletta said. "It might have nothing to do with you at all."

"Yesterday the local sheriff attempted to scare me away."

"Ha!"

"Yes. It was amusing."

"Are you armed?"

"My handgun," he said.

"Get something heavier, just in case. And, Travis, I *am* going to send Judah."

"Give me another day or two, would you? There is a state trooper here who seems honest. I do not think she trusts me yet, but I can work with her."

"You have a very short leash here. And I want you to call in again tonight so I know you're all right."

"You need not worry about me."

"I always worry. Worrying is my job."

"I hear sirens. I should go."

"Travis? Find Ransom. Find your father and come home."

"I am working on that as we speak. Good-bye, Mother."

He hung up and squinted over the tall grass. Red and blue lights washed over the horizon near the turnoff into the gravel parking lot. He had two or three minutes before company arrived. He pulled up Skottie Foster's cell number and sent a quick text message.

NEED ASSISTANCE. HOW SOON
CAN YOU GET UP HERE?

He put the phone in his left coat pocket to balance the weight of the Eclipse, then found a trail back through the punishing grass. He walked up to the parking lot with Bear at his heels, stopped at the edge of the grass, and watched an ambulance pull into the lot, followed by a squad car skidding over the gravel. The car doors opened and Sheriff Goodman stepped out. On the other side, the deputy, Christian, jumped out and ran around the front of the car to the driver's side, stood next to the sheriff, and leveled his shotgun at Travis.

Goodman touched the brim of his hat, wiped his chin, and grinned. "We meet again." He unsnapped his holster and drew his gun.

Before Travis could open his mouth, a hundred and forty pounds of muscle and teeth and claws silently launched past him and plowed into the sheriff. Goodman fell backward against the car and his deputy fired the shotgun, missing everything but giving Bear a split second to change direction and knock Christian to the ground.

"Bear," Travis shouted. "Bear, *haltu!*"

The dog grabbed the barrel of the shotgun in his mouth and shook it from side to side, then dropped it as the sheriff rose to his knees, bringing his pistol up. Bear pushed him back down with one massive paw as Christian rolled over and grabbed for the abandoned shotgun.

"Bear, *haltu!*"

Bear did stop then, standing on the sheriff's chest, looking up at his master. Goodman stopped, too, and the deputy. Everything was perfectly still for one long moment.

"Bear," Travis said, "*kaśu.*"

The mastiff snorted, turned around and, obeying the command to hide, disappeared once more into the tall grass.

# 2

A silver Ford Escort with a red streak down its side idled against the curb across from Ruth Elder's house. Its passenger-side door was emblazoned with the words SHERIFF'S DEPARTMENT, and the warning CALL 911 was stenciled above the gas cap. As Skottie pulled up in front of Ruth's mailbox, a deputy stepped out of his car and crossed the street toward her, his hand resting easy on the butt of his gun.

Skottie's phone vibrated and she looked down at it. The screen flashed a text message: NEED ASSISTANCE. HOW SOON CAN YOU GET UP HERE?

Skottie rolled her window down as the deputy reached her.

"Keep on driving, amigo," he said. He was young and good-looking, with a wide forehead, friendly eyes, and skin the color of Emmaline's antique mahogany china cabinet.

Skottie flashed her ID and the deputy leaned forward to read it, his lips moving a little, then straightened up and pushed his hat to the back of his head. He took a step back so that Skottie could open her door and get out of the car, but he kept his eyes on Ruth Elder's house. Skottie glanced over at the house and saw a curtain move behind the big window that overlooked the front yard.

"What's going on?"

The deputy gave her a nervous glance and bit his lower lip. "I'd appreciate you moving along, Trooper. I'm trying to keep this street clear."

"Planning a parade?"

He shrugged. "Sure. You should watch out for the little old guys on tricycles."

She put her ID away and stuck out her hand. "I'm Skottie. What's your name?"

The deputy gave her hand a skeptical look before shaking it. "Ekwensi Griffith," he said. "Most people call me Quincy. Look, we got a complaint from the man of this house here that somebody's been hassling his wife."

"Ruth Elder's husband called you?"

"I guess. He's up in New York somewhere."

"Yeah, the man of this house." She pointed so he wouldn't misunderstand. "This house right here? He's long dead, Quincy. So who called you?"

"I dunno. Some guy. He calls the sheriff last night and tells him to run some other guy off. And the sheriff was ready to do it, too, but then he got a call out to the lake this morning. I guess I just don't know enough." He looked at Skottie and pursed his lips. "But maybe you know something."

Skottie shook her head. She was putting two and two together, but it didn't quite add up. Ruth Elder's husband was dead, but Rachel Bloom was temporarily living in the house and her husband must be around somewhere. Maybe he was in New York. Had Ruth's son-in-law decided he didn't want anyone prying into her life anymore? Rachel Bloom hadn't seemed agitated when they left her. She had cooperated with Travis, had answered his questions willingly. Change of heart?

"The man who called in, the one who filed the complaint, was his last name Bloom?"

"I have no idea."

"What about the other guy," Skottie said, "the one your boss was gonna chase off. Is his name Travis Roan?"

"I don't know any names. Sheriff just said he was some kinda foreigner. A white guy. You working with him? That what you're doing out here today?"

Skottie didn't bother to answer him. She walked around the front of her car and stepped up onto Ruth's immaculate brown lawn.

"Whoa," Deputy Griffith said. "Hey, I can't let you go up there."

"I just need a minute, brother. Want to ask the lady a question."

She turned and started up the walk, but Quincy rushed forward and put a hand on her arm. Skottie stopped and looked at him, and he must have seen something dangerous in her eyes because he immediately removed his hand and his neck turned a deeper shade of walnut.

"Listen," he said, "I let you go up there and bother that lady . . . well, it's my ass. Tell you what, you let me call this in and get the sheriff's permission, okay? Then everything'll be cool, right?"

The sun was peeking through a cloud, bathing the deputy in a halo of light. Skottie squinted at him, at the dirty collar of his uniform shirt, the razor bumps on his jaw, and the stubble on his shaved scalp. She wondered what time it had been when the sheriff had summoned poor Quincy, whether the kid had been able to grab a bite to eat before taking up his lonely post on Ruth Elder's block.

"All right," she said. "Let's see what Goodman says."

She walked with Quincy to the silver Escort. She could tell he was uncomfortable, that he didn't want her listening in, but he left the car door open and sat sideways with his feet stuck out on the pavement. He thumbed the button on his handset and asked the dispatcher for Sheriff Goodman's car.

Skottie heard the usual crackle of static and then a woman's voice. "He's back here already, Quincy."

"That was quick."

"You want him? He's in his office."

"Yeah, thanks, Phyllis." While they waited for Goodman to pick up, Quincy squared his shoulders. He avoided looking at Skottie. She could see the tension rising in his shoulders as he prepared to talk to his employer, and he began to breathe faster. He jumped when a male voice blared through the speaker.

"That you, Quincy boy?"

"It's me, Sheriff. Listen, I'm at that house you told me to watch, and there's a woman here."

"'Course there's a woman there. Didn't you pay attention when I told you—"

"I mean there's *another* woman. A different one. This lady came to talk to the homeowner, and I don't know if that's okay or not."

"Who's that? You weren't supposed to scare her friends and neighbors. You know what, why don't you just come on in? The situation resolved itself at this end while you was out there jerkin' off."

"What?" Skottie reached for the handset, and Quincy reluctantly gave it to her. She stretched the cord across his chest and leaned forward. "Sheriff? This is Trooper Skottie Foster from the Hays office. What situation are you talking about? What was resolved?"

"Foster? What are you doin' there?"

"I came to talk to Rachel Bloom about her mother. Your deputy did his job and stopped me before I even got out of my car." She saw a flash of gratitude in Quincy's eyes and she almost smiled at him. "What's happening?"

"Don't see how that's any business of yours, Trooper. You're way out of your league."

"Sheriff, I sent you a message about a suspicious man who was on his way up here. Driving a rented Jeep."

"Oh, that was you?" Goodman's tone changed. There was an undertone of curiosity now, overlaying the arrogant entitlement. "And, what, you followin' up on that?"

"I am. Did something happen with him?"

"You know what, why don't you come on in with that young Quincy. Let's have us a little talk."

"Did—"

"Quincy, you still there, son? Give that nice lady a ride on in. You're done out there anyway. Goodman out."

Quincy hung up and squinted at Skottie. "Am I supposed to arrest you?"

"I don't think so," Skottie said. "I think we're friends now."

Quincy jerked his head at the passenger seat. "Well then, hop in, amigo. I can bring you back to your car after you see the sheriff."

Skottie ran back to her civilian vehicle, a 2014 Subaru Legacy, and grabbed her purse. She picked up a manila file folder from the passenger seat that held the transcription of Ruth Elder's journal, then changed her mind and left it there. She locked the doors and crossed the street again. She glanced back at Ruth Elder's house as she got in Deputy Griffith's squad car, but the curtains were pulled tight across the windows.

Quincy started the car and they rolled away from the curb. "I think you and Sheriff Goodman are gonna get along great," he said.

Skottie detected a note of sarcasm in his voice.

# 3

Muffled voices squawked over the car's radio. A conversation or a song, Travis couldn't be sure which. He knew he was dreaming, but he couldn't make himself wake up. He turned off the radio, but the voices grew louder for a few seconds before cutting out completely. He thought he had heard a few half words, a staticky phrase in some other language, and maybe a melody in the background, but he couldn't place the tune. Fog had settled over the Flint Hills, and Travis could only see as far ahead as his headlights. He slowed to twenty miles an hour and glanced over at his traveling companion, who was having trouble staying awake.

Bear looked up at him, his tongue lolling. His left ear was flipped inside out, but he didn't seem to mind. He laid his head back down and dozed off.

The two of them floated along quietly, the highway scrolling slowly by under their vehicle, jagged rock walls looming up on either side. Occasionally Travis saw naked men jumping from rock to rock or running along with them, matching the speed of the car from high above. The dim headlights of other vehicles crept past them on the other side of the median, and Travis thought he saw some sort of large creature on the shoulder, big as a house, chasing them. He sped up and it fell back, swallowed up in the fog.

Travis didn't hear the hoofbeats until Bear perked up and shook his black mane. The dog waited for Travis to roll down the passenger-side window and then stuck his head out. The sound was unmistakable but alien, echoing off the hills and the asphalt and seeming to come from all around them. Travis took his foot off the accelerator as a pale horse materialized in front of them, charging straight at their car. Travis reacted instantly, braking and swerving. The horse swept past, clipping the side mirror as it went, and disappeared.

"Was that real?"

The dog pulled his head back into the Jeep and blinked at Travis. He had the sudden feeling Bear could talk, had always been able to talk.

Travis turned on his hazards and pulled a U-turn, bounced over into the grass median and back up on the shoulder, heading the wrong direction. Bear put his heavy paws on the dashboard and watched the road ahead.

A minute later a silver car zoomed past them, its blue headlights blinding Travis. He caught a glimpse of a dented fender and a long red streak down the side of the car that obscured the phone number beneath a cartoon badge and the number 911. He took his foot off the gas and let the Jeep cruise forward, already dreading what he knew he would find.

The horse lay at the edge of the road, a colorless shape on the dark grass. Travis pulled over and got out. Bear jumped down behind him and followed.

When it saw Travis coming, the horse tried to get up. It scrabbled at the ground and craned its neck. But its legs failed and it grew tired. There was a gash open along its side, and Travis could see the bone in one of its front legs. He turned and went back to the car, but couldn't find his gun. He thought he ought to have a sugar cube or an apple. Anything. But he didn't. He looked back and saw that the horse was talking to Bear now, telling him something, and Bear was responding, but Travis was too far away to hear them.

Bear saw Travis watching and came to him and pressed against his legs. Travis bent and put a hand on the top of Bear's head, felt the warmth and the faint pulse beneath the fur. Then he sank to the ground and wrapped his arms around Bear's massive neck.

After a long moment, he stood again and looked back at the horse, but it was gone.

"It got a taste of freedom," he said. "That's something, isn't it?"

The dog walked away from him and trotted off into the spongy gray nothingness. Travis looked around for their car and suddenly couldn't remember where he had left it. He sat down in the middle of the road and closed his eyes, prepared to wait for Bear to return, for the horse to reappear, for some sort of insight.

He woke up then and reached out for Bear, but the dog wasn't there. He sat and stared at the polished metal toilet in the corner, the bare walls without windows, the locked door, and the wooden chair that was missing part of one leg. Travis felt a sharp pain and he touched his face, probing carefully with his fingertips. A dried nugget of dark blood fell into his lap and he winced. He wondered if anyone knew where he was, and he remembered how the sheriff had promised he would disappear if he chose to remain in Kansas.

# 4

The Burden County sheriff's station was in a modified double-wide trailer, all mint-green siding and white trim. Except for the sign out front, it looked exactly like one of the starter homes that lined the other side of the street. Deputy Ekwensi Griffith pulled into the parking lot beside the building and they got out. They had stopped at a KFC on the way back, and Quincy balanced two buckets of chicken and a big bag of sides. He kicked his car door shut and the bag swung around, banging into his leg.

Skottie stood for a long moment looking around, her boots scuffling in the dirt. There was a pen behind the lot where three German shepherds paced around in circles, growling and throwing themselves against the wire walls of their enclosure. Skottie waved at them and held the station's front door for Quincy, then followed him inside, where she could still hear the dogs barking. A woman who might have been Phyllis the dispatcher sat behind a long counter in the middle of the front room.

Quincy motioned for Skottie to wait there and he crossed to a door behind the counter. He went through, and Skottie caught a glimpse of a dim hallway before the door closed again. The woman smiled at Skottie and nodded at a row of plastic chairs, then returned to flipping through a fashion magazine.

Skottie sat and waited. The decor reminded her of a chiropractor's waiting room more than a police station. There was a plastic tree in the corner behind the front door and a cheaply framed Norman Rockwell print on the wall next to the tree. She perused the collection of magazines on the end table and picked up a copy of *Family Handyman*, passing on *Deer & Deer Hunting*. She read an article explaining how to build a tree house in twelve easy steps and had just settled into a review of this model year's riding mowers when the inner door opened again and Sheriff Goodman sidled into the room. Skottie stood and took a step forward, but the sheriff didn't make a move to shake her hand. The skin around his left eye was purple and splotchy, and his jaw was noticeably swollen. He frowned.

"I know you," he said. "Seen you before."

"We met once a few weeks ago," Skottie said. She tossed the *Family Handyman* on the table. "That wasn't my favorite day."

Goodman squinted at her, then laughed, three sharp barks, as if he had read what laughter was supposed to sound like.

"What'd I do?"

"You don't remember?"

"Did I hit on you? 'Cause I get a little flirty sometimes."

"You made damn sure I knew what my place was and who was boss around here."

He studied her for a minute. "Well, if I didn't get flirty, maybe I still got a chance."

"Not likely," she said. "What happened to your face?"

"Nothing to worry about," he said.

"Hunting accident?"

"Something like that." He nodded at her. "Okay, let's you and me have a talk."

"Yes," Skottie said. "Let's." She smiled at the woman, who might as well have been holding her magazine upside down for all the attention she was paying it. She didn't smile back.

Skottie followed Goodman around the counter and through the door, past a kitchenette that smelled like fried chicken and a unisex bathroom with the door standing open. She glanced in and saw a plunger sitting on the toilet seat. Down a brief hallway, they came to three doors, two of them open. One of the rooms was empty and contained a low cot, a chair, and a metal airplane toilet installed in the corner. She guessed that the closed door next to it hid a similar room. Deputy Griffith emerged from it, closed the door again behind him before Skottie could see inside, and brushed past them.

A young guy with a brown shirt and a sandy brown buzz cut was waiting for them behind a desk in the third room. He had his feet up and was picking chicken out of his teeth with the corner of a folded five-dollar bill. A paper plate piled with bones sat on the desk in front of him, and he used his free hand to pat his stomach.

"Shoulda saved you some," he said. "I know how you people like chicken."

"Dammit, Christian," Goodman said. "Getcher feet off my desk."

Christian moved the chair back and stood. Skottie noticed his left arm was bandaged and there was an ugly welt on the side of his neck. The brass name badge pinned to his chest read c. PUCKETT. He saluted Goodman, then walked past Skottie with his eyes averted and closed the door behind him. Skottie could hear him in the hallway, talking in low tones with Quincy.

"Sorry about him," Goodman said. He used the side of his hand to brush the plate into a trash basket next to his chair. "Take a seat."

Skottie ignored the offer and stood across from Goodman, looking down at him across the desk. "Guess it's hard to find decent help."

"Christian's my nephew. My sister thought he'd get some discipline if he come to work for me. He's a decent kid, just young, is all. He'll grow into the job."

Skottie couldn't bring herself to care one way or another about Sheriff Goodman's opinions or his relatives. They could think what they liked about one another and about her. None of it mattered. She had a job to do, and the worst that these men could do was get in her way, irritate her, and make her lose her cool. So she kept her mouth shut and smiled, but the smile didn't mean a thing.

"So," Goodman said, "what can I do for you, since you already made the long haul up from Hays on your day off?"

Skottie raised an eyebrow.

"Oh, yeah," Goodman said. "I know you're not here in any kind of official way. I put in a call down there when Quincy picked you up." He pointed in the general direction of the waiting room and, beyond it, to the highway. "You got no reason to be here, far as anybody knows. So let's go forward on the understanding that I'm being nice to you."

"Great," Skottie said. She hoped she sounded sincere. "I appreciate that."

"Since we're friends now, I'm curious. You gave me a heads-up about this guy Roan, and now he's a suspect in a murder we got out at Kirwin. If you know something about him, I'd appreciate hearing it. Might go a ways with me."

Skottie considered how much she should tell him. Goodman didn't seem to know that she'd been in contact with Travis since the traffic stop, but once he found out he would drop the friendly act. She might have a brief window of time in which he'd share information with her, if he thought she was cooperating, but he'd be suspicious if she volunteered anything too easily. "What does that mean, it might go a ways? What do you think you can do for me?"

Goodman looked at her and his eyes narrowed. When he stood up, Skottie rocked back on her heels and then silently cursed herself for doing it. She hadn't meant to show him any kind of weakness or indecision. Goodman crossed to the filing cabinet in the back corner of the room. As he passed the window, Skottie's gaze was drawn outside to Deputy Griffith, who was leaning on the hood of his squad car in the parking lot. He was watching the office, though Skottie was reasonably certain he couldn't see in past the blinds.

"You want something?" Goodman had pulled a pint of Dewar's from the top drawer, and he held it out to her, waggling it back and forth.

"No, thanks," Skottie said.

"Suit yourself. Five o'clock somewhere, right?" Goodman grinned and poured three fingers into a paper Dixie cup from a stack on top of the cabinet. He crossed in front of the window again, and this time Skottie avoided looking out at the lot. Goodman sat down, and now Skottie sat across from him.

"What we got," Goodman said, "is a woman murdered sometime in the last few days and dumped out at the lake in the Kirwin preserve. You know it? The lake?"

"I used to go out there when I was a kid. In high school."

"I didn't know you grew up around here."

"No reason you should."

"Whereabouts?"

"Why?"

"I grew up here, too. Feels like I oughta know you."

"You don't wanna know me," Skottie said. "Anyway, what makes you think Dr. Roan is connected to the woman you found?"

"Don't know yet. Still looking into it." Goodman regarded her over the lip of the paper cup. He took a sip of scotch. "What's the deal with the Bloom chick? Her husband calls in and complains somebody harassed her, gives a description of Roan. Next thing I know, you're popping up over there, too."

"I visited her yesterday. I was going back to ask her a couple of follow-up questions."

"About Roan?"

"No."

"Then what?"

Skottie decided to change the subject. "What's your victim's name?"

"Margaret Weber. She was a teacher out at the middle school in Hays. Somebody did a real number on her. Took his sweet time."

Skottie recalled her conversation with Travis at the bar. He had talked about killing as a last resort. "Roan's only been in the area a couple of days, right? So why's he a suspect?"

"I don't think he did the killing," Goodman said. "I think he dumped the body. Found him practically standing over it. Which means he's got an accomplice that did the actual work. Like, maybe he came out here in the first place to help somebody finish poor Margaret off and hide the crime."

"That's ridiculous."

"Is it?" He sipped from his cup again without taking his eyes off her.

"You think it's me?"

"Is it?"

"So you're thinking I killed a schoolteacher in Paradise Flats, and then Dr. Travis Roan, a person I've never met before, caught a flight out here to help me cover it up. Why?"

"You got a daughter. She go to the school Margaret Weber teaches at? *Taught* at, I mean. Maybe you had a run-in with her, maybe she gave your girl a bad grade and it was the wrong time of the month."

"My daughter's not in middle school yet." Skottie spoke through clenched teeth, but held her temper. She knew Goodman was trying to rattle her. "I've never met your victim."

Goodman waved his hand at her, swiping it through the dust that floated in the sunlight over his desk. "Ah, I don't think it was you. Just wanted to see what you'd say." The dust floated back.

"You don't think Roan had anything to do with your case."

Goodman shrugged.

"So why keep him?"

"He's weird," Goodman said. "I don't like him."

"Not good enough, and you know it. You're going to have to turn him loose pretty soon, unless you've got some real evidence."

Goodman nodded. "Yeah. But I can make him nervous for a while. Meanwhile, you wanna tell me how you know him? Aside from you two colluding in a murder, that is." He smiled to let her know he was just kidding around.

The light changed in the office as the sun went back behind the clouds, and Skottie glanced out the window again. A white Explorer had pulled into the slot next to Quincy's car, and a uniformed state trooper was standing behind it, engaged in conversation with the deputy. Skottie recognized the trooper as Lieutenant Keith Johnson. Goodman followed her gaze and swiveled in his seat. He pulled the blinds aside.

"There we go," he said. "Wondered how long he was gonna take to get out here. Those SUVs y'all use don't move very damn fast, do they?"

"You called my lieutenant?"

"Told you that. Called soon as Quincy ran into you."

"Why?"

Goodman let the blinds drop back into place. He set his scotch down and folded his hands under his chin.

"You got your neck of the woods and I got mine. You stay in your neck or you tell me why. Today I tell your boss you're up here interfering in my investigation, tomorrow maybe I arrest you because now the groundwork's been laid, you see?"

"You can't arrest me."

"Maybe I can't hold you, but I can sure as shit put you in a room for a few hours and make your life hell while I got you."

Skottie leaned forward over the desk. "What's your problem, Goodman? Why are you making this adversarial? Are you so insecure about what's happening in your 'neck of the woods'?"

Goodman made his strange laughing noise again. He held up his hands, palms out, placating her. "Okay, okay. Let's go back to being friends again." He picked up the paper cup, saw that it was empty, and his eyes darted to the filing cabinet, but he set the cup back down and centered it on the desk, staring at it while he talked to her, moving it slowly back and forth. "You know how often we catch a murder in Burden County? I'll tell you, it's one, maybe two, in a year. It's always some guy gets liquored up and hits his wife too hard. Too hard this one time. Or somebody pushes somebody else, maybe hits a guy in a bar, and they don't get back up. But what we don't get is a woman's body with a dog collar on her neck, sunk down in the lake. That don't happen here, and I'm guessing you can sympathize with me how I don't like seeing it." He looked up at her for a second. "I just don't like seeing that. And your friend Travis Roan either happened to stumble on it or he's involved with it in some damn way." He glanced at the filing cabinet again, then smacked his lips and turned his gaze back to Skottie. "Like you say, he's been in the area for two days and, also like you say, I can't hold him very long. But I don't like him and

I don't like coincidences. So . . . would you be so kind as to tell me, Trooper Foster, did he divulge anything to you in your encounters with him that I might find of interest? Anything I can use to help solve this murder I got?"

He sat back in his chair and raised his eyebrows in a silent invitation to open up.

"Right," Skottie said. "Cards on the table?"

Goodman nodded.

She almost opened up, but at the last moment stuck with her instincts and lied. "He never told me why he was here."

Goodman sighed. "Then why were you at Ruth Elder's house this morning?"

"I wasn't. I saw your deputy parked there and I stopped to see what was going on. Curiosity, that's all."

"You happened to be driving past the house where your buddy Roan was yesterday? And where you say you were? That's what you're telling me?"

"I guess so."

"More coincidences, huh? Your day off, you drive all the way up from Hays and then decide to drive down a residential street where I got Quincy watching a house and where you been before by your own admission. Amazing. Somebody should call *Ripley's Believe It or Not!*, if that's still a thing."

"It's not a coincidence," Skottie said. "I got a text from Roan this morning. It said something happened up here and to come right away."

"Can I see that text?"

"I'm not giving you my phone."

"But he had your number."

"He got it from the dispatcher yesterday. Lied and told her he was a friend of mine. You can ask my lieutenant about that if you don't believe me."

"And you have no idea what Roan's doing here in Kansas, why he's snooping around a dead woman's house or why he got himself found near another dead woman's body?"

"None."

"But you come running because he texted you."

"It was that or clean my oven and make a pumpkin pie. It's my day off, and I really didn't have anything better to do. I'm just as curious about this guy as you are, Sheriff."

Goodman watched her for a long time, maybe waiting for her to say something else. When she didn't, he finally stood up again and she followed suit.

"I'm gonna pretend I believe you, Trooper," Goodman said. "But from now on, Travis Roan is my problem, not yours. Unless you got something concrete to give me, something helpful, you stay the hell away from Paradise Flats, you stay away from Rachel Bloom, you stay away from Travis Roan, and you let me do my job."

"You got it." Skottie saluted him and turned to leave the room. Behind her, she heard the filing cabinet scrape open.

# 5

She stepped out of the pale green building and saw Ekwensi Griffith headed toward her, his boots crunching on the gravel lot. The dogs were barking, still throwing themselves at the sides of their chain-link enclosure. As he drew near, Quincy waved his hand and shouted as if he wanted the sheriff to hear him inside. "I guess you'll be need-ing a ride back to your car, Trooper."

Behind him, Lieutenant Johnson was waiting, leaning against the back of the Explorer with his arms folded across his chest. He pushed himself away from his vehicle and cleared his throat. "No worries, Deputy." His voice boomed across the lot. "I'll give her a ride out there."

Quincy turned, walking backward, and nodded at the lieutenant. "Okay. Yeah, that's great." Then he turned again and bumped into Skottie before she could step out of the way. He grabbed her arm and pressed a piece of paper into her hand. "Whoa! Sorry. You okay?"

"Yeah," Skottie said.

Quincy leaned in and whispered, "He asked me to give this to you. It's my ass if Goodman finds out. Trusting you, amigo." He patted her on the shoulder and moved away, trotted toward his car without looking back.

Lieutenant Johnson was watching Quincy, frowning. Skottie took advantage of the distraction and stuffed the paper into her pocket.

Johnson turned his gaze back to her. "You ready to go, Foster?"

"Yeah."

Skottie went around to the other side of the Explorer and got in. Johnson started the engine and reversed out of the lot onto the resi-dential street. Behind them, Deputy Griffith's squad car pulled out and drove away from them in the other direction. The shaft of sun-light Skottie had seen from the window of Goodman's office was well hidden now. The sky was a slate sheet stretching to the horizon.

"Which way we going to your car?"

She pointed. They drove in silence for a moment before Johnson spoke. "We don't know each other too good yet, I guess."

"Lieutenant?"

"I mean, you might be thinking I'm the same as that sheriff."

Skottie shrugged.

"Goodman calls and I come running. I can see where you might think me and him are friends, and I don't want that going through your head. I'm here 'cause I was concerned about you, okay? Long and short of it. How'd he treat you?"

"I'm okay."

A handful of tiny snowflakes settled on the windshield, and Johnson turned on the wipers at their lowest setting.

"You ready to tell me what's going on?"

"Turn left up here," Skottie said. "I can tell you what I know, but there's not much."

"I'm all ears."

She told him everything that had happened in the last two days, starting with spotting Travis Roan and his unleashed dog at the highway rest stop. She ended with her trip in Deputy Ekwensi Griffith's squad car.

Lieutenant Johnson pulled up next to Skottie's Subaru and put his vehicle in park. They sat there watching snowflakes melt on the warm windshield while she finished her story. At last Johnson shook his head. He looked puzzled. "What did Goodman want with you?"

"He's got a murder and he likes Roan for it, but he can't pin it on him. There's no evidence, and it doesn't make any sense to me that Roan could've done it or would've done it. This isn't a guy who came here to carry out a hit on some woman. He's chasing an old Nazi to serve him with papers."

"And what? The sheriff thought you could cough up some clues for him?"

"I don't know."

"Something's not adding up for me," Johnson said. He maneuvered in his bucket seat until he was comfortable and could see Skottie without craning his neck. "But look, like it or not, Kurt Goodman is the duly elected sheriff of this county. Unless you have a legitimate reason to think he's doing something illegal, you need to step off. If he's trying to deal with a homicide case, you're not gonna make it easier for him or for this Roan guy or for yourself by butting in."

"I wasn't butting in. He's the one who—"

"Skottie. Just . . . You're back on duty tomorrow, right? So let's worry about our job, let Goodman worry about his. Travis Roan can call a lawyer if he's innocent, okay?"

"Yes, sir."

Johnson sighed. "Hey, this stuff is supposed to pick up here pretty soon." He pointed out the window at the lowering sky. "Better get yourself home before it opens up on us."

"I will," Skottie said. "And Lieutenant? Thanks."

"See you tomorrow, Trooper."

She opened the door and hopped out next to her car. Johnson sat there for a second while Skottie found her keys, then he put the Explorer in gear and drove away, down the street and around the corner.

Skottie had been so caught up in the events of the day—and thinking about the note in her pocket—that she opened the car door without first hitting the button on her key fob. She didn't realize until she was sitting in the car that she hadn't unlocked it. It had already been open. She immediately checked out the back seat and the glove box, looking for anything that might be missing or that hadn't been there before. The file folder with Rachel Bloom's translation of her mother's journal was gone, but nothing else seemed to have been disturbed. She started the car and got out, stood next to it looking up and down the street for anything suspicious.

The theft of the transcript didn't bother her much. It would be easy enough to print it out again. But she didn't like the idea that someone had been in her car without her knowledge. She circled the car, looking for scratches around the locks. Either she had left the car unlocked in the first place (which wasn't like her at all) or someone had used a slim jim to loid the lock and then hadn't thought to lock it back up behind them. *Of course,* she thought, *the person most likely to have a slim jim in a town the size of Paradise Flats would be a firefighter or a cop. Like maybe a sheriff's deputy.*

She let her car run, warming it up, and finally reached into the front pocket of her jeans for the piece of paper Quincy had given her. She leaned back against the open driver's-side door, unfolded it and smoothed it out, and read it.

*Please find Bear at the lake.*

*Do you remember the word?*

She read it two more times, then folded it back up and stuck it back in her pocket. She was angling herself into the car when she saw the curtains at the front of Ruth Elder's house fall back into place.

She closed her car door and walked up the path to the front door. She held her thumb against the button, listening for movement inside the house, watching the curtains for a suspicious eye.

She knocked and rang the doorbell again, but got no response.

All she needed was a squad car turning the corner at the end of the street. She headed back to her car, trying to see both ends of the road. There was no movement, no chirping birds, no sign of life. She glanced at the sky above her. It was almost black. A storm was blowing in fast, and Skottie remembered she had to pick her daughter up at school. She glanced at her phone. She only had an hour.

And she still had to get out to the lake to find Travis Roan's dog.

# 6

Travis was sitting up at the edge of his cot when the door opened and Quincy entered. The deputy shut the door behind him and crossed over to Travis. He was carrying a paper plate with two pieces of fried chicken and a dollop of mashed potatoes.

"Sorry, I think they got a little cold," Quincy said.

Travis took the plate and set it down next to him on the cot. "What, no biscuit?"

"The sheriff ate yours, I think."

"Understandable."

Quincy shuffled from one foot to the other and crossed his arms, then uncrossed them and ran a hand over his scalp. Travis waited for him to figure out what he wanted to say.

"I, um . . . I gave Trooper Foster your note."

"Thank you again."

"I hope I did the right thing there. I mean, I hope I didn't just aid and abet, or whatever."

"Well, you did aid me," Travis said. "But there was no criminal intent, so you need not worry about abetting."

"I took a risk for you. And I'm not sure why I did it. But if the sheriff finds out, I don't think he'll care whether you think there's criminal activity or not."

"Then why help me at all?" Travis stood and leaned back against the wall. He stuck his hands in his pockets. He wanted a cigarette, but he'd given them up. Bear's sinuses were too sensitive. "Sheriff Goodman hardly seems like the type of man to associate with people who are, let us say, different than he is. Is that why you passed my note along to Officer Foster?"

"I don't understand you."

"Was helping me a way for you to get back at your sheriff?"

"Get back at him for what?"

Travis shrugged.

"Oh, you mean you think he's racist," Quincy said.

"Is he?"

"He's set in his ways and he's not real tolerant, but he pretty much hates everybody equally. Black, white, men, women. He's fair-minded about it, at least. Besides, he kinda had to give me a job. He's my father-in-law."

Travis raised his eyebrows, genuinely surprised, and Quincy laughed.

"Yeah," Quincy said. "My wife, Angela, the sheriff's daughter, when she told him about us, he wasn't too happy. But she doesn't back down from anybody ever, not even her own dad. He could see he either had to get on board with us or she was gonna up and leave with me. I don't know where we were gonna go, but if she said we were gonna leave, well . . . I guess we were going somewhere. And knowing her, she probably never would've talked to her dad again."

"And so he gave you this job . . ."

"To keep Angela around. He loves her. And he's getting used to me."

"So why did you give Skottie Foster my note?"

"It felt like the right thing to do. She's a cop, and I guess you're something like a cop."

"As are you," Travis said.

"And Sheriff Goodman . . . Well, I think maybe he's in over his head with whatever's going on around here. Maybe I can help nudge things so we don't all get caught in a shitstorm. Anyway, I hope to God I'm right about you."

"As do I, Deputy Griffith."

"Enjoy your chicken."

Quincy left the room, and Travis heard the lock engage. He sighed and picked up the greasy paper plate.

## AUGUST 1970

The Baptists had moved to a new tin building on Broadway and the old church sat empty, a window on the west side boarded up, another window missing a pane of faux stained glass. Judging by the rest of the window the pane might have been purple and blue, but now it looked black, no light shining through the hole. There was a For Sale sign jammed into the lawn in front, weeds growing up around the metal stakes.

Jacob led the way around to the back and used a key to open a gray metal door. The bottom of the door scraped against concrete as it opened, and Rudy caught a whiff of must and rat droppings.

"Been abandoned for years now," Jacob said. "No offers on it."

"Nobody wants an old church?"

"I guess it runs against the grain to turn it into a doughnut shop. Better to let it sit. More pure or something."

"Something."

The two of them stepped inside and Jacob felt along the wall until he found a switch. Electric sconces blinked slowly to life, revealing a long hallway with oak doors staggered along both sides.

"Got 'em to turn the power back on for us. Water, too, but that's gonna take a day or two."

"I'm in no hurry," Rudy said.

He moved down the dim passage, opening doors and turning on lights. This area of the church had apparently been used for Sunday school and evening Bible classes. There were three old cribs in one room and an open toy box with grimy plastic animals spilling out of it. Another room held an old upright piano, the keyboard cover propped up and three ivory keys missing. There was a bookshelf that was half-filled with dog-eared paperbacks. Titles like *The Power of Faith, Lay Your Hands, Follow My Shepherd.* Rudy wondered how quickly they would burn if he lit a match. He pictured piano wire shriveling and popping, discordant music playing to a house of ghosts.

"In there's the changing room," Jacob said. "Where the altar boys put on their robes. The choir, too, I guess. Whoever."

Rudy could have figured it out for himself. There was a wardrobe against the back wall with its doors standing open. A handful of wire hangers dangled from a rod.

"And through here you got the main church. Pews, altar, big cross and all."

Rudy looked through the high arched portal and saw what the lightning had done. Sunlight shone through a hole in the ceiling, and the floor was covered with feathers and bird shit and wet paper around a pit that was charred black around the edges. A permanent shadow reached out from the altar toward the abandoned pews that sat helpless, row after row, like soldiers on the front line.

"But come this way first."

Jacob ducked into a doorway and Rudy followed him down a narrow staircase. At the bottom of the stairs to their right was a shuffleboard court, blue and red painted lines dead-ending at a cinder-block wall. To their left, an accordion-style partition had been pushed aside and three steps led down into a big meeting hall with a pass-through to a kitchen. Rudy could see an industrial oven and an avocado-colored refrigerator.

"Gas is turned on, too," Jacob said. "Ovens work."

Rudy smiled.

"And here's the big surprise." Jacob found another key on the ring and unlocked a door next to the pass-through, revealing yet another staircase, narrower, cement with gritty black strips to keep people from slipping and falling. He flicked a switch and beckoned to Rudy and they descended together into a subbasement, murky and dank. The ceiling was low, but the room extended the entire length of the church above, as far as Rudy could tell, and perhaps half its width. The walls were painted gray, and four light fixtures were inset at regular intervals above them. There was a furnace at the far end, next to a water heater, and stacking chairs were piled beside folding particle-board tables against another wall. The floor sloped to a drain in the middle of the room.

"This isn't on the plans," Jacob said. "I didn't even know it was here until I came to look the place over yesterday. What do you think?"

"This could be very useful," Rudy said.

"That's what I thought. Too much traffic out by your place these days. That shed is harder and harder to get into without somebody asking why you don't mow your grass more often."

"I worry about the boys. They're at an age where they're exploring everything. And Magda worries me, too."

"She suspicious?"

"I don't think so. But this pregnancy has been harder on her, and she puts Kurt and Heinrich out of the house more often. They're very curious boys. Eventually they'll think to look inside the shed."

"It's good for boys to be curious."

"Of course."

"But a church . . ."

"Nobody would think twice about a preacher visiting his church at any hour of the day or night," Rudy said.

"We can fix this up pretty nice, I think," Jacob said.

"We can indeed, Deacon Meyer." Rudy smiled again and turned around and around in the big gray room, planning it out in his mind. The cabinets would go here, the steel table would go there. Perhaps there would even be room for a second table. And the ceiling was solid enough that he thought he could hang a considerable weight from it. If he had strong enough chains.

"Come on," Jacob said. "Let's see if they left any wine in the kitchen."

# CHAPTER FIVE

## 1

I t was early afternoon, but dark clouds gave the landscape an aura of dusk. Snow was coming down harder and there was a cold breeze gusting off the water. Skottie parked next to the rented Jeep, got out of her car and walked toward the lookout, with its useless rusted telescope. The surrounding trees were bare, and the raised platform gave her a good view of the park. Crime scene tape was strung out from tree to tree along the lakeshore, snapping in the wind, keeping time to the ripples that floated ashore. A pair of abandoned goggles had rolled into a thicket, its rubber strap swaying like a river snake.

She was going to be late picking her daughter up, which meant Maddy would be shuffled off to the after-school program for snacks and SunnyD and four square in the gymnasium. Maddy would be happy. She loved the extra time with her friends. But now there would be an extra charge for child care services on the monthly bill from the school. Skottie was thinking about maybe getting a second job in the evenings to help make ends meet. There were always freelance guard jobs listed for police, but Skottie hated to take even more time away from her daughter. They were having enough trouble.

She listened to the sounds of her boot heels on the wooden floor of the lookout, the splashes of nearby water rippling against iced-over shallows, a chickadee singing its "hey, sweetie" song somewhere above her. But there were no sounds she associated with dogs. And there wouldn't be, would there? Bear didn't make noise.

The note Travis had written for her said that Bear was at the lake. Skottie assumed the sheriff had left Bear behind, and of course Travis would be worried about leaving the dog out in the wildlife refuge all night. The weather report had predicted freezing conditions all week.

She scanned the tall brown brush all around her, looking for some sign of movement, but there was nothing.

"Bear?"

She listened again and heard a faint rustling in the grass that might have been the wind.

She cupped her hands around her mouth and shouted, "Bear! Bear, come!"

She closed her eyes and tried to think. In the note, Travis had asked if she remembered "the word." He had taught her a word to use with the dog. A word in some other language. He was trusting her to recall it because he wouldn't have dared to write it down for her. For all he knew, the note might have been intercepted before it got to her and Bear's safety would have been compromised.

The sound of an engine and the crunch of gravel behind her broke her concentration. She turned and saw a familiar silver car pull into the lot and park beside Skottie's Subaru. Deputy Ekwensi Griffith stepped out and made a show of stretching his arms, pivoting in one direction and then the other. He relaxed and put his hands in his pockets, walked out toward Skottie.

Skottie took a step back and felt the railing press into her spine. Her boot prints across the deck were dark against the fine dusting of snow. "What are you doing here?"

"I read your note," he said. "Before I gave it to you. Sorry."

"I would have read it, too, if I were you. But that doesn't really answer my question."

Quincy stopped at the edge of the lookout, one foot up on the first step, but he didn't ascend to the platform. He pulled his hands out of his pockets and held them up in a gesture of surrender. "I come in peace, amigo."

And Skottie suddenly remembered the special command word for Bear.

"You're smiling," Quincy said. "That mean you're happy to see me?"

"Goodman know you're out here?"

"No way. He'd kill me." Quincy looked up at the charcoal sky. "I mean, literally kill me."

"Then why follow me out here?"

"Something's going on. I knew Mrs. Weber. Not real well, but she was a nice enough lady. I can't believe anyone would kill her like that. Then there's Roan, who just decided to trust me with that note, even after the sheriff worked him over pretty good. He seems like a decent guy. And there's you, too. How do you fit in with all this? I guess I wouldn't be much of a lawman if I don't at least try to figure this thing out."

Skottie waved her hand at him. "Back up a second. Goodman beat Travis up?"

"A little bit, I guess. Said Roan resisted arrest."

"How was Margaret Weber killed?"

"Strangled. And some other stuff. Real nasty stuff."

"Travis has a gun. I saw it myself. If it's not the murder weapon—"

"Just because he has a gun doesn't mean he didn't strangle her."

Skottie shook her head. "Yeah, right. But it doesn't make a lot of sense, does it?"

"That note," Quincy said. "It said you should look for a bear. But that's the dog's name, right?"

"That so?"

"That dog attacked the sheriff, and Christian, too."

"Attacked them? That's why they're bruised and battered?"

"It could've hurt them, I think. It really just knocked them down. And Christian wouldn't say it, but I think it scared the shit out of him. He said it's the size of an actual bear. Maybe it is one. Anyway, it ran off." He waved his hand aimlessly. "Somewhere out here. They've had people all around the lake these last couple hours trying to find it, so I think it's long gone."

"Okay," Skottie said. "Thanks for the info."

"Look, amigo, if I'm in trouble I wish you'd say so. I'm out of my depth, and I'm afraid maybe the sheriff is, too. My wife's having a baby. It'd be nice if I could keep my job, if we could keep our house. And it'd be nice if I had some idea we were doing the right thing. If I knew I was on the right side of whatever's going on. Does that make sense?"

Skottie nodded and settled her weight against the railing. The back of her jacket was now wet against her skin and the wind off the lake cut through her.

"I think if Goodman sent you to talk to me, you wouldn't be alone."

"I said—"

She held up a hand to cut him off. "Right. So there's a Nazi somewhere around. Been hiding near here for, what, maybe sixty years? I don't know. Or maybe he was somewhere else and he just got here. Anyway, that's what Travis Roan's doing in Kansas. At least, that's what he says he's doing. He's chasing a bad guy. Goodman's gonna have to release Travis, probably later today, and it would be a good idea if you made sure nothing happened to him between now and then. Make sure he doesn't have some sort of tragic accident right after he leaves your station. If he's for real, then I don't think you want to be on the side that's protecting a Nazi."

"Nobody's protecting any Nazis. Sheriff Goodman wouldn't do that."

"Maybe."

"What are you gonna do now?"

"I'm just looking for a bear."

"Well, keep an eye out for lions and tigers while you're at it. Makes as much sense as Nazis hiding out in the sorghum."

Skottie chuckled and pushed herself away from the railing. "Thanks."

Quincy opened his mouth like he wanted to say something else, but he closed it again and shook his head. He turned and walked back to his car, started it up, and drove away. He waved once at Skottie before his tires spun out on the wet asphalt and he had to concentrate on keeping the car on the road.

When he was out of sight of the lookout, Skottie stepped down off the deck and took a deep breath. She cupped her hands around her mouth again and shouted at the white-capped trees.

*"Amiko!"*

A moment later a shadow broke away from the trees and the tall weeds rustled, parting as an enormous shape crept out onto the strip of manicured grass that edged the parking lot.

Skottie had forgotten how big the dog was. She estimated he must outweigh her by at least twenty pounds. Her hand automatically went to her belt, but she wasn't carrying her Taser today. Bear stopped six feet away from her and yawned, showing his long yellow fangs. He shook his mane and the skin rippled under his thick fur.

*"Amiko,"* Skottie said again. *"Amiko,* Bear."

He closed the distance between them, his paws melting the skin of new snow. She held out her hand, bracing herself, and Bear sniffed it. He licked her hand and sat. Skottie let out a long shuddering breath. "Good boy," she said. "Good dog."

# 2

Skottie could see smoke, a thick black plume rising and mingling with the low-hanging clouds, but she couldn't see a fire. She glanced back at Bear, who had perked up and was sniffing the air. The radio handset was sitting in Skottie's lap and she picked it up.

"One-Eleven Norton. I'm off duty and headed south on 183," she said. "Possible ten-eighty-five in progress."

The dispatcher's voice came back at her a moment later. A man she didn't recognize. Somebody new had taken over Sarah's desk for the day. "Ten-four. Officer is on the scene. Are you nearby?"

"I think so. I'm just north of Stockton. Looks like a pretty big fire, but it's hard to say how far off the road it is."

"You're right on top of it, One-Eleven."

"Who's on the scene?"

"Thirty-Two."

That would be Ryan Kufahl. Skottie knew him well. He had shown her around when she'd first transferred back to Kansas. He was alert and reliable with a quick smile and a laid-back manner that had helped to make her feel at ease. "Does he need backup?"

"One-Eleven?" Ryan Kufahl's voice crackled over the radio. "Hey, I'm on the access road and I'm looking at a tractor on fire."

"Fire truck on the way?"

"Yeah, but . . . Skottie, there's a body inside this thing. I wouldn't mind another pair of eyes on this."

"Give me two minutes." She hung up the handset and pulled her Subaru onto the side of the highway. She threw the vehicle in reverse and sped backward along the shoulder, then maneuvered onto a dirt access road for utility vehicles. It paralleled the highway, rising up until it dead-ended at a rusty metal gate near the overpass. Shrubs and weeds grew wild along the trail and obscured her view, but before she reached the gate Skottie saw the bonfire. At its center was the hazy bulk of a tractor, its tires deflated and melting. The flames swirled around it and rose to a spiraling point a dozen feet high, and a cold breeze from the north was blowing the smoke away from her. Officer Ryan Kufahl stood next to his cruiser ten yards from the fire. He waved at her as she pulled up next to him, then walked over to her car.

"You said there's a body?" Skottie stuck her phone in her hip pocket and opened her car door.

"You can see it better over the other side there." Ryan had to shout to be heard over the billowing flames.

Skottie opened the car's back door and Bear jumped out. Kufahl held his ground, but Skottie could see him tense.

"That's one hell of a big dog," he said.

"He won't bite." Skottie hoped she was right about that.

"You got a leash?"

"I'll get some rope from my car," she said. "In a minute. What've you got here?"

Kufahl pointed and led Skottie around the tractor, close to the edge of the drop-off and the highway below. Bear padded along at Skottie's side.

"See it?"

"Yeah," Skottie said. A dark shape was propped up in the driver's seat of the tractor. The moving flames made it look as if the body were twitching and dancing in place. "A man."

"I agree," Ryan said. "Too big to be a woman."

"Any idea who it is?"

"Ambulance is on its way. Once the county coroner gets hold of the body, we might be able to ID him."

"I doubt it," Skottie said.

"Well, there's not gonna be much left of him. But somebody's gonna come forward in the next day or two. How it always goes. Somebody's missing this guy and they're gonna come looking for him. We'll get it figured out."

"Why would a farmer bring his tractor up this road? It doesn't lead anywhere." Skottie skirted the blaze and walked up the trail to the gate with Bear at her heels. The metal was badly rusted but solid, and a new steel padlock dangled from a chain wrapped around the posts. She grabbed a crossbar and shook the gate. It moved a little, but she could see that it was solidly moored in a concrete slab at the base. She knelt and Bear pushed his head against her, nearly knocking her over. She scratched him behind the ear while she examined the padlock. "This looks brand-new."

Ryan crunched up the trail to her. He bent and peered at the lock, then over at her. "Not a scratch on it."

"How often do these get replaced?"

"No idea," Ryan said. "I've never seen it done. Unless somebody stole one, I don't know why you would. Half the time they don't even get these locked back up after the trucks leave."

Skottie stood and wiped her hands on the front of her jeans. They walked back to their cars and stood watching as the flames began to die down. From far away, Skottie heard a faint siren. The ambulance making its way up the highway toward them. She shook her head and sighed. It was far too late to do anything for the charred man in the tractor. The paramedics might as well take their time.

Ryan looked away from the fire and scuffed a toe in the dirt. "You think this guy came out here to kill himself?"

"And replaced the lock on the gate?"

"Maybe he didn't wanna be followed. Didn't want anybody stopping him before he got his fire lit," Ryan said.

"It's possible," Skottie said. But it looked like murder to her. And she wondered if it had anything to do with the dead woman at the lake or the Nazi hunter being held in Paradise Flats. She pulled out her phone and checked her texts, but there was nothing new since the one she had received from Travis that morning.

NEED ASSISTANCE. HOW SOON
CAN YOU GET UP HERE?

She assumed he would text again or call when Goodman released him. It was beginning to look like Bear would have to spend the night with her. She stuck the phone back in her pocket and listened as the ambulance grew closer. She estimated it was still five minutes out. Another siren joined the chorus, this one only a stone's throw away, and a moment later Skottie saw the flashing lights of a Burden County squad car coming up the dirt road. It pulled up behind her vehicle, and Deputy Christian Puckett jumped out.

Bear's mane bristled and his ears went flat against his massive skull.

"Bear, no," Skottie said. She started to reach for the dog, to restrain him, but then pulled her hand back. She had no idea how Bear would react when he was on guard, whether he was as likely to attack her as anybody else. In the absence of any sound but the roaring fire behind them, the dog was somehow more terrifying than if he were barking or growling.

"Whoa!" Christian scrambled around his car and peeked out at them, his gun raised high in the air. "Wondered where that dog went. Trooper, you step away from that animal."

"Bear, no," Skottie said again. *"Sit."* She wasn't sure Bear would respond to a command given in English and she couldn't remember what language Travis had used with him. She wasn't about to forget *amiko*, but she wasn't sure *friend* was the right word to describe Goodman's deputy. If Travis and his dog stuck around much longer, she decided she would need to learn more commands.

To Skottie's great relief Bear sat, but he didn't take his eyes off Christian.

"Deputy, put your gun away," Kufahl said. "This animal's not threatening anyone."

"I beg to differ, Trooper," Christian said. Skottie could barely see the top of his head through the car's windows. "Earlier today, that thing attacked me and my sheriff. Almost killed me."

"It bit you?"

"Well, no." Christian poked his head back up. "It kinda . . . It knocked me down."

"And then what did it do?" Skottie was glad for Kufahl's presence. His objective questions were efficiently defusing the situation.

"It ran off," Christian said. "Hid itself in the woods out by the lake. We been looking for it all day. And now I found it. And now I'm gonna shoot it."

"A dog knocked you over and ran away. That right?" Kufahl sniffed and turned to Skottie. "Trooper, is this dog dangerous to either myself or the deputy?"

"I'll vouch for him," Skottie said. "The dog, not the deputy."

"Had his shots?"

Skottie hesitated for a second, unsure about her answer, but the silent dog next to her had earned the benefit of the doubt. "Absolutely."

"Put the gun away, Deputy," Kufahl said again.

After a moment Christian stood up and came around the back of his car, holstering his weapon as he walked. He ambled over to them, without ever taking his eyes off the dog, and stood beside Kufahl.

"If it bites me, you're gonna answer for that, Trooper."

"Got it."

Christian pointed at the fire. "Don't that beat all?" The two men clearly knew each other, and it was just as obvious that Kufahl didn't much like Christian.

"There's an unidentified man in there," Skottie said. "You people are gonna have your hands full this afternoon."

"Us people?" Christian looked at her, then looked away at Kufahl. His upper lip quivered. "Hell, we already got our hands full. This one can wait. He ain't goin' nowhere."

Skottie narrowed her eyes. "You got here pretty fast," she said.

Christian looked at her, then looked away at Kufahl. "So I'm fast."

"You couldn't have got the call and made it out here by now. I've been driving twenty minutes already since I left Paradise Flats."

"You mean since you left Kirwin, right? Yeah, I been following you. Sheriff told me to make sure you got over the county line."

"So you were right behind me?"

"Yup."

Skottie wasn't so sure. If Christian had talked to Quincy, he would know that she had been out at the lake. She couldn't think of a single reason Sheriff Goodman would have her followed when he had a murder investigation to deal with and only two deputies on duty. Unless he was completely paranoid, he didn't need to make sure she had left Burden County.

But there was no point in arguing. "Come on, Bear," she said. She walked back to her vehicle, conscious of the giant animal shadowing her. She decided to let him ride in the front seat this time. He intimidated Christian, and that was worth something to her. Besides, the blanket she had laid over the back seat was already rumpled and covered in fur.

When she glanced back, Christian was watching her. He stuck out his index finger, cocked his thumb like a gun, and mimed shooting at her. He winked and nodded, then turned his back to her.

She pulled around his squad car, its lights still flashing. The ambulance passed her on its way up the road and she had to pull over into the grass, then she gunned it and sped out to the highway. There was nothing she could do for Officer Kufahl or his burn victim. And she had a sick feeling in the pit of her stomach.

Travis Roan had asked her how quickly she could get to him that morning, but she had been unable to help him. She had also failed to talk to Rachel Bloom. And Lieutenant Johnson didn't seem entirely pleased with her. She was batting a thousand for the day.

She wondered again if the tractor fire had been started as a distraction or if it was connected in some way to the murdered woman at the wildlife refuge. Someone was playing a very dangerous game. But the playing field was shrouded in smoke and fog, and Skottie couldn't see the ground well enough to know whether she was making the right moves.

# 3

The door opened again and Sheriff Goodman entered the makeshift cell. He had a paper plate, which he set down on the end of the cot farthest away from Travis. Goodman closed the door and leaned against it, stood for a moment regarding Travis through half-closed eyes. When he finally spoke, he seemed tired, his voice low and flat.

"Brought you a biscuit. I ended up with a little more than I could eat."

"Thank you," Travis said.

"Put some butter on there and heated it up in the microwave a few seconds. Should be 'bout as good as new, I'd guess."

"Kind of you. Is there any chance you have a cigarette?"

"Got some chew if you want."

"No."

"Listen, I been thinking on you."

"And?"

"Why'd you stick around? I gave you plenty of chances to go."

"I have a job to do."

"Right. Catching Nazis. I looked up that company you're with." Goodman made a dismissive gesture. "It don't look so important to me. Nazis was a long time ago. You're on a wild-goose chase here."

"Perhaps I am."

"Yeah." Goodman moved the plate with the cooling biscuit closer to Travis and took a seat. He shook his head at the wall and puffed out his cheeks, let his breath out in a long sigh, then busied himself fixing the sharp crease in his uniform trousers. Travis could smell whiskey in the air. "There's things I don't like here," Goodman said. "And it's my job to get to the bottom of things I don't like."

Travis waited while Goodman gathered his thoughts. The sheriff's eye was turning a darker shade of purple, and Travis felt a momentary pang of regret.

"Since you got here," Goodman said, "a lot of weird stuff's been happening. All at once. Like you brought it with you. While you been right here in this room, another body got found. All burned up. We don't get a whole lot of dead people in Burden County. We don't even have our own coroner. I keep the peace pretty good, believe it or not. But now, it's just . . ." He snapped his fingers twice. "People disappear. One after another. I wanna think it's a coincidence, you being here and bad things happening. But I don't like coincidences. Don't really believe them. There's a reason for things."

"There are always coincidences," Travis said.

"You better eat that biscuit before it goes cold."

Travis reached for the sheriff's peace offering and broke it in half, letting the crumbs fall to the floor. He took a small bite.

"Cards on the table, I don't like you, Dr. Roan."

"That is hardly a revelation," Travis said. He took another small bite of the biscuit.

"I don't expect you like me much, either. But I keep thinking you're not going away." He threw his hands up. "So just explain to me how all these things come together. How you and two dead bodies happened in my county."

Travis swallowed the last bite of biscuit and rubbed his hands together. "These people I hunt have been hiding for more than seventy years, here and there, all over the world. They have different names, they work now as bakers and plumbers and all manner of things, blending in with the people around them. They rarely make mistakes.

But always there is someone who sees them, someone who recognizes them. And every time I go to verify these sightings, there is someone who asks me about the coincidence."

"Still," Goodman said, "it's one thing when people are living in the same place. They're bound to bump into each other. You can't live in a town like Paradise Flats or Phillipsburg or even Hays without knowing just about everybody around you. Like if your Nazis all stayed in Germany, I guess they'd get seen a lot. Hard to hide there. But we're talking about people who ran thousands of miles away from each other. And it's been decades. It's too much to think they'd spot each other now. It don't wash."

"The world is getting smaller, as they say. People travel more. And if you pass someone in a mall that you once saw at another mall, that is a much different thing than if you pass someone in a mall who tortured you or starved you or raped you." Travis frowned. "Please excuse me. I become angry sometimes. I understand your disbelief, Sheriff, but these are not people you would forget if you had spent years of your life being hurt by them."

Goodman squinted at him and picked up the empty paper plate from the cot. He folded it in half and began to twist it in his hands.

"An example," Travis said. "Many years ago, when I was starting out in this job, and this was before Bear and I crossed paths, I was sent to London to find a man who had been seen there. Not a Nazi, but a man who had helped hide many Nazis, who had helped them travel. They had escape routes they called 'ratlines' to move Nazis out of Germany to places like South America and Africa, you understand?"

"Sure."

"I was staying in a hotel in Greenwich and I went out into the city every day looking for him. Every night, I would return to the hotel, a very good place, but old. Every night, I would order a hamburger and a baked potato from room service. I would sign the bill without paying attention, and then eat and fall asleep. I would wake up the next morning and start again. One night, the man brought me my hamburger on the big tray with the tiny bottles of ketchup and mustard and the tiny shakers of salt and pepper, but this time I decided to pay with cash. I was worried that I had put too much on my room charge and my father would scold me."

"Your father?"

"He is in charge of the Foundation. Since my grandfather died. So I asked the man who had brought my hamburger to wait a moment. This was the same man who had brought my dinner for, what? Five nights in a row? He had been my room service waiter the entire time I was there. You see this coming?"

Goodman's mouth twisted into a smirk. "He was the guy you were looking for."

"I went to find my wallet, and there on my desk was the file with his photo clipped to it. He was older, you know, and had shaved his mustache, changed the color of his hair, even tattooed his neck and hands with bright distracting patterns. But I made the connection at last. He saw the photograph at the same time I did." Travis sat back and rubbed the side of his nose with his index finger.

"And you caught him?"

"Sorry?"

"You caught him, right?"

"Oh, yes. He never even tried to run. When he realized I was there to find him, he surrendered. I think he was relieved. Happy to stop hiding." Travis sighed. "But it was a big coincidence. It was a coincidence that someone saw him there and called the Foundation. And it was a coincidence that he brought me a hamburger every night for almost a week without someone else working that shift. If he had only taken that night off, maybe he would be a free man even now."

"So," Goodman said. "Coincidences."

"Maybe they are not what we think they are. Maybe we pull at one another's threads all the time. Spiders and flies crawling across webs we cannot see."

Goodman stood back up and stared at the twisted paper plate in his hand. "I wish to God you'd just left Burden County when I asked you to."

"Perhaps if you had been more polite about it."

Goodman chuckled. "Well, soon's as I finish processing your paperwork, I'll let you go. I'm gonna ask you real polite to just head on back home. If there's somebody here like you say, you leave him to me." He nodded once, as if settling the matter, and opened the door. "You hang tight now, Doc." He left, and Travis heard the lock engage.

Travis settled back on the cot and looked around at the bare walls.

"Spiders and flies," he said.

# 4

There was a rented Ford Mustang parked in front of Emmaline's house and a man was sitting on the porch next to Maddy. It took Skottie a long minute to recognize him, and when she did the brief spike of alarm at seeing a strange man with her daughter was replaced by a different sort of worry.

"How did I not recognize that man right off?"

Bear shifted in the seat next to her and looked up as if trying to figure out what she was asking.

"Talking to myself, boy," she said. "Great. How often do I do that?" *About as often,* she thought, *as I mistake my husband for a total stranger.*

When she pulled into the driveway, Brandon Foster stood and stepped down off the porch. He wasn't smiling, but he didn't have his angry face on. While Skottie took that as a promising sign, her own expression didn't change.

Skottie jammed on the brake and put the Subaru in park. Maddy was hanging back on the porch. She looked tense and ran down the steps close behind her father.

"Mom, Dad's here. He even picked me up early and we got ice cream." Her face brightened when she saw Bear. "Is that our dog?"

"No," Skottie said. "Maddy, go in the house."

"She can hear us," Brandon said. "It's healthy for kids to know that their parents argue."

Brandon was big and blond, with freckles dusted across the bridge of his nose, solid under a layer of fat that he called his "bulletproof belly." Skottie had once liked that softness that hid his strength. They had met nearly a dozen years ago. Brandon was a beat cop then, and Skottie was in the academy. There had been a string of drive-by shootings, and Skottie had spotted the perpetrator's car and called it in. Brandon had been the first responder, and they had both been excited and proud of their roles in the case. They had gone for a drink at the end of their shift to wind down and had woken up next to each other the next morning. Three weeks later they were married, and ten months after that Maddy had joined them. She favored her mother in nearly every way, but she had her father's freckles.

"Maddy, I told you to go in the house."

"Grandma wouldn't let him inside," Maddy said. She was ignoring Skottie, too keyed up and distracted. "Whose dog is that, Mom?"

"A friend's. We're taking care of him for tonight. *Just* for tonight."

"What's his name? Can I pet him?"

"No." Next to her daughter, Bear was as big as a horse. Maddy could probably ride the dog around the front yard if he let her, and Skottie knew that thought had already occurred to Maddy. "I mean, try not to surprise him."

Brandon was watching them, patiently waiting, maybe even hoping Skottie was as distracted as Maddy was, that his presence would be accepted along with the dog's. Skottie felt jangled and uptight and wanted to get her husband off Emmaline's property. But she didn't want to upset Maddy.

"His name's Bear, baby. Hold out your hand and say *amiko*, okay? *Amiko*."

"What does that mean?"

"Just do it!" Skottie immediately regretted raising her voice. Why had Brandon forced them into an adversarial situation by showing up with no notice? How could that help anything? "Please, Maddy, it means *friend*."

"Where did you get that dog?" Brandon said. "Is it dangerous?"

*"Amiko,"* Maddy said. "Hi, Bear. *Amiko*." She held out her tiny hand for Bear to sniff while Skottie held her breath.

Bear licked Maddy's palm and sat down in the snow. Maddy approached and ran her fingers through the dog's thick black mane. Bear looked up at Skottie, and she could swear he was smiling. She let out a sigh of relief.

"Honey, he's been out at the lake all day," Skottie said. "He's probably dirty."

"I don't mind, Mom. Does he know other words?"

"I think so, but most of them are in another language, honey, and I don't remember what it is. Portuguese, maybe?"

"I can look it up," Maddy said. Now that she had a task, she had forgotten that she didn't want to go inside the house and leave her father and mother to face off against each other. "Come on, Bear!"

She turned and ran up the porch steps and Bear stood up.

"Wait, baby," Skottie said. She put a hand on Bear's head, wondering if she'd be able to hold him back if he decided to chase Maddy. "Don't run, okay, Maddy? That might make Bear excited. And why don't you leave Bear with me for a minute. I'll bring him in when I'm done out here."

"You're not gonna leave him outside all night?"

"No, I think we'd need a fence or a little house for him. It's gonna get cold tonight."

"You do what your mama says," Brandon said.

Maddy nodded and trudged the rest of the way across the porch. As soon as the screen door shut behind her, Skottie could hear Emmaline scolding the girl. There was no love lost between Skottie's mother and Brandon.

When Brandon had moved up to detective and then to homicide, Skottie had opted for the Illinois Highway Patrol. This division in their careers had led to divisions in their marriage. Brandon had belittled the IHP, had told her once that her whole job was to sit in her car all day and pass out tickets while he was out there risking his life to make the world a better place. She had not forgotten the comment and had not accepted his many apologies. Brandon had begun to drink more, had stopped coming home after his shifts. And Skottie had been fine with that. When he did come home, there was usually a fight.

"You didn't need to back me up," Skottie said. "I told her to go inside, she was gonna go inside."

"I know that," Brandon said. "That wasn't disrespect. I was helping."

"I don't need your help."

"It's good for kids to see parents back each other up. So Maddy can't play us off each other."

"What, did you just read a book about raising kids?"

"As a matter of fact, yeah. Look, Skottie, I'm trying to be better. It's been six months. That's a long time for my family to be apart from me, but I stayed outta your way, gave you space like you asked. You have any idea how hard that was for me?"

"You waited six months to see your daughter."

"Can we just talk? I know I screwed up, and I'm doing my best here to show you respect."

"I don't have anything to talk about," Skottie said.

Brandon took a step toward her and Bear nudged her aside, moved closer to Brandon. The dog's mane was crackling as if a wave of static electricity were moving through it. Skottie was struck again by how eerie the dog's silence was, and Brandon apparently felt it, too, because he stepped back and raised his hands.

"Call the damn dog off," he said.

"He can feel the tension. Nothing I can do about that, so maybe it's safer for you if you keep your distance."

"You know I'm not gonna hurt you, Skottie."

"Do I?"

"That was *one* time."

"You don't get two chances."

Brandon looked away. He ran his hand through his hair and sighed. "You got no idea how sorry I am for that. You gotta know I'd do anything to make it up to you and Maddy. You know me. You know . . ." His voice trailed off, and Skottie almost felt sorry for him. Then she remembered.

During a particularly vicious argument one night, Brandon had hit her. They had stood there for a moment, both of them stunned, then Skottie tried to hit him back. He blocked her fist and she swung again. He blocked her blow again, but when she raised her hand the third time she saw something in his eyes, a subtle change in his expression. He left his hands down at his sides and let her hit him.

He had apologized then, had cried and begged her, had reminded her that it was the first time and promised it was the last. But Skottie had quietly packed a suitcase, put Maddy in the car, and driven away.

Six months gone by.

Brandon sat down on the porch steps. He kept his eye on Bear, but the dog was relaxed again. It seemed as long as Brandon kept his distance, Bear would leave him alone.

"I got the papers you sent," Brandon said. "But I don't think you want that. You don't want to put Maddy through that."

"No," Skottie said, "I don't. But it's the next step, and I've got to move forward with my life. I don't wanna go back to Chicago, and I don't wanna be with you anymore, Brandon."

"I waited too long. I should have come before now."

"It wouldn't have made any difference." *I didn't even recognize you at first*, she thought. *I moved on whether I really meant to or not.*

Brandon folded his arms across his knees and watched a shaggy *V* of geese migrate across the sky, a month later than all the others and with no hope of catching up. Finally he nodded. "Okay. I'll give you more time. But I want Maddy. You can't keep her from me."

"I won't let you take her back to Chicago."

"You want her to grow up in Hays? What's she gonna do here? At least in—"

"Hey, *I* grew up here."

"You were the only black girl in your graduating class. You told me yourself."

"So more black people is what I needed? More than my mother?"

"You got out of this town the first chance you got."

"And the last person who hurt me was you."

He blushed. "I found a good divorce attorney, Skottie. He's expensive and I'd rather not—"

"I thought you were worried about putting Maddy through this stuff."

"Just . . . Dammit, just let me have her for the weekend. I'm at a hotel here. That big one down the road. I took some vacation days. Let me have some time with her and I promise I'll bring her back after. Not playing games with you, Skott."

"No."

The screen door opened again and Maddy took the porch like an invading army. "It's Esperanto, Mom. I looked it up. *Amiko!*"

"Esperanto," Skottie said. "That's right."

"Bear," Maddy said. "Bear, *venu ĉi tien*. Is that right, boy? *Venu ĉi tien?*"

Bear pulled himself to his feet and shambled up the porch steps to Maddy, knocking Brandon into a snow-covered hedge, seemingly by accident, but Skottie wondered whether it was a purposeful snub. The dog seemed to pick up on physical cues like a second language. Esperanto and body language. He pushed against Maddy, nearly knocking her over, and she squealed in delight.

"How did you . . ."

"The computer has a recording of how to say things. All you have to do is put in what you wanna say and it says it for you."

"Even in Esperanto?"

"We can talk to him, Mom! I bet he knows lots and lots of words. He's like a code dog! Bear, *amiko*!"

The dog obligingly licked Maddy's face, covering her from chin to forehead in slobber. Maddy laughed and fell down and Bear lay next to her. The dog was so big that Skottie couldn't see any trace of her daughter behind him.

Brandon regained his feet and brushed the snow off his jeans. He shot the dog a nasty look, but let it go at that. "What do you say, Skottie?"

Maddy's head popped up from behind the mass of black fur on the porch. "Mom, can I go? Dad'll bring me home in time for school Monday, right Dad?"

She'd been listening. Skottie shook her head, not turning her daughter down, but registering the fact that she couldn't win this fight without hurting both Maddy and Brandon. And maybe herself, too.

Brandon looked at her and raised his eyebrows. He pressed his lips together in a half smile, an expression of questioning innocence that had always worked with her.

"Come back Friday, after lunch," Skottie said. "Can you do that?"

"I'll be here," Brandon said.

"Yay! Thanks, Mom!"

"Don't be early," Skottie said. "I'll have her ready at two o'clock."

"You'll see me then," Brandon said. "And Skottie, pack a bag for yourself, too, if you decide you wanna come along."

He didn't wait to see how she might respond to his suggestion. He walked away across the top of the snow to a rental car parked across the street. Skottie noticed that Bear's eyes followed Brandon until the car pulled away from the curb.

# FEBRUARY 1977

The frequency of Rudy's seizures had decreased over the years to a point where they occurred at regular intervals every few months and rarely interfered with his routine. He associated them, correctly or not, with the perfectly round smooth scars that skipped down his chest and abdomen and ended at his groin. The lightning had affected both his brain and his body in unexpected ways. Neither his hair nor his toenails had grown back, and he had lost all the hearing in one ear, but he had learned to read lips, so he appeared at all times to be thoughtful and attentive, carefully watching people's faces when they talked. Yet he often heard disembodied voices and saw strange people and objects in the corners of his vision.

Magda had died giving birth to their third child, a girl, and Rudy subsequently spent less time at home on the ranch. The life he had once craved as an American family man he now looked back on as an interlude between the more crucial periods of his work. His children were looked after by a succession of nannies, and Rudy had moved most of his personal belongings to a small house on the border of the churchyard.

His flock had grown steadily over the years, lost souls attracted by rumors that Reverend Rudy of the Purity First Church had the power to heal sickness and dispel doubt. Lightning had infused him with the electric mastery of Divine Will. He had not just seen the light, it had moved through him, His wonders to perform.

In Sunday school the children of his parish were taught that Reverend Rudy had spoken directly with God during that fateful storm, and they learned that his spells were holy messages from on high, were clarifications of the Word. A depiction of the red pattern of his scars had been painted from ceiling to floor in every room of the church, and each livid circle represented the first letter of one of the tenets of the faith: "Power Resides in Us," "Unity Brings Strength," "Rebirth, Not Death," "Invest in Ourselves," "Treat Others as They Deserve to Be Treated," "A Yielding Nature Is Divine." Taken together, the letters spelled the word *PURITY*, which his congregation chanted at the start of morning and evening masses.

The same red dots also festooned the sides of a Volkswagen minibus, bought as a tax write-off and used for church outings. From a distance, the bus strongly resembled an ice-cream truck, and when the church's youth group wasn't away on a picnic or visiting a museum, Reverend Rudy enjoyed driving his bus through neighboring towns, taking pleasure in the inevitable disappointment of small children who followed along behind him, quarters clutched in their little hands.

These excursions also served a second, more satisfying, purpose.

Twelve teenagers had disappeared from western Kansas over a period of seven years. All of them had been girls between the ages of ten and eighteen, but investigators had not found a single connection among them. Two of them had attended the same school, but none of the twelve had known one another, so far as anyone was aware. Three of them had been black, two Jewish, six Hispanic, and one had been visiting from an American Indian college in eastern Kansas. No bodies had been found, and the police departments of three counties had concluded that the girls were runaways. Flyers were handed out, appeals for information were made on the local television and radio stations, photographs were stapled to telephone poles, but no new leads were uncovered.

Had anyone ventured down the stairs to the subbasement of the Purity First Church, down beneath the shuffleboard court, the communal hall, and the cozy kitchen, they might have uncovered some sign of those twelve missing girls. They might have found evidence of other men, women, and children who had been there, had spent their last moments on Earth staring at six red scars before moving on. Reverend Rudy had put a great deal of work into renovating that cold room, with its concrete-block walls and its hulking furnace. The walls had been soundproofed, covered with thick insulation and another layer of concrete. The ceiling had been stripped to the joists and reinforced, gaps filled, and the whole thing replastered, then carpeted. This had the unfortunate effect of making the room smaller, but Rudy had convinced himself that sacrificing some space was worth it in the long run.

Two stainless steel tables had been brought in and bolted to the floor. The tables were heavy and awkward, and the stairs leading down to the subbasement were steep and narrow. No one could see Rudy's secret room, no one could know it even existed, and so he and Jacob had done all the work themselves. It took them a year and a half. When they had finished with the heavy work, Jacob had traveled alone to Boston with a shopping list provided by Rudy. He returned four days later with a trunk full of surgical equipment. Scalpels, shears, rib spreaders, clamps, specula, drills, and a variety of bits. Rudy unpacked the trunk with little gasps of excitement, setting each new tool in its preordained place on the aluminum racks against the walls.

The doctor's mission had become a holy mission.

They were careful. After finishing the room, they waited. It was important to establish the church, as both an alibi and a safe haven, and that took a lot of work. It was another six months before Rudy took his own shopping trip and, when he went, he did not take the colorful Purity First bus. He paid four hundred dollars cash for a 1964 Buick Skylark and parked it in an abandoned barn on over-grown farmland adjacent to his Third R Ranch. He removed the station wagon's back seat and welded a dog cage into the cargo compartment.

That first night he drove south to Hays and cruised slowly through the slush that had formed along the streets out by the highway. The trip wasn't as productive as he'd hoped, but he learned the lay of the land. On his next trip, he spotted a young man holding a cardboard sign and standing in the grass beside the on-ramp to I-70.

Rudy pulled onto the shoulder and turned on his hazards. He let a Camaro pass him, and when the ramp was empty, Rudy leaned across and cranked the passenger window down. He turned on the dome light so the boy could see him.

"Hey," he said, "where you headed?"

The boy stuck the sign under his arm and hoisted a backpack over his shoulder. He ran to Rudy's car and leaned in the window. His breath was visible, drifting away to the west.

"Thanks, man! I'm on my way to Chicago, but I got people in KC, if you're going that far."

Under the yellow light of the dome Rudy could see that the boy was pale and fair-haired. Hidden by the shadows on the side of the road, he had looked darker, swarthier. Rudy frowned.

"What's your name, son?"

"Jonas, sir. Jonas Miller. Oh my gosh, ain't you the Rev? From up in Paradise Flats? I know you. My aunt goes to your church, man. How you doin'?"

Rudy smiled and nodded, leaning farther forward so he could read the boy's lips. "Jonas, yes. You were in Bible camp two summers ago, am I right?"

"Damn." Jonas shook his head. "Sorry. I mean, dang, Rev. You got a good memory."

"Indeed I do. I'm sorry, Jonas, I just remembered I've forgotten something back at the church. I'm afraid I can't give you a ride tonight." He fished his wallet from his back pocket and pulled out two ten-dollar bills, which he passed out the window to the boy. "Here, it's getting dark out. You'd better find a motel room for the night. And get yourself something to eat."

"You sure, Rev? I don't wanna take money from you."

"Think of it as help from the church. Next time you're up my way, you can pay us back by taking some meals to our elderly parishioners."

"You bet I will. Thanks, Rev!"

"Be careful out here, Jonas. You never know what kind of people are out and about at night."

"I can take care of myself, sir. Don't you worry about me."

Jonas Miller adjusted his pack and backed away from the Skylark. He trotted a few feet down the shoulder and turned and waved. Rudy waved back and rolled up the window. He turned off the dome light and pulled a U-turn, going the wrong way down the ramp until he got back to the main thoroughfare. He headed north, back toward the church, back home. He would have to try again another night. Jonas might remember seeing him in Hays, might wonder why Reverend Rudy was going east in the middle of the week.

Rudy pounded his fist against the steering wheel and cursed his luck.

He noticed the blinking hazard warning on the dash and belatedly flicked the lights off.

The Skylark continued quietly along the road at exactly the posted speed limit and did not stop again until Rudy was home.

# PART TWO

# THE LORD

## of

# LIGHTNING

# CHAPTER SIX

## 1

They released Travis that afternoon. Ekwensi Griffith opened the cell door and handed him his jacket, belt, keys, phone, and wallet. Travis checked the wallet and nothing seemed to be missing. His phone was password-protected in his favorite obscure language, and he felt confident no one had tampered with it. There were three missed calls from his mother. He asked if his rented Jeep had been impounded and was told it was still at the lake, but nobody offered to drive him back to it. He did not ask about Bear.

If Sheriff Goodman was in his office, he didn't bother to come out and wish Travis well.

He walked to his motel. The sky was the color of his peacoat, and his loafers sank into the new snow with every step he took. By the time he reached the Cottonwood Inn, his socks were soaked through and his feet hurt. The motel room seemed cavernous and cold without the comforting presence of Bear.

He took a long hot shower, then selected a slate suit with a subtle pinstripe, a light gray shirt, and a black tie. He changed his wet pea-coat for a silvery-gray waterproof jacket. After a moment's thought, he retrieved a flat leather pouch from his suitcase and slipped it into his breast pocket. At last, tired but refreshed, he dropped the old suit off at the front desk to be cleaned and used an app on his phone to call a car.

Thankfully the young man who drove him out to the wildlife refuge kept to himself, humming quietly along with a Townes Van Zandt album. Travis was able to tune out the music and think about his next moves.

The body of Margaret Weber had not been weighted down. Someone had been in a hurry to get rid of her or had expected her to wash ashore. The killer was either a careful planner or a clumsy amateur, so there would be a great deal of forensic evidence on the corpse or there would be none at all. Unless there was a third scenario he hadn't thought of. There was always a third option, and Travis had long ago learned to keep an open mind. But until that option presented itself, he would have to proceed with what he knew.

He didn't think Sheriff Goodman's office would be sharing any lab results with him and he didn't want to bet his freedom on the idea that the killer was a clumsy amateur. So he would act as if he were up against the careful planner, unless and until he found out otherwise.

But why would someone want Margaret Weber's body to be found? Had the killer purposefully set Travis up to discover her corpse? He didn't think so. His visit to the wildlife refuge had not been sched-uled and he hadn't told anyone he was going there. It had been a random whim, a convenient nearby place to let Bear run free for a few minutes.

And yet the sheriff had arrived at the lake almost immediately after Travis called in his gruesome discovery. Goodman had already been nearby. Was that a coincidence or had he been alerted even before the body was found?

As the car approached the Kirwin Refuge's visitor center, Travis looked around them in every direction. He saw nothing except a gray sky pressing down on leftover brown stalks of corn, a bare scrubby tree, and a narrow two-lane road that rose toward the clouds in front of them and disappeared in the blank silver haze of snow far behind them.

The song "Home on the Range" popped into his head, and he smiled sadly at the thought that there must be a season when Kansas skies were not cloudy all day. He had seen the sun exactly twice since landing at the Kansas City airport.

His driver plowed through a snowbank and stopped in the middle of the parking lot. Travis found a five-dollar bill in his jacket pocket and tipped the kid, then stepped out and squinted at the silent landscape. The car backed up and turned around and bulldozed back through the snowbank, turned left, and chugged off down the road. Travis spun in a circle, looking at everything through fresh eyes now that he knew it was a crime scene. The lookout and its rusted telescope, the skeletal trees, and the water iced over in places. His Jeep was still parked in the same spot, and its windows were intact.

Travis had no trouble finding the path he and Bear had made through the tall grass. It had been widened by the boots of deputies and paramedics and by the wheels of a gurney, the grass trampled, the snow melted and dirty. He walked down to the lake and stood at the water's edge.

Margaret Weber's body was gone, but she had left an impression. He bowed his head and murmured a few words for her, then scanned the shore in both directions. He saw no fresh dog tracks in the snow.

"Bear!"

He listened, but there was no movement beyond the fluttering of a few startled wings in the brush.

"Bear, *sekura*! *Venu ĉi tien*, Bear!"

Nothing. No answer. He hoped that was a good sign. He did not want to have to speak any prayers at this lake on behalf of his closest friend.

He turned and trudged back up to the parking lot and over to his rental. He walked around the Jeep looking for footprints and signs of tampering, surprised to find none. He had assumed the sheriff would jimmy his way in. Travis keyed it open and slid in behind the wheel. It was dark inside. The windshield was already blacked over with snow and ice crystals. He switched on the dome light and checked the glove box. His gun was still there. He took it out and popped the magazine, checked the chamber. As far as he could tell, no one had touched it.

"Curiouser and curiouser," he said.

He slipped the gun in his pocket and started the vehicle. It turned over easily, and within seconds the vents began producing warm air. He grabbed his driving gloves from the box, slid back out onto the ice and gravel, and left the Jeep to warm up.

If someone had seen him at the lake and warned Goodman, there was exactly one comfortable place that person might have hidden without being seen. Travis walked across the lot to the glass doors of the visitor center, stepping high and watching carefully for the best places to put his feet. The hems of his trousers were already wet, and he was mildly concerned about his leather boots. He stamped up and down on the welcome mat under the concrete awning and cupped his hands around his eyes. There was no movement in the vestibule, and so he opened the door and stepped inside. As soon as the doors swung shut behind him he felt a few degrees warmer. He rubbed his hands together and blew into them while he looked around at the bulletin board on the wall, the racks of pamphlets and brochures. Nothing had changed since morning, but now he was paying closer attention, looking for something. He wasn't sure what, but he thought he'd know it if he saw it.

A staggering variety of community notices and advertisements were tacked to the board with colorful pushpins: a haunted corn maze; an auction of the estate of Dorothy Franklin; three Christian rock bands giving concerts on different dates, two of which had already passed; a food program; a flu shot clinic; a pancake feed at the firehouse. There was a poster asking for information about a woman who had disappeared from the area, and he counted four xeroxed flyers with photos of missing children. Travis studied their faces in the grainy pictures, but wasn't sure what he expected to see. If he had been born in a place as colorless as Burden County, he might have run away as a child. He moved on to look at the business cards for house-painters, personal health-care providers, DJs, day cares, house cleaners, craftsmen, and lawn services. Travis took a few of the cards and put them in his pocket. He tore the phone numbers from some of the notices.

The rack held magazines with titles that reflected the neighboring area codes and wildlife. There were flyers enticing visitors to look at salt mines and giant hay bales and local history museums. One leaflet proclaimed that the word of God was *Purity* and that this purity could only be achieved by rejecting "others"—and yet people new to the area were welcomed at services every Sunday morning. The contradiction amused Travis and he took one of the leaflets, folded it in half, and stuck it in his pocket with the business cards and phone numbers.

But nothing struck him as significant.

He turned to the vestibule's inner doors and pulled the handles. They were locked, which didn't come as a surprise. He considered a moment, then retrieved the flat leather pouch from his hip pocket and withdrew his snap gun and a torsion wrench. A moment later he opened the door and stepped inside the center's main room. He put his tools away in the pouch and returned it to his pocket, grateful that his motel room had not been searched while he was in his cell. Many of Travis's tools and weapons were illegal to carry in the state of Kansas.

All the windows had blinds, shut tight against the pearly sky, so he turned on the overhead lights. The visitor center was one big room with a high ceiling and two offices at the back, their doors standing open. A sign on the back wall outlined the various interactive displays throughout the room. Travis turned three hundred sixty degrees, looking carefully at the fish tank, the reptile habitat, the board covered with fur and feathers and scales for children to touch and compare. He squatted and looked at the floor, angling himself so that the overhead lights shone across the linoleum. He saw scuff marks and dirt and a few small puddles that he had caused by tracking snow inside. He stood and walked to the back, inspecting each of the two offices in turn. He lifted the blinds in the first office and saw the straggly tree that bordered the two-lane highway. The second office shared an outside wall with its mate, which meant that neither office gave a view of the lake or the outlook post. If someone had been waiting in the center, they would have had a clear view of anyone coming or leaving, but nothing else.

He went back to the first office. As he lowered the blinds back into place, something shiny caught his eye, a smudge of red on the white sill. He squinted at it, moved his head this way and that, watching it reflect the light, then took out his leather pouch again and selected a flat pick. He scraped the red dot off the windowsill and smiled when he saw that it flaked away, rather than coming off in one piece. The tiny bits left behind sparkled in the overhead fluorescent lights. He deposited the flakes in a tissue from a box on the desk behind him and folded it up inside the pouch.

He made one last circuit of the visitor center without seeing anything else unusual. He turned off the lights, locked the door behind him, and trekked back out to his Jeep. The windows were fogged, but it was warm inside. He pulled off his gray leather gloves and called his mother at the Foundation. After reassuring her that he was all right and filling her in on his arrest, he asked for a quick bit of research from her, then hung up and found Skottie Foster's cell number in his recent calls log. He turned on the Jeep's defroster and listened as the phone automatically dialed.

# 2

Maddy was in the kitchen. Skottie could hear her in there, banging cupboard doors, opening and closing drawers. Bear padded through the living room, past Skottie, and on into the kitchen as if he belonged there. Her phone rang and she glanced at it, saw it was Travis Roan. She was mildly surprised that Goodman hadn't held him longer and was curious to hear details, but decided to call him back later. She started to follow Bear, but Emmaline caught her arm.

"You okay?"

"I'm fine, Mama."

"You're gonna let Maddy go with him?"

"He's her father."

"You should take his keys. Make him leave something here so you'll know he's not gonna leave. Disappear with Maddy, you never see him again."

"Mom, please."

"I don't trust him. I told that man he could not come in my house." Emmaline's voice cracked and rose as she grew angry all over again at the memory. Skottie saw that her mother's fine dark hair had all been replaced by silver wire. There were deep grooves beside her mouth, and crooked little lines circled her eyes. Skottie wondered when all these changes had occurred. How had they crept in so quietly?

"I told him," Emmaline said, "and he went and sat on my porch anyway. That porch is part of my house. Told him I was gonna call the police, he didn't move."

"Brandon *is* the police, Mom. That's not gonna worry him."

Emmaline blinked at her.

"And, Jesus, you don't have to call anybody anyway. *I'm* the police."

"Who I would've called is police*men*." Emmaline emphasized the last part of the word, making it clear that her daughter could not possibly be an effective officer. It was an old insult, but it still stung.

But Skottie shrugged. "Too late now, I guess." She meant that Brandon had gone, that there was no longer a reason to call for help. And she meant that she was already a police *officer*. She had taken that decision out of her mother's hands long ago.

"Well," Emmaline said, "I don't want that man here again. You see him, you tell him that. He comes back here, I'm gonna dial the operator then and there."

"You shouldn't call the operator anymore, Mom. Call 911 if you need help."

"I know that—"

"And don't worry. I'll deal with Brandon myself from now on."

She walked away, proud of herself for not taking the bait, not re-hashing the ancient argument about what she did for a living. But she was angry, too. She and Maddy had needed a place to stay, and she had been grateful to Emmaline for taking them in. But it meant she couldn't be herself, couldn't risk offending her mother, and she wasn't sure whether she had refrained from fighting because she was taking the high ground or because she was afraid Emmaline might kick them out.

She felt like she was losing on every front.

In the kitchen, Maddy was standing on the counter, straddling the sink. She had moved the drainer with last night's dishes to the small Formica-topped table in the corner and had dragged over a chair to help her climb. She was holding the handle of an open cupboard door for balance. Bear sat in the middle of the floor watching her, and when Skottie entered the room, the big dog stood and turned his sad brown eyes to her. He looked worried.

"Get down from there," Skottie said. "This instant."

"I can't find any bowls big enough. I don't know where anything is here."

"I said get down."

"Bear's thirsty, Mom." She looked like she wanted to stamp her foot. "At home we have that big silver bowl, but there's nothing here."

Skottie brushed past the dog and lifted her daughter off the counter and set her on the floor with a thud that shook the cabinet door shut. She hadn't meant to be rough, but Maddy was getting heavier. *Everybody around me is changing,* she thought, *and I haven't been paying attention.* Maddy spun around and surprised Skottie by wrapping her arms around her and burying her face in Skottie's stomach, cutting off the lecture Skottie had ready about the dangers of climbing on the kitchen counter. Skottie hesitated for a moment, then hugged her daughter back. Maddy's shoe had left a smudge on the chrome faucet, but she decided not to mention it. She would clean it later, hopefully before Emmaline noticed.

She waited until Maddy let go, then knelt in front of her and took her daughter by the shoulders.

"What did you and your dad talk about? Before I got here?"

"Nothing."

"I don't want you to—"

"Bear's *so* thirsty."

Skottie took a breath. "Look at me. I want you to have fun this weekend, okay? But this is our home right now. You know that, right? Me and you."

Maddy rolled her eyes. "I guess so."

Skottie realized she had squandered her two days off. She might have taken Maddy to a park, or taken her shopping for new jeans at the outlet mall. Instead, she had put a couple hundred miles on the Subaru and gotten herself in trouble with Lieutenant Johnson. And she had given Brandon an opportunity to manipulate their daughter. "Okay, let's get Bear some water."

Maddy looked back at the counter. "You didn't need to be worried. If I did fall, he would cushion me. Bear's a big fluffy pillow."

Skottie glanced at the dog and he closed his eyes, then opened them slowly as if mildly insulted. Skottie reached out and scratched him behind his ear. He wagged his tail and came closer, and Maddy sank her fingers into his mane.

"Can we take him for a walk?"

"Sure, we can do that. I need to make a quick phone call."

"We need to get food for him," Maddy said.

"We'll go down to the Dollar General. Except, looking at this big boy, he probably eats steak all the time. Maybe we better go to the IGA."

"Can I bring my phone?"

"No. You can play that game on your own time. I need you to pay attention and help me with Bear. I'll make my call while we're on our walk, okay?"

"Where does Grandma keep the big bowls?"

"Let's find out. But this time, I'll look high and you look low. And put that chair back where it belongs. We don't want your grandma to yell at us."

Maddy hopped to it and Skottie opened a cupboard over the stove, grateful, for the moment, that they had a project.

# 3

Travis's phone vibrated on the console between the seats and he pulled over to the side of the road before picking it up. The sun had suddenly come out again and the snow was already melting, turning into sludge that spewed up from beneath the Jeep's tires. He checked the caller ID and smiled.

"Skottie Foster, thank you for returning my call."

"I take it you're out of jail, Dr. Roan?" She sounded a little out of breath, and Travis could hear ambient traffic noise near her.

"I am free now, thank you. And the sun has decided to grace us with its presence. Surely a good sign. Where are you?"

"About a block from my house. It's still overcast down here. Tell me, what does Bear eat?"

Travis leaned back against the seat and smiled up at the mottled sky beyond the Jeep's roof. "I was quite worried, but I trusted that you would find Bear and take care of him. He will eat whatever you are eating. He likes people food."

"So we shouldn't get him dog food?"

"Oh, my lord, no. Would you eat dog food?"

"I don't think so, but I'm not a dog."

"No, you are most definitely not."

"What?"

"You are not a dog."

There was a long pause, and he wasn't sure what to say to fill the silence. He reflected on his statement and couldn't find anything wrong with it. He sat still and waited.

"I wasn't getting dog food anyway," she said at last. "I thought maybe he'd eat a steak."

"Oh, yes. He likes steak very much."

"That's what you ordered for him the other night. At the Roundup." He heard her breathing hard and he waited. Finally she spoke again. "He was hiding that whole time out at the lake. There were tons of people tramping all over there and nobody found him. But he came right out when I called him."

"Yes, he is a good boy. Trusting when there is reason to trust."

"Esperanto, right? I mean, the language you use with him. That did the trick."

Travis heard another voice, high and excited. "I'm the one . . ." The voice trailed off and there was a rustling sound, followed by a muffled exchange. Then Skottie came back.

"My daughter did some research online and figured out a little more about that language. We're trying it out on Bear. He knows a lot of words. *Sidigu.*"

It was Travis's turn to be quiet. He closed his eyes and thought.

"Dr. Roan?"

Travis opened his eyes and smiled again. "Please, I asked you to call me Travis."

"Is something wrong, Travis?"

"No. But that is my private language with Bear."

"Why Esperanto?"

"My father taught me. It was my first language."

"Like German shorthand."

"No. Nothing like Ruth Elder and her daughter. My father was not encouraging some special bond with me; he was simply testing my ability to learn and adapt. My brother, Judah, was to follow in his footsteps while my . . . while I provided research, linguistics, and weapons. I hope you will not misunderstand. I am extremely grateful to you for rescuing Bear. I only—"

"No, no, I do understand, but we had to—"

"Yes, of course. Please, I should not have said anything. Skottie, I have a question that might be perceived as odd."

"Ha! Sorry, I mean what is it?"

"Would you tell me, what color of fingernail polish do you use?"

"Fingernail polish? I don't wear colors. I use a clear coat."

"Really?"

"You sound surprised."

"No, but that is a nice bit of synchronicity. I use a clear polish on my own nails. It strengthens them."

"Um, yeah, it does. Why are you asking me about fingernails?"

"I promise to explain when I see you next."

"When will that be? We're on our way to the grocery store right now. For the steak. I think maybe we'll all have steak tonight."

Travis heard a happy squeal in the background.

"That's Maddy again," Skottie said. "My daughter."

"Please tell her hello for me. And thank her for figuring out how to talk to Bear." He looked around him at the bare trees and the mottled fields, brown stalks jutting pointlessly up through the thin layer of snow, waiting to be plowed under in the spring. "I am not entirely sure where I am, but I believe I can be in Hays within the next two or three hours."

"Hays isn't that far from you. Shouldn't take that long."

"I am running out of time to complete my mission here, so I decided to prioritize and make good use of the daylight I have left. I was on my way to the church."

"What church? And why are you running out of time?" She sounded more engaged than she had been. She had a police officer's curiosity about people's movements and motives. He realized she might still be suspicious of him.

"The Foundation is going to send someone else soon. I have not made the progress that was expected of me. But I asked them to run a background check on our mutual friend the sheriff."

"Goodman?"

"Of course. I believe Mr. Goodman became sheriff because his father arranged it."

"Who's his father?"

"A man named Rudy Goodman. In the 1970s, he founded something called the Purity First Church."

"Oh, crap," Skottie said. The background sounds had changed.

There was a hollow echoing quality to her voice, and Travis guessed that she was now inside a building.

"Where is Bear? Is he still with you?"

"Yeah. I mean, sort of."

"You have arrived at the grocery store?"

"Yup. Gotta hurry. Maddy's waiting outside with the dog."

"Bear would never let any harm come to her."

"Which is why I left her out there," Skottie said. "But I still need to hurry."

"Very well. A minute ago you cursed. Why?"

"That church you mentioned is weird and famous."

"Famous?"

"At least locally. They travel around with some kind of recruitment drive inside a tent that they put up in parking lots. At the mall, at Walmart, sometimes out by the movie theater. They go all over the place. Did you see those signs coming in? On the highway? 'Repent unless you're a bad seed.' Stuff like that."

"'Unless ye be of impure stock.'"

"Right."

"One sign said 'Their breed fears the storm.' Another said 'Lesser men are but cattle.' That one included a citation that does not match anything I remember from the Bible."

Skottie didn't say anything, and Travis thought the call might have been dropped.

"Skottie? Are you there?"

"I'm here."

"So those people put the signs up? The Purity First people?"

"They like to sit down in front of temples and synagogues, movies and concerts, too. Keep people from going in and out so they have to listen to their spiel. They show up anywhere there's something they don't like, and they don't like much of anything. Or anyone."

"It seems quite clear whom they dislike."

"Yeah."

"And our sheriff is one of them."

"That explains a thing or two."

"And creates another mystery or two."

"It fits the Nazi profile, doesn't it? Let me know what you find out. I plan to check on the body you found. Maybe forensics can tell us something useful."

"Good. Skottie, is Bear doing well? Is he happy?"

"He seems okay. Can he eat cookies? I'm getting cookies."

"Are they oatmeal?"

"Oreos."

"Ah, he likes Oreos even more than oatmeal, but chocolate will make him sick."

"They're the vanilla kind."

"Not as tasty, I think, but much better for him." Travis thought about his dog sitting outside a grocery store in western Kansas, like some pet. At least he wasn't chained to a signpost, and he had Skottie's daughter for company. Travis shook his head, though he knew Skottie couldn't see him. Bear was not used to being treated like a dog.

"I could come get him now if you like," Travis said. "I can wait and visit the church tomorrow." He hoped she would ask him to come right away, even though the roundtrip would take the rest of his afternoon. He missed his canine friend more than he missed his books and the silk sheets on his own bed.

"Hang on a second." She apparently covered the phone with her hand, but he could hear her talking to someone. A moment later, the quality of the sound changed again. He heard wind and cars and he guessed she had rejoined her daughter in the parking lot.

The phone hissed and Skottie was back on the line. "We can keep him a little longer."

Travis heard another squeal of delight in the background and assumed Skottie's daughter was campaigning to keep Bear in their home.

"He's pretty low-maintenance for a dog," Skottie said. "But I really don't want Maddy to get too attached. So if you can still pick him up tonight . . ."

"That should pose no problem for me."

"It's probably better if you get to the church today anyway. I'm guessing they'd be closed tomorrow for the holiday."

"You think a church would be closed on a holiday?"

"That church might."

"I see. All right. Expect me before eight o'clock."

Skottie gave him her address and he memorized it. "I'll leave a light on for you," she said.

"Skottie?"

"Yeah?"

"Thank you for taking care of him."

"My pleasure. Maddy's really taken to him."

"Of course. He is extremely personable."

Travis ended the call and set the phone down with a sigh. People were messy and complicated, with needs and motivations Travis sometimes found confusing. Bear was easy to understand, easy to rely on. Still, he had confidence in Skottie, and his separation from Bear served a dual purpose. He needed an ally in Kansas, and looking after his dog would bind Skottie to him in subtle ways. It was a big step forward on the road toward mutual trust.

# 4

"It must be expensive to feed him if he eats steak all the time," Maddy said. "We don't even do that, and we're people." She was walking a little ahead of Skottie and her hood was up, her face hidden from view, but she sounded happy, swinging Bear's makeshift rope leash back and forth.

"I think Bear gets treated differently than most dogs," Skottie said. The plastic bag full of steak and Oreos and small golden potatoes smacked into her leg with every other step she took.

"Probably because he's smarter and bigger and cuter."

"He's cute?"

"In a scary kind of way."

"I think it's probably because Travis doesn't have anyone else," Skottie said. "I guess I'd treat a pet differently if I didn't have you to worry about."

"You can always let me go live with Dad," Maddy said. "Then you wouldn't have to worry about me at all."

Skottie wasn't sure whether she had walked into a trap or had accidentally taken the conversation in a bad direction. At some point, she had lost her sense of such things. Bear led the way, stopping at the occasional tree or fire hydrant or parked car to sniff around. Maddy kept her head down, and Skottie couldn't tell what her daughter was thinking or how best to approach her, how to get her talking again. And they'd been having such a good afternoon.

"Is that where he is?" Maddy broke the silence, pointing up at an eight-story concrete building. Her voice was flat and emotionless now.

Skottie knew what she meant. "Yeah. That's your dad's hotel."

"Will he be coming for Thanksgiving tomorrow?"

"I don't think so."

"So you're making him stay at that place all alone on Thanksgiving?"

"That's his choice. I didn't ask him to come here."

"Of course he came here. He loves me. You can't just take his kid away and expect him not to care."

Skottie felt her face flush and she clamped her mouth shut so she wouldn't say the first thought that had popped into her head: *If he really cared, why did he wait six months to come see you?* Instead she stared at the blank outer wall of the hotel. They were behind it, cutting through the parking lot of a strip mall a quarter mile from Emmaline's house, and the hotel's architect hadn't bothered to make the back of the building attractive. Skottie wondered whether Brandon was staying on the other side, the pretty side, or was somewhere up there watching them from the window of his room. What kind of view did he have? Was he lonely?

"He's probably lonely," Maddy said.

Startled, Skottie stumbled over a crack in the pavement, the grocery bag bouncing up high before slamming back into her thigh.

"I'm sorry," Maddy said. "I shouldn't have brought it up."

Bear had found something interesting under a twiggy hedge at the side of the parking lot, and they stood there for a long minute waiting for him to finish exploring.

"I understand," Skottie said. "You miss your dad. Sometimes I miss him, too."

"Then let's invite him over tomorrow."

"Um . . . I don't . . ." Even if she wanted to ask Brandon to dinner, she knew Emmaline wouldn't let him past the front door. But she didn't want to remind Maddy how deep the division in their family had become.

"Just think about it? It might not be so bad, you know?"

"I'll think about it, Maddy, but don't—"

"That's all I want, Mom. I'm just asking for a little reasonable discourse, is all."

"Reasonable discourse? Is that something you heard me or your dad say?"

"No," Maddy said. "I can talk. I'm not a baby."

"I know it," Skottie said.

Maddy peeked at her from under her hood and then looked away. "Mom, don't look at me like that, okay?"

"Okay."

"I mean it."

"I know," Skottie said. "I get it that you're grown up now and all you want is a little reasonable discourse."

She reached out and put her arm around Maddy's shoulder and was grateful when Maddy let it stay there for the rest of their walk.

# 5

Driving through Paradise Flats, looking for the church, Travis noticed that many of the businesses in town and more than a few community landmarks were named for the Goodman family. A few others, including the 4-H community center, had been founded by people named Meyer. These two families appeared to be the big movers and shakers in the area. He wondered how easy it had been for

Kurt Goodman to get himself elected sheriff in a county saturated with members of his own family.

Purity First was housed in a large stone edifice, one step removed from being a cathedral. By contrast, many of the other churches Travis had seen in the area looked like administration buildings or new brick schoolhouses, complete with American flags dangling over dead yellow lawns. Purity First's campus gave it the air of something old and steeped in tradition.

Travis parked on the street and got out. The sun had disappeared again and ominous clouds had begun to roll in. Across from the church was a community garden with a hand-lettered sign that said *Free! Take some vegetables!* There was a box at the near side of the garden with a slot and another sign asking for donations. Travis took a five-dollar bill from his wallet and dropped it into the slot, then crossed the road and looked up at the church. It was surrounded by a high wooden privacy fence, stained a shade of cedar that matched the anachronistically modern steeple above. Travis was tall enough to see over the fence if he hopped, so he grabbed the top edge and pulled himself up. Inside the compound was a tennis court with lawn chairs set out beside it and a little table with an umbrella that had gathered a big pile of crispy leaves. The net had been taken down for the winter, and a basketball hoop was similarly net-less, waiting for the sun to bring the church youth back outside. Two flags hung limp from a pole outside the church building: an upside-down American flag, and beneath it a plain white field decorated with a stylized wolf's head. Small prefabricated outbuildings lined the inside of the fence, each big enough to house three riding lawn mowers. Travis caught a whiff of chlorine and assumed there was a swimming pool nearby. He wondered why it hadn't been drained and covered yet.

He dropped down and walked around the block, looking for a

break in the fence. The wooden privacy fence was succeeded after a few feet by a wrought-iron railing with a locked gate. There were doors behind the gate at either end of a short walkway that ran parallel to the fence. Travis presumed the more modest entrance might lead to a church office, adjacent to the sanctuary. Across from it were big double doors, taller and wider and more ornate, with small stained glass inlays. He walked past the church and kept going to the end of the block. The road curved to the right, and the houses on both sides of the street were connected by the same cedar fence that surrounded the church. Many of the homes had been refurbished with gray aluminum siding and storm windows, giving them a uniform facade despite radically different architectural touches. Some of the homes might have been there for a hundred years or more, unique and dignified, before being slathered over with suburban banality. There was a moving van in front of one house, but there were no movers to be seen, nobody outside. The front door of the house was closed and curtains were drawn over the windows. Travis made note of the address as he passed it: 437.

Small signs were posted every few feet that said PROPERTY UNDER 24-HOUR VIDEO SURVEILLANCE. Travis waved at one of the signs and kept going. He didn't see any cameras. A wide alley between the church and the first row of houses was lined with garbage cans and protected by a padlocked gate. The fence was visible here and there, a blank connective tissue, for at least three blocks in every direction, and Travis's feet were wet and cold by the time he got all the way back around to where his Jeep was parked. He was afraid his boots were ruined.

It appeared to him that the church had purchased every house and lot nearby and then continued to expand, encroaching on the neighborhood like a virus. A plague of Purity.

It took Travis twenty seconds to pick the lock on the iron gate. He waited a moment to see if anyone would come out of the church and shoo him away, then he slipped inside and closed the gate behind him. He bypassed the public entrance and went through into the wide courtyard next to the tennis court. There was a path butted up against the church wall, and he walked parallel to it in the grass. The fence was buttressed on the inside surface by thick iron bars bracketed to the wood. A backup generator sat silent, and Travis traced cables from it back to the church. He tried the door of the first small outbuilding he came to, expecting it to be locked, and he was not disappointed. He made his way around to the back of the building and looked through a greasy little window that faced the fence. Inside were two sets of bunk beds, a small table with a hot plate, and a minifridge under a shelf that held slim battered paperbacks with titles like *Your Enemy Wears a Badge*, *The Slave Mentality*, and *Tame the Mongrel*. The thin blankets on three of the beds were mussed and stained. Travis glanced through the windows of some of the other sheds without seeing anything different, then walked past a big double garage that looked as new and prefab as the outbuildings and followed the fence around to where the alley led into a small parking lot.

The only thing that seemed out of place was a dirty white semi-trailer truck parked in the far corner of the lot, well hidden by the high fence. There was nothing painted on either side of the trailer, no logo or even an advertisement for the church. There was a half-inch gap between the big doors at the back and a lingering scent of sweat and old food that he hoped wasn't coming from him. He jiggled the handle, but it was locked. He wondered why anyone would bother locking a truck when it was parked in a secured private lot.

Tucked away out of sight next to the trailer was an old green Volkswagen minibus with bright red spots scattered across its sides like spattered blood. It looked like something a clown might drive on a dare. Travis cupped his hands and tried to look inside, but the windows were tinted black. He wrote down the license numbers of both vehicles, then crossed the lot back to the church, aware that he was now being observed.

As he drew near the grand stone building, he could hear voices chanting something unintelligible. They stopped and a man's voice shouted something, then the voices started up again in response to the man. The sounds were coming from somewhere low to the ground, behind the heavy shrubbery that ringed the foundation. Travis guessed there was a basement conference room hosting a meeting, but he couldn't tell how many people were down there.

The double doors opened inward as he reached them.

"Welcome, friend." A middle-aged man stood blinking at him from the warmth of the vestibule. His thin blond hair fell across his face, and he held his free arm up as if warding off the outside atmosphere. He was tall and wide and bore a passing resemblance to Sheriff Goodman around the eyes and mouth. But where the sheriff was rough-hewn and tanned, this man was pale and precise in his movements.

Travis smiled at him. "Is this a bad time?"

"No, my friend, it's never a bad time to embrace the Word." The man stepped back and waved his arm across the threshold. "Did someone leave the gate open?"

"Apparently so," Travis said.

"Well, now you're here, please come in."

Travis stepped inside and wrinkled his nose at the smell. It was a strange mixture of must and body odor, like a high school dance held in a tomb. He stamped his feet on the mat.

"Seems quiet," Travis said.

"It's Thanksgiving," the man said. "Happy Thanksgiving."

"Today?"

"Tomorrow. Most of our parishioners have gone home."

"This is not their home?" Travis thought of the outbuildings inside the fence and all the bigger houses surrounding the church that fronted the street.

"In the larger sense it is, but they've gone out to spread the Word."

"And what is the word?"

"Welcome," the man said. "The Word is welcome."

"That is usually a good word."

"If it falls on the right ears."

Travis looked around him. There were pews against two of the walls and a stained glass window that depicted Isaac lying on an altar, his father brandishing a knife above him. "You saw me with your cameras out there?"

"We have eyes everywhere."

Travis nodded, but he didn't believe the man had been watching the cameras, if there were cameras. If so, he would have come out to greet Travis as soon as he breached the fence. The myth of video surveillance might be nearly as good as actual cameras, yet cheaper and easier to maintain.

"We must protect everything we are and everything we have from the baser elements of this world," the man said.

"And what about the trailer you have out there? Are you protecting whatever is in it?"

"There's not much in the trailer," the man said. "Just some banners, our tents, and some equipment. The valuable stuff is in here."

"Protected by more than cameras, I presume."

The man shrugged.

"The sheds?"

"Our youth group raises money for the church by doing yard work around the town, Dr. Roan."

If so, Travis thought, the youth group was forced to pick grass and leaves by hand, since there was no room in those sheds for any lawn equipment. "You know me?"

"You're Dr. Travis Roan. I'm Deacon Heinrich Goodman. I'm the director of this place." His brown shirt was unbuttoned too far down his pale chest.

"Goodman? The son of Rudy Goodman? The brother of Kurt?"

"He was once my brother. No more."

"No more? What happened?"

Heinrich Goodman smiled like a snake in a hamster cage. "Would you like to take a quick look around the place?" He walked ahead and Travis tagged along, his hands clasped behind his back. He felt like whistling to ward off evil spirits.

"You seem like a man of the world, Dr. Roan," Heinrich said. "I hope our little church doesn't disappoint you."

"I will try not to track any of the outside world on your carpets."

Heinrich turned and squinted at him. "Don't worry about that. We have it cleaned weekly. Every Monday morning, like clockwork."

They were in a wood-paneled hallway with plush red carpeting. The walls were lined with portraits of major donors to the church coffers, all of them old white men. Travis recognized one of the faces. The brass plaque under his photograph read JOSEPH ODEK. Travis stopped and sucked air in through his clenched teeth.

"What's that?" Heinrich turned back again, a concerned look on his face.

"Nothing, Mr. Goodman. I suppose I am surprised by how big this place is."

"Wait until you see the nave. We spared no expense in renovating it the second time."

The final two portraits at the end of the hall were separated from the others and dwarfed them in size. They were mounted in elaborate gold-leaf frames and depicted a pair of middle-aged men in 1970s fashions: wide collars, facial hair, heavy black glasses. Like Odek, each of them was identified by a discreet brass plaque. Travis paused to study the photo of Reverend Rudy Goodman. He had a thick salt-and-pepper beard and his head was bald, but his eyes blazed with righteous authority. The man next to him was named Jacob Meyer. Travis had never heard of him, but he inspected the photo carefully. Meyer projected a different sort of personality. There was something pleasant about his toothy smile, and the laugh lines around his eyes made him look like he had just told a dirty joke, whispered so the nearby wives and kids wouldn't hear. Travis wondered if one of the two men was a Nazi in hiding. They were both roughly the right age for it.

Heinrich stopped in front of huge double doors with his hand on the push bar. "Is something wrong?"

"No," Travis said. "You mentioned you had to renovate again. Why?"

"That would have been after the second lightning strike in 2004."

"You were struck by lightning twice?"

"I wasn't. My father was. The hand of our Lord reached down from the heavens to anoint him."

"Reached down through the roof?"

"What could stop it?"

"Not the roof, I suppose."

"No, sir. When the Lord has something to say, He comes right out and says it."

"But only to your father, right?"

"He's the chosen one."

"Is he still alive, your father?"

Heinrich nodded gravely. "Yes, but his health has suffered in recent years. His seizures have come back and increased in severity." He looked away when he said it, and his cheek twitched. Travis hoped for his sake that he didn't play poker. "I'm afraid he won't be able to see you."

"Pity."

Heinrich pushed the doors open, and Travis followed the red carpet through to a cavernous room with exposed rafters high above and purple windows along the walls on either side. There was a wide main aisle leading up to the sanctuary and two narrower aisles on each side, bordered by pews. Travis estimated five hundred people could comfortably sit through a service there—maybe the entire population of Paradise Flats—but at the moment there was only a single figure hunched over in a pew at the front. The church didn't look quite like anything Travis had seen before. The stained glass windows told a story, from the back of the nave to the front: a man on fire was surrounded by what seemed to be dots of energy, then the man was laying his hands on a wailing woman with a hunchback, and in the third window the woman was in the cloud of dots and had lost her hump. There were more pictures in more windows, but Travis's eye was drawn to the chancel. There was a podium with track lighting above it and a huge round window in the back wall high above the altar that depicted a thunderstorm in progress. Where he expected to see a cross there was a stylized lightning bolt, bright gold, its wicked tip piercing the altar, its top intersecting with the stained glass tempest above.

Travis pointed. "The lightning that struck your father?"

Heinrich tipped his head. "When the Lord blessed Reverend Rudy, He also saw fit to clear this church of the sinners who were using it. The building became available to us. The lightning was a sign pointing the way."

"What do the dots mean?"

"More signs and symbols."

"Purity First," Travis said.

"It's an acronym. Power, Unity, Rebirth, Investment, and so on."

"Truth? Is that what the T stands for?"

"No," Heinrich said. "'Treat others as they deserve to be treated.'"

"A bit like the Golden Rule. But not quite, is it?"

"It's something my father always said. It became a tenet of the church. Who knows how these things come to be or what they origi-nally meant. Words have a power of their own without needing any greater meaning."

"I see." Travis felt that words ought to mean something, or else why say them? And he was sure the fifth tenet of Purity First meant exactly what it seemed to. But he said, "What would I find behind that door?" and pointed at the archway behind the altar.

"Oh, I'm afraid we aren't prepared for a full tour today. Tell me, though, would you be our guest for a very special Thanksgiving cele-bration tomorrow? It would be my honor."

"You said most of your parishioners were away for the holiday. What kind of celebration do you have planned?"

"Many of our people are away at the moment, yes. But there are those who don't have homes or families or are unable to travel. Some have special duties to attend to and we couldn't spare them. There's Kenny, you see." Heinrich pointed to the hunched person in the front pew. "We invite these friends to our family dinner here at the church. In the basement."

"The basement?"

"Yes, there's a community space down there and a small kitchen. There's a shuffleboard court, too, if you know how to play, but I'm afraid I don't. It doesn't get a lot of use."

"I have never played, either," Travis said. He wandered down the aisle and stopped next to the pew where the man sat. "Your name is Kenny?"

The man stared straight ahead at the altar without acknowledging Travis's presence. Travis moved between Kenny and the altar and looked down at him. Kenny was perhaps sixty years old, with a large nose and dark deep-set eyes. Drool cascaded off his chin, soaking his sweater, which looked like it had been put on backward and inside out. Kenny's eyes were glazed, and there was a curved scar that arced up over his temple where no hair grew.

Travis felt his skin crawling and his hands automatically clenched into fists. The shape of Kenny's scar didn't look accidental. Someone had hurt the poor man, had taken his soul from him and left his body to inhabit the church.

Heinrich joined Travis and smiled at him. "I'm afraid Kenny doesn't speak much."

Travis swallowed his anger and put his hands in his pockets. "What happened to him?"

"He is one of the Lord's special creatures. It makes him happy to gaze on the lightning. We keep the nave open for him around the clock, since he wanders in at odd hours."

Travis looked up again at the dazzling lightning bolt that split the altar in two. He wondered if it was solid gold or plated. "Well, thank you for the kind dinner invitation," he said. "May I think it over?"

"Of course," Heinrich said. He pulled out a wallet and removed his card, handed it over to Travis. "Here. My private number is the one at the bottom. Call me up by tomorrow morning, would you? One way or the other, so I know how many to expect around the table."

"Thank you." Travis glanced down at the card before tucking it away in the breast pocket of his jacket. It was plain white with black type across six red dots. "I will show myself out. You need not trouble yourself."

"As you wish."

"Kenny, it was good to meet you," Travis said, but there was no response.

Travis walked up the red carpet without looking back to see if Heinrich was following him. When he got to the double doors, he shut them behind him. Alone in the hallway, he took out his phone and snapped a picture of each of the church elders' portraits. He took one of Joseph Odek, too. Then he put his phone away and walked quickly out of Purity First and into the bracing autumn air.

He looked around, trying again to locate the cameras. The sound of a metal door scraping against concrete caught his attention and he poked his head around the corner. A large man in a denim shirt strode quickly across the basketball court to the parking lot. A moment later, Travis heard a vehicle door creak open, then slam shut, and an engine roared to life.

Travis sprinted down the path and around the corner in time to see the semitrailer truck bounce out of the alley and down the street, knocking over a garbage bin along the way.

"Where is he going in such a hurry?" Travis looked at the rows of matching houses, but there was no one around to respond.

# 6

Heinrich bounded down the stairs three at a time and crossed the shuffleboard court. He entered the communal hall and glanced at the closed door next to the kitchen, the door that led to his father's workshop, before turning to look at his people. They stopped chatting and looked back at him, waiting. There were more than twenty of them now, in matching brown shirts, handpicked from the Purity First congregation. They were the most devoted to the cause, their Lord's army. Heinrich thought about the bags he had packed and waiting nearby, and he wondered what would become of this little army after he left them. They were enthusiastic, but they required a firm hand.

"It has begun," he said. "Today an emissary has come to us, dressed all in gray to symbolize the mixing of our races."

A low murmur rolled through the crowd, and Heinrich held his hand up for silence.

"Yes, it is the same man Lou-Ellen told us about, the one who travels with a great black beast. And . . ." He held up his hand again. "And he is working with the black woman."

"Purity First," a boy in the front row said.

"We are the true minority," Heinrich said, his voice rising as he settled into the familiar sermon. "We are beset on every side by our enemies, who outnumber us and try to force us to conform to *their* standards. And yet *we* built this civilization from the ground up. *We* created language and math and science. *We* tamed the beasts and seeded the fields. Could *they* have accomplished all that we have? I say to you *they could not*! They outnumber us ten to one, but they lack the intelligence and the ambition, the talent and the skill. No, the black, the Jew, the Mexican, they take the food from our table! And what do they give us in return?"

"*Nothing!*"

"And yet they are envious of us. They *hate* us."

"*Hate!*"

"They attack us on every front. But we fight back," Heinrich said. "They have sent their man in gray to confuse us, to obstruct us, but we will not bow to his agenda."

"Tell us what to do, Deacon," Donnie Mueller said.

"I'll kill him," Stanley Mayhew said. Stanley was a giant of a man with a heavy unibrow over dark dead eyes, and while many nodded in agreement, those closest to him in the back row inched away to the farthest edges of their chairs.

"Thank you, Stanley," Heinrich said. "The man in gray will return here tomorrow afternoon. He will expect us to resist, but he doesn't know what we are capable of. And when he comes, we will be ready for him."

"*We will be ready!*"

"We will push back," Heinrich said, "against him and against all those who would corrupt our way of life."

"*We will push back!*"

Heinrich shook his fist at the tiny windows up near the ceiling of the big room. "Purity First!"

"*Purity First!*"

He stretched out his arms and waited for his followers to settle down again. "This is what we have waited for. Go and prepare yourselves for tomorrow."

"*Purity First!*"

They stood and folded their metal chairs, returned them to the rack at the back of the room, threw away their coffee cups, and exited in small clusters, whispering to one another, their faces shining with excitement and pleasure.

Heinrich called to one of the men as he passed. "Donnie, would you stay for a minute?"

"Of course, Deacon."

"I have a special job for you."

## JUNE 1992

Amy Romita was sixteen and had suffered from severe acne for three years when she came to one of Reverend Rudy's Sunday sermons. Tears streamed down her cheeks and her voice broke as she explained to the enraptured congregation how ostracized she felt, how friendless she was, and how much she longed to be rid of her affliction. People in the front pews reached out to her, touched her, reassured her. They swayed back and forth and prayed out loud for Amy to be released from her burden. Rudy closed his eyes and felt the room hum with electricity. He put his hands on her face and then rubbed them down the length of her back and felt the familiar jolt of power that always flowed when the lightning was working through him. Amy fell unconscious on the sanctuary steps and had to be carried to a front pew, where she woke up an hour later, confused about where she was and what was happening around her. Three weeks later, her skin clear and beautiful, Amy met Reverend Rudy at the Econo Lodge in Phillipsburg and expressed her gratitude to him with great enthusiasm.

Donnie Mueller was nearly catatonic when his sister Kim wheeled him into the reverend's office on a quiet Tuesday afternoon. His eyes were closed behind enormous sunglasses, and a pillow was duct-taped over his head to keep out ambient noise. Donnie's shoulders were hunched and his limbs were stiff and atrophied. He was unable to attend a sermon, unable to leave the house except under the most extreme circumstances because of migraines. Kim explained that any sound or light caused her brother crippling pain. Rudy smiled and nodded and brushed his hands against Donnie's temples. Afterward his sister wheeled Donnie back out, helped him into her car, folded the wheelchair, and put it away in the trunk. She forgot to take it back out when they got home because Donnie limped up the path to the front door by himself and crawled into bed on his own. He attended a Purity First tent service the following Sunday, and Heinrich put him right up front so everyone there could see him grinning and clapping his hands in time to the music.

Now Amy and Donnie volunteered for the church, and this Sunday they were working the room, going up and down the aisles while Liz Wimberly and her choir girls, all in red robes, got the crowd on its feet. The musicians played behind Liz, and supplicants lined up in front of the pulpit, and Reverend Rudy prepared for his sermon, and Amy and Donnie searched the congregation for volunteers.

Rudy and Jacob had spent a great deal of time debating the pros and cons of healing various ailments and disfigurements. Amputees looked good, of course, but although Rudy was often able to cure them of phantom limb syndrome, aching stumps, and other difficulties, they *didn't* grow their limbs back. At least, not quickly enough to dazzle a restless congregation on a Sunday afternoon. Limps, sore throats, chronic fatigue, allergies . . . these were all either too minor to impress or too hard for Rudy and his assistants to verify. He didn't want any fakers. They would undermine everything he was trying to build. And he didn't want the congregation getting bored, either.

Jacob had always told him, "Good theater puts butts in the seats and money in the collection baskets."

So Amy and Donnie were looking for people who clearly needed help, people who might provide the drama Reverend Rudy required. And they thought they had struck pay dirt with two new parishioners. One was Gary Gilbert, a truck driver who had gone through the window of his eighteen-wheeler the previous summer. He had suffered a concussion and broken eleven bones, including both his arms and a leg. The bones had healed, but he had lost nearly seventy pounds and his vision came and went. He had not been able to hold down any solid foods and he carried a bag with him in case he couldn't get to a restroom before vomiting. The other prospect was Lou-Ellen Quinlan, a former underwear model. When she was twenty-three years old, Lou-Ellen had been hit by a car while crossing against a light at Forty-Fifth and Broadway in New York. She had flown several feet through the air before slamming face-first into a fire hydrant. Her neck had broken in three places, minute particles of bone chipping off and ricocheting about under her skin like glass, tearing up the soft flesh of her throat and embedding in her lungs. She had undergone eighteen hours of surgery and her doctors had been optimistic about her prospects, but she had never woken up from anesthesia. She was now thirty-one and had spent all of her remaining twenties and the start of her thirties lying on a twin bed in the basement of her parents' home in Plainville, Kansas. She had a physical therapist who visited three times a week to exercise her arms and legs and rub her down. Her mother gave her sponge baths and whispered encouraging words in her ear, waiting patiently for Lou-Ellen to open her eyes.

Gary Gilbert was sitting at the back of the church on the aisle, ready to leave at a moment's notice if his stomach began to act up. He was listening to Reverend Rudy's sermon, but his eyes weren't working well and he didn't see Amy approach him. He jumped when she leaned close and whispered in his ear, but stood and followed when she took his hand and led him to the front row by the pulpit.

Lou-Ellen Quinlan was in a wheelchair next to the door to the narthex. Her mother, Marybeth, smiled at Donnie when he touched her elbow and she nodded when he beckoned to her. Donnie waited while she wiped her daughter's chin and tucked a blanket in around Lou-Ellen's scrawny legs, then led the way down the side aisle and motioned for Marybeth to sit next to Gary. Gary scooted over for her, and Donnie moved into her place behind Lou-Ellen's chair, ready to roll her forward when the time came. Amy stood beside him and reached out with her pinkie finger to touch his hand. A flicker of a smile twitched across Donnie's lips.

"And finally," Reverend Rudy said, his voice rolling across the sea of upturned faces before him, "you *know* who you are! And you *know* that you cannot keep yourself secret from *Him*! You know in your *heart* if you are a wolf or a butcher, a lamb or a gardener! You know if you are *worthy* and you know if He has *chosen* you! And, my people, if He has chosen you, then you are among the *pure*! And you will be *welcomed* at the last! Purity First! *Purity First!*"

The congregation took up the chant. "PURITY FIRST! PURITY FIRST!" Nearly every person there had descended from someone in Germany or Poland or Ireland or Sweden. There was a first-generation Scottish American and there was a woman who claimed her ancestors had arrived on the *Mayflower*. One man had come to Kansas from Austria when he was a boy and still remembered the mountains. Their voices rose, drowning out the reverend, who had stepped away from the microphone.

Another volunteer named Judy rushed forward with a towel for him, and he mopped his brow. That was the signal for Donnie and

Amy to get moving. Donnie wheeled Lou-Ellen's chair forward so that Amy could help Gary out of the pew and into a second wheelchair. They trundled across in front of the waist-high railing, a short procession of four, while the congregation watched and hummed and nodded in time to Liz and her girls, who were softly harmonizing, scatting a little, just keeping a rhythm. Two large men came forward and lifted Lou-Ellen's chair up the three steps to the sanctuary. They turned her around so the crowd could see her, set her down in front of Reverend Rudy, and locked her wheels. Donnie leaned in and whispered in the reverend's ear.

"Comatose," he said. "Name's Lou-Ellen Quinlan. Pedestrian hit-and-run. Her mother's in the front row."

Donnie went back down the steps and stood off to the side next to Amy, while Gary's wheelchair was lifted up the steps and rolled up behind Lou-Ellen. Under the hot lights, beads of sweat stood out on Gary's forehead and he clutched his barf bag tight. He was grateful for the use of the chair because otherwise he thought he might pass out.

Reverend Rudy tossed his towel to one of the beefy men and knelt by Lou-Ellen's chair. Liz held up her hand and the choir stopped singing. A hush fell over the congregation, and the people in the front moved forward, straining to hear as the reverend cocked his head, apparently listening to Lou-Ellen. Rudy murmured something in her ear and listened again to the silent girl. Then he raised his fists in the air and tilted his face toward the ceiling, where scorched timbers surrounded fresh wood, marking the spot where the church had been marred by that long-ago storm.

"This girl suffers!"

"*She suffers,*" the congregation repeated.

"Our sister Lou-Ellen has lost the way!"

"*Mmm. She's lost.*"

"She's lost inside herself and can't find the way out!"

*"Find the way. Find the way."*

"She hurts and needs our help!"

*"Help her, Reverend Rudy."*

"But if she is pure, if she has that *purity* that comes from the blood, I can help her!"

*"Lay your hands on her, Reverend Rudy."*

"Let the lightning work through me!"

*"Let it flow."*

"Let it flow!"

*"Let it flow!"*

"I say . . ."

*"Let it flow!"*

Liz raised her hands in an echo of Rudy's gesture, the sleeves of her shiny red robe swinging wildly, and the choir started up again, louder this time, the tempo faster. The crowd picked up the cue and started clapping in time. Rudy was still as a statue, on his knees, his hands in the air. Whether he was surrendering or anticipating victory over Lou-Ellen's coma was unclear. In one smooth movement, he turned and lowered his hands to the girl's head. He held them there, then ran them down her neck, over her torso, lingering for only a moment on her emaciated breasts, down her abdomen and into her lap, then back up again. To the congregation it looked like he had stuck his finger in a light socket. He trembled and shook, but his hands moved with a sure purpose. At last he fell back, and one of the beefy men caught him under his arms. The man picked Rudy up and stood him on his feet and held him there while he got his balance and recovered. The people in the front row could hear his ragged breathing over the sound of their own hands clapping.

An old woman screamed *"Her eyes are open!"* and fainted.

Someone else took up the cry. *"She's awake!"* And more people shouted and fell about, excited to see Lou-Ellen's pretty blue eyes.

Marybeth rushed to her daughter's side, stumbling on her way up the steps. Those men in the front pew who were not trembling and speaking in tongues could see Lou-Ellen's lips moving as she spoke to her mother for the first time in eight years.

Bert Holstrom waved at Marybeth to get her attention. "What did she say? What's she saying, Mama?"

"She said . . ." Marybeth looked at Bert, then raised her tear-filled eyes to the rafters. "She asked me what hit her."

And Marybeth started to laugh.

# CHAPTER SEVEN

## 1

When he saw the blue and red lights, Travis almost pulled over. He frowned at the rearview mirror and tried to see through the windshield of the car behind him, but the setting sun reflected bare branches overhead against the opaque safety glass and the driver was invisible, save for a dark human shape with an ungainly hat stuck atop it.

He checked his speed. Fifty-five miles an hour. Well within the speed limit, not far below it. He was reasonably certain his brake lights worked. He had not rolled through any stop signs.

He shrugged and pressed the accelerator to the floor. The Jeep leapt forward and the squad car behind him fell back.

Around a bend, Travis shifted gears and pulled off the road, rammed the Jeep into a copse of brush and young trees. A flock of starlings burst from the thicket, beating their wings perilously close to the windshield before taking to the air. The birds were far out over a field by the time the silver patrol car whizzed by. It sped away into the distance without slowing as it passed the poorly hidden Jeep. Travis couldn't be sure whether the driver had seen him. He waited, surveying the road. A drop of rain hit his windshield and rolled slowly down. He watched it merge with other drops, growing larger and heavier. After a moment he pulled out his phone and typed *starlings* into the Internet app.

"Ah," he said. "A murmuration." He looked out across the field at the faraway formation of fluttering brown specs. "You are called a murmuration."

Satisfied, he shut down his browser and pulled up his contacts. The squad car had not reappeared, so Travis backed out of the thicket and executed a U-turn. As he headed back the way he'd come, toward Paradise Flats, he punched up Skottie's number and listened for the first ring.

"But why a murmuration?"

# 2

"What?" Skottie held the phone away from her face and looked at the screen. She put it back up to her ear. "A what?"

"Skottie?"

She was getting used to the husky whisper of Travis's voice and didn't have to strain to hear him. "Yeah," she said. "This is Skottie."

"Did your phone just ring?"

"Yeah. Twice."

"Mine did not."

"Travis? Why did you call?"

"I have some bad news for us both."

"Does it involve a murmuration?"

"Ah, you heard me," Travis said. "I was talking to myself, but did you know a flock of starlings is called a murmuration?"

"Yeah, and a bunch of crows is called a murder, and hippos are a bloat. I have a ten-year-old kid. I get to hear a lot of this stuff. Did you know toads can live forty years in captivity?"

"Toads?"

"Travis, what did you want? What's the bad news?"

"I believe the sheriff is having me followed."

"I think he had me followed, too, when I left his office. That white-power deputy of his showed up right on my tail. He beat an ambulance to a fire."

"A fire? Are you all right?"

"Yeah," Skottie said. "I'm fine. And Bear's fine, too. I forgot to tell you earlier. Somebody burned a tractor on a frontage road out by the highway. There was someone in the tractor."

"And one of Goodman's deputies was there?"

"Had to be nearby. So either he was already in the vicinity or he followed me there."

"Now I understand what the sheriff was talking about," Travis said. "Goodman mentioned another body had been found. He seemed genuinely mystified, though, not like he had anything to do with it."

"Doesn't let the deputy off the hook."

"The one following me attempted to pull me over."

"You didn't stop?"

"Why would I stop? I ran through the possibilities in my head and none of them favored me."

"You're supposed to stop," Skottie said.

"I evaded whoever was driving the squad car, but as soon as they catch up to me again, things might become unpleasant. I have a difficult thing to ask of you, and I understand if you would rather not do me any more favors right now. I have imposed on you more than I wished to."

"You want me to hang on to Bear tonight?"

"Would you?"

"Sure."

"If I go there now, I may be leading these people to your home."

"I said sure. He ate his steak and he's having a nap. Maddy's in love with him."

"Bear likes children."

"As long as he doesn't like to eat them."

"Oh, my lord, no."

"It was a joke."

"I see. I will wait until morning to get him. Perhaps by then this situation will have resolved itself."

"Resolved itself? How?"

"We are being chased all over the board and people are dying. I think something must be done to drive our villain from the shadows."

"'Something must be done'?"

"I have no plan yet. But I would feel better knowing Bear is safe."

"Don't do anything stupid, Travis."

"I appreciate your confidence."

"I mean it. I'm a police officer. You do something illegal and you and me are gonna end up on different sides."

"I would not wish that."

"I'll take care of your dog. But you have to get him tomorrow. My daughter's getting attached to him, and it's gonna break her heart if he's around much longer."

"I forgot. You said you have to work tomorrow."

"The holidays work out so if you work Thanksgiving you don't have to work Christmas. It's better for Maddy."

"How will I get Bear from you?"

"You could pick him up here. My mom'll be around." She realized as soon as she spoke that she didn't want her mother to deal with Bear and Travis on her own. "Or better yet, I can take him along with me on patrol."

"They allow that?"

"He's not exactly high maintenance, Travis. I don't think anybody would even know if I had him in the car."

"Text me where to meet you. As early as possible."

"Will do. Earlier is better. It's Thanksgiving, and I have a lot to get done as soon as I go off shift." The thought of the holiday meal suddenly made her picture Travis and his dog eating a microwave pizza. The restaurants in Paradise Flats would all be closed. "Wait a second," she said. "Do you have somewhere to be tomorrow?"

"I have a room at the Cottonwood Inn."

"No, I mean do you have anyone to celebrate Thanksgiving with? A place to go?"

"I have been invited to attend church tomorrow."

"No, I'm serious," Skottie said.

There was a long silence. Then: "I will have Bear. We will be fine."

"Listen, my mom and I are cooking a turkey. Why don't you come? You can eat some stuffing and mashed potatoes and watch a football game."

"I am not sure—"

"So you're gonna sit alone in your hotel room?"

"I—"

"Just come."

"Since you insist," Travis said. She could hear a smile in his voice. "Thank you for inviting me. I would be delighted."

G ary Gilbert heard the congregation chanting, but at the same time that the reverend was shouting and the choir was singing something about God choosing "the finest from among us," he recognized Marybeth Quinlan's voice. She had briefly been a babysitter to his girls before the accident with her daughter had turned her into a virtual shut-in. She was somewhere nearby, laughing and crying and gasping for breath. Barely audible among all this chaos was the small, sad voice of a girl asking where she was and what was happening. No one was answering her, and Gary reached out toward the sound of her, thinking maybe he could comfort her with a pat on the shoulder or a friendly smile, and he dropped his bag. His stomach chose that moment to do a double roll, and he reached for the pocket where he kept a couple of Zofran tablets in case of an emergency, but he was too late. He got his hands up just in time to spew a mouthful of bile and Diet Sprite out between his fingers.

He could smell it right away, bitter and rancid, and he hoped he hadn't hit anyone with the spray. Somewhere in the back of his mind, he felt himself trying to form an apology. But he couldn't get it out. Instead he slid straight forward onto his face and blacked out. He had no idea he was directly in front of the enormous gold lightning bolt that split the altar. No idea that, to the congregation behind him, it looked like he was prostrating himself before that sacred icon.

Gary woke up, to a degree, several times during the rest of that day and night. Each time, he slipped back under before he could speak or move. But he could feel people touching him and, later, carrying him. He felt the sanctuary's carpet against his cheek, which was replaced by a cold metal surface. He smelled his own vomit, then bleach, and then dust and oil and blood. He heard snippets of conversation from different men in different rooms, but they made little sense to him.

"Praise be."

"Heal your brother."

"He's waking up . . ."

". . . didn't work."

"Gary Gilbert is not of us. You see how . . ."

"Impure stock. This man has lied to you. His blood is . . ."

"Just get him off to the side until . . ."

"What do we . . ."

"Damn, he's heavier than I . . ."

"Fold up his legs."

When he finally woke up again it was dark. He couldn't tell what time it was or where he had been taken. His mouth tasted terrible and he felt dizzy, but his stomach was calm. He tried to move his arms and legs, but they were bound to the surface beneath him. His back hurt, and he wiggled into a slightly more comfortable position. He could feel the air against his skin, raising goose bumps, and he knew that he had been undressed. He could make out vague shapes in the darkness, ambient light glinting off glass or metal next to him, and he wondered whether his vision had returned or his head was playing tricks on him. His brain sometimes supplied him with colors and shapes that weren't really there.

"Hello? Is there somebody here? I can't move."

He listened, but there was no movement, no response, just his own labored breathing. He struggled against his bonds, tried to sit up, but eventually gave in and waited. He had no idea how long it took for someone to come, but he had just begun to fall back to sleep when a light flicked on above him. He blinked and gasped. The room he was in was bright and clear, and he knew it couldn't possibly exist in his imagination. He was lying on an inclined metal table with his feet slightly elevated above his head, and his wrists and ankles were secured with thick leather straps. There was a lamp on a swivel arm above him and two high metal stools, one on each side of the table. His clothes were draped over one of the stools. A rolling cart was positioned near his head, and Gary could see an array of scalpels, clamps, spreaders, tongs, and sponges spread across a stained white towel on the cart's surface. There were other instruments there that he didn't recognize. And strewn atop them were items from Gary's own wallet. He recognized his driver's license with its donor sticker, his library card issued by the Hays Public Library, and a credit card he hardly ever used because it was almost at its limit and he hadn't paid it down in months. Across from him was another table like the one he was lying on, this one unoccupied, its straps unbuckled and hanging empty. The walls were lined with metal shelving units like the ones Gary had in his own garage, but the shelves were piled high with medical paraphernalia.

A door opened and Reverend Rudy entered, wiping his hands with a red cloth.

"You're awake, Mr. Gilbert," the reverend said. "Good. I was beginning to worry about you." His voice was soft with a warm undercurrent, completely unlike the harsh spitting rasp he used when shouting from the pulpit.

"Where am I? What am I doing here? The last thing I remember—"

"You made a bit of a mess in my sanctuary," Rudy said. He pulled one of the stools, the one that wasn't currently occupied by Gary's khakis and button-up shirt, closer to Gary's table and sat on it. "It took poor Liz more than an hour to clean up your sick, and even though we've got fans drying the carpet, I think we're going to have to replace it. I can still smell your vomitus in there."

"I'm sorry," Gary said. "But my stomach feels fine now. And I can see. My vision is . . . You really did it. You healed me."

Rudy tapped a finger against his lips and stared off into the middle distance. "Funny," he said. "I didn't feel the tingle when I laid my hands on you. The energy didn't move through me. Are you sure you feel all right?"

"I . . ." Now that the reverend had cast aspersions on his health, Gary noticed that his stomach had in fact started to feel a little queasy. And his peripheral vision was going blurry again. "Yes," he lied. "Yes, I feel good. I feel perfect. Could you let me up now? I think all the blood is going to my head."

Rudy continued to tap on his lips, but he looked at Gary. "You're in what's called the Trendelenburg position, heels over head. Named after Friedrich Trendelenburg, a great surgeon. A great *German* surgeon."

"Oh." Gary wasn't sure what else to say. He wished the reverend would untie him, but he understood he was in a delicate situation of some sort and he didn't want to push Rudy too hard. He thought it would have been enough to lay him on a couch until he woke up. He wasn't likely to roll off and hurt himself, so strapping him to a table was definitely overkill.

"Listen," he said, "I'm grateful, but I don't understand what's—"

"Mr. Gilbert, how many fingers am I holding up?"

Gary panicked, realizing the fuzz had crept without warning inward from the edges of his vision. He could still see somewhat clearly, but only within a small area directly in front of him. He wasn't sure where Rudy's fingers even were, much less the number of fingers he was holding up.

He guessed. "Three?"

"Interesting," Rudy said.

Gary heard the stool squeak as Rudy moved. Then Rudy was standing above him.

"You can't see much at all now, can you?"

"I could for a little bit there," Gary said. "When I first woke up. Maybe if you try again?"

"The power of suggestion," Rudy said. He took off his glasses and wiped them with the red cloth. "You tricked yourself into thinking you were healed because you believed in my energy. But only briefly. Without that energy, you're slipping back into ill health. You need the lightning. My lightning."

"Please just let me go home now. Let me go home." Gary could hear the wheedling tone in his voice and was ashamed, but he suddenly realized he could live with his problems. He was used to them, and they were uniquely his. Being strapped to a table while the reverend talked about German doctors was not something he wanted to get used to.

"Tell me," Rudy said, "do you have any family in Paradise Flats? I didn't see anyone at church with you today."

"My wife left. But I have two little girls."

"Two girls? Where are they now?"

"I, um . . . They're with my dad."

"Your father. And where does he live?"

"Well, he's still in Stockton, actually. But that's pretty close by, you know. I could call him, if you want. He doesn't drive much these days, but he'd come pick me up. I know he would. It's not that far. It's not far at all."

"Hush now, Mr. Gilbert." Rudy smiled at him, put his glasses back on, and tossed his red cloth on the cart. "Sometimes it doesn't work. Sometimes the lightning doesn't come, doesn't flow from me. I used to blame myself. Do you have any idea how awful that made me feel, this notion that people needed my help and yet I couldn't deliver? How could that be? Why was I able to heal one person and not another? The answer, of course, was right in front of my eyes. And my eyes work much better than yours, Mr. Gilbert. Still, it took me a long time to see it."

"See what?"

"That the problem wasn't with me; it was always the other person, the person who had come to me. The lightning did not respond well to those people. Just as it didn't respond to you. I mean no offense; it's simply a fact."

"But I wanted to be healed. I did." Gary's vision was fading fast. He turned his head and saw the other table, the empty table, through a pinprick of light. He knew that it might be the last thing he would ever see, and he drank in every detail. The reverend kept talking, but Gary didn't hear him. He was staring at that table, and it was puzzling him. There was something odd about the dimensions of it, something that didn't seem right, even though it was fading fast, being eaten up all around the edges by the creeping fuzz. He blinked and tried to bring it into focus, but that only made things worse, and everything disappeared at once in a gray smear.

"Mr. Gilbert, are you listening to me?"

"What?"

"I asked if I might call you Gary, since we're becoming such intimate acquaintances. May I?"

"Yeah, um, sure. Just, can you let me up from here, please?"

"There's a story I sometimes tell, Gary," the reverend said.

Gary took it as a bad sign that Reverend Rudy was selectively ignoring him, but he still couldn't wrap his head around the situation. He had been in a church and he thought of churches as safe places.

"I never tell this story up there, not at the pulpit," the reverend said. "This story is not for them. It's for my guests down here. But not all of them, either. I don't tell it often, but I think it's sometimes useful to revisit our history, don't you think? It keeps us humble. Would you like to hear it? This story of mine?"

"Just let me go," Gary said. His throat had closed and he could barely force the words out. "I promise I won't tell anybody about all this, whatever it is. I swear, man."

"When I was a boy, my father would sometimes take us into the city. My sister and I. She was younger, and very beautiful, with long blond curls, and our mother made the prettiest little dresses for her. But she's not important to this story, my sister, even though she was there."

The reverend's voice floated through the charcoal air, and Gary stopped struggling against the straps. A small part of him had accepted what he knew was going to come. He tried to keep the worst of his panicked, rabbity thoughts at bay and sent up a silent prayer for rescue.

"As I say, sometimes our father would take us with him on his trips. He would have work to do, business acquaintances to meet, I suppose, and he would give us coins—I no longer remember how much money it was, a Reichsmark or two each, perhaps—and he let us roam about, just so long as we promised to stay together. My sister always spent her coins right away on treats and on ribbons for her hair, while I pocketed my money and saved it. I had a box under my bed at home, and I would put my unspent coins away after each of these trips. This hoarding of wealth, I guess you'd say, was a habit that would later serve me well. But one time, on one of our outings, we were walking along a busy street, holding hands, and my sister was sucking on a hard candy of the sort she liked best, when we saw a crowd gathering. We were small, and it was easy to push our way through to the front of the crowd. In a little clearing in the middle of all the people was a man who was lying still, just lying there on a rug that had been spread out on the ground. And next to him was a second man, who was kneeling in the dirt and talking to us all and calling out to passersby, calling to them to stop and see the miracle. Stop and see the miracle. I remember feeling concerned that he was soiling the knees of his trousers and thinking that Mother would be cross with me if I were ever to do what that man was doing. But even though my sister tugged on my hand, trying to pull me away, I stayed and watched those two men. My sister was already bored, and I don't know why I wasn't bored as well, but . . . well, I wasn't. I stood and listened as the man talked. I wish I could tell you exactly what he said, Gary, but it has been a great many years, and so much of what happened in my youth has faded from memory. I can't even remember my sister's face anymore." Rudy sighed, and it was a long moment before he resumed his story. "I do go on, don't I? It's nice to be able to hear myself talk without all the yammering that goes on up there in the church. It's quiet down here sometimes, so peaceful. But where was I? Oh, yes, the man was talking, saying something about a certain kind of sickness. He told us that the man on the ground had this sickness, that he had a growth in his body. In English we would call this sickness a cancer, of course, a tumor, but that's not what we called it then and there, and it's not what the man called it that day. I remember that much at least. But we knew what it was, even we children had heard about such things. The man on the ground was conscious and he was crying, much as you are crying right now, Gary, anxious about what was to occur and hoping for that miracle the man was shouting about. Or that's what we were led to believe. Perhaps he was, perhaps he was innocent and truly full of cancer and sincerely hoping to be cured by this man kneeling in the dirt by his side. I would like to believe that, I would, but the man lying down was no doubt the healer's accomplice, a con man, and I've spoiled the first part of my story, haven't I? Because, yes indeed, the kneeling man was a healer, and he had a box next to him with the lid open and a few coins scattered along the bottom of it to prompt those of us in the crowd to add our own coins to the meager few in there, to donate to the spectacle, to show our appreciation for the afternoon's entertainment. And when he was satisfied that he had a big enough crowd he went to work, talking all the time about what he was doing. Magicians call it a patter, talking about one thing while you do another, distracting your audience and binding them to you through speech. As I am binding you to me now, Gary. And while he talked, the healer, the magician, he opened the other man's shirt and he ran his fingers up and down his torso until he had found the tumor under the skin. At least, that's what he told us he was doing, searching for that pesky tumor. He found it, of course. Told us he'd found it. My sister and I watched, awestruck, as he dug into the man's stomach with his bare hands, blood pouring out from between his fingers, poking and prodding and digging, and talking to us the whole time, and the man lying there without showing any signs of pain, any indication that he was being wounded by the magician's prying fingers. The healer looked at my sister as he worked, seemed to be talking to her, and I could not blame him. I do remember that she was beautiful, and I do wish I could call her face to mind now. She watched the man work, staring right back at him, and I don't think she was bored anymore. Then he pulled a bloody growth out of the other man's belly, produced it for all to see, showed it to us in the palm of his hand, and it was roughly the size and appearance of a large slug. He rose to his feet and passed it triumphantly under the noses of everyone gathered there, but my sister, whom he was most trying to impress, I think, turned suddenly away and made a retching sound and asked me again to leave. But I could not move. I was stuck to the spot, Gary, mesmerized. I wondered at it, at every bit of it: the showmanship, the goriness, the truth or fiction of it. What did it mean to use a man's agony for the entertainment of strangers? I confess I was thrilled. And then the magician used a bucket of water to gradually wash away the blood that had pooled on his patient's stomach. As the water ran over and down his skin and soaked into his shirt and pants, the blood was diluted and just . . . it just disappeared, just like that, leaving no indication of a wound or . . . or anything at all. The man on the ground was wet, but otherwise fine, and the magician said that he could rise and return to his home, that he was cured and would go on to live for another decade or more. I suppose that man with the tumor is dead by now anyway, whether he lived for another decade as promised or another fifty years. But on that day he did get up, and he smiled and did a little dance to show that he was unharmed and cancer-free, though why could he not dance, even if the cancer remained inside him? I did not question it. Not then. The man who was now without cancer, if he had ever had it, dropped a few coins in the magician's box, and that was to prompt the rest of us to do likewise—I know that now, but at the time I did not, and so I stepped forward and took the coins that my father had given me that morning, took them from my pocket and put them in the box, and the magician smiled at me and nodded. I tried to talk to him then, tried to ask him how he had done it, what else he could do with such amazing powers, but he didn't wait around for questions, mine or anyone else's. As soon as he saw that he had all the coins he was going to get from the crowd, he grabbed up his box and he marched away down the street. I tried to follow, waving at him, crying for him to come back and teach me how to do what he did, but my sister tugged at my hand and led me away in the opposite direction, back to the shops where she could buy more sweets and more ribbons and lace, because she had not given the magician her own coins. She still had her money and I had nothing, and so I could only follow my sister from place to place, thinking all the time about the miracle I had witnessed. That night I pulled my own box of coins from under my bed and counted them, wondering how many more I would have if I could do what that healer had done. It was a seed, you see. A seed had been planted in my mind, and it would grow and grow over the years, even when I did not know that it was there. I know what you're thinking. You're thinking that the things I saw that day inspired me to become a healer, but you'd only be half right. You haven't heard the whole story yet. On that day I only knew I didn't want to be my sister, who had seen something glorious and paid no attention. Now I was aware of the magic that surrounded me. There was more in the world than I had previously dreamt. I grew withdrawn and rebellious, bored by the mundanities that others gladly suffered. I looked everywhere for opportunities to thrive, to be different and better than the people around me, better than my sister, who married a baker's apprentice, a pauper, and moved away from me.

But my attitude served me well when the party came into power, when the Führer made it possible for individuals with vision and talent to rise and come into their own. I finally thrived.

"You look uncomfortable, Gary. Is it your stomach again? I think it must be. I have these pills from your trouser pocket. Would you like one? Open your mouth and raise your tongue. There you go. Let it dissolve." Rudy smacked his lips as if he were the one taking a Zofran, but Gary couldn't see him at all anymore, not even as a vague shape in the shadows. He concentrated on the sweet taste of the pill in his mouth and half listened as Rudy began to talk again.

"I was about to tell you about the camp," Rudy said. "It was grand, Mauthausen-Gusen, with so much vital industry, so many people, and I was at the center of it all. I had been given the responsibility of keeping the trains running on time, so to speak. But my superior was a weak man, an alcoholic, and so I did everything. I ran the entire camp, whether I ever received proper credit for that or not. They called me the Wolf because I was fiercely loyal to the men who served under me. As I say, I thrived. I had a room built for me, much like this room, so that I could explore and discover and experiment. I'm not really a scientist, but I am curious about the world around me, a good thing to be, and I'm adaptable. Why is this person not the same as this other person? Why are the *Juden* and the black different from the white man? Why does the lightning not work when I try to employ it for the benefit of your kind, Gary? I must know. And you can see that, if the lightning itself rejects you, we were not wrong in the things we did back then, during the war. Before I knew anything of the lightning I was doing its work, but I never did understand, and I still don't understand. I have had many opportunities over the years because I am the chosen of the storm. I am the conduit for the energy, and it is my responsibility to move that energy properly. Before I knew this, I suspected it, and I would walk about the camp and choose from among the prisoners there, point them out and they would be taken to my special room, the one like this room. And one day as I was walking among the *Juden* and the homosexuals, I saw a familiar face. He had changed a bit over the years. It had been a decade since I had seen him in the street, but I recognized him. It was the magician, of course, but he did not know me, and why would he have? I was no longer a child, even if I still had a child's thirst for knowledge. I had him cleaned up and brought to me, the magician, that man who had created a miracle in the street, and I asked him, now that I finally had my chance, I asked him how he had done it. At first he didn't want to tell me—can you imagine? That he would hold so tight to his secrets even in that place where all was laid bare for everyone to see? Madness. But I made him talk, and now I wish I hadn't. He was a charlatan, of course. A part of me knew that all along, but I did so want to hang on to that feeling that there was magic in the world, in the air, in the sky above us and moving through us. I made him tell me and it spilled out of him, how he hid the bit of meat between his fingers along with the balloon full of pig's blood, and squeezed it out onto the other man's belly, worked it around and produced that piece of meat, pretended it was the cancer. It turns out, and this may not surprise you, the other man did not even have a tumor. That, too, was a lie. All of it a trick to get money from people on the street, people like me. I look back now and see that, in her way, my sister was wiser than I was. She kept her money, at least for a time, until she spent it on other things that didn't last, and perhaps my belief in the magic gave me the same pleasure as her sweets and ribbons brought her. Perhaps that belief lasted longer and gave me more than she got. I don't know. But in any event, the news that I had been tricked did not sit well with me, and I'm afraid I didn't react well. And here we reach the end of my story. I thank you for listening, Gary, though I suppose you had no choice. It is good to relate these things every once in a while."

Gary heard the scrape of one steel instrument against another.

"Oh," Rudy said. "I left off the last bit of the story, didn't I? Do you know what I found when I cut open that magician? When he was on my table at the camp that was so very much like this table in this basement room? You will hardly believe. Hidden away in his bowels were three perfect diamonds. He had swallowed them to try to keep them when he was brought to the camp, and I suppose he must have excreted them and reswallowed them again and again, his ultimate secret, a treasure with real worth beyond his lies and his tricks. He had brought me the beginnings of real wealth, and I kept those diamonds until I needed them. I did not spend them frivolously. I saved them and used them to purchase safe passage to America, where I am safe and respected, where I was able to purchase a ranch, where I was available for the storm to speak to me and through me, where I ultimately bought this church and saved it from the wrecking ball. And I have done so much good here for so many people, all because once, when I was a young boy, I stopped and paid attention when I thought there was magic happening. Isn't that a sort of magic itself, Gary? If I had not paid attention to that magician on that day, I would not have recognized him later and I would not have had those diamonds delivered to me so that I could later make my escape and find my destiny here. I believe the lightning was speaking to me then, urging me toward the direction I needed to go to survive and, as always, thrive. But maybe you're wondering how I could have done all of this with just three diamonds. You see, I learned that day the thing I had been so curious about. I learned the difference, what it was inside the *Juden* that made them different. It wasn't only the diamonds. Some of them had coins and other small pieces of jewelry, gold and silver and gems. Do you know how much gold is in a gold tooth? In a thousand gold teeth? I kept it all. And I still look for it, Gary. I don't find much these days, but I hold out hope. There are always possibilities, as long as I am willing to pay attention and look for the magic. And that truly is the end of the story." Rudy chuckled. "Now, let's see what you have inside you, why don't we?"

Before he started screaming and all thoughts were driven out of his mind by pain, Gary realized what it was that had bothered him about the other table, sitting there across from him, empty save for the leather straps at each end.

It was child-size.

# CHAPTER EIGHT

## 1

Lieutenant Keith Barent Johnson hated to work late, but it was the night before a holiday, which meant that there were housekeeping duties to perform and paperwork to finish up. He fervently hoped that the new trooper, Skottie, would be able to get through the morning's shift without too much trouble. Thanksgiving wasn't likely to be as bad as the Fourth of July or New Year's Eve, or even Christmas. He didn't anticipate a lot of drunk drivers, but the roads were a little slick from the melting snow, and street crews would not be operating. There wouldn't be sand or ice melt spread across the blacktop. And there would be a lot of travelers out and about, headed to Grandma's house for a slice of pumpkin pie or to the local Chinese restaurant after the turkey burned and the gravy seized up in the pan. If Keith had to guess, he figured Skottie would be facing at least four or five accidents, cars in a ditch or up a tree somewhere. He just hoped there wouldn't be any fatalities. Those were tough to deal with under any circumstance, but were especially difficult during the holidays. If Skottie ran into any trouble, he would come in and help, of course, but he was afraid Gwen wouldn't like that at all. Not after he'd missed taking the girls out trick-or-treating last month. That hadn't been his fault, and he knew she understood that, but the knowledge didn't make things a lot easier. Gwen was getting a little frayed around the edges, trying to cope with a teenage boy and twin girls, none of whom were inclined to listen to her. She needed a little help, and he'd promised her he'd be there, at the very least so he could deal with his parents when they showed up. He thought she'd appreciate it, too, if he made his famous butterscotch pie for everyone and maybe did the dishes afterward while she relaxed for once.

But it all depended on Skottie Foster handling things on her own.

So he was getting things ready for her, trying to anticipate whatever she might run into and squaring away any distractions. He had just decided there was nothing else he could do and his holiday was in the hands of fate and proper planning, had his keys out, ready to lock up, when his computer chimed. He shook his head and flicked out the lights in his tiny office, then sighed and flicked them back on, crossed to his desk, and clicked the Safari icon in the dock at the bottom of his screen. He had a new e-mail from Captain Clayton, and he leaned forward over the back of his chair to open it.

The captain had written a single sentence: *Look into this, Keith.* Below that was a forwarded message from Major Thomas. The New York address of a law firm was at the top, followed by six paragraphs. He had to read it all before he was able to process it.

Dear Major Thomas:

My name is Mary Loftus, and I am an attorney with Morrison, Ellis, and Moore. I am contacting you on behalf of one of our firm's partners: Jason Bloom.

This CEASE AND DESIST ORDER is to inform you that the actions of State Trooper Scotty Foster, including the persistent harassment of Jason and Rachel Bloom, have become unbearable for them. As Officer Foster is a law enforcement officer representing the state of Kansas and you are her supervisor, you are ORDERED TO STOP and prevent her from engaging in such activities immediately, as they are being done in violation of the law.

Morrison, Ellis, and Moore will pursue any legal remedies available against you if these activities continue. These remedies include but are not limited to: suing Scotty Foster, you, and all of her commanding officers for damages in civil court, and seeking criminal sanctions against the Kansas Highway Patrol and all responsible parties within the hierarchy of the Highway Patrol.

Officer Foster must IMMEDIATELY cease all contact with Rachel Bloom, and you must send me written confirmation that you will order her to stop such activities. You risk severe legal consequences if you fail to comply with this demand.

This letter acts as your final warning before we pursue legal action. At this time, I have not contacted the authorities or filed a civil suit against you, as I hope we can resolve this matter without authoritative involvement. This order acts as YOUR FINAL CHANCE to cease illegal and unwanted activities before we exercise our legal rights against you.

To ensure compliance with this letter, and to halt any legal action we may take against you, I require you to fill out and sign the attached form and e-mail it back to me within two (2) days of your receipt of this letter. Failure to do so will act as evidence of your infringement upon Jason and Rachel Bloom's legal rights, and we will immediately seek legal avenues to remedy the situation.

Sincerely,

Mary Loftus

Mary Loftus wrapped up the e-mail with a long boilerplate disclaimer about their exchange being private and confidential, and there was an attachment that Keith downloaded to his desktop.

He wondered why Jason Bloom, if he was actually a partner at a big New York law firm, hadn't written his own threatening letter. And he wondered if the damn letter was legitimate at all, since they'd misspelled Skottie's name.

Either way, it had rolled downhill through the chain of command and had landed on his desk. He rolled his chair back and slumped down into it. He swiveled back and forth a few times, staring into the shadows in the corner of the room. At last he reached for his phone.

# 2

Skottie ended the call and stared at her phone for a long minute. Her head was spinning, and she knew she needed to organize her thoughts, to figure out some plan of action.

But Maddy needed to get ready for bed, and Bear had complicated their nightly routine. The big dog was a constant distraction for Maddy, who couldn't seem to keep on task for more than thirty seconds. Emmaline came home from church and brought a flurry of energy with her into the tiny house. She waved Skottie away and took over with Maddy, prodding the girl to turn off her music and brush her teeth.

Skottie went to the kitchen and filled another bowl of water for the dog and glanced out the window. It had started to sprinkle again, creating a frozen crust on top of the thin layer of snow in the backyard. She checked the overnight forecast and saw that a major storm system was rolling in. A huge digital cloud of green, ringed with yellow and red highlights, was moving fast from the northwest. She went outside with Bear, letting him run and slide around the tiny yard while she watched the sky and mulled over the conversation she had just endured with Lieutenant Johnson.

He had sounded tired. Whatever Skottie had done to make Rachel Bloom sic a lawyer on the KHP, he told her, she had better not do again. And if she was *still* doing something, she needed to stop immediately. She had tried to explain to him that she had no idea what was going on, but he hadn't been interested.

"All I care about is that we don't get sued, Skottie," he had said. "That clear?"

It was clear. But what wasn't clear was why there was talk of being sued in the first place. She had visited Rachel once, at her deceased mother's house. Everyone had been cordial, the meeting had ended on a sad and troubling note, but Skottie couldn't recall any hostility. She wondered if Travis had visited again and said something to trigger a lawsuit. She'd brought up that possibility with the lieutenant.

"Stay the hell away from that guy, Skottie."

She didn't mention to Keith that she was watching Travis Roan's dog, that she had invited the Nazi hunter to Thanksgiving dinner.

"I'm gonna get him checked out," Keith said. "See if he's even who he says he is. But in the meantime, you steer clear. You do your job, help fix a flat tire, give out a ticket or two, and keep your head down. Hopefully this goes away on its own."

And if it didn't? Skottie hadn't asked, but she could read between the lines. Her job was in jeopardy. She wasn't sure she could follow the lieutenant's advice. She was being bullied, and she didn't like it. She was used to standing up for herself, and the thought of backing off and letting someone else take control left a bad taste in her mouth.

When Bear went back to the door, she took him in and locked up for the night. He followed her and watched as she checked the latches on all the windows. She grimaced at the fresh trail of muddy paw prints on the floor.

"I don't even wanna think about trying to give you a bath," she said. "But we should've got a brush for you, huh? When we were at the store. Spruce you up a little?"

She rummaged around in the linen closet and found a pile of old sheets and blankets from the queen-size bed that was still back in Brandon's house in Chicago. They didn't fit any bed in Emmaline's home. She bunched them up in a corner of the living room and showed Bear that he should lie down on them. She pantomimed for him, lying down and pretending to sleep, and then stood and motioned him over. She felt foolish, but he finally padded over and curled up, watching her the whole time.

"We're a little bit the same, you and me," she said. "Suspicious of everybody, but holding out hope, huh?"

Bear snorted and stood, turned in a circle, and lay back down. She shook her head and silently scolded herself for talking to the dog as if he could understand her. Maybe if she spoke in Esperanto . . . She was beginning to understand why Travis Roan trusted the dog more than he did other people. But she still couldn't understand why he had trusted her so easily.

She cleaned out the coffeepot for the following morning, poured herself a glass of wine, and sat in Emmaline's old rocking chair by the window, staring out at the darkness while fat raindrops hit the glass every few seconds. She didn't think she had many options.

Her first instinct was to drive out to Ruth Elder's old house in Phillipsburg and confront Rachel in person. But she knew that would be the end of her career in Kansas. The more she thought about the situation, the angrier she got, so she decided to sleep on it, come back to it fresh in the morning with a clearer, and possibly wiser, head.

But that still left the question of why. Why threaten her with a lawsuit in the first place? Skottie hadn't even met Jason Bloom and had barely spoken with his wife. She was more convinced than ever that there was indeed a Nazi in the general area. But she felt certain there was something else going on, and she was too good at her job to leave it alone.

She sat down with a pen and a notepad and wrote down everything she had seen or heard about since arriving back in Kansas, everything that didn't seem to sit right or that was currently unsolved. Then she put the list in order from major crimes to minor, big questions to small. The hidden Nazi wasn't at the top of the list.

There were two dead bodies. Possibly both homicides, although one or both might also be suicides or accidents. Two bodies gave her something to work with. She grabbed her phone and dialed Keith Johnson back. He picked up after the first ring.

# 3

The street looked radically different in the dark, with rain pelting down on the slick pavement and the gritty shingles. He stood in the shadows near the community garden and watched the quiet houses, all connected by the wraparound privacy fence that extended for three city blocks around the church.

The moving van was gone, and there was a lamp in the window of number 437. Travis moved quickly. Despite the signs warning that the neighborhood was under video surveillance, he still didn't see any cameras in use. But if they were hidden somewhere under the eaves or behind cracks in the fence, the rain would decrease their range and effectiveness. Unless the church had sprung for something state of the art and very expensive, right now the entire street would look like a grainy blur. The cameras, if there *were* cameras, were there to discourage vandals, not a trained huntsman.

He darted across the road and flattened himself against the fence, slid along until he came to the covered porch of 437. He vaulted the railing and stood for a moment in front of the door, scanning the street in both directions for any sign of movement. When he was confident that he hadn't been observed, he knocked lightly on the door. He listened and heard nothing from inside. The quality of lamplight in the window didn't change; no shadows moved across the glass. He knocked again and tried turning the knob, then pulled out his bump key and unlocked the door.

Inside it was dim and empty, the single lamp shedding more light on the street outside than it did inside the front room. Boxes had been stacked randomly along the walls, next to plastic-covered furniture. Travis locked the front door and moved quickly through to the kitchen, which was in a similar state of disarray. A box had been opened on the island counter and silverware was piled next to the sink, crumpled newspapers strewn carelessly on the floor. He flicked a light on in a tiny bathroom and checked the empty medicine cabinet, then went back through the kitchen and up the stairs to the second floor. There were three bedrooms along a hallway, two on Travis's left and one on the right, and a small bathroom at the end with the door standing open. Travis looked in the first bedroom on the left and saw several sets of iron bunk beds, identical to the beds he had seen in the church's outbuildings. They were shoved into the room with no space between them so that it would be virtually impossible to use them, or even to close the bedroom door. The bedrooms across from it looked the same.

When he was satisfied that he was alone in the house, he returned to the front room and uncovered an armchair. He folded the plastic sheeting and set it on a heap of boxes all labeled *living room* in Rachel Bloom's distinctive handwriting, then dragged the chair so that it faced the dark kitchen. He sat and took his Kimber Eclipse from the holster under his arm.

Then he waited.

# 4

"Put that away," Skottie said. "Time to wind down for the night."

Maddy surrendered her phone with a minimum of fuss.

"I caught a Horsea today," she said.

"Is that good?"

"It's a Pokémon. You know?"

"Oh. Well, is it good?"

"It's okay," Maddy said. "It's not good for fighting electric monsters."

"Then maybe we should stay away from electric monsters." Skottie glanced at the small bookcase next to the bed. Like the bed and the room, the books there had once belonged to her, and looking at them now she felt oddly wistful. She remembered reading them under her covers in this same room. The top shelf held books by Walker Percy, Harper Lee, Walter Mosley, and Ralph Ellison, but the shelf beneath that was filled with older books that had been passed down to her by her mother, from Emmaline's own childhood. Skottie scanned the titles and smiled. There were *Raggedy Ann and Andy and the Nice Fat Policeman* and the first three Oz books sitting next to the Anna Apple series about a spunky British girl: *The Wandering Wood*, *The Faery Fountain*, *A Balloon to the Moon*, and her favorite, *The City Under the Sea*. Anna Apple had always fallen into strange adventures and emerged better off than before, thanks to the friends she made along the way. Skottie remembered them fondly: the kindly old nutcracker, the Babushka that contained endless smaller versions of herself, and the strange twins, Margaret Marigold and Peggy Petunia, who were never in the same place at the same time. Skottie had read about them so many times that the books were falling apart.

She reached out and touched their spines.

"You okay, Mom?"

Startled from her reverie, Skottie jumped. "Of course, baby. Why?"

"You have a funny look on your face."

"I just remembered something, that's all. Do you want me to read to you like I used to?"

"No," Maddy said. "I want Bear to sleep in here with me."

"Absolutely not." Skottie sat down on the edge of Maddy's bed and smoothed the blanket over her daughter's thin body. The blanket was festooned with cartoon characters she didn't recognize, elastic dogs and vampire girls, and she wondered where it had come from. Emmaline must have gone shopping. "Did you brush your teeth?"

"Of course I brushed my teeth," Maddy said.

"Don't tell me 'of course.' You didn't brush 'em last night."

"Can Bear sleep in here or not?" Maddy smacked her hands silently down on the blanket.

"I already said no," Skottie said. "Did you wash your face?"

"Yes. But where will he sleep?"

"I put some old blankets on the floor in the living room for him. You can read for fifteen minutes, and then I want you to turn off your light. It's been kind of a weird day, and you need your sleep."

"Bear will get lonely out there. And scared. He's never been here before."

"He's a dog. They usually sleep outside. He'll be fine." But Skottie already saw a chink forming in her armor. Travis had said something about Bear sleeping in hotel beds. He was no ordinary dog.

"I'll stay in the living room with him," Maddy said. This compromise seemed to make perfect sense to her.

"No, you will not."

"Why don't you like Bear?"

"I like Bear very much." Skottie smiled as she realized that she really did like the dog. But she also realized she would have to lay all her cards on the table or Maddy would never accept her decision. "He's a good dog, baby, but he's also a stranger to us. I'm responsible for you, and I don't know what Bear might do tonight. I need to keep you safe, and I don't know him well enough to feel good about you two sleeping in the same room."

As if on cue, Bear padded into the room, his claws ticking gently against the hardwood. He glanced at the bed and sniffed, as if acknowledging that it was too small to accommodate him, then turned in a circle and plopped down on the floor at the foot of Maddy's bed. He smacked his lips and yawned wide, rested his head on his paws, and closed his eyes.

Maddy grinned at her mother, silently daring her to drag the dog back out of her room. Skottie frowned and weighed her options. She was reasonably sure she could order Bear to leave and he would, but Maddy would be devastated and there would be a fight. The dog had brought her daughter out of her shell—only a little, but it was progress—and Skottie didn't want to create yet another wedge between them.

"Fine," she said.

Maddy wiggled happily and Skottie saw her involuntarily lean forward, about to give her mother a hug. But she caught herself and sat back, clapped her hands instead. Bear looked up at the sound, saw that he wasn't needed, and laid his head back down. Skottie noticed that one of his eyes didn't shut all the way, and she wondered if he slept like that all the time, always on partial alert.

"I give up," she said. "He can sleep in here. But your door stays open all night, and if you get scared or you feel uncomfortable, I want you to holler. I'll be right across the hall."

"I know where your room is, Mom. For God's sake."

"I'm just reminding you. And watch the language."

"Can I have my phone back? I won't play with it."

"If you won't play with it, then what's the point of having it?"

Maddy shrugged.

"I'll plug it in in the kitchen," Skottie said. "You can have it in the morning."

"Okay. Thanks, I guess."

"You sure you'll be okay?"

"I'll be fine," Maddy said. "You don't need to worry about me."

Nothing could sound less true to Skottie, but she was glad for the moment, and grateful to the dog for helping to create it. She stood and kissed Maddy on the forehead and left the room, glancing back once to make sure Bear was staying put.

"Sleep tight, you two."

# 5

Travis had just finished writing a text message when he heard muffled footsteps and the unmistakable sound of a door being opened at the back of the house. He hit send and put his phone away, then sat up straighter in his chair and picked up the Eclipse from his lap.

A light went on in the kitchen.

"Hello!" A voice carried through to the living room, deep and masculine, with a faint German accent. "I've come alone and unarmed. Don't shoot me."

A moment later an old man stepped into the light and stopped, framed in the doorway. Travis recognized him from his photograph in the church hallway. He was using a cane to steady himself and his shoulders were stooped a bit, but he seemed strong and healthy in all other ways.

"The right Reverend Rudy Goodman," Travis said. "Or should I call you Rudolph Bormann?"

"No, no, I haven't been called that in many years. May I come in? This knee gives me fits in wet weather. I'd like to sit."

Travis gestured at the plastic-covered couch against the wall close to Rudy. "By all means."

"Thank you." Rudy sat and rested the cane beside him against the cushions. He put up his hands and smiled. "You aren't going to shoot me, are you? I assure you, I'm as harmless as I look."

"I doubt that." Still, Travis lowered the gun back to his lap.

"You know my names, but you haven't introduced yourself."

"I am Dr. Travis Roan."

"Like the horse."

"Like the Noah Roan Foundation, which sent me to find you."

"Well done, boy."

"Where is Rachel Bloom?"

"I'm sorry?"

"Rachel Bloom. These boxes are all from her mother's house."

"Ah, may I?" Rudy reached for his jacket pocket, and Travis tightened his grip on the Eclipse. "Just my phone," Rudy said. He pulled out a flip phone and opened it, peered down at the tiny screen. "The Bloom woman is getting on a plane even now. I'm . . ." He shook his head and smiled again at Travis, then patted his chest and found a pair of reading glasses in another pocket. "The vision goes along with the hearing at my age." He put the glasses on and looked at his phone again. "I'm mistaken. Her plane took off an hour ago, almost. On her way to New York, to her husband, and good riddance."

"On a plane?"

"Yes, her husband works for my law firm. I should say, it's not my firm, but this church is one of their biggest clients."

"You are lying. Why would you have kept her mother's things?"

"What a boring woman she must have been. I haven't found a single thing of interest in these boxes. But I'll keep looking."

"I do not believe you let Rachel go." Travis pointed the gun at Rudy and waved the barrel in the direction of the front door. "Stand up. You and I are going to move this conversation somewhere less private."

"Not necessarily. Are you, by any chance, related to someone named Ransom Roan?"

Travis hesitated.

"I thought as much. There's a resemblance." Rudy sat back and folded his hands over his small belly.

Travis lowered the Eclipse back to his lap. "Is he still alive?"

"Yes." Rudy snorted and wiped his lips with the back of his hand. "Well, not by much, but he is among the living."

"How did you catch him?"

"It was surprisingly easy."

"I do not believe you."

Rudy shrugged. "I really don't care whether you believe me." He leaned forward and picked up his cane, passing it back and forth between his hands as he talked. "You've met my son Heinrich? He's currently keeping Ransom Roan company. In a few minutes, he will kill him. He will do this unless I arrive, alone and unharmed, at their location."

"Call him. Tell him to bring my father here."

Rudy shook his head. "That would be foolish of me. No, we're working on a deadline here, and my knees are no longer what they once were. It will take me a bit to get there and give him the order to stand down. So we ought to get down to business."

"How long? How much time?"

Rudy glanced at his watch. "We have roughly fifteen minutes."

Travis calculated quickly. His father had to be somewhere within the church compound, but there was no way to check every room of every surrounding house in fifteen minutes, much less the church building itself. Unless Rudy was lying and Ransom was already dead at the bottom of the lake.

"What do you want?"

"Not much. I'm an old man, Dr. Roan. May I call you Travis?"

"No."

"Petty of you. Anyway, I don't have long to live. I've made my peace with that. The lightning showed me what waits beyond all this." He waved a hand at the stark room, indicating the world outside its walls. "It will be glorious. And this place, this existence has given up all of its secrets to me. There's nothing left for me here."

"Then end it. Kill yourself. You can use my gun."

Rudy chuckled. "No, thank you. I have loose ends to tie up before I go. Family matters, mostly. Miles to go before I sleep, isn't that what they say? I would like to walk those miles unmolested. I want you to leave here, go back to your Foundation and tell them their witness was wrong. There is no evidence left anyway. Ruth Elder is dead, her daughter is under my control. Everyone else you might have talked to is dead now. Every single strand of your case against me has been cut. You have nothing. So go home, Dr. Roan. Go home and live your life and let me live mine. That's all you have to do. Absolutely nothing. In a month or a year, perhaps five years, I'll be dead of natural causes. And this will all be over. My church will continue on, but I will not. The slate will have been wiped clean. Maybe you'll even come to my funeral, just to be sure it's really me in the coffin."

"And what about your victims?"

"Which ones?"

"You were responsible for the deaths of thousands in that camp."

"Ancient history. Did you know them personally? No, of course not."

"They deserve justice."

"Oh, they got justice. Perhaps it's not the justice you would prefer. Maybe I was always on the right side of things and you are a self-righteous child who doesn't understand the ambiguities of history. Who's to say you're right and I'm wrong?"

"There is no gray here. You are a murderer and a monster. And I think you have continued your murderous ways, even here and now."

Rudy sighed and pushed himself up from the couch. "Be that as it may. We will agree to disagree about my level of responsibility. We won't talk about all the people I've helped through my church and my charitable acts, the people I've rescued from starvation, cured of illness and disease, the wounds I've healed, the bones I've knitted back together. Who's to say how it all balances out in the end? I won't be judged by you. I'm going to walk out of this room and you're not going to stop me unless you want your father to die." Rudy looked again at his watch. "He has less than ten minutes left. If you're thinking of shooting me and rescuing him, I should tell you that you'll never find him. At least, not in time."

Travis sat unmoving and watched Rudy limp away. From the kitchen, Rudy's voice came again. "Go home, Dr. Roan. Go home." The back door opened and then closed, and Travis heard a latch catch. He picked up his gun and put it in his shoulder holster and stood. He put the chair where he had found it against the wall and left by the front door.

The rain had stopped while he was in the house, but sheets of water still poured off the porch overhang. Travis walked through it, stepping carefully on the slick steps. A thick fog had rolled in with the breeze, and he felt the icy cold all down his spine.

He put up his collar and ran to the neighboring porch. There were no cameras he could see under the eaves, and he crossed the porch, peering through the windows next to the front door. A man sat on a sagging couch watching TV, the blue light casting demonic shadows across his broad face. He had a single bushy eyebrow that ran the width of his face and wore the same sort of brown shirt that Deacon Heinrich had been wearing. Travis guessed the man must weigh three hundred pounds, and a fair amount of it looked like muscle. There was no sign of anyone else in the house, but Travis didn't like his odds against the giant.

He jumped down and ran toward the next house, slipping on the wet grass, but keeping his feet under him. He didn't have a plan yet, and his mind was churning through the possibilities. He knew he could get back into the compound through the main gate, but he assumed that would be guarded now. He needed to find a way back onto the church grounds without being discovered, and he hoped one of the other houses would be empty. He was certain Rudy Goodman had lied to him, but his lies might be mixed with kernels of truth. Purity First might indeed be holding Ransom Roan captive, and it was possible Rachel Bloom was on a plane bound for New York. But Travis had no intention of taking the Nazi's words at face value.

A pair of headlights switched on halfway down the street, the beams diffuse and otherworldly. The driver's-side door opened and a figure stepped out onto the blacktop, his face concealed by the wide brim of his hat.

"If you go back in alone, they'll kill you," the man said. "Come on. It's cold out here, dammit." Illustrating his point, he got back in the car and slammed the door.

After a moment's hesitation, Travis walked out to the street and got in the car. The driver turned to him and nodded like he was picking up an old conversation.

"We got a lot to talk about, Doc," Sheriff Goodman said.

PART THREE

RANSOM

## OCTOBER 2018

eat right, sleep well, and keep my conscience clear." That was Rudy's stock answer when people asked him how he had remained so well preserved. Of course, he also believed the lightning was responsible for his vitality. It healed others, but it had always lived in him, even if it was aging as he aged.

For a ninety-four-year-old man, he was remarkably fit and flexible, and his face was unlined so that in a certain light he looked almost childlike.

He rarely left his house behind the church. He didn't give sermons anymore or walk the few yards across the compound to heal the sick and injured. Every once in a great while Heinrich would bring someone to his kitchen door who was afflicted with arthritis or shingles or cataracts, usually someone who had donated a lot of money to Purity First and in return had demanded to see Reverend Rudy. In those rare instances, he would lay his hands on them, but the energy that passed between them was always weak now, a mere shiver of lightning, an echo of thunder.

Sometimes, in the early morning, Rudy would get one of the church boys to take him out for a spin in the church bus. The original

Volkswagen had been replaced by a newer van around the turn of the century, painted in the same bright colors and polka-dot pattern as the first bus. But he had made some improvements to the inside.

Everyone thought it quaint that Reverend Rudy liked to ride around in his folk-band-church-social-clown van as if it were still 1976. People smiled as he passed them, and if they were members of his church they waved at him. Sometimes other people threw things at the van or yelled curse words at him. Those people were outsiders, and they mattered to him not at all.

For a long time he had been careful, driving the Skylark, never having anything on him that could help the police identify him or trace him back to the church. But over time he realized that the church bus gave him protective coloration. Purity First wasn't well liked, he knew that, but Midwesterners were raised to treat a church and its trappings with deference, and that courtesy extended to the van. He had been pulled over only once while driving it, and only because a taillight had burned out. The trooper had never looked inside, never asked him to open up the back. The Christmas-colored bus had cloaked him in respectability and made him feel safe, free to go about his business in peace.

In the old days he would keep an eye out as he drove and pull to the curb when there were no adults nearby and the group of children was small. He preferred one or two kids at a time, and girls were better than boys; girls with olive skin and dark hair were best of all. His little princesses. He had kept candy in a box behind the front seat and had given it to the children indiscriminately. Sometimes he would invite a child to ride with him around the block or through a park. He would watch carefully to see if anyone had observed him from a window or a shadowed doorway. And if he felt safe, he would take the child back to the church with him.

Everyone kept secrets within them, but children had the best secrets of all.

He had taken women, too, given them rides to his special basement room. And there had been men as well, a handful over the years. Gary Gilbert sprang to mind. The secrets men kept were bitter and hard, and men didn't make the right noises when fear overtook them, when they lost all hope for mercy or rescue. No, children were always preferable.

But lately he had slowed down. Now he only ventured out once or twice a year, and there was no real urgency about his trips. In fact, he was likely to give away all his candy and come back home with an empty van, and that was all right with him. His headaches weren't as bad as they used to be, but he didn't have much energy these days.

The business with the old woman bothered him. He had grown a beard when he got to America, lost his hair after the first lightning strike, started wearing glasses in the seventies when his eyesight had begun to grow weak. When he looked in the mirror, he saw no trace of the man he had been, the failed doctor, the reluctant administrator. His German accent was faint beneath the acquired drawl of his western Kansas dialect. But the woman had recognized him nonetheless, and she had told her friend, the teacher. And the teacher had told her son. So many threads that still had to be cut or the cloth would come unraveled.

And that singular coincidence had brought back memories that he had thought dead and buried. He was experiencing lost time, and he found himself coming awake in strange places, in the bathtub or standing in the middle of the basketball court or down in his secret basement room, with the taste of ashes in his mouth. For the first time, the church and the family he had built from nothing began to feel like a prison.

He wondered how many years he had left.

So when the vibrant blues and greens of summer faded to brown and yellow, Rudy decided to take a trip, maybe find a new distraction to bring back home with him, something to ease his cabin fever. Donnie Mueller had proven himself trustworthy, and although Rudy hated the fact that he could no longer drive himself, he enjoyed the man's company. He sent for Donnie and waited impatiently for him to open the gate and nose the van down the alley and out onto the street. Rudy got in and they meandered around the neighborhood, waved at some of the passersby there, taking their time, and then drove to the turnoff for US-283 and headed south.

Traffic was light and they left the highway in WaKeeney earlier than Rudy had expected. Donnie drove around the little town, stopping at the parks and schools, but never lingering. There was a Pizza Hut where the high school kids sometimes hung out, and Donnie pulled the van into the parking lot late in the morning. The place had just opened up for lunch, and there was only one other car parked with its nose facing the main door. But there was also a bicycle in the rack around the side of the building. A single bicycle, pink, with tassels hanging from the handlebars.

Donnie parked at the opposite end of the lot from the car, a rental with Texas plates. Rudy got out and went inside, leaving Donnie to mind the van. They had been there a few times before. Every few months Rudy sat at the back of the big dining room and had pasta from the buffet and watched the high school kids horse around with one another. His scars itched, and he tried not to scratch them as he ate. And the children were so caught up in their private dramas that they didn't notice him.

He recognized one or two of the employees who were bustling

about, getting the buffet ready for the lunch rush. There was a young Hispanic girl waiting at the counter. She was holding a crumpled dollar bill, and Rudy guessed she might be waiting to get change for the video games that were located in a small alcove beside the front door. The pink bicycle outside would belong to her.

The door opened behind him, and an older man walked in with a *New Yorker* under his arm. He looked around the room, then went to a corner table, sat, and opened his magazine. He was dressed impeccably in a sharkskin suit that set off the silver highlights in his long gray hair. Rudy felt mildly self-conscious in his red track suit, but after a moment's reflection decided he looked all right. At least he wasn't drawing attention to himself as an outsider.

Rudy stepped up to the counter and stood behind the girl, watching the cooks pull pizzas out of the ovens and slice them with a big rocking blade that reminded Rudy of a scythe. The girl turned around to look at him, then turned away again. She looked like she might be anywhere between twelve and fifteen.

Rudy could remember a time when there were no Hispanics in the area, no blacks, no Jews. In the early eighties, a black family had moved into Paradise Flats. But they hadn't stayed long, and they hadn't changed anything about the community. Rudy had known, though, that they were merely scouts and there would be more. Like ants who sent out one or two or three at a time to establish scent trails. Once you saw the first ant, it was too late. The swarm was coming. Now there were six black families living in the area around Paradise Flats, and Rudy had stopped counting the spics.

"They're pretty busy," he said to the girl's back. "Might be a while."

The girl shrugged.

"You need change for the games?"

She shrugged again. The talkative sort.

"I've got change," he said.

At last she turned her head and squinted at him. She shook her head. "I don't mind waiting."

"Here." Rudy reached into his pocket and pulled out a small rubber coin purse. He squeezed it open and poked around inside until he found six quarters. He fished them out and showed them to the girl in the palm of his hand.

"I only have a dollar," the girl said.

"That's okay. Take them all."

"I don't think—"

"Honestly," Rudy said, "they're heavy. My pants are gonna fall down with those in there."

She wrinkled her nose at him, but he smiled to show her it was a joke. "Go ahead," he said.

At last she reached out and scooped the quarters out of his palm, replaced them with the dollar bill. It was moist with her sweat. He disguised his revulsion with another friendly smile. Just a nice old man waiting for some pizza. He watched her scamper away toward the machines and then stepped up to the counter and waited to be helped. He eventually paid for the buffet, and found a table as far as he could from the man in the sharkskin suit. The stranger was watching him over the top of his magazine, like someone out of an old spy movie, and Rudy wished he would just go away.

Rudy ate two pieces of sausage pizza, wiped his hands with a paper napkin, and stood up. He left the girl's sweaty dollar bill as a tip and moved toward the front door, managing to get there just as the girl finished playing Ms. Pac-Man. She stepped back from the machine and almost bumped into him.

He chuckled. "Done with the games?"

"Last quarter."

"Oh, that's a shame."

She shrugged yet again. He wanted to pry her mouth open and pull her tongue out. If she wasn't going to use it, why have it at all?

But instead he opened his eyes wide and snapped his fingers. "You know what? I think I might have more quarters in my bus." He was careful not to call it a van. Kids these days were taught to be suspicious of strangers.

"Bus?" Sure enough, she craned her neck to see out the big windows at the front of the Pizza Hut. The green-and-red van was visible from a distance no matter where it was parked, and he could see the subtle change in her expression. How could something that looked like a holiday on wheels be threatening? She looked back up at him. "I don't know, mister."

He had her that easily. The promise of some nonexistent quarters. It was nearly always that easy, though, and his triumph didn't show on his face. He was sure it didn't.

"Come with me."

He didn't look back, just swung the door open and walked out onto the chilly blacktop. He could hear her behind him. He motioned to Donnie and the side door slid wide, revealing its dark interior. Rudy leaned in and grabbed a tool that was sitting ready beside the center console.

"You know," he said, turning to look at her, "I'm not sure exactly where they . . ."

The girl was running away across the parking lot, and in her place was the stranger in the sharkskin suit, the *New Yorker* rolled up under his arm, an umbrella held loose in his left hand. He was much taller than Rudy was, and broader across the shoulders. The stranger reached into his jacket with his free right hand, and Rudy could see that there was a shoulder holster there under his left arm.

"Am I right in thinking you're Rudolph Bormann?"

Rudy hadn't heard that name in more than sixty years and it didn't immediately register, but an alarm went off somewhere in the recesses of his lizard brain. He jabbed out with his Taser, not thinking, not planning, not at all careful, the way he was usually so careful. But the Taser was there in his hand, ready for the little girl who had now disappeared completely, having enjoyed the benefit of Rudy's quarters and not having paid him back in any way; it was there and he used it. An instinct.

The stranger stumbled back, his eyes wide, and dropped his umbrella with a clatter. Rudy hit him again. The third time the man went down in a quivering mass on the blacktop, the *New Yorker* flapping its reluctant way across the field behind the van.

Rudy looked back and forth between the highway and the big front window of the Pizza Hut, but no one came running, there was no outcry. The driver's-side door creaked open, and Donnie came running around the front.

"Oh, shit," he said softly, as if to himself.

"Help me," Rudy said.

Donnie started to open the passenger-side door.

"No," Rudy said. "Help me put him in the van."

"Oh, shit," Donnie said again.

Donnie got the man under his arms and Rudy stooped and lifted his legs. Even with Donnie's help, it wasn't easy. Rudy's knees hurt, and the stranger weighed a good deal more than the little girl would have. They had to rest the man on the lip of the doorway until Rudy could catch his breath. Then he bent and pushed up, folding the stranger's legs up against his chest while Donnie scrambled backward and rolled him onto his side so Rudy could close the door.

When it was done, Rudy leaned against the van and waited, panting and watching.

A hawk flew overhead and screeched, banked toward something unseeable in the field, and disappeared in the grass. Rudy watched it and felt his pulse at his wrist, counted, calmed himself.

"We should go," Donnie said. Rudy had already forgotten the boy was there. Sometimes he wondered if his mind was beginning to go.

"I want to know who he is," Rudy said.

He climbed back in the van, crawled over to the stranger, and felt his pulse. It was slower than Rudy's, but steady. The man wasn't going to wake up soon. Still, Rudy used one of the chains bolted to the floor of the van and secured the man's body. Then he went through the man's suit pockets and found a car key.

Donnie started the van and sat behind the wheel, bouncing in place, anxious to get going. Rudy ignored him. He stood in the parking lot and pointed the big plastic end of the key at the rental car with Texas plates. It beeped and unlocked for him. Inside, the car was clean and smelled new. Nothing behind the visor or in the glove box. But there was a wallet in the console, and Rudy took it with him back to the van, sat in the passenger seat, and removed the contents, spreading them out on his lap, while Donnie started the van and drove back to the highway and away from WaKeeney.

According to the man's driver's license, his name was Ransom Roan. A small stack of five business cards identified Ransom as "chief investigator" for something called the Noah Roan Foundation. Rudy had never heard of it. A family business? Had Ransom Roan followed Rudy from the church or was he at the Pizza Hut by coincidence?

Rudy had a lot of questions for his new friend Ransom. He shoved the contents of the wallet back inside and put it away in the glove box, then reached back and used the Taser again on Ransom's limp body. Then once more for good measure. He didn't want Ransom to wake up before Rudy was ready for him.

He felt as if he had woken up from a long nap, and there was a familiar tingle in his fingertips. He whistled tunelessly as Donnie drove, and anyone who saw him would have said he looked much younger than his ninety-four years.

# CHAPTER NINE

## 1

Skottie had become increasingly frustrated with Lieutenant Johnson. He insisted on following protocol and wouldn't sign off on her involvement in the tractor fire investigation. With the threat of a lawsuit hanging over the department, he said he needed to be able to show that everything had been handled properly and aboveboard. Skottie had not been the first to arrive at the scene of the fire, she had not been the officer in charge, and she had left before the coroner showed up, so the lieutenant had elected to keep her on the sidelines.

After putting Maddy to bed, Skottie had called Trooper Ryan Kufahl. When he'd picked up, his voice sounded thick with sleep.

"This is Skottie. Did I wake you?"

"Hmm. No," Ryan said. "Actually, yeah, I guess you did. Fell asleep in front of the TV again."

"Sorry," Skottie said.

"No, it's still early. I'm gonna have a hell of a time getting to sleep later."

"Listen, I won't keep you. I was just wondering if you could fill me in a little on that burn victim you found."

"Wish I could," Ryan said. "I was supposed to go along and witness the autopsy, but I caught a three-car pileup that took me past the end of my shift."

"They delayed the autopsy?"

"Right," Ryan said. "Supposed to go in first thing tomorrow so I can view it and sign off."

"Who was handling it? Was it Iversen or one of his assistants?"

Dr. Lyle Iversen was the coroner and forensic examiner for the twenty-third district, which covered four Kansas counties that butted up against one another in a sideways $L$ shape. In his spare time, he acted as assistant coroner for the other districts in western Kansas, as well as parts of Colorado and Nebraska. He was based out of a mortuary near Hays in Victoria, but he kept his Dopp kit ready because most of his time was spent on the road or in the air, traveling to small towns to analyze crime scenes and sign death certificates. He had a Cessna gassed and ready to go at a moment's notice. Skottie hadn't met him, but she had heard stories about the adventurous doctor. If he was somewhere away at the fringes of his territory, one of his two assistants would have responded to Ryan Kufahl's call.

"It was the man himself," Ryan said. "But I didn't get much of a chance to talk to him. Like I say, I had that accident I had to respond to, so I left the doctor to his business and never made it back up there."

"Did he identify the body?"

"I don't know, Skottie." Ryan sounded annoyed. "What's this about, anyway?"

"Yeah, sorry. I was thinking this might tie into something else I'm working on."

"Working on? Like what?"

"Don't worry about it," Skottie said. "Kind of an off-hours thing. Do me a favor and don't mention this to the lieutenant? That we talked about this?"

"Sure, I guess," Ryan said. "But if there's something I should know about, you'll clue me in, right?"

"Of course. Sorry I woke you up."

"No problem. I should probably eat something anyway. I'm surprised you can't hear my stomach grumbling."

Skottie ended the call and paced around the room while she considered her options. She could call Dr. Iversen and ask him the same questions she'd asked Ryan Kufahl, but she didn't know whether Iversen was strictly by-the-book. She hadn't caught the call, so he might be as reluctant as the lieutenant to give out any information. Kufahl and Lieutenant Johnson were the only people he was officially obligated to talk to about the case. On the other hand, Skottie now knew where the body had been taken.

She decided it might be best to cut out the middleman and take a look at the evidence herself.

# 2

Three men sat in a car across the street from the house, two of them in the front seat, one in the back. When they saw Skottie come out and get into her car, the man in the back seat leaned forward and flicked the ear of the man behind the wheel.

"We should follow her," he said.

"Why would we do that?" Theoretically the man in the back seat was in charge, but the driver was used to making decisions.

"I don't . . ." The man in the back seat slumped back down with a sigh. "I guess, like, maybe we don't even have to go in the house?"

"She's probably armed right now. I don't wanna get shot, do you?"

Skottie's car roared past them to the end of the street, and the three men got a glimpse of her face as she passed, but her eyes were focused on the road ahead and she didn't look to either side. She paused at the stop sign, turned left, and was out of sight.

The man in the passenger seat chimed in. "She probably keeps her gun under her pillow. We're gonna get shot no matter what."

"No," the driver said. "She won't do anything with her kid and the old lady around, right? That's when she's gonna be most vulnerable and scared. So we wait, we go in, and we leave. Safe and easy."

Neither of the other two spoke, and the driver relaxed. It was just like he said. Safe and easy, in and out. As soon as they delivered their message, they could go home.

# 3

Nine miles from Hays was tiny Victoria, Kansas, named for Queen Victoria by Scottish and English settlers in the late nineteenth century. There was nothing on Main Street to indicate that its history had been preserved. It resembled every other small town in the area, with agricultural co-ops and John Deere suppliers, small construction companies and dusty mercantiles. Hudson Brothers Mortuary was sandwiched between a bank and an insurance agency. The digital readout on the bank's sign informed Skottie that it was past eleven o'clock and the temperature was thirty-nine degrees Fahrenheit. She pulled up in front of the mortuary's white brick building and turned off the engine. A half-track was parked in the wide alley across from the mortuary, and a stray calico with one ear stopped to scowl at Skottie's car before trotting casually away. Despite the mist that still clung to the ground, Skottie saw fingers of lightning reaching down to touch the horizon. The moon's diffuse glow lent an eerie cast to the empty street, and Skottie half expected to hear boot heels clicking toward her across the pavement or a distant wolf's howl. She got out and went to the door, situated well back from the street under a wide arch. She pressed a buzzer on the wall and waited, stamping her feet against the cold. After a very long time, she heard footsteps on the other side of the door and a latch was thrown. The door opened inward, and a stout man in an ill-fitting blue uniform peered out at her.

"We're closed," he said. His hair was thin and greasy, and he had three chins stacked neatly atop the huge knot of his navy necktie.

Skottie flashed him her badge. "Yeah, sorry. I'm following up on a case, and it can't wait till morning."

"We're closed tomorrow, too," the watchman said. "Thanksgiving, don't you know?"

"Well, that's just it," Skottie said. "If I wait two whole days, this case is gonna go cold."

"Oh, yeah?"

"Speaking of cold . . ."

The watchman blinked his eyes and stared out at the street, as if he might be able to see the temperature. He hopped back on his heels and opened the door wider. "Oh, sorry," he said. "Weather's been freaky, ain't it?"

"Supposed to rain again later," Skottie said. She squeezed past him into the stuffy vestibule.

"Snow and fog and rain. We're getting the whole shebang this week, huh?"

"Welcome to Kansas."

The watchman squinted at her. "Don't gotta welcome me. I been here near on forty-five years. My whole damn life."

"It was just a joke."

His brow furrowed with effort. "Huh. Anyway, never saw weather like this, I'll tell you that."

He turned his back to her and waddled away through the dim vestibule. Skottie followed him into a small waiting area decked out with wooden chairs and ancient wood paneling. There was a tiny desk in one corner of the room that evidently served as a guard station. An empty Styrofoam cup of coffee was tipped over perilously close to the edge of the desk, and there was a tattered paperback laying facedown, open to a point roughly halfway through.

"We only got one body right now," the watchman said. "Waiting for a viewing on Saturday. That what you're after?"

"Actually, I'm wondering about the case Dr. Iversen's working on."

"Iversen? Oh, that ain't part of the mortuary, per se. They got their own area in the back. I don't go in there. It's where they do the autopsies and stuff."

"Exactly," Skottie said. She decided since she was here under false pretenses, she might as well go for the big lie. "I was the trooper who found the body today. I need to get some information for my file. Trying to get the paperwork squared away so I can enjoy the holiday."

The watchman led the way down a narrow hall, turning on lights as he went. "Got a big turkey?"

"And all the trimmings," Skottie said. She had seen the turkey in the basement refrigerator, but had no idea what else Emmaline was planning for the holiday feast. She felt a sudden flash of gratitude and sympathy for her mother, who had welcomed Skottie and Maddy into her home, fed them and cared for them. Then she boxed up these feelings and put them away for later.

"Well, this is the lab back here. I can unlock it for you, but then I really oughta get back to my post." He drew himself up taller as he mentioned his responsibility, and Skottie wondered whether he had anyone at home, up late prepping a turkey and potatoes, or whether he was looking forward to a TV dinner and a six-pack in front of the football game.

"I'll let you know when I'm done in there so you can lock it back up," she said.

The watchman nodded. He unlocked a thick wooden door, then lumbered away, back to his lonely vigil.

Skottie could smell all the familiar hospital chemicals. She brushed her hand against the inside wall of the room until she found a light switch and flicked it. Overhead lamps blinked to life, revealing a long room, bright white and sterile. Support beams divided the room into sections, and two stainless steel tables had been situated between the beams with easy access on each side of them so there was plenty of empty floor space. Dr. Iversen would be able to move around freely as he worked without bumping into anything. Counters lined two of the walls, with cabinets above and below painted candy-green, deep metal sinks with arched faucets, and soaps and towels and squirt bottles of varying colors. A bulletin board was hung over an old-fashioned wall phone with a long cord. Two desks with iMacs were positioned near the back of the room, and the wall to Skottie's left as she entered the room was dominated by a huge refrigerated cabinet with eight heavy doors fronting storage bays designed to keep corpses fresh. There were paper cards in slots on three of the eight doors, indicating those cabinets currently held bodies.

Skottie had been in rooms like this, in Chicago, in Kansas City, in Milwaukee. They were always the same, even if the details differed. Clean and orderly, an attempt to boil the ugly uncertainty of death down to facts and statistics. Skottie could see how the rooms comforted some people, gave them lists they could check off and file away, but they made her skin crawl. A woman had been drowned and a man burned, their bodies left for strangers to discover, and there were no facts that mattered except that two people were gone forever.

She knew she would have to open the cabinets, pull out the drawers, and look at the bodies, but she wasn't ready for that. She went instead to the first desk at the back of the room and tapped the space bar on the computer keyboard. The monitor sprang to life, showing a desktop picture of a smiling man holding a baby, squinting into the camera, deep purple beneath his eyes. A proud sleepy father. Skottie assumed this computer belonged to Dr. Iversen's assistant. A gray box sprang up, obscuring the young father's face, and a blinking cursor prompted her to input a password.

"Damn," Skottie said.

"What are you looking for?"

Skottie started and looked up from the monitor. A very tall man in a heavy brown trench coat and a white Stetson stood in the doorway, a ring of keys in his hand. He had gray hair and glasses and a neatly trimmed mustache. Skottie judged him to be in his midfifties.

"Dr. Iversen?" she guessed.

"Who are you?" Iversen hesitated in the door, torn between curiosity and outrage. "I thought—"

"You were expecting Trooper Kufahl, right? I'm afraid I lied to your watchman out there."

Dr. Iversen dropped his keys in a pocket of the big coat. "He said the trooper who found the body was here. That's not you. So I'll ask again, who are you?"

"I really am with the Highway Patrol. Can I show you my badge?"

Iversen nodded, and Skottie took out her badge holder, flipped it open so he could see the shield inside. He seemed to relax. He unbuttoned his coat and hung it on a peg behind the door while Skottie talked.

"Trooper Kufahl asked me to come out here and check on something for him," Skottie said. She didn't want to lie to Iversen—lies seemed to be piling up behind her at an alarming rate—but the truth was far too convoluted. She had no legal or procedural reason to be there, and she didn't want the doctor to start making phone calls. Once word got back to Lieutenant Johnson, Skottie knew she would be in an enormous amount of trouble. "I didn't want to disturb you at home, so I thought I'd just take a quick look at the file for him and leave you a note for the morning. Sorry if I startled you."

Iversen hung his hat on a peg next to the trench coat and used his fingers to smooth his hair. He shook his head.

"Why didn't Ryan come out here himself? Have I met you before?"

"Only over the phone. My name's Foster. Call me Skottie."

"Okay."

"Ryan's still caught up with that other case, the pileup," she said. "Long day."

"Right. Helluva day. Why I came back. Thought maybe I could get a jump on tomorrow. Two suspicious bodies, one right after the other—well, it's not a record, but we're not really set up for that, not to mention the ordinary bodies we've got to deal with." He held out his hands like he was surrendering to the mysteries of life, or the Fates, and shook his head again. "Anyway, what was it Ryan needed?"

"I know it's early yet, but if you've got anything on the John Doe from today, the burn victim . . ."

"Not much, of course," Iversen said. He went to the refrigerated cabinets and adjusted his glasses, reading the cards attached to the doors. "We got lucky with a couple of details, though, and I'm waiting on an e-mail from the hospital." He settled on one of the drawers and unlatched it, pulled it out on its rollers, looked in, and closed it again. "We'll know more when I get him on the table tomorrow, but . . ." He grabbed a file from a rack on the counter next to him and went to a large light box on the wall, opening the file as he walked. He stuck a rectangular sheet of film in the holder at the top and pushed a button on the side. A moment later, the light box flickered to life. "Look at this."

Skottie watched as he clipped two more X-rays up on the wall. Sections of the dead man's skeleton were illuminated in no particular order, like a gruesome jigsaw puzzle.

"Here." Dr. Iversen pointed to a spot on one of the X-rays. "See that?"

Skottie moved closer and squinted up at a blurry white spot on the reversed-out shadow of an arm. "That line, is it a fracture?"

"Not just one. Three fractures, close together here. And here, too. And see there?" He pointed again, but Skottie didn't see anything unusual.

"Harder to see," Iversen said. "But those dark spots there, the head of the radius has been dislocated enough times that scar tissue built up in the joint. Monteggia fractures of the proximal forearm. These are old injuries, set well and healed. Probably childhood trauma."

"Abuse?"

"Not necessarily." He held his arm out and hit the heel of his hand against the counter. "You put your arm out to break a fall and the pressure gets transferred up the line and breaks at the weakest point, which is your ulna . . . here." He pointed at his forearm. "It probably wouldn't happen this way, especially with the dislocation at the wrist, if he had been hit with something from above or from the side. If I had to guess, I'd say he spent a lot of time on a skateboard. Or maybe a bicycle or in-line skates. Fell often enough that he broke that arm three different times."

"Ouch," Skottie said.

"Well, yes, but a lucky break for us, so to speak. Lucky *breaks*, I should say. We ought to be able to use those to help us identify him. He was too badly burned for much else."

"What about dental records? Or a DNA test?"

"Dental records, sure. Sarakay's going to get on that first thing. But I'm afraid a DNA test would take weeks and cost more than the county will probably want to spend."

And Skottie knew that a DNA test, aside from being slow and costly, was no guarantee of any real results. There had to be something to match the DNA to in order to make an identification. It was a long shot.

"But if he's a murder victim . . ."

"Oh, I think that's beyond any doubt."

"Really?"

Iversen pointed to another X-ray. "See that?"

"Okay, it's a skull," Skottie said. "Besides that, what am I looking at?"

"Here." Iversen tapped his finger on a line that looked like a curly hair had fallen across the negative.

"Another fracture," Skottie said. "But it's—"

"Not a fracture. A piece was cut out of this man's skull. He's had brain surgery."

Skottie felt her level of excitement rising. "That should make it easier to identify him."

"Maybe. There's one more thing you can tell Ryan, although I'll show him all this tomorrow anyway."

Dr. Iversen led the way to the refrigerated cabinets and pulled out the same one he'd opened before. This time he rolled it all the way out and waved Skottie over.

"Look at the side of his head there," Iversen said. "Isn't that interesting?"

"I don't see it."

The man's head was badly burned, most of the skin blackened and thin as parchment. His hair was burned away, and the flesh that was visible along his scalp was a livid pink. His features were obscured by a mound of blisters like mushrooms on an old log. Skottie wanted to look away, but she didn't want to embarrass herself with Dr. Iversen.

"It's hard to spot," Iversen said. "This poor man. But if you know what you're looking for, and I was curious after looking at the X-rays, right in here you can see it. A puckering of the flesh along the temple. There was a recent wound; you can see the indication of stitches all along here."

"You're saying that surgery on his head"—Skottie looked away toward the X-rays—"he had that done right before he died?"

"I'm certain of it."

"So maybe he was confused. He drove that tractor out there when he shouldn't have been driving at all, and something went wrong."

"I can't speak to his state of mind," Iversen said. "That's outside my job description. But between this and those fractures he's suffered to the proximal third of his right ulna, I think he'll be very easy to identify, even without DNA testing."

"That's great news."

"Like I said, I'm waiting on an e-mail from the hospital, but I wouldn't expect anything for a few days yet. A lot of the older files haven't been computerized yet, so the victim's childhood injuries might not be readily available. And it's very possible he didn't grow up around here. If he came here from Wichita—or New York or Russia or something—it's going to take a lot more digging. But I'm optimistic."

He rolled the body back into the cabinet and went to the light box, turned it off, and took down the X-rays. He put them back in the file and returned it to the rack on the counter.

"I'll get a look inside as soon as possible tomorrow," he said. "Could be we'll find something more to go on. It's hard to think of a better example than this one, in terms of being able to identify a body this far gone. We'll figure him out."

Skottie's excitement at the possibility of progress was tempered by the realization that she might not have a job by the time the burn victim was identified. She might never get the chance to follow up, to help solve the case. And there was a possibility the dead man had nothing to do with any of this. She was far out on the ice and no longer knew how to get back to shore. She wasn't sure she wanted to.

Dr. Iversen took a step back and tapped his chin with an index finger. "Come to think of it, why did you say Ryan needed this information tonight? If he's working on something else, why couldn't this wait?"

"You know how it is," Skottie said. "Curiosity. It's hard to sleep when you've got something gnawing away at you."

"So he sent you."

Skottie shrugged.

"And you were looking at Sarakay's computer when I came in. What did you think you would find there?"

"I just thought maybe there was a file on the case. Maybe you'd found some identification."

Dr. Iversen walked over to the desks and glanced down at his assistant's computer. He tapped the space bar, just like Skottie had done, and seemed satisfied when the gray box popped up prompting him for a password. He turned and went to the other desk and sat down. He entered his own password and nodded at the monitor.

"No harm done, I guess," he said.

The computer chimed, and Iversen rocked back in his chair. His eyebrows shot up.

"Well, what do you know?" He looked up at Skottie, his suspicion of her dissolving in the face of a new discovery. "An e-mail from the hospital. Might be what you're looking for."

He moved the mouse and clicked it, studying the screen, while Skottie moved closer to the desk, holding her breath. Iversen spent a long minute reading the e-mail, then looked up at her with a smile.

"They got a match already," he said. "For the arm fractures, not the damage to the victim's skull, but it seems to me that matching those three breaks makes it fairly conclusive. Especially if the surgery to the skull is as recent as I think it is."

"Are you sure it's a match? I mean, wouldn't the hospital have a record of brain surgery?"

Dr. Iversen gave her a grim look. "If it was done at a hospital. That cut looked ragged to me. Like I say, I'll know more tomorrow when I can get a closer look at the actual work done."

"So what's his name?"

"Wes Weber," Iversen said. "Thirty-three years old. Unmarried. As of six months ago, a resident of Hays."

"Weber," Skottie said. "I've heard that name before."

"Yes . . ." Dr. Iversen stood, sending his chair rolling backward to the wall behind him. He strode to the refrigerated cabinets and bent forward, pulled his glasses down on his nose while he read the cards on the three occupied drawers. He reached over and grabbed another file from the rack and held it up.

"Same last name as our other mysterious victim," he said. "Margaret Weber. Drowned at Kirwin Lake. Coincidence?"

Skottie shook her head. And then she remembered the other place she'd heard Wes Weber's name. On Monday she had found his abandoned green pickup truck at a rest stop and had arranged for it to be towed.

Except now she was certain he hadn't meant to abandon it.

# 4

"She's back!"

The man in the back seat awoke with a start and wiped his mouth. His left shoulder was wet with drool. "Huh?"

"The statie," said the man in the driver's seat. "She just got home."

The man in the passenger seat was snoring softly.

"Don't wake him up," said the man in the back seat. "We got a while. Might as well let him rest. Me too. Wake me up a half hour after the lights go out in there."

He flopped back and was breathing deeply within seconds.

"Right," said the driver. "Yeah, you guys rest while I sit here and watch a house. Jackasses."

"What?" The man in the back seat was only half-awake, his voice thick and drowsy.

"Nothing," the driver said. "I didn't say a damn thing."

# 5

Maddy was a light sleeper. She had been living in her grandmother's house for nearly six months, but she was still waking up every night, lying in the dark, staring up at nothing and listening for her parents' angry voices. Her father wasn't around anymore to argue with her mother, but that was disturbing in a different way, and she hadn't decided which was worse, the constant fighting or the quiet Kansas nights.

So at first she wasn't surprised when she woke and heard people whispering in the living room. She checked the clock next to her bed and saw it was after midnight. Sometime during the night, while she was asleep, the rain had stopped. Now there was only the steady plink of water falling off the roof and hitting the lawn chairs on the patio outside her bedroom window.

She slid from under her blanket to the floor and waited for her eyes to adjust to the dark. Bear was standing at her bedroom door and Maddy tiptoed over to him. He looked at her when she patted his head, but he didn't move from his post, and it occurred to Maddy that the big dog was blocking the doorway, protecting her from whoever was out there.

At the same time, it occurred to her that the people talking didn't sound like her mother and her father, or her grandma Emmaline. There were strangers in the house.

"It's okay, boy," she said in a low voice even she could barely hear. "You stay here. I'll check it out."

She slipped out into the hallway. Her mother's door was open, and she was softly snoring. The voices coming from the front of the house were louder now, and Maddy could make out isolated words.

"... *got a gun?*"

"*Hurry, I ...*"

"... *trash it first, make it look ...*"

She snuck across the hall and up to her mother's bed, reached out and touched her on the shoulder. Skottie came awake right away, squinting and reaching out to stroke Maddy's hair.

"What's wrong, baby?" Skottie's voice was soft and hoarse, trying not to wake Grandma Emmaline in the next room.

"There's people in the house, Mama."

Soft light from a streetlight outside stretched across the blankets and made Maddy's T-shirt glow pink. Bear's shadow moved across the wall as he padded around to the other side of the bed.

"You're having a bad dream," Skottie said. "It's just the rain. Let me—"

"There's two men. Maybe three. They're in the living room."

Skottie sat up and swung her legs over the side of the bed, frowning now, concern creasing her forehead and digging grooves alongside her mouth. "You sure, Maddy?"

Maddy nodded and pointed at the open door and they both held still, their eyes wide as they strained to hear. Again, snippets of sound drifted through the air, the low rumble of faraway thunder, the whistle of a distant train, and low male voices in another part of the house. Maddy could no longer make out whole words, but there were at least two people out there.

Skottie was out of bed in an instant and she crossed the room to her gun safe in two long strides.

"Take Bear with you and go to your room. Get under the bed."

"What about your bed?" Maddy cast a suspicious eye at the shadowy space beneath the edge of the bed skirt.

Skottie crouched in front of the safe and looked up at her with a grimace. "No room. Grandma's stuff is under there, remember?"

Maddy recalled the day they had moved in, the two of them shoving boxes of her grandmother's clothing and linens under the bed in order to make room for their own things. She instinctively glanced at the tiny closet. It was so full the door didn't close properly. For the first time it occurred to her that they had imposed themselves on Emmaline.

"Hide under your own bed, Maddy," Skottie said. "Hurry up. Don't try to get the dog to go under there with you, and don't come out until I come for you."

Skottie worked the dial on the safe's door, and Maddy backed up, then turned and crept out into the hallway again. She glanced at her own door, but the thought of hiding under her bed like a helpless kid held no appeal. Which left her with two options: she could wake her grandmother or she could scout the situation in the living room. There was no one else there to help them. Her mother had a gun, but if the men were armed, too, Skottie would need to know that. And she would need to know where the men were. Someone was going to have to call the police, and Maddy wanted to call her father. There was a lot to be done, and her mother already had her hands full.

Maddy made up her mind and snuck down the hall to where it widened out into the big communal space where they ate breakfast. She felt a soft presence and reached out, twined her fingers in the fur at Bear's throat. She could see three figures, all in dark clothing, moving slowly through the living room, in and out of shadows. But they weren't paying attention to the television or Emmaline's antique vase or even the spare change in the jar by the front door.

Maddy couldn't tell whether they had guns. She moved to her right and into the kitchen and Bear followed her, massive yet insubstantial as a ghost. The back door was standing ajar, the tiny window above the dead bolt broken, glass and ice dusting the linoleum. Cold air blew hard against Maddy's legs. Light from a street lamp pushed through the kitchen window, silhouetting a wooden knife block on the counter. Maddy reached out for a butcher knife, then pulled her hand back. She could barely breathe and her pulse drummed against her skull. Stabbing a grown man wasn't something she could do, and she knew it.

Then a creak in the hallway. Someone moving toward the front of the house. Her mother had a gun and was going alone against three burglars.

Maddy saw her phone on the little table where her mother sat to pay the bills. She unplugged it and swept the phone's home screen up, ducked and yelled "Hey, you guys!" Then she thrust the phone high above her head, aimed it at the pass-through above the counter, and snapped a picture.

She ducked down and crawled toward the living room, hoping the flash had distracted the men long enough to give her mother an advantage.

She could hear male voices shouting behind her, heard an earth-shaking crash, and then Bear had the back of her pajama top in his teeth and she was off her feet, carried across the kitchen, over the threshold, and deposited on the frozen grass outside.

# 6

First, the temperature in the house had suddenly plummeted. Then there had been a flash of light and the sound of glass breaking. Skottie heard Maddy yell and she stood frozen in place, trying to pinpoint the sound. She couldn't fire without knowing where Maddy was. She was carrying her shotgun, a Mossberg 500, which held five rounds, and her Glock was in the waistband of her yoga pants, at the back, giving her another seventeen shots if she needed them. There were two rifles in the open gun safe if she had to retreat to her bedroom. Unless an army had broken into the house, Skottie felt confident she could protect herself and her family. But the element of surprise would be useful. If she could get to the living room quickly and quietly, she might be able to get the intruders to stand down and end the situation peacefully. Unless they had Maddy. Maddy was supposed to be under her bed, out of harm's way. But of course she wasn't. Skottie silently cursed herself for letting the girl out of her sight.

Skottie wished she could move her ears independently, the way Bear did. There were too many ambient sounds, and it was hard to pick out the exact location of the intruders.

A shadow materialized at the end of the hallway and lunged at her, too tall to be Maddy or Emmaline. Skottie didn't hesitate. She raised her gun and slammed it butt-first into the intruder's gut.

The shadow hollered and dropped, hit the floor hard. Behind Skottie, Emmaline's bedroom door opened.

"What's going on out here?"

"Get back in your room, Mom. *Go!*" Skottie jumped over the writhing shape on the floor and left the hallway in a crouch. To her right, across the kitchen, the back door was wide open and banging into the wall. She couldn't see Maddy anywhere. She put her back to the end of the counter and poked her head low around the side. The dining room was empty. There was a short wall in front of her where the end of the hallway extended into the living room, making room for her own bedroom on the other side. Skottie crossed to it and flattened herself out, then snuck a look into the living room. The big picture window was broken and two figures stood beside the front door, in the act of pulling it open, their backs to her.

She stepped out and pumped the shotgun to get their attention.

"Step back from the door and raise your—"

But she was too late. The door was open and the two men were through it before she could finish her sentence. She chased after them, across the living room and out onto the porch, the shotgun resting on her shoulder. She flicked on the light above the door with her free hand, knowing it would make her more visible to them, but wanting them to see that she was armed. She considered chasing them down, but halted on the top step. Maddy and Emmaline were still in the house with one of the intruders.

Somewhere out in the darkness an engine started. Two car doors slammed shut and a vehicle squealed past her with its lights off. She saw a red streak on silver paint as the car turned the corner and fog swallowed it up.

She went inside and closed the door, locked it and switched off the porch light, then turned on the lamp next to Emmaline's favorite chair. Curtains billowed in the cold air from the broken window, but she didn't see a lot of glass on the floor. She went through the kitchen to the back door and glanced outside, but the yard was empty. She closed the door and threw the bolt and walked back through the kitchen, turning on lights as she went.

"Maddy?"

No answer.

"Maddy, you can come out now, baby."

Emmaline was kneeling at the near end of the hallway, holding one of the rifles from the safe. When she saw Skottie, she used it to push herself up from the floor and stand.

"I took care of this one," Emmaline said.

The man Skottie had hit was lying on the floor in a fetal position. His wrists and ankles had been tied together behind him with a long orange extension cord, and he was grunting in pain, shouting into the throw rug beneath him.

"Police," he said. "I'm police!"

"Deputy Puckett," Skottie said, "what the hell are you doing in my house?"

# 7

Donnie saw the girl and he slowed the car, followed her at a walking pace down the street with the headlights off. They were a block over from the trooper's house and there wasn't a light on anywhere. He figured she heard the car, but she didn't look up.

"That's the statie's kid."

"Go," Lance said. "Just get out of here."

"No," Donnie said. "If we got her kid, we got the upper hand."

"Fuck you, that's federal. Besides, my arm hurts, man."

Donnie knew what he meant. So far, they were guilty of breaking and entering, probably a home invasion. If they got caught, kidnapping would carry a much higher sentence. But playing it out in his head, Donnie thought they could get away with it.

"Get me to the hospital, Donnie," Lance said.

"It's not that bad. If you didn't stick your arm through the window—"

"I got startled."

"One thing at a time," Donnie said. "If we got her kid, the statie's not gonna call the cops," he said.

"Hell she won't. She *is* a cop. They look after their own."

"She's a state trooper. They got their own territory out on the highway, not here in town. Hell, they don't even know the regular cops, the ones who respond to 911 calls." Donnie wasn't sure this was correct, but he needed Lance to calm down long enough to listen to his newly hatched plan. "Anyway, she won't call the cops because she's gonna get fired if she causes any more trouble. The reverend's lawyers made sure of it."

"This is *us* causing *her* trouble. Why wouldn't she call for help?"

"Well, she won't call right away. She's gonna wanna see what we have to say first."

"So we can trade her the kid for Christian."

"We can't leave him in there. But we're not gonna hurt anybody. She gets the kid, we get our friend. And this whole thing might be scary enough she decides to leave town. Mission accomplished."

"What if she doesn't wanna do what we say?"

"It's her *kid*," Donnie said.

"Those people don't care about their kids like we do."

Donnie shrugged. "Everybody cares about their kids. Even animals. On YouTube one time I seen a mother giraffe chase a buncha lions away from its baby. It's some kinda instinct."

"Pride."

"Just nature, I think."

"No, a buncha lions is called a pride," Lance said.

"Oh, yeah. I knew that. Anyway, you in?"

"Yeah, I guess. Long as she doesn't call the rest of the cops."

"I'm telling you, she won't," Donnie said.

"But then we gotta go to a hospital. My arm, man."

"After this we'll go see the reverend and he'll fix it up hisself."

Donnie pulled the car to the curb and put it in park, left the motor running. Lance got out on the passenger side and Donnie turned on the headlights. At the same time he popped the trunk open from inside so they'd have a place to put the girl. When the lights hit her, the girl stopped and turned around with a scared look on her face. Donnie chuckled and jumped out of the car to help Lance grab her.

The fog closed in around him as soon as he stepped away from the car, but he could see a moving shape off to the side that he assumed was Lance. Donnie moved out into the street so he could flank the girl. She was backing away more slowly than he was advancing, holding her phone up close to her face.

"Hey, girl, whatcha doing out so late?"

She held the phone up. "Waiting for you to get close enough I could do this," she said. There was a flash of light. "I already called the police and I just got your picture."

Donnie didn't figure she'd called the police. If so, they'd still have her on the line. "Too foggy," he said. "You got a pic of fog, is all."

That confused her and she looked down at the phone. As soon as her eyes weren't on him, he leapt at her and grabbed the phone out of her hands. He got his elbow around her neck to hold her still and glanced at the phone's screen. She'd already exited the camera app, and there was a green bar directing her back to her phone call. His stomach turned over. She really had called the police. He threw the phone to the ground and stomped on it with his boot heel, hoping that would end the call, that the police hadn't traced the phone. At the same time, somewhere off to his left, Lance started screaming.

"Lance?"

"Get it off me!"

"Where are you, man?"

"Donnie!"

Donnie held tight to the girl, who was struggling harder now, digging into his arm with her fingernails, and dragged her along with him through the fog.

"I can't see you," he said. "Lance?"

Lance had gone silent.

The girl bit into his hand and Donnie yelped, let go. She ran and disappeared in the darkness. Donnie froze in place, listening for her footsteps.

"Donnie, where you at?" Lance's voice was no more than a step or two away.

Donnie gave up on the girl for the moment, shuffled to his left until he almost tripped over his friend. He squatted and put his hand on Lance's chest.

"You hurt?"

"Can't tell. My arm's real bad, though. Feels cold, but like it's on fire."

Donnie squinted, looking his friend up and down. The arm really was bad. There was a pool of blood under Lance, and it was growing.

"Can you get up?"

"Shhh. It's still out there, man. It attacked me."

"What attacked you?"

"It was like a werewolf," Lance said. "Swear to God, running around out there in the fog."

"There's no—" But Lance grabbed him and cut him off, pointing at something behind Donnie.

Donnie turned and saw a black lion step out of the mist. Donnie stiffened. The beast stood silently, watching him for a moment. He didn't realize it, but Donnie was waiting for the animal to growl, to snarl, for some warning that it was going to attack. When that happened, his fight-or-flight response would kick in and he would act. But when it finally did move, there was no signal or sign. It was on them in an instant, its hot breath in Donnie's face, its black lips drawn back, its fangs dripping. Lance was screaming again, but that was the only sound Donnie could hear. His bladder let go, warmth spreading down his left leg, and he fell back, smacking his head against the pavement.

"Bear!" The little girl's voice, somewhere out there behind the curtain of fog.

And the beast was gone, responding to the girl's summons, a dark blur, gray upon gray, and then nothing.

Donnie lay next to Lance in the middle of the street, waiting for his friend to calm down. When Lance's screams turned to gasps, Donnie rolled over and pushed himself up.

"Shut up," he said.

"Huh?"

"Shut up and lemme listen."

Lance stopped whimpering, even held his breath, while Donnie stared into the fog and concentrated so hard that he gave himself a headache. At last he got to his feet and held out his hand to help Lance up.

"C'mon," he said. "Unless your arm's falling the fuck off, we gotta get moving."

"The werewolf," Lance said.

"That's the guy's dog." Donnie was embarrassed that he'd thought it was a lion, but at least he wasn't blubbering about it like Lance was. His wet jeans were starting to feel icy cold, and he kept his body angled away from Lance so he wouldn't notice the dark spot. "The foreign guy. It's a big damn thing, but it's just a dog. I killed dogs before."

"What are we gonna do?"

"We're gonna hurry the hell up. That dog's so big, it can't move quiet in this. The crust of ice on the snow. It's breaking through every time it takes a step. You can hear it, you listen close, but we gotta hurry or we'll lose it."

"I don't think I wanna find it."

"You wanna get Christian back from the statie or go back to the reverend empty-handed? That's his nephew or something, man."

"We can't go faster than a dog, Donnie."

"We can if it's going slow. Like if it's trying to stay close by a little girl."

# 8

"Mom, I can't find Maddy!"

Emmaline glared at Deputy Christian Puckett, who wasn't looking at anyone, just rocking back and forth trying to get his arms free from the electrical cord wrapped around them.

"Where's my granddaughter?"

"I don't know, I swear."

"Your friends took her?"

"No way!"

"Check her room," Skottie said. "I told her to hide under her bed. Maybe she went back in there."

Emmaline nodded, her angry expression replaced by one of concern. She turned and scampered down the hall to Maddy's room. Skottie propped her shotgun against the wall in the living room and went to where Christian was lying, braced herself behind him, and yanked him up by the arms. He squirmed, but she kicked him in the back of his knee and he went limp. Skottie retrieved her gun and leaned against the wall.

"What was the plan here, Deputy?"

"We weren't gonna hurt nobody."

"That's why you break into my home? *So you won't hurt me? So you won't hurt my daughter?*"

Emmaline emerged from Maddy's room and stood at the other end of the hall for a moment before crossing into Skottie's room. Skottie poked Christian with the barrel of the shotgun.

"Don't move," she said. She walked past him and glanced in through Maddy's bedroom door before looking in her own room. Emmaline was on her hands and knees, her head under Skottie's bed.

"Mom?"

Emmaline pulled her head out and sat back, smoothed her nightgown over her knees. Her hair was in a net and her face was free of makeup. She looked small and vulnerable, something Skottie had never noticed about her before.

"I can't find her. She's not here."

Skottie went back down the hall. Christian had just gained his feet, sliding himself up the wall, and she kicked his leg again as she passed him, forcing him back down. He stifled a yelp.

She hurried through the rest of the house again, checking behind the sofa, under the dining room table, and opening the cabinet doors. She unlocked the back door and stepped outside too fast, skidding out onto the patio, snow arcing up over her bare feet. Moonlight through the fog made the backyard glow as bright as sunrise, but there was no sign of movement, no sense of a living creature anywhere. Bear's paw prints were everywhere, crisscrossing over themselves, but the only human tracks she could see were her own.

"Maddy?"

No answer. Nothing moved in the floating white.

"Maddy? Baby, are you there?"

If Maddy had been hurt, she might not be able to respond. Then again, she might not be alone.

"Bear?"

The quiet dog didn't materialize.

"Bear, come. Come here, boy." She wished she knew the right words, the right language. But she didn't think the dog was there. The yard had an empty feeling.

Fighting her rising panic, Skottie backed away from the door and closed it. She went back through the kitchen to the hallway, where Christian had regained his feet and was hopping as fast as he could from an angry Emmaline, who had found a broom and was swatting him with it. Skottie grabbed him by the collar of his uniform jacket and hauled him forward, faster than he could hobble. She stood aside and let him fall on the living room floor where there was more room to maneuver than there was in the narrow hallway. Then she turned him over and pulled his face up to hers.

"You tell me where my daughter is, you son of a bitch."

"I don't know. I never even saw her, I swear to you."

*"Where is she?"*

"I don't *know.*" Christian had begun to cry, and Skottie let go of him. She had enough experience with missing person cases to know that she had a limited amount of time before it would be too late and her daughter would be far out of her reach. But somebody had Maddy, or at least knew where she was.

"Goodman did this, right? The sheriff ordered this?"

"No," Christian said. His voice was a blubbering wheeze, and she had to lean in close to understand him. "He doesn't . . . He doesn't know about any of this. Oh, shit, I am so screwed."

"Boy, that's the first true thing I've heard you say," Skottie said.

# 9

Bear padded along next to Maddy. The breeze had now changed direction and was coming from the west, and the dog blocked most of it with his bulk. Still, Maddy was shivering, hugging herself against the cold, dressed in nothing but her T-shirt and leggings. She thought of her phone, cracked and broken in the middle of the street behind her, and wondered if the 911 operator had taken her off hold already. Would they still be able to trace the call? Maddy knew she couldn't count on it. There was only one other place she could think to go for help, one other person she knew she could trust.

"It's this way," she said to Bear. But she wasn't at all certain that they were going in the right direction. She had lived in her grandmother's house all summer, but she had spent most of her time outside looking down at her phone. She scanned the street for familiar landmarks, things she had seen during their walk to the grocery store, but she could see only a few feet ahead.

"Bear, do you know the way? The grocery store? Do you remember?" Her teeth were chattering, and she didn't know the word for *groceries* in Esperanto, and she didn't want to go to the store anyway, but she knew her father's hotel was somewhere between her house and the IGA. "Steak, Bear," she said. "Steak?" She had spent an hour before dinner with Bear, looking up words online to test him, and now she struggled to remember some of her new vocabulary. Grocery store and *steak* were too specific, but maybe something simpler. What was the word for *food*? "Um . . . *Manga Joe*, Bear?" That wasn't right, but it was close. She stopped walking and closed her eyes, put her hands and face in Bear's warm fur and concentrated. "*Manĝaĵo!* That's it!"

Bear snorted and flicked his left ear at her, then nudged her into motion. He crossed the street and waited for her, then led the way in a direction Maddy was sure was wrong.

"No, Bear, the grocery store. Food. *Manĝaĵo.*"

Bear kept moving and Maddy had no choice but to follow along, picking her way carefully across the crust of snow and swiveling her toes a little with each step, digging in the way her father had taught her during their harsh Chicago winters together.

And two blocks later she saw the looming outline of the hotel. Bear had understood and had led her back along the route they'd taken in daylight, reversing the walk from the grocery store.

"This is it, boy. You did it! My dad's here, and he'll help us."

Bear stopped and looked back at her, his fur blowing gently in the wind.

She knew he didn't understand and she felt a pang of regret for tricking him. He probably expected more steak, and he wasn't likely to get it tonight.

"Tomorrow," she said. "I bet my grandma can make something special for you for Thanksgiving, okay? I'll tell her."

She grabbed Bear's mane and he allowed her to pull him down the sidewalk and around the side of the building to the front. Orange light spilled out through the glass doors and was whisked away by the mist.

"Stay here, Bear. *Restu*, okay? I'll be right back."

She left Bear sitting next to a concrete fountain that had been drained for the winter and she scooted through a revolving door. The rush of warm air made her cheeks flush, and her nose started running. She wiped it on the back of her hand and walked as calmly as she could to the registration counter. No one was in sight, but there was a bell and she rang it. A minute later a skinny guy came out of a back room. He had thick black-rimmed glasses and a neatly trimmed beard and was chewing something. When he saw her, he swallowed whatever was in his mouth and came around the counter toward her.

"Hey, you okay?" He bent at the waist, and she was afraid he was going to kneel down in front of her. She wondered how bad her hair looked and wished she had a jacket to cover herself with. Her pajamas were thin and inadequate, and looking down at the little flowers all over her leggings, Maddy felt more like a little kid than she wanted to.

"Where are your parents?" He looked up at the revolving door and the big window next to it as if he might be able to see the parking lot through the blanket of white fog.

"I need to talk to my dad," Maddy said. "He's a guest here."

"Your dad's here in the hotel?"

"Yeah, but I don't know what room."

"What's his name?" The guy seemed relieved to have something he could do. He went back around the end of the counter and tapped on a keyboard.

"Brandon Foster," Maddy said. "He's a policeman."

The guy nodded and tapped some more keys, peered at a monitor. "Yeah, he's in 514. I can ring him, but it's pretty late." He looked up at her and shook his head. "Never mind. Lemme call him for you."

She spotted the elevator in the far corner of the lobby. "It's okay, I can find it."

"Well, I really need an adult to vouch for you. It's the middle of the night." He pointed to a couch next to the counter. "Tell you what, wait here, okay? Lemme find your dad for you."

Maddy nodded and went to the couch, which was decorated with the same sort of flowers as her pajamas, but bigger. She fell backward into the cushions and watched the guy pick up a phone with a long cord. He punched four buttons and waited. Maddy could hear a phone ringing at the other end and then a muffled voice.

"Mr. Foster," the desk guy said, "I have a girl here who says she's your daughter?"

The muffled voice said something in response. It sounded like a question.

The guy looked over at Maddy. "What's your name?"

"Maddy. Tell him Mom's in trouble."

"Sir, her name's Maddy. She came in here pretty cold and wet, and she says her mother's in some kind of trouble."

The muffled voice, her father sounding much less sleepy than when he'd answered the phone, said something sharp and short and the desk guy hung up the phone.

"He's on his way down. Lemme get you a blanket. Laundry just came out of the dryer, so it'll be nice and warm." He smiled and she smiled back at him.

The guy returned to his back room, and Maddy watched the elevator. The lobby felt empty and sterile, and now that she knew her dad was coming to help she realized she was shivering. She wiped her nose again and glanced over the counter to make sure the guy wasn't coming before she rubbed the back of her hand on the arm of the couch. Her eye was drawn to movement outside and, as she watched, a man appeared on the other side of the big window. He put his face against the glass, shielding it with his hands and looking around at the lobby. Then he saw her and pulled back, but not before she recognized him.

He was one of the men who had broken into her house, the one who had grabbed her and smashed her phone.

"Bear!"

The dog was alone out there. Without thinking, Maddy jumped off the couch and ran across the lobby. There was an emergency exit next to the revolving door, and she slammed into the push bar and through. She vaguely heard her name being called, but the door shut behind her and she pressed on into the foggy night.

"Bear! *Venu*, Bear! *Venu!*" She remembered how to tell him to come to her, but she couldn't remember the word for *danger*, even though she was sure she'd studied that one.

Something moved, almost within arm's reach, and then she saw him. Bear materialized in front of her, fog rippling around his imposing frame. At the same time she felt warm air behind her, heard the door *snick* open, and a yellow wedge of light spilled out over the sidewalk at her feet.

"Maddy, get down!"

She started to turn toward the sound of her father's voice, but there was a bright flash of light and the deafening roar of a gunshot next to her ear. She staggered sideways and fell, but her father caught her and scooped her up before she hit the ground.

"Bear," she said.

"Oh, honey," her father said. "Was that the dog?"

# 10

Before she did anything else, Skottie fetched her handcuffs and secured Christian. Then she put Emmaline in charge of watching him, pulled on a pair of boots, and left the house.

She dialed 911 as she walked along the street, scanning every shadow, every hedge and tree and patch of black ice, looking for some sign of Maddy. The emergency dispatcher put her on hold before Skottie could say anything, so she hung up and called Lieutenant Johnson on his cell.

He picked up after two rings. "Skottie? You know what time it is?" He didn't sound like he'd been asleep.

"Yes, sir," Skottie said. She was slightly out of breath, jogging fast, keeping her eyes peeled. "I've got trouble here."

"Yeah, listen, can we talk about this Monday?"

"No, sir. Three men, at least three, just broke into my house."

"Oh, damn." She could hear him sit up straighter, his voice suddenly alert. "I thought you were talking about the other thing again."

"No, sir, that can wait." Skottie reached the end of her block and turned the corner. Something glinted in the middle of the next street, and Skottie hurried across, squatted down to see it more closely.

"Skottie? You there?"

"Just a minute," she said.

The shiny thing in the street was a phone, crushed and deformed into a rough parallelogram. The screen was cracked, but when Skottie pushed the home button it displayed a faint green bar indicating that a call was in progress. She touched it but it didn't respond. She picked it up and turned it over, recognized Maddy's *Adventure Time* phone case.

"Skottie?" The lieutenant's distant voice reminded her that she was still on a call of her own. She stood up and stuck Maddy's phone in her jacket pocket, then started walking again and put her own phone back up to her ear.

"Sir, my daughter's missing right now."

"Skottie, you need to hang up and call 911."

"I did. They put me on hold. I was hoping you could—"

"Right. Hold tight and let me make a couple of calls, okay?"

Skottie turned the corner again. Her vague plan was to search the block around Emmaline's house, then expand out another block, keep spiraling outward.

"One of the men was Sheriff Goodman's deputy," she said.

"The black kid? Quincy?"

"No, sir, one of the other ones."

"Skottie, don't do anything until I call you back."

"I'm looking for Maddy right now. I'm gonna keep doing that."

"Of course."

She hung up without saying good-bye and dialed Brandon's number. She had deleted it from her speed dial weeks before and was surprised to find that she still remembered it. He picked up right away, sounding like he hadn't been sleeping, either.

"What's going on over there?" he said.

"Maddy's missing. How fast can you—"

"I've got her, Skottie. She's here."

Skottie stopped walking. She went over to the curb and sat on it, took a deep breath. "Is she okay?"

"She's fine," Brandon said. "Just cold. I was about to call you. Skottie, what's she doing out in the middle of the night? For God's sake, she doesn't have any shoes. Her feet are practically frozen."

"You think I let her wander the streets?"

"No, I don't . . . Hey, I think I've got a legitimate right to be concerned here."

Of course he did. Skottie realized her relief had somehow turned immediately to irritation at the sound of her husband's voice. "Sorry," she said.

"Maddy won't talk to me, just keeps crying about that dog."

"Dog?"

"I didn't realize it was the same one. It startled me, is all."

"What are you talking about?"

"I shot at it. That dog you brought home was following her. I mean, it came out of the fog like some kind of . . . I don't know if I hit it. It didn't make any noise."

"He wouldn't. He's mute."

"Huh."

"You really shot Bear?"

"I don't know. You can't see anything out there, so much fog."

"Jesus, Brandon."

"What happened over there?"

"We had a break-in. Maddy must've made a run for it."

"A break-in? You okay?"

"I'm fine. Mom's fine."

"Skottie, you need to come home where I can—"

"Not the time. I'm just glad Maddy's all right."

"Yeah, she'll be good. They're putting a rollaway in my room."

"You're keeping her?"

"I thought . . ."

Skottie nodded to herself. It wasn't a bad idea to let him hold on to her for the night. She had crossed her legs under her, and there was a pebble digging into her ankle. She stood back up and stepped over to the sidewalk. The adrenaline was leaving her system, and her muscles felt like jelly.

"You're right," she said. "Keep her there, let her sleep. Things might be hectic around here for a while."

"You want me to come over there?"

"No, I got it under control." She waited for him to scoff or contradict her. She was grateful when he didn't.

"Sure," he said, and he sounded like he meant it. "But if you need anything, you know—"

"Yeah, thanks. And you need to find that dog. His name's Bear. You can't leave him out there tonight. Maddy knows how to talk to him when you track him down."

"I'll do my best," Brandon said. "And if, you know, if you wanna come over here, there's room."

She almost smiled. "Thanks, I'm okay."

She ended the call and let her arm drop to her side. Her fingers were tingling. She walked through the fog to the corner and turned onto her own street, completing the square block. A light came on over the porch next to where Skottie was standing, and a woman opened the screen door. She was white, wearing a pink terry-cloth bathrobe and her orange hair in a net. She was holding a flip phone.

"Is that you, Officer Foster?"

Skottie stopped, one eye on the car idling halfway down the street. "Yes, ma'am. It's me."

"Did you hear a commotion earlier?"

"Commotion?"

"I told Henry to get up and go look, but he went back to sleep. Anyway, I was thinking I should call the police." She held the phone up as if to show her intentions. "But I saw you patrolling out here and I just want you to know that it makes us all feel safe having a police officer right here on the block."

"Who's 'us all'?"

The woman shrugged. "Everybody here. Thank you."

Skottie felt herself softening. She was tired and worried and nearly certain that this same woman had snubbed her just days before at Dollar General, but it was good to feel needed. "I think it was just some rowdy kids," she said. "But I checked it out just in case."

The woman nodded and clutched her phone between her hands. She turned and went inside without another word and turned off her porch light, leaving Skottie in the dark.

# 11

"We have to check on him!"

"Maddy, honey, calm down." Brandon was standing with one foot on the rollaway bed, pushing against the upright half, trying to open it up.

"If he's hurt . . ." Maddy was wearing the oversize slippers and robe from the closet. She looked ridiculous and charming, a tiny head sitting atop a shapeless mass of fluff.

"If he's hurt, he might be dangerous." The rollaway tipped over and

Brandon caught his balance before he fell. He took a step away from the bed and glared at it. "Anyway," he said, "I don't know if I hit him or not, but either way I'm not gonna be able to find him in the fog. We'll get some sleep and I promise we'll look for him in the morning."

"You told Mom you were gonna look for him right now."

"I never said that. I told her I'd look for him, and I will. It just makes more sense to wait till morning."

"No."

"What?"

"No. If you won't look for him now, I'll do it by myself."

Brandon gave Maddy a look she'd seen a million times before. He was trying not to lose his patience and she knew it, but she also knew that Bear might be long gone by morning. Or he might need a veterinarian right away. Brandon shook his head and attacked the bed again and finally opened it up, but it was too close to the wall and there was a loud *thump* as the corner of the frame punched a triangular hole through the drywall. He hopped back and looked at Maddy, his eyes wide. There was an answering *thump* from the other side of the wall, someone pounding at them to be quiet. She almost laughed, would have if she weren't so worried about Bear.

"Fine," Brandon said. "I'll look."

"Me too," Maddy said. "I'm helping."

"Absolutely not. You stay right here where I know you're safe."

"Dad!"

"I'm not kidding."

"If he's hurt, he won't come to you. He won't come to you, anyway. You don't know his secret language, and he doesn't know you."

"Well, what am I supposed to say to him then?"

"Let me help," she said. "I'm gonna be all worried anyway. It's not like I'll be able to sleep."

Brandon had always been a pushover when it came to his daughter. "Fifteen minutes we'll look, but if we don't find your dog in fifteen minutes, that's it, okay?"

"Okay." She had no intention of quitting before they found Bear, but she was willing to say whatever she needed to in order to get her dad moving.

Brandon took another look at the rollaway and sniffed, then led the way out of the room to the elevator. On the ride down he looked her over and frowned.

"Wish we had something better for you to wear. We get down there, you stay in the lobby where it's warm. I'll scout around a bit and see if I can spot your dog."

"I'll just go right outside, under that arch, okay?"

"Maddy, could you just do what I say without all the argument?"

"Probably not, Dad."

"Stay in the lobby. And tell me what I need to say if I see the dog."

"His name's Bear."

"Okay."

"Tell him this, say *amiko*. It means *friend*. That way he'll trust you."

"*Amiko?*"

"Right."

"Not sure that's gonna help, since I shot at him already."

"Yeah," Maddy said, "there's a pretty good chance he's gonna eat you."

The elevator doors opened and they stepped out into the lobby. Without saying a word, Brandon pointed at the couch next to the registration counter, ordering her to sit, and she veered off in that direction. Brandon walked to the revolving door and out. The hipster came out of his back room and smiled at her.

"How's that rollaway working for you? Not too lumpy, I hope."

She put a finger to her lips, motioning for him to be quiet, and she went to the emergency door, pushed the bar as slowly and quietly as she could, and slipped outside. The fog seemed like it was lifting, but she thought the air felt colder and wetter than it had before. She went to the fountain where she had told Bear to stay and walked around it, bent low, looking for tracks in the snow. She saw the dog's big paw prints and followed them around the fountain, back toward the doors, then away again. There was a black smudge in the snow, and she scowled at it, kept walking slowly with her head down and saw another dark spot, then more. She knelt, her knees immediately freezing cold, and poked one of the spots, brought her hand up to her face. Her fingers were wet and red.

"Dad!"

Brandon came running, slipping and sliding past the big window. "I told you to stay in—"

"Dad, it's blood. He's hurt."

"Let me—"

Brandon started to bend down, and Maddy saw someone move behind him, coming around the other side of the fountain. The fog made her think it was the hipster at first, but when the person got closer she recognized the man who had broken into her house. He was holding something that looked like a length of metal pipe.

"Dad!"

Her father looked up at her and started to turn around just as the other man brought the pipe down hard on Brandon's head. Brandon fell forward into the snow. The man pointed at Maddy with the pipe.

"You're a real pain in the ass, kid, you know that?"

# 12

Skottie took a helpless look around her. The house was a shambles. Curtains blew into the living room in the breeze through the broken picture window, the TV was turned onto its screen on the floor, and Emmaline's best armchair was upended. Also there was a white man on the kitchen floor with his wrists handcuffed and his ankles bound together with duct tape. Christian Puckett was sitting upright with his back against the dishwasher, his head hanging down and his legs sticking straight out in front of him at an awkward angle. Emmaline leaned against the kitchen counter across from him. She looked up when Skottie entered, her eyes wide with worry.

"Maddy?"

"She's okay," Skottie said.

"Oh, thank God," Emmaline said. "You found her?"

"She's with Brandon."

Emmaline shook her head. "That don't mean she's okay."

"C'mon, Mom."

"This ain't legal," Christian said. "I got rights."

"You want me to call the police?" Skottie said.

Christian looked away and sniffed. His nose was running, and Skottie could see damp traces of tears on his cheeks.

"'Cause if I call the police, they're probably gonna ask you what you were doing here in the first place," Skottie said.

"Just let me go, man."

"Maybe after you tell me what you were after."

"Ain't telling you shit."

Emmaline kicked him.

"Mom," Skottie said. "Be careful you don't leave any bruises."

Skottie went back to the living room and picked up her mother's chair. She moved it out of the breeze from the window and tipped the television upright. She pulled both her own phone and Maddy's from her pocket and set the broken phone on an end table. At least Maddy was safe with Brandon. She felt a delayed wave of relief and gratitude toward her husband. He had definitely earned an invitation to Thanksgiving dinner, provided Emmaline could be talked into letting him in the house. The thought of Thanksgiving dinner made Skottie feel how tired she was, and suddenly she wanted nothing more than to crawl into bed with a glass of wine and sleep for two or three days.

Her phone rang.

"Skottie here."

"Skottie, this is Keith."

"Keith?"

"Your boss. This is my landline."

"Right. Yeah, I was expecting . . ." She switched the phone to her other ear and went to the kitchen door. "I'm sorry, Lieutenant, I forgot to call you back. A lot's going on here. Maddy . . . My daughter's okay. She's with her father."

"Did he take her? This a domestic kidnapping?"

"No, she ran off and he found her."

"She . . . Great, okay." He didn't sound happy. "I better call some people back, let everybody know the situation's resolved itself there. Except you had a break-in, right?"

"Right."

"So you need to get hold of the local cops so they can get a report from you. Go ahead and tell them about one of their guys working for the Burden County sheriff. You have any idea what they wanted?"

"I don't know what they were after, sir."

Emmaline gestured to her.

"Hang on a second, sir." Skottie lowered the phone. "What, Mom?"

Emmaline pointed at the deputy on the floor. "They thought they could scare you."

"How do you know that?"

"I stepped on his knees."

"Mom!"

Emmaline waved her off. "He'll be all right."

"Did he say what it's all about?"

"No, but I could step on him again."

"Never mind, I think I have a pretty good idea." She put the phone back up to her ear. "Sir? Sorry about that."

"This related to the Nazi hunter thing, Skottie?"

"Yes, sir. I think it is. They're trying to scare me off the investigation."

"There *is* no investigation. Not officially. And if there were, threatening you wouldn't help them."

"I think these guys have a long history of getting away with things. I don't think they ever considered they might get tripped up, and they're panicking now."

Keith grunted. "Damn, Skottie."

"I know, sir. You told me to stay out of all this, but things were already in motion."

"Look." He paused, and Skottie had begun to think the connection had dropped when he spoke again. "Take the morning off. Take a few days off, okay? I'm gonna get someone to cover for you."

"I can work, sir."

"No, you can't. I'm serious. You're on vacation until I tell you otherwise. Got it?"

"I don't have vacation days yet."

"So it's unofficial."

"Sir—"

"I'll call you back after the holiday. We'll sort this out."

"Yes, sir."

She hung up and stared at her phone, feeling slightly dizzy and nauseated. A text had come in from Travis while she was talking to the lieutenant.

NEW INFO. ON MY WAY TO YOU.

She didn't bother to text back. The dizzy feeling was being rapidly replaced by anger and frustration. She hadn't done anything wrong, but she was dangerously close to losing her job. She needed to take control of her situation, find the man pulling the strings, and put him down before he could cause more trouble for her.

"Baby?"

Skottie looked up at Emmaline and tried to smile. "It'll be okay, Mom."

"I know it will be. In your whole life, you never let anybody drag you down, and you sure ain't gonna start now."

Skottie's smile felt genuine, if only for a second. She took a deep breath. On her way out of the kitchen she turned back. "Mom? You can step on him again if you want."

## OCTOBER 2018

R ansom Roan opened his eyes with difficulty and tried to sit up.
"You're finally awake," Rudy said.

"What the hell?" Ransom strained against the leather straps buckled tight around his wrists and ankles. He was bound to a metal table in a brightly lit concrete chamber that looked like a bunker.

"Bless you for trying," Rudy said. "You're not going to break those straps."

Ransom forced himself to relax, to conserve his energy. "Hello, Rudolph Bormann."

Rudy shook his head. "I haven't been that person in a long time. But I remember him the way you remember *einen alten Schulfreund.*"

"You call yourself Goodman now."

"That's who I am."

Ransom glanced back down at the metal table and then around the room, looking for anything that might give him a clue as to his whereabouts. His eyes locked on a drooling man who sat hunched on a stool in the corner.

"Excuse me," Rudy said. "I should introduce you to my friend

Kenny. Kenny, this is Mr. Roan. Mr. Roan, this is Kenny. You needn't bother conversing with Kenny. He lacks a brain."

"How do you know who I am?"

Rudy held up Ransom's wallet. "I looked up your Noah Roan Foundation. It's funny, you'd think I would have heard of it. But I suppose I've been too busy to care what you people have been doing."

"Whether you have heard of us matters very little."

"You should be very proud of yourself. What you do, sneaking around, spying on people."

"I am proud," Ransom said. "And you must know I am not the only one hunting you."

"Hunting? As if you have some real purpose or power? As if I'm the deer and you are the wolf, circling and sniffing after me?" Rudy threw Ransom's wallet at him and slammed his fist on the metal table. "No! I am the wolf, not you. I am the hunter and I am also the healer. I take life and I give it. I bring down the weak and the worthless, the Jew and the black, and I will teach you to respect me."

"Rudolph, *no one* respects you. At least, nobody worth knowing. You run a church full of mouth breathers who do not have the foggiest idea who you really are. I know all about you. Your army out there, they are all sheep, too stupid or unaware to know what you really think of them."

Rudy sat back and composed himself. "You're right about one thing. They are sheep. But they're *my* sheep, my flock, and I am their shepherd."

"They would follow anyone. When I arrest you, they will find someone else to follow. And there will always be someone willing to exploit their gullibility."

Rudy smirked. "Neither of us is going anywhere, Mr. Roan. If anyone is gullible, it's you. You seem to be under the impression you're going to walk out of here unscathed. I assure you, that's not the case."

"If you were going to hurt me, you would already have done so. As you say, it has been a long time since the camps. I am not so sure you want to slide back into your old ways. Life has been good for you in America, and you would not want to jeopardize that, would you?"

Rudy swiveled in his chair and picked up a red rag from a cart next to him, revealing an array of silver instruments beneath it. He dabbed at his eyes with the rag. "You amuse me, Mr. Roan. May I call you Ransom?"

Ransom looked at the instruments on the cart. "Perhaps I misjudged you. After the camps, you kept it up? The torture? The killing?"

"The camps were only a stop along the way. I've always had my work, my studies." Rudy scowled. "Tell me, how many others like me have you found out there?"

"I have found seven of you."

"Impressive."

"And my research has helped others. As I said, they will hunt you. If I disappear, someone else will find you. My investigation into you is on file with the Foundation. You cannot stop this by killing me."

"No." Rudy stood up and walked away toward the corner of the room opposite Kenny, who was watching something imaginary crawl up the wall. Rudy stretched his arms high over his head and groaned. "I strained my back lifting you into the van, Mr. Roan. I might be getting too old."

"You are going to be subpoenaed and dragged out into the light," Ransom said. "You will be hounded and vilified and spat upon until you are finally deported. You will lose everything you have built here, and when you find yourself back in Germany, you will most likely be put in prison. If it is any consolation, you will probably die of old age before you are convicted of your crimes."

"Then why come after me at all?" Rudy started back toward the table. "Why not let me be?"

"You mean nothing to me as a person. I had not even heard of you before a witness came forward. But you are a symbol of the evil that men do. You represent an ugly time in our shared history, and it helps to see you brought down."

"Helps who?"

"Everyone. Society."

"*Your* society?"

"You have to know this is wrong. All of this." Ransom's gaze took in the entire basement room, the cart, the metal table, the sound-proofed concrete walls, poor Kenny. Even the old yellowed poster with the struggling cat on a tree branch. "Or maybe not. Maybe you like this ugly little room."

"This room is my sanctuary."

Rudy picked up electric clippers from the tray and turned them on. He raised his voice, ensuring that Ransom would hear him over the buzzing sound that echoed off the cinder-block walls.

"Killing is not my ultimate goal," Rudy said, "but I don't shrink from it."

He moved to the head of the table where Ransom could no longer see him. Ransom felt a tug at his scalp and the cold business end of the clippers.

"I am a student," Rudy said. "Yes, even at my age. When we stop learning, we might as well go ahead and die, don't you think?"

"And what will you learn from my death?"

"I had actually hoped to keep you alive. You present a number of problems for me. As you say, you've come to arrest me. Obviously, I can't let you do that."

Ransom saw a clump of hair, long and silver, land on the floor next to the table, and he shivered.

"If you kill me," he said, "my sons will come for you."

"And if I kill them?"

"You cannot kill everyone, Rudolph."

"Yes, yes, an unending wave of Nazi hunters will come. How did you find me, by the way?"

"You made the same sorts of mistakes you people always make."

Rudy cleared his throat. "You said there was a witness? Someone from the camps saw me?"

Ransom shook his head. "No."

"I think so. When I have finished with you, I will find this witness and dispose of him. Or is it a woman?"

"No witness." The pile of hair was building. Ransom wondered how long it would take him to grow it back. He wondered if he'd have the chance.

"I can't spend the rest of my life in disgrace or in prison, Mr. Roan. Surely you understand that."

"Whatever you do, that is the inevitable end of this. Unless you die first. You could kill yourself, you know. You have enough tools in here to do yourself in many times over."

Rudy chuckled and the buzzing sound stopped. "No. That's not what these tools are for. You've met Kenny. Kenny, show Mr. Roan your scar."

The drooling man came to attention at the sound of his name. He jerked forward and pulled his hair back so that the arc of scar tissue at his temple was visible.

Ransom looked away. "You did that to him?"

"Thank you, Kenny," Rudy said. "That will be enough. Why don't you go upstairs and play with the girls? Go upstairs, Kenny. Hold the railing so you don't fall." He moved back into view and set the clippers on the tray. He looked at Ransom and smiled. "I should make him wear a helmet, he falls down so often. But I don't suppose there's much left for a helmet to protect."

Ransom pulled at his straps again and tried to push himself away from the table. Rudy sat back and watched until Ransom had exhausted himself.

"To answer your question," Rudy said, "yes, I did that to him. Or *for* him, depending on your point of view. He was a desperately unhappy man, and now he's cheerful. He doesn't talk much, but he still knows a handful of words and he has a smile for everyone he encounters. He helps out at the church when he can, doing menial work—sweeping the floors, picking up between the pews, that sort of thing. So who's to say his operation was such a bad thing for him?"

Ransom closed his eyes and concentrated on his breathing. He felt a sudden certainty that he was not going to escape this time. The Foundation would send someone after him, but it would be too late. Ransom wondered which of his remaining children would follow him to Kansas. Would it be Judah or Travis? Poor Travis had been through so much already, and he was finally dealing with his anger issues. It would be better if Judah came. Judah was stronger.

When Rudy started talking again, his voice was soft and thoughtful. Ransom could barely hear him. "Did you know I was struck by lightning two times, Mr. Roan? Two times is a lot when we talk about lightning. It's rare, but it happens. I'd be willing to bet you've never been struck by lightning even once. But there's a man in South Carolina who's been hit ten times. A park ranger in Virginia was struck seven times. You see, when it hits someone, it's more likely to hit them again. And no one seems to know why, but if you ask any of us, those of us in this special club, we could tell you. It has chosen us, marked us. Look here. Come on, take a look."

Ransom opened his eyes. Rudy rolled up his sleeve and turned his arm back and forth under the fluorescent lamps. Vivid blue scars snaked down toward his wrist, forking out from a thick central line, like the branches of an upside-down tree or a simplified coral formation.

"See that? The lightning etched itself on my skin, like a tattoo, like a brand. Letting me know that it owns me. But maybe I own it, too." He rolled his sleeve back down and patted Ransom on the shoulder. "For some people, Mr. Roan, the lightning hurts them, damages them physically and psychologically. But for others, like myself, it changes them for the good, gifts them with insight and energy. Isn't it possible that one man's torture is another man's freedom? You say I'm a symbol of evil, but who are you to decide that sort of thing?"

"I am not the one who decided that." He was going to say something more, but Ransom's throat had closed so that it was painful to speak.

Rudy waved his hand at the ceiling. "Up there is my church. And it wouldn't exist without my talents."

"A talent for hurting people? For killing?"

"If the lightning chooses a person, I can heal them, transfer a small part of my energy to them. I do *good* in this world, which brings us back to the subject of you. I can't let you stop my ministry before I'm ready."

"Rudolph—"

"You said you have sons?"

"They have caught monsters as delusional as you."

"I have sons as well. Or I did. At least Heinrich stayed with the church. But you must understand the concept of a legacy. Having work that matters and someone to carry on the work." Rudy moved the cart closer to him and examined the tools arrayed there. "But I worry that despite Heinrich's best intentions, my ministry will disappear after I die. People are drawn to the church because of my abilities. Will they still come if there's no one here to help them, to take away their pain? I don't know the answer to that question. Do you?"

"Enough of this," Ransom said. "Unbuckle these straps."

"I had an idea a few years ago," Rudy said. "A vision. It was after the second time the lightning came to me. I was fearful at first. I knew it would come again. It would never stop. I would never be able to relax, because at any moment I would be struck again. But maybe there was a reason for it all. Maybe I was being given more energy than I needed so I could pass it on to someone else. And when I do that, I can finally end all this, I can silence whatever's in me that calls the lightning. The energy will move on to someone else and let me be. Its legacy will be preserved, and so will mine."

"Do you ever get sick of your own voice?"

"Don't be rude. The problem is that lightning is unpredictable. I can't very well ask people to stand with me under a tree in a storm and hope that something amazing might take place. I need a way to control the transfer of electricity, to directly affect a man's brain. But how? And what part of the brain?"

He pointed to a short tool with an electric cord. It looked like a wood burner that had been altered and glued back together.

"I made that myself. It provides a charge that I can direct. I touch a person's brain with lightning, and perhaps someday I'll create another like myself."

"That does not . . ." Ransom needed water, his throat burned and fought him, but he forced the words out. "You are not magic. That is madness. You use the power of suggestion to dupe people into following you, into thinking they have been cured of whatever they bring to you."

Rudy sat back on his stool and a thoughtful expression drifted across his face. "Yes, I have thought of that. Perhaps the migraines go away when the boy thinks they will go away. Perhaps the girl wakes from her coma because she hears someone tell her to do so and she believes it is time. It is what you call the placebo effect, right? If you have enough faith in the cure, your own brain will convince your body to cure itself. Something like that. But even if you are correct and this is what I'm doing, does it negate the work itself?" Rudy shook his head. "No, the lightning works, one way or another. Understanding it is a *human* requirement, Mr. Roan."

"And what do you think you are, some kind of god?"

"Oh, I am very human. All saints are human at first. And I didn't say I had no need of understanding, it's just that I need to understand different things than you do. For instance, I would like to understand *you.*"

Rudy reached for the cart. He pulled it closer and picked up a short electric saw. He held it up for Ransom to see and he winked. "This comes later. For the skull." He set the saw back down on the cart and selected a scalpel. "But first this."

## CHAPTER TEN

## 1

The parking lot of the Hays Walmart was nearly empty, stretching to the white-frosted grass at the edge of the highway. They had left Travis's rented Jeep outside the compound and Sheriff Goodman had driven to Hays, where they parked close to the store and got out of the silver cruiser. The moon through the clouds had burnished the sky to a pearly sheen, but lightning lit up the horizon far out beyond the overpass.

"Big storm coming," Goodman said.

Travis nodded. Kansas was living up to its reputation and he had resigned himself to the idea that the day could bring any kind of weather.

"Still don't see why we need to stop off here," Goodman said. "I got the rifle and shotgun in the car. You're welcome to whichever of those. And you got your automatic."

"I do not know how many people I will need to shoot before I find my father. I would not care to run out of bullets."

"I know a guy not too far from here can set you up with just about any weapon you want."

"We are here already."

An old man in a blue apron smiled at them as they entered. "Happy Thanksgiving," he said. "Got your turkey yet? Need help finding anything?"

·"I know where it is," Goodman said.

"Thank you," Travis said to the man. He followed Goodman to the back of the store, past displays of snow tires and Christmas decorations, toy cars and furnace filters. He knew they were in the right department when the aisles of golf clubs and sleeping bags gave way to compound bows and shotgun shells. There was a long glass counter showcasing knives and scopes of varying lengths and an array of shotguns and rifles on view in a larger glass case behind it. An employee saw them and approached. He had a neatly trimmed salt-and-pepper goatee, and his apron had been recently starched.

"You fellas looking for anything in particular?" He moved behind the counter.

"Yes," Travis said. "I would like a Remington shotgun, the 870 Express, and the Winchester 54." He shifted his attention to the glass case in front of him, where knives sat cradled between dark felt runners. "I will also require the Buck Special there. The six-inch blade, please, with the sheath, and the PakLite Skinner. What is your best scope for the Winchester?"

The man blinked at him.

"Leave the Winchester," Goodman said. He spoke to the employee. "What's your name, sir?"

He pointed at his name tag. "Caleb."

"Caleb, my friend doesn't know what he wants, so I'll order for him. He's gonna want that Weatherby up there, not the Winchester."

"But I do want the Winchester," Travis said.

"The Weatherby's gonna outperform it."

"I am buying the rifle for short-term use," Travis said. "I am comfortable with the Winchester."

Goodman held up his hands, backing out of the argument.

Travis turned back to the employee. "Caleb, please also give me the Colt semiauto, the .270 Short Magnums, and a half-dozen magazines, if you have them. I will require a rain suit, a good pair of binoculars, an adequate bow, along with arrows and a quiver for them, and a machete."

"That's a whole lotta gear," Caleb said. "What're you hunting?"

"What is in season right now?"

"Um, wild turkey, but those firearms are gonna blow a turkey all to hell. Deer season doesn't open for a few more days."

"I am getting an early start," Travis said. "Do you have anything that might punch through a cinder-block wall?"

"Um, what?"

"Never mind."

Goodman cleared his throat. "He's not from around here, but I'll vouch for him." He flashed his badge and winked at Caleb.

"Thanks, Sheriff."

"All right," Goodman said. "Let's get this show on the road."

"I'm gonna need you to register first," Caleb said, turning a countertop computer around. "Just fill out the form there. Only takes about a half hour to hear back. They most always okay people, no problem."

"I told you, Doc," Goodman said. "I got a friend can hook you up easier than this."

Travis smiled at him. "But this is one-stop shopping."

# 2

Skottie heard footsteps on the porch. She put down the roll of tape she was using to seal up the broken front window, grabbed her Glock from the end table, and went to the door. Travis stepped over the threshold.

"I apologize for the hour," he said, "but I need your assistance. The situation has escalated."

"We're all wide awake here."

He caught the door before she could close it. "I brought a . . . Well, I brought someone else who might be helpful."

He gestured and Sheriff Goodman stepped into the light from the open door. He had his hat in his hands, and his thin hair was flying about in the breeze. "Trooper Foster," he said. "Good evening to you."

"Travis," Skottie said, "have you lost your mind?" She kept her gun down at her side, but she was extremely conscious of its weight in her hand.

Before Travis could say anything, Goodman held up a hand. "Ma'am, I know you and me didn't hit it off, but I never meant any harm to you. And I think I might already be a part of this situation you got."

"And what situation is that?"

"Well, now you mention it, I'm not so sure what *your* connection is to all this. But I got two dead bodies up in my county. And this fella's missing his dad." He pointed his thumb at Travis. "So we got a stake in this."

"I have spoken with the sheriff and I believe he has—"

Skottie cut him off. "My connection? Look at this place. *Somebody* must think I'm involved."

"What happened?" Goodman's lips were pulled tight, and without his hat he looked somehow vulnerable. Skottie realized she wanted Goodman to argue with her, wanted someone she could push back against and yell at. But it was clear that he wasn't jockeying for position.

"We had a break-in." Skottie sighed. "Come on. You're letting in all the cold."

Goodman entered and closed the door behind him. He looked around and raised his eyebrows at the sight of the plastic bags billowing into the room. Skottie and Emmaline had vacuumed up the broken glass and set the couch upright again, but duct tape and plastic garbage bags were the best solution they had come up with to temporarily replace the big window.

"Are you all right?" Travis said.

"Yeah."

"Your daughter?"

"She's with her father."

"And where is Bear?" Travis was looking around as if his dog might be hiding behind a door, waiting to spring out and surprise him.

"He's with Maddy," Skottie said. She hoped that was true. She hadn't spoken to Brandon since he'd told her the dog was lost and wounded. "We caught one of the intruders." Skottie motioned for them to follow her and led the way into the kitchen, where Emmaline was leaning on the counter, her shotgun still aimed in the general direction of Christian Puckett's head. "Sheriff, I think you two have met."

Goodman made a sound like a gasp and a cough uttered at the same time. He took a step back and balled up his fists, torqued his body, and pulled his arm back. A second before he punched the wall, he took a deep breath and opened his hands.

He spoke to Skottie without looking at her. His gaze was fixed on the pots and pans hanging from a rack above the oven. "Sorry. Don't mean to cause you more trouble. This boy broke into your house?"

Skottie nodded.

"Nobody got hurt?"

"Well, *he* did. And one of the other guys might've cut himself. There's blood."

"You sure he wasn't trying to stop them other fellas?"

"Sheriff—"

He held his hands up in a gesture of surrender. "Okay, I believe you. But this is—"

"So I guess you didn't send him here," Skottie said.

Goodman glared at her. "Ma'am." He tipped his hat at Emmaline before turning his attention back to his deputy. "Nephew, what're you doing in this nice lady's house?"

Christian glowered up at him, but didn't speak.

"Heinrich put you up to this?"

The deputy looked away.

"What's my brother want with these people?"

There was no answer.

"I surely do wish you'd turned out worth a damn." Goodman looked at Skottie. "Tell me, how'm I supposed to explain this to my sister?"

"I'm sure she knows her son's no good."

"Don't make it easier to say it out loud. What're you gonna do with him?"

"As soon as I arrest him, I'll have to take him in and explain what happened here. That might get me in some trouble with my boss right now."

"You know what he was doing here?"

"I think they were trying to run me out of town, but I want to find out more from him before I do anything. My lieutenant is gonna want details, and I don't have any."

"Well, it don't look like my nephew wants to talk to nobody just yet. Maybe when his bladder starts cramping up you'll get him in a gabby mood."

They left Emmaline to her lonely vigil and returned to the living room.

"Mind if I sit? Been a long night," Goodman said.

Skottie motioned toward the couch and Goodman lowered himself with a sigh that he dragged up from somewhere deep in his body. Then he took the pistol off his belt and leaned forward, put it on the end table nearer to Skottie than himself. Goodman held his empty hands up in a gesture of peace. He took off his hat, put it on the back of the couch behind him, sat back, and crossed his legs.

"Now," he said. "I'm hoping me and you can bury the hatchet here so we can go after the killer of that woman at the lake and the fella in the tractor fire. Could be my hands are officially tied. But maybe we can help each other out."

Skottie put her Glock on the table next to the sheriff's pistol, and a moment later Travis took his Eclipse out of its holster and set it with the other two weapons. Three chunks of metal that were largely useless without a hand to point them.

"What is it you want?" Skottie said.

"Take a look at this," Travis said.

He sat next to Goodman on the couch and handed a file folder to Skottie. She took it and sat across from him in Emmaline's best armchair. The manila folder had the Noah Roan Foundation logo embossed on the front, and there was a label on the tab that read *BORMANN.*

"They are holding my father captive," Travis said.

"Who is?"

"My dad's church," Goodman said.

"Purity First?"

"That's the one."

"You know that for a fact?"

"I have not seen him," Travis said, "but Reverend Goodman is using my father as leverage against me. Against the Foundation."

"You need to call the authorities," Skottie said.

"Ma'am, I *am* the authority," Goodman said.

"So what's this?" She opened the folder and looked at the first densely typed, single-spaced page on Roan Foundation letterhead.

"Each of us has information," Travis said, "and I need everything I can get if I am to plan what to do. I have to find out if my father is even still alive."

"This is your whole file on the Nazi?"

Travis leaned forward and tapped the letterhead. "You see, Ruth Elder's death probably would have caused our investigation to dead-end if we had known, but since we had no idea our witness was dead, we kept poking around. While my father was out here doing the leg-work on this, my mother was busy trying to corroborate and strengthen the claim against Bormann from our end. And yesterday she found a second witness."

Which Skottie could see for herself. The second page in the file was a list of names culled from a newsletter subscription pool. The sixth name on the list was circled: Winnie Shrimplin.

"Armed with Ruth Elder's information, Rudolph Bormann's name, and the camp he was assigned to in the war, my mother went looking for other survivors who might remember him. We try to keep track of everyone who came out of the camps, everyone who might be willing to help us. Winnie Shrimplin was briefly in Ravensbrück but was shipped out to Mauthausen-Gusen, probably on the same train that took Ruth Elder."

"Where is she now?"

"Living in Spain. She is not well enough to travel. But we do not really need her here. Earlier this evening, I sent photos of two men to my mother and she passed them along to Mrs. Shrimplin. We are waiting to hear back from her. It has been a long time, of course, but it is possible she will be able to make a positive ID from one of those pictures."

"You said Sheriff Goodman's dad is holding your dad," Skottie said. "So that's the Nazi, right?"

"Undoubtedly."

"But you still need another witness?"

"To connect him to the war crimes, yes."

"Where'd you get the pictures?"

"From the church," Goodman said. "My brother, Heinrich, hangs this stuff in the hallway. He's in charge of the church now. The guy with the glasses is my dad. The other guy's my uncle Jacob. Not my real uncle, but he was my dad's best friend for as long as I can remember. He died a few years back, and Dad doesn't leave the house or church grounds much since that happened. If what the doc says is true, my dad pretty much has to be this Bormann guy you all are looking for."

Skottie turned the page and looked at printouts of the photos Travis had taken. They were pictures of pictures, blown up and grainy with a smeared reflection of overhead lights across them, but the men's features were clear. Neither of them looked familiar to her, but she stared hard at them anyway, trying to see something evil in their eyes or in the set of their jaws. She paid special attention to the man with glasses, wondered what Goodman was feeling, knowing what his father must have been. Finally she turned them over and moved on.

"I thought you said there were two pictures," she said. "Who's this?" She held up a third printout of a man slightly younger than the first two. He looked vaguely familiar to her, but she couldn't place him.

"That," Travis said, "is Dr. Joseph Odek."

"I know that name."

"He is definitely not Bormann, but he is . . . Well, he is a very bad man just the same, and if the church is somehow tied to him . . ."

"He's from South Africa," Skottie said.

"Yes," Travis said. "He has been arrested twice for human trafficking and poaching, but he managed to skate away both times."

"He was on the news."

"He has been on our radar for a very long time." Travis's voice was even lower than usual, and he seemed to be forcing his words out through clenched teeth. "I even met him once."

Skottie's eyes opened wide. "Is that who cut you? Your throat?"

"Odek is a problem for another day," Travis said. "But I would very much like to find out how Bormann knows him."

"What kind of doctor is he?"

"Why?"

"If Odek's a doctor, maybe he did something at the camps," Skottie said.

"He is too young," Travis said. "I believe he was a medical doctor at one time, but he found better ways to make money. Better for him."

"Does that . . . I mean, what kind of—"

A familiar tune started playing in the dining room. Justin Timberlake's "Cry Me a River," her ringtone for Brandon. The phone had slipped down onto a chair and it took Skottie a minute to find it, but just as she picked it up, it stopped ringing. She opened her recent history and saw that the call had indeed come from Brandon. She decided he could wait. She returned to the living room, sat back down, and kept the phone in her lap on top of the file folder.

"Sorry," she said. "Can I ask you something?"

"What is it?" Travis said.

"I asked you before what kind of doctor you were and you changed the subject."

"Does it really matter?"

"Not really. But I'm curious."

"I am a doctor of theology." Travis waved a hand in the air, and something about the gesture made Skottie think he wanted a cigarette. "God and morality and that sort of thing."

"Why didn't you just say so?"

"My views have evolved over time and are complicated. I do not share them lightly."

Skottie looked at him a moment longer, then turned her eyes down, back to the file. "Anyway, there's not a lot of new information in here."

Travis narrowed his eyes. "It is a pending investigation," he said.

"I didn't mean anything by that," Skottie said.

"No, you are right. I am tired and I am worried. When the file was put together, we were waiting for more information from my father."

His eyes held a brittle sheen, and Skottie almost reached out to pat his hand. She stopped herself and shook her head again.

"I only meant I think I can add to this," she said. "I did some digging of my own. You know Ruth Elder was with someone at the café when she saw Rudolph Bormann."

"Yes," Travis said. "Her friend Peggy."

"And Peggy's a nickname for Margaret. One of Maddy's books has characters in it who are twins, but they turn out to be the same person: Peggy and Margaret."

"Margaret Weber was Ruth's friend Peggy?"

"I think so."

"Then we must assume Bormann killed Mrs. Weber because Ruth told her something."

"Which gives us a motive."

"I'm still having trouble with this," Goodman said. "If you told me somebody in my family was a Nazi, I'd guess it was Heinrich, not my dad."

Travis nodded. "I am sorry."

"Besides, my dad's not exactly a young guy. Hard to see him running around killing people."

"Look, it was Margaret Weber's son who burned up in that tractor fire. He was just identified a few hours ago."

"He was murdered," Travis said. It wasn't a question.

"The coroner hasn't officially determined that," Skottie said. "But yeah."

"So are we thinking the Nazi killed our witness? Then killed the witness's friend, and then killed the friend's son? Why the son?"

"Maybe Margaret told her son about Bormann, or maybe he didn't have any idea what was going on, but he tried to protect her or went looking for her and stumbled on something. When was the last time you heard from your dad?"

"Two days after he arrived in Kansas," Travis said. "He talked to Ruth Elder, and she had described Rudolph Bormann. She told my father her story, or parts of it. Enough that we were able to go to work at our end, my mother was, and find our second witness in Spain. My father was supposed to call again after he had scouted this area a bit."

"But he didn't."

"No," Travis said. "Which is unusual for him."

"He was supposed to check in with Ruth Elder again, too. When she didn't hear anything from him, she wrote everything down in a diary and hid it among her things for her daughter to find."

"Why go to so much trouble? If she wanted my father to have the information, why hide it?"

"In case Bormann got to her first," Skottie said. "Remember, she was trained in shorthand so she could help in the war effort, but German officers couldn't necessarily read it. Then for years after, it became a secret language between her and her daughter. She was trying to make sure her account of things would outlast her. She must have been terrified."

"And rightly so."

Skottie nodded. "But could a ninety-year-old man do all this?"

"How old was Wes Weber?"

"Had to be a lot younger than ninety. Unless Bormann snuck up on him and pushed him off a cliff, then dragged his body into a tractor to burn it . . . Well, I don't buy it."

"So he has some help," Goodman said. "My brother?"

"I think he has a whole army of helpers."

"The church?"

Her phone rang. Brandon's number again. She swiped the green button to answer.

"Brandon? Maddy okay?"

There was a hesitation before the person at the other end responded. "Was Brandon the fat guy?"

Skottie stopped breathing. "Who is this?"

"You need to listen real careful now."

"No, you listen to me—"

The connection ended. Skottie stared at the phone, then looked up at the room. Travis and Sheriff Goodman were watching her.

# 3

"What has happened?"

"Somebody just . . ." Skottie left off and shook her head. She could barely breathe. She pulled the last call up and dialed the number back. The phone rang once and a different male voice answered.

"Is this Skottie Foster?"

"What is this?" she said.

"I apologize for my friend, ma'am. He gets excited."

"Who are you?" Skottie held a finger up at Travis, who had stood and was hovering over her, trying to hear the other end of the conversation.

"Well, ma'am, I'd rather not say."

"What do you want?"

"You didn't call the police," said the man on the other end of the call. "Or they'd be here by now."

"No," Skottie said. The man had used the word *here*, which meant he was nearby, watching the house. She looked at the front door, then walked to the window and used her free hand to peel a strip of duct tape from the corner of the garbage bags that covered it. Travis saw what she was doing and went to the other side of the window. He cut a small slit in the plastic with a sharp knife that seemed to have appeared from nowhere. He put an eye up to the slit and peered out at the street.

The man on the phone kept talking. "He still there in your house? Our friend?"

"You mean Deputy Puckett?"

"He still alive?"

"Well, I didn't kill him yet, if that's what you're asking. But if you've done something to my daughter, I swear to God—"

"All right, ma'am. We haven't killed anybody, either. So let's say we arrange a trade. Your girl for our friend."

Travis took his eye away from the window and nodded to her. He moved quickly across the living room and into the kitchen. Goodman followed him, grabbing his hat from the back of the couch. Skottie felt a cold breeze as the back door opened and then heard the soft click of the latch as it shut behind them.

"You there?" The guy on the phone sounded nervous.

"Give me a second," Skottie said. "I don't understand what you want."

She heard the sound of muffled talking, the phone being dragged across cloth. Then the first guy was back on. "What's to understand, bitch? Give us Christian back and maybe you get to see your baby girl again, right? You get that?"

Faintly in the background, Skottie could hear the second guy. "Give me that back."

"You're not doing it right, Donnie. You gotta—"

"You just told her my name!"

Skottie felt the room spinning around her and she struggled to stay calm. They were obviously amateurs, and one of them was a little smarter than the other. The dumb guy needed to prove himself, a situation that could easily lead to violence. Brandon would no more lose his phone than he would lose his gun or his badge. Had they killed him to get it?

She interrupted the argument on the other end of the phone. "Let me talk to my husband." She hated herself for choosing Brandon. If she asked to talk to Maddy, the men would assume Maddy was most important to her and they might hurt her to get Skottie's cooperation. She was throwing Brandon under the bus, making him the bigger target, but he would do the same if it meant protecting their daughter.

The men were silent for a moment. Another burst of static noise. Then the smarter of the two answered. "He's, uh . . . They're not here with us."

"Where are they?"

"Don't worry. They're somewhere safe."

"How do I know—"

The man hollered and it sounded like he dropped the phone. She could hear snippets of anxious conversation.

"Who are you?"

"Gun it! Drive!"

"Oh, shit, Donnie, shit, man!"

There was the sound of an engine, a car door slamming, and someone shouting, his voice growing fainter in the background. Another car roared to life on the street outside the house. Skottie ran to the front door and opened it in time to see two sets of taillights at the corner, red dots in the mist, diminishing to pinpricks and fading away.

Goodman walked out of the darkness pulling something heavy behind him. As he drew closer, Skottie could see that he was dragging a young man who was crab-walking along, trying to keep up as the sheriff hauled him backward by his shirt collar. Goodman stopped and picked the kid up by the front of his shirt and heaved him up on the porch.

"There were two of them," Goodman said. "Watching your house from the street. The other one drove off, but the doc's following him in my cruiser."

"They have Maddy," Skottie said. "And my husband, Brandon."

"They weren't in that car," Goodman said. "None of 'em. There was just the two guys. I got the license number off their car. You wanna call it in, Trooper, or should I?"

The young man tore at his shirt, yanking it out of Goodman's grasp, and tried to scramble away, but the sheriff stomped on him, held him down with his foot while he lit a cigarette. "See this gun on my hip, youngster? Yeah, you see it. So stay put and stay quiet." Goodman put his lighter away and looked up at Skottie. "What do you say we ask this boy some hard questions?"

# 4

One of them was following him. Donnie had no idea what they'd done with Lance or Christian, but the trooper and her people were dangerous. The two big guys had come up on Donnie's car without a sound, opened the passenger door, and pulled Lance out without any trouble at all. Donnie hadn't wasted any time in getting away from there, but now they were right behind him.

He still had the phone he took from the trooper's husband, and he pulled up the keypad with his left thumb, glancing at the screen when he could. He kept the accelerator depressed as far as he dared, zooming through residential streets, moving into a quiet industrial neighborhood, passing the hotel where they'd snatched the girl and her dad. It took him three times to dial the right number, and he felt a tremendous wave of relief when he heard Heinrich Goodman's familiar voice.

"Who is this?"

"Deacon? This is Donnie. I'm in big trouble."

"Where are you calling from?"

"Um, I stole a phone."

"Good," Heinrich said.

"That trooper, it's her husband's phone."

"How did it go?"

"Things got complicated."

"Are you with the police?"

"No. I'm driving, but they're following me and I don't know where to go."

"Following you in a car? Tell me everything, but do it quickly, Donnie."

"Yeah, I'm in my car. We went in, but the trooper got Christian. So we grabbed her daughter and her husband."

"You have them?"

"I brought the girl in. You can ask the reverend."

"And the husband?"

"I stopped the truck and put the husband on it. He's gotta be half-way to Mexico by now."

"I'm not sure you should have done that, Donnie. Why didn't you call me before doing something so drastic?"

Donnie had wanted to handle things himself, to make the deacon proud. He had thought maybe Heinrich would promote him past the rank of acolyte. Maybe he would even get another audience with Reverend Rudy. "I don't know," he said. "I'm sorry."

"And the trooper is following you now? Looking for her child?"

"No, it's the other one, I think. The hunter. But there were two of them, maybe more. They have Christian and they have Lance, and I'm about out of gas."

"You can't lead them here, Donnie," Heinrich said. "You need to slow them down, create a distraction while I prepare the church for their coming."

Donnie's stomach somersaulted, and he felt beads of sweat breaking out on his forehead. "Where am I supposed to go?"

The deacon spoke slowly. "It's your time now. You've served your purpose and I commend you, but it's time to join the lightning."

"Are you sure?" Donnie could barely breathe.

"Do you have a weapon?"

"I got a gun I took off the trooper's husband."

"Good," Heinrich said. "Use it. Use it on as many of them as you can before you turn it on yourself. It will unnerve them, give us a psychological advantage and give me time. Go, Donnie. Go in glory."

Deacon Heinrich's voice was replaced by a terrible silence, and when Donnie glanced down at the phone again, he saw that the connection had been broken.

# 5

"You don't wanna talk," Sheriff Goodman said. "I get it."

Christian and Lance sat next to each other on the kitchen floor. Lance's arm was bleeding, but the sheriff had handcuffed his wrists behind his back. Skottie had tried appealing to the two young men, begging them to tell her where Maddy was, even showing them photos of her daughter in hopes of humanizing her for them. But they had adopted identical defiant stares, neither of them volunteering a single word. At last Goodman had stepped in.

He looked at Lance. "I seen you around, haven't I? What's your name?"

Lance shook his head.

"Nice friend you got, Christian," Goodman said. "Guess you met him at church, right?"

Both captives were quiet.

"Since you're not feeling chatty, how 'bout I do all the talking here and you just tell me if I'm right or not?" Goodman said. "And since you're not being cooperative, we'll make it interesting." He went to the living room and came back with his gun from the end table. He cocked his head to the side and shook it, holstered the pistol, and pulled out a stun gun from a clip on the other side of his belt. He held the stun gun up so they could see it and pressed a button on its side. An ominous buzzing sound filled the tiny kitchen.

"Yeah, that's more like it," he said. "These things hurt like a sonofabitch."

Skottie took him by the arm and led him around the corner, out of earshot of the two captives.

"This makes me uncomfortable," she said. She kept her voice low. "We don't torture people."

"You wanna get your daughter back," Goodman said. "So trust me."

"Why do you even care?"

"I'm just doing my job."

"I thought your job was keeping people like me from moving into the neighborhood."

"The hell with you." He turned and started to walk away, then turned back, holding the stun gun dangerously close to Skottie's face. "You're from Chicago, right? So you don't know me, and you sure as shit don't get to come out here and judge me."

"I was born here."

He took a step back. "I'm on your side here."

"It's the way you're going about it."

"I get that, but principles are a luxury at a time like this. They're for when your little girl is back with you."

He returned to the kitchen without waiting for her response. "Where were we? Oh, yeah. Maybe I can guess where the girl is. I been Burden County sheriff for a long time now. Christian, you know the score up there. That church runs the town, and the town runs the county, and the county pays me a whole lot of money to look the other way and make sure things go smooth for the church. Ain't that right?"

Christian said nothing, so Goodman moved in closer to the two men and pressed the button on the stun gun again. Both men jumped, and Goodman stepped back.

"Just testing this thing," he said. "Make sure the batteries still work. Anyway, y'know, I did what my dad and my uncle Jacob wanted me to do, but I grew up in Paradise Flats, ran around that lake up there with my friends, kissed my first girl, and married her, too. That's my home. My friends live up there. I know you get it, fellas. Your friends live there, too, right? Like that guy who just drove off and left you here?"

Christian spat at him, and Goodman buzzed the air near Christian's ear with the stun gun.

"Behave yourself, Nephew. Now, when my buddy Mike's little girl disappeared a couple years back, I got busy looking into that, until I got word I should stop looking. Now why, I wondered, would the church want me to stop looking for a missing kid? You got any idea about that or was it before you started working for my brother? Girl's name was Drew. Ring any bells?"

Christian looked away from him. Goodman arched an eyebrow at Lance, but got no response from him, either.

"Well, I got an idea or two, 'cause I been pokin' around. What I think, the church has a whole lotta you guys going around and finding kids, maybe some women, maybe even some men, I don't know. You're a good recruit for them, Christian. I bet that patrol car lets you get real close to kids." Goodman's voice grew tighter and deeper as he continued speaking. The muscles in his jaw tensed and rippled. He was shaking. "Do you use that official car I gave you to grab children off the street, Nephew?"

He leaned forward and touched the stun gun to Christian's throat. The younger man jerked and squealed, bucked against the handcuffs and duct tape, his head banging into the counter behind him. Skottie started forward, but Goodman held out his hand to stop her.

"I tell you? I never did find Mike's little girl."

Skottie took a deep breath. She stepped back and crossed her arms across her chest.

Goodman glared at Christian. "I think you boys hang around the bus stops and the mall down here, maybe you go all the way out to Wichita, for all I know, but you snatch kids up and you deliver them to the church. Maybe keep 'em in those houses all up and down the street over there until you got enough of 'em to make a package deal? Does my dad know about that part or is it just my brother? Your grandpa, is he the one put you up to this?" He shook his head. "I think you take these kids, you stick 'em in a truck and send 'em down to Mexico or thereabouts. I'm pretty sure about most of that. Part I'm not so sure about is the trip back. Does that truck bring Mexicans up this way? Sure a lot more Mexicans around here lately, working the kitchens at Chinese restaurants."

Goodman looked around Emmaline's kitchen like maybe he expected to see a Mexican worker. He sniffed and took a step closer to his nephew. "What do you think, huh? Am I at least close? In spitting distance?"

"I don't know what you're talking about," Christian said.

"Oh, hey, you *can* talk," Goodman said. "So I'm gonna ask you one more time. Where is Trooper Foster's daughter?"

Christian lunged forward, pushing off the counter, clearly intending to head-butt Goodman in the groin, but he fell short and thunked to the floor at his uncle's feet.

Goodman reached down with the stun gun and pressed the button again, watched Christian rise up and bounce off the floor. Goodman backed up and spat a brown gob at the deputy.

"No use to anyone."

He turned and left the kitchen, handing the stun gun to Skottie as he passed.

"Well, anyway," Goodman said, "that's what I think's going on up there, Trooper. I figure your girl's on a truck bound for Mexico right now."

# 6

The streets were dark and empty. Travis kept Goodman's silver cruiser a few yards behind the other car, just close enough to see it through the mist, but far enough back that he might not be noticed. Either the driver knew he was being followed, in which case fear and anxiety would lead him to make a mistake, or he didn't and he would lead Travis somewhere interesting. A frightened mouse scurries for his hole.

But the driver pulled into a vacant lot across from an abandoned gas station and shut off his headlights. Travis cruised past and circled around at the next intersection. The lights from a nearby building loomed through the fog. He drove slowly back down the street, going the opposite direction, and saw the driver was out of his car, standing in front of it with his arms out. He was holding a gun loosely in his right hand. No mouse hole for this one.

Travis pulled into the lot and parked four yards away. The man's eyes were closed and his lips were moving. Travis sat and counted to a hundred, waiting for the man to move. His Eclipse was back in Skottie's house on her end table and the weapons he had purchased from Walmart were locked in Goodman's trunk, out of reach for the moment. Travis opened his door and stepped out of the cruiser. His boots crunched on brown grass that had sprouted between cracks in the blacktop.

The other man opened his eyes. "What's your name?"

"Travis." He kept his hands out at his sides, showing the man he wasn't armed.

"You're the one who came to bust up the church," the man said. His voice was shaky.

"That was not my original intent, but it seems to be the course I am on. What do you call yourself?"

"My name's Donnie."

"Donnie, you could give me your gun and we could talk."

"I can't do that."

"Why not?"

"I got orders."

"From whom? Who gave you these orders?"

Donnie shook his head. "This is it for me," he said. "For you too, I guess."

He raised the gun and pointed it at Travis. Travis didn't move. "What will you do after you shoot me?"

"I guess that won't be any of your business," Donnie said. "What I do after you're dead." There was desperation in his voice, something Travis had heard before in people who thought they had reached the end of the road. He knew there was no way he could reason with Donnie; they were past all that. Whoever had given him his orders would probably never give another thought to Donnie, but his hold on the poor man was complete, and Donnie had clearly reached the end of his usefulness as far as his master was concerned. Travis felt a great sadness wash over him. Everything about the situation was ugly.

And Travis was standing exposed in an empty lot with no cover. He realized he had made a mistake in not considering how desperate Donnie might be. He could only hope poor visibility and fear would cause the man to miss his shot.

Travis had just begun to tense, watching Donnie for the moment he pulled the trigger, when the mist parted and a massive creature appeared from out of the darkness. It slammed into Donnie, who went down in a limp tangle of arms and legs, the gun skittering away across the pavement and stopping in a clump of dead weeds. It took a fraction of a second for the scene to change, and then it all came into focus again. Bear's jaws were fastened about Donnie, and the dog's massive head swept back and forth, slamming Donnie's body into the ground again and again.

"Bear!" Travis ran forward. *"Haltu!"*

Travis banged to his knees and Bear came to him, covered in blood. The dog snuffed at him, licked his face and knocked him over, nudged at him with his head. Travis felt through the fur for injuries and found a deep wound in the dog's withers, a groove running across the top of his shoulders and along his back. The lesion was oozing, and Travis was careful not to aggravate it. There was more blood, flecks of it coating Bear's mist-slicked fur, but Travis probed with his fingertips and found no other injuries beneath the thick pelt. The blood was mostly Donnie's.

Travis picked himself up and went to Donnie's body, Bear padding silently along behind him. He knelt and felt for a pulse in Donnie's throat. It was there, and steady. He pulled out his cell phone and dialed Goodman's number.

"I could use some assistance," he said when the sheriff picked up.

He gave his location and cut the connection, sat on the broken blacktop and beckoned for his tired dog. He made Bear lie down, cradled his head in his lap, and waited.

# 7

Sheriff Goodman ended the call and went looking for Skottie. She was on the phone, pacing up and down in her bedroom, grabbing guns out of her safe and throwing them on her bed. She pulled the phone away from her ear and said, "Just a second, Ryan." She gave Goodman a questioning look, and he could see that her wide eyes were red-rimmed, her skin puffy, her hands shaking.

"That was the doc," Goodman said. "He caught the other kid. I'm gonna go pick him up."

"Did he find out anything about my daughter?"

"I don't think so."

"We need to get going. Do you have any idea what Maddy's going through right now?"

"No, ma'am, and neither do you. Thinking about the worst of it . . . Well, it might not be as bad as you think anyway. Not yet. You're better off rounding up as many people as you can to help find her."

"That's what I'm doing. The Highway Patrol's putting out an APB. Who else do you know who can help?"

Goodman could tell she was close to hyperventilating. He reached out to put his hands on her shoulders, then pulled back. "Well, shit, I ain't much good to you. I got my best deputy on his way already, but he's the only one I trust. Burden County ain't all that big, but a lot of the people there are likely in that church or have family there. And everybody's related to everybody. I don't know who else I can call. Hell, the bad guys got people in my family, in my department . . . I don't even know I can trust my wife right now. Don't tell her I said that."

"I don't know—"

"Listen, they're not too far away. They're probably not expecting us to be on 'em yet, and they're gonna be going slow. If I'm right, they won't wanna get pulled over with what they got in the back of that truck. We got a little time to prepare. We might catch 'em with my Crown Vic or your Explorer, but maybe think about who's got the fastest car you know and give him a call. I'll be right back with the doc. It's gonna be okay. I promise."

He tipped his hat and turned away, hoping she hadn't seen the doubt in his eyes.

# 8

They took Donnie to the emergency room at Hays Medical Center.

"A stray dog mauled him," Travis said. "It came out of nowhere."

"It mighta been a wolf," Goodman said. "Should probably treat him for rabies. All the injections."

The on-duty nurse gave Travis a clipboard with a form to fill out. He set it on an empty chair, and when no one was looking, he and Goodman left.

By the time they made it back to Emmaline's house, Deputy Quincy Griffith had arrived with a giant thermos of coffee. It was his night off, but he had jumped in his patrol car as soon as Goodman called him and had made record time getting to Hays. Quincy took Emmaline's two captives to the Ellis County sheriff's office with instructions that they were to be held for the holiday and would be picked up after the weekend for transfer to Burden County. Quincy promised to return as soon as possible.

When she saw Bear, Emmaline took him by the scruff of the neck to the bathroom.

"Let's get him cleaned up, and I'll take a look at that cut," she said.

Skottie came down the back hall, her phone calls complete and her arms full of the guns she had taken from her bedroom safe.

"We're wasting time," she said. "I think I have enough weapons here for all of us."

"I have a few more in the back of the sheriff's car," Travis said.

"This boy went on quite a little shopping trip tonight," Goodman said. "Pretty near cleaned out the sporting goods department."

"Travis, I know you want to find your dad," Skottie said.

"My father would be disappointed in me if I did not help you."

"Thank you," Skottie said. "We're gonna get Maddy back tonight."

"You find a fast car?" Goodman said.

"Better than that. I remembered I know a guy with an airplane."

## NOVEMBER 2018

Ransom was nodding off in his rocking chair when he heard the door handle. Rudy came in and closed the door behind him and looked around the tiny room as if he had never seen it before. They were in one of the sheds that lined the inside of the church's fence. The books on the shelf next to the door had titles like *Stay Invisible, Black Like Them, Dark Matters*, but Ransom had no desire to read them. He wasn't sure he could read them if he wanted to. He spent most of his time watching shadows on the wall and thinking about his children.

Rudy sat across from him on the edge of one of the two bottom bunks, propping his cane between his legs. He watched Ransom rock back and forth. Ransom couldn't help it; he needed to rock all the time or he felt anxious. His fingertips tingled, and the side of his head burned where the half-moon incision was beginning to heal.

"Didn't sleep?" Rudy said. "I understand. I don't sleep much myself."

Ransom glared at him.

"How are we today?" Rudy said.

Ransom didn't answer. He formed several responses, but his mouth wouldn't make the words.

*Fuck you,* he meant to say.

*If I could move any faster, I would kill you.*

*Wait until my sons get their hands on you.*

He said none of this, but he took some satisfaction from the apparent fact that Rudy didn't know he could still think clearly. Whatever Rudy had done to him, Ransom was still whole inside. It was just that his brain couldn't communicate very well with his body.

"I wanted to tell you that I'm very proud of you," Rudy said. "I can't call you a complete success, but our time together has taught me a great deal. If you could understand my work, you might even thank me for allowing you to be a part of it."

"Fuck," Ransom said. He grinned, proud to have blurted out the one word that summed up all his feelings.

"Probably not," Rudy said. He leaned back and stroked his beard. "I don't imagine you'll be doing that ever again."

Ransom slumped in his chair, exhausted by the achievement of speaking that one word. Rudy grabbed his cane and pushed himself up from the bed. He went to the mini-fridge under the shelf and opened it, grabbed two longneck bottles of imported German beer, and held them up.

"Drink?"

Without waiting for an answer, he took his keys from his pocket and popped the caps off with a bottle opener on his key ring. One of the caps went flying and he retrieved it from the floor, setting his keys on the edge of the shelf above, pushing the books back toward the wall to make space for them. He tossed the caps in the small trash can and straightened back up with some difficulty, holding the small of his back with one hand. He passed a beer bottle over to Ransom and sat back down on the bunk bed with a huge sigh.

"I'm getting old," he said. "But you understand. You're no spring chicken yourself."

Ransom concentrated on moving his arm. He considered throwing the bottle at Rudy, but knew the attempt would fail. Rudy was three feet away, but he might as well have been on the moon. Ransom brought the bottle up to his mouth and took a shaky sip of beer.

"I'm very close," Rudy said. "I feel as if my life's work is finally . . . Well, I'm making progress, and you've helped show me the way. I really think that."

Ransom lowered his bottle and stared at it.

"I have someone new on my table," Rudy said. "A girl. She's got mixed blood. I wonder which race is stronger in her. Later, I'll bring you back down to my laboratory and let you watch as I work. It's sort of a tradition. You may recall I let Kenny sit in on your transformation." He shook his head. "Poor Kenny. He didn't turn out as well as you have."

"Where?" Ransom said.

"Where's Kenny? Oh, you might say he's gone for a swim. One day soon Deputy Puckett will take you out to see him." Rudy took another sip of beer. "You know, I think I'll miss you, Mr. Roan. But we must always move forward, never look back. This little mixed girl they found for me, she seems strong. She'll last me quite a while, I think." He raised his bottle to Ransom in a toast. "To the next generation, my friend."

Ransom tried to raise his arm, but lost control of his fingers. He dropped his bottle and it exploded against the floor, foamy beer dripping away through cracks in the plywood.

"Look what you've done," Rudy said.

Ransom saw his opportunity, the only opportunity he was ever likely to get, and focused every ounce of thought and energy into standing. He pushed himself up from the chair and used the rocking motion to help propel him forward. He took one agonizing step forward, and then Rudy stuck his cane out and tripped him. Ransom fell, putting out his arms and grabbing the shelf. It came free and he smacked the side of his head and right shoulder against the wall as he fell. Books spilled down on top of him.

Rudy braced himself and rose. "I'll send someone along to clean this up."

He stepped over Ransom and opened the door hard, banging it into Ransom's arm. He looked up at the sky, then stepped over the threshold and closed the door behind him.

Ransom listened to his captor's footsteps until they faded away, then he rolled over and began the long process of pushing himself up. He got his knees under him and unclasped his fist, stared at the keys he had grabbed from the shelf. Then he got back to work. The first step was to stand up, then he would concentrate on getting out of the shed and walking around the empty swimming pool to the parking lot.

# CHAPTER ELEVEN

## 1

Skottie watched out the windshield over the plane's nose. Every once in a while she saw a pair of headlights below, but traffic was sparse. The Cessna's shadow moved across the fog beneath them at what looked like a walking pace, and Skottie had to will herself to sit still and be patient. She knew they were traveling much faster than any truck could, but patience wasn't her strong suit, even in the best of circumstances.

Travis leaned forward, and Skottie turned to look at him. He was in the seat behind Dr. Iversen, and next to him was a big stack of towels and blankets from Emmaline's hall closet. He reached out and gave her shoulder a squeeze.

"We will find her," he said. The steady roar of the Cessna's engine made it hard to hear his low rasping voice. "Finding people is what I do."

Skottie nodded in response, unable to put her fear into words.

"I'm guessing they've probably crossed into Oklahoma by now," Dr. Iversen said. "Or pretty close to it."

"How long until we get there?"

"Not long," Dr. Iversen said. "Just hang tight. They'll be going the speed limit. Won't want to get pulled over with what they're carrying. We'll be on top of them soon enough."

The coroner had met them at Hays Regional Airport, his Cessna 172 gassed and ready to go. Skottie wasn't sure if he'd been asleep when she called him, but he was alert and eager to help as soon as he learned about the situation. Travis had loosely estimated the truck's lead time based on when the first call had come from Donnie, and they had determined there was no way to catch up to it on the ground. After hanging up with Dr. Iversen, Skottie had called Ryan Kufahl again. The trooper had still been awake and, based solely on Sheriff Goodman's guess that Maddy and her father were on that truck, he had begun coordinating a ground search, pulling in state troopers across southern Kansas and Oklahoma. They were gambling that the truck would indeed head south. If they were wrong, Maddy could be anywhere to the north, east, or west of Hays. She might never be found.

Skottie didn't want to think about what her daughter was going through or what would happen if they caught up to the truck and Maddy wasn't on it.

Lightning flickered and faded somewhere behind them. The plane crossed over several acres of featureless farmland, following the invisible thread of US-183 south, then leapt back up above a wooded area, the trees mired in swirling mist in a way that reminded Skottie of the dead bleached trees that reached up to break the surface of Kirwin Lake. She wondered what was beneath the water back at the nature preserve, what had been dumped there over the decades, how many tortured bodies with strange scars.

The Foundation's file on Rudolph Bormann didn't mention bodies in the lake or human trafficking, it had contained no clues to Maddy's whereabouts, but Skottie had read it through twice already, hoping to find something that might lead her to her daughter.

Bormann had arrived in Kansas sometime in the fifties or sixties, carrying false identification. There was no record anymore of where he had come from, how he had escaped Germany after the war, who had given him his papers, but at some point he had acquired four thousand acres of pastureland in Burden County and had dubbed it the Third R Ranch. Skottie assumed the name was a reference to the Third Reich, and it astonished her that he would be so bold, so open about who he was and where he came from. But apparently no one had ever connected the dots. Kansas was a long way from Mauthausen-Gusen.

In 1971, Rudy had bought an abandoned church in Paradise Flats and had moved into town with his family. The church still owned the ranch property. Skottie made a mental note that the land should be checked for buried bodies. How long would it take to inspect four thousand acres?

And where had Rudy's money come from? Even in the 1960s and '70s, that much land wouldn't have been cheap.

Skottie hoped she would have a chance to ask Rudy in person.

However he had purchased it, once the church was established, young women and girls began disappearing from the area. Not too many, not enough to cause a panic, but there was a pattern, and the Roans had eventually pieced much of it together from decades' worth of local newspapers on the Internet and microfiche files.

Meanwhile, Sheriff Goodman had been pursuing a parallel line of investigation. Rudy had tried using his son's position to help cover his tracks, but when Kurt Goodman began to realize the extent of his father's crimes, he had left the church and severed ties. It had

not been easy for him to reconcile the man he thought he knew—
a prophet, a preacher, a magician in every sense of the word, but a
largely absent and unavailable father—with the monster who began
to emerge when Goodman started tracing missing person cases
back to Purity First. Reluctant to jump to conclusions, the sheriff
had spread his inquiries out farther, to eastern Kansas, Nebraska,
Colorado, Oklahoma, Missouri, and Texas. Missing children, grown
women, and men all seemed to funnel through the church and disappear. The pattern later established by the Roan Foundation had already begun to take over a file cabinet in Sheriff Goodman's spare
bedroom. But Goodman hadn't known what to do about it, hadn't
been able to put together enough legal evidence to act.

Until Ruth Elder had spotted Rudy Goodman in a diner in Phillipsburg and made that half-remembered connection between an old
monster and a new saint.

But the monster didn't know he'd been seen until Ransom Roan
came to Kansas. Skottie wondered whether Roan had directly approached Rudy or had simply asked the wrong question of the wrong
person. In whatever way Rudy discovered Ransom's presence, the former Nazi had acted quickly. And then Rudy, or someone working for
him, had panicked. The smooth and efficient machinery by which
Purity First had abducted dozens, maybe hundreds of people, had
broken down. Maybe Ruth Elder had died of natural causes; maybe
she had been murdered in such a way that it looked natural. She was
an old lady, and no one had looked closely at the cause of death. But
she had told others about Rudy Goodman, and those others had been
silenced, too.

From beyond the grave, Ruth Elder had pointed her finger at the
saint of wolves and butchers. Rudy and his people were lashing out

blindly. They had grown complacent after a half century of peace and safety, and their plans were out-of-date. They had thought they could control Skottie by sending lawyers after her, by breaking into her home, by kidnapping her daughter.

Skottie balled her fists up in her lap. First she would find Maddy, then she would end the danger of Rudy Goodman, no matter what it took.

"Is that it?"

Dr. Iversen was pointing out the window on Skottie's side. They had outraced the fog, broken into flat grassland, and she could see the pale rectangular roof of a semitrailer truck moving along the highway below them.

"Travis," Skottie said, "is that the truck you saw in the church parking lot?"

He was looking out his window behind them. "I have no idea. There were no markings on it."

"Chances are good that's it," Dr. Iversen said. "It's right about where it should be, given when we think it left and how fast it must have been going. There's not a lot of traffic down there."

"But there are other trucks," Skottie said. "Pretty much all the traffic this time of night is gonna be trucks."

"Yeah," Iversen said. "It's a gamble."

"I'm calling it in," Skottie said. "How does this radio work?"

"Dodge City Regional's probably the closest," Iversen said. "But the tower closed at ten and it won't open until six. There's nobody there to take a call right now. Just use your cell. It'll work."

Because of the cease and desist, they had decided an APB should come from Ryan Kufahl rather than Skottie. She called him and, after consulting with Dr. Iversen, gave the trooper the approximate location of the white truck. After ending the call, she stared out the window at the truck below, trying to sense whether her daughter was in there, caged in the dark, helpless and frightened.

"Hang on, baby," she whispered. "I'm coming."

"I'm circling around," Iversen said.

The plane dipped and banked in a long curve over the denuded trees, and Skottie lost sight of the truck. Minutes later they were lined up again with US-183 and cruised back over the length of highway.

"It's gone," Skottie said. "Where's the truck?"

"Perhaps it sped up," Travis said.

They waited for the white roof to come back into view, but there was nothing below them except the long straight stretch of empty pavement.

"He saw us," Skottie said. "The driver saw us or he heard us up here and he got spooked."

"Damn," Iversen said. "Hang on."

Skottie's stomach lurched as Dr. Iversen pushed his Cessna into a dive and angled westward. Scattered trees multiplied and clustered until they were above a wooded area that hadn't yet shed its colorful leaves. It felt like they were skimming the tops of the uppermost branches, and Skottie unconsciously pulled her feet up off the floor of the little plane. Tributary roads split off from the highway and disappeared under the leafy canopy. Mile after mile disappeared behind them, but there was no sign of the truck. Iversen shifted direction again, taking the plane back to the highway and crossing over it. Ten minutes later, Skottie exclaimed and pointed down at a splinter of darkness, a two-lane gravel path built for farm machinery. The truck was speeding along, a blur of white that wove in and out of the cover of the trees.

"That's got to be it," Skottie said.

"It is too big for that road," Travis said.

Iversen picked up the radio and held it close to his lips. "DDC FBO . . . DDC FBO . . . N 123 LH, you copy me? N 123 LH, calling Dodge City with a priority request. Over." He looked at Skottie and said, "It's worth a shot. They're officially closed, but they may have someone up—"

There was a squawk of static over the speaker and a woman's voice. "N 123 LH, this is DDC. State your request. Over."

"This is N 123 LH. Does the Highway Patrol have a plane in the air right now? Over."

"Negative, N 123 LH. Over."

Iversen looked at Skottie. He raised his eyebrows and shook his head. "Well, this is gonna sound a little bit crazy, DDC. I'm just south of Coldwater, about sixty miles south of you. Gonna try landing in a field here. Over."

"N 123 LH, are you experiencing difficulties? Over."

"You might say that. What's your name, DDC?"

"Samantha."

"Samantha, this is Lyle Iversen. I have a situation here and I need the local authorities to ping my GPS and respond ASAP. We might need some ambulances."

"Did you say ambulances? Like, more than one?"

"As many as they've got, Samantha."

"Will do. Please stay on the line. And good luck."

Dr. Iversen put the handset in its cradle and nodded at Skottie. "We're gonna have a lot of company in a few minutes. Hope we're right about this."

He brought the plane down low, almost scraping the treetops.

"Tell me you can actually land this here," Skottie said.

"Landed worse places than this. Most of the landing strips around here are just grass. Not a problem, long as they keep it mowed short enough."

Ahead the gravel road widened into four lanes to provide a turn-around, and Iversen aimed for that. He coasted over the top of the truck and put the Cessna down with a jolt that made Skottie feel like her head had popped off. They taxied forward, the air brakes squealing and gravel flying, and stopped six feet short of a strand of sickly looking elms.

Skottie jumped out, leaving Iversen to communicate the successful landing to Samantha in the tower. Her ankle twisted when she hit the gravel, but she barely noticed. She pulled out her Glock and angled sideways toward the ditch at the side of the road nearest her. Travis was just behind her and he ran the other way, covering the opposite side of the narrow throughway.

A minute later, the truck barreled out at them from the dark tunnel of trees. The Cessna completely blocked the way forward, and through the windshield Skottie could see the driver shouting at himself in the cab while he turned the wheel. His neck was as wide as Skottie's torso, and he had a long white beard. The set of his shoulders made it clear he was stomping as hard as he could on the brake. The truck came to a screeching halt beside her and Skottie leapt up, favoring her injured ankle, and grabbed the door handle on the passenger side. The driver leaned across, but was too late to lock the door. Behind him, Travis swung open the door on his side and pointed his Eclipse at the driver. The man sat back in his seat and put his hands in the air.

# 2

The driver didn't resist. He followed Travis's prompting and stepped down from the truck's high cab. Travis handcuffed him and forced him against the side of the truck. Skottie checked under his seat and found a sawed-off shotgun. She took the keys from the truck's ignition and went around, careful of her twisted ankle, and threw the heavy latch.

When she opened the doors, a Hispanic woman launched herself at Skottie, screaming and clawing. Skottie stepped sideways and caught the woman under her armpits, got her hands behind the woman's head, and immobilized her until she stopped struggling.

"Do you speak English?"

"Little," the woman said.

"I'm police," Skottie said. "You're okay. I'm here to help you."

"*Policía?*"

"Not to arrest you. Help. Help you." She tried to remember her high school Spanish. "Ayud? I mean, yudar, *ayudar.*"

The woman nodded and Skottie let her go, hobbled backward. The woman turned around and regarded her apprehensively. Skottie ignored her and pulled herself up onto the rear bumper. She peered into the dark trailer, unable to see beyond the first few feet, but she could hear movement back in the dark.

She turned back to the Hispanic woman. "Ask them if there's a little girl named Maddy in there. Hurry!"

She didn't wait, but pulled out her phone and used the light on it to lead her in. Young women moved past her toward the exit, shrinking away from her as she went farther in. She could hear the first woman asking about Maddy. Small girls lay against the hard slats at the sides of the trailer, and she checked them to make sure they were breathing, to make sure they weren't her daughter. She kept going. All the way in, lying with his head propped up against the wall behind the truck's cab, Skottie found Brandon. His eyes were swollen nearly shut, but there was a glint of light when the phone's lamp hit them and he murmured something in a damaged voice. Skottie squatted next to him. Even at his worst Brandon had been strong and vital; to see him broken caused a swell of grief and pity in her.

"Brandon? Where's Maddy?"

"Not here," he said.

Skottie's legs failed her and she fell backward. Brandon reached out to her, tried to raise himself up with his other hand and gasped in pain. His head banged against the wall of the truck and he closed his eyes.

"They separated us," he said. "Give me a second and I'll—"

"No," Skottie said. "You can barely even move."

He shook his head and gasped again. "You have to find her, Skottie." He felt for her hand and squeezed it once, hard, then his hand fell limp at his side.

"Of course I will."

She picked herself up and left him there, stumbled back out, following the women and little girls in their exodus from the truck. Travis was there passing out blankets and towels from the plane. Dr. Iversen had his black bag open on the bumper of the truck and was shining a penlight into a girl's eyes. He reached into his pocket and produced a lollipop, which he handed to the girl. She gave him a tentative smile in return.

"She's not here, Travis."

"The church?"

Skottie nodded. She felt dizzy and nauseated with worry, but she tried to force her thoughts back along practical lines. Panic and fear would do nothing to help Maddy.

"My husband, Brandon, is in there," she said. "He's injured. He's all the way at the back."

Dr. Iversen picked up his bag.

"Well, let's get some more light in there so I can see what needs doing," he said.

# 3

A dark blue 4x4 pickup with lights flashing came down the narrow road and pulled in behind the trailer truck. A Comanche County deputy stepped out, a rangy man with a Sam Elliott mustache, and gave the Cessna a skeptical look before approaching Skottie. He introduced himself as Tucker, and they exchanged greetings and credentials. A minute later, three Highway Patrol cruisers came zooming in.

The truck had been carrying fifteen women and children, as well as Brandon. They were frightened and dehydrated, but they were all relatively healthy. The troopers passed out bottles of water, and Travis finished giving Emmaline's blankets away.

Brandon had a concussion. There was a head wound that started bleeding again when Dr. Iversen cleaned away the clotting, and the doctor put twelve stitches in Brandon's scalp.

"He should be all right," Iversen said. "But concussions are tricky. He needs to get to a hospital as soon as possible."

Deputy Tucker walked Brandon carefully back to his truck and waited while Brandon threw up in the dead leaves by the side of the road, then bundled him into the passenger seat and took off for the nearest emergency room, his array coruscating and his siren screaming.

The Highway Patrol had many questions for them, but Skottie was too impatient to answer them. The truck full of women and girls had not made it over the state line into Oklahoma, so the FBI wouldn't necessarily become involved. But either the Highway Patrol or the Comanche sheriff's office would call in the Kansas Bureau of Investigation. Meanwhile, whoever was buying girls from the church would soon be looking for their latest shipment. They would begin making inquiries of their friends in Paradise Flats long before the KBI could get rolling. And evidence would begin to disappear. If Maddy was still alive, Purity First might dispose of her as soon as they discovered their truck hadn't arrived at its destination.

So Travis dealt with the troopers as quickly as he could. He said they knew very little, only that the truck had come from the Purity First Church in Burden County. The sheriff there had called for help, and Skottie had recruited Dr. Iversen and Travis to assist. There would be many more questions later, but Skottie had a badge and the officers on the scene had their hands full.

Skottie sat in the back seat of the Cessna this time. Travis took the copilot's seat, and Dr. Iversen got the plane in the air.

"How long will it take us to get back?"

"Be a lot faster now," Dr. Iversen said. "I know where I'm going."

# 4

The mist was rolling away and the horizon was multicolored under the far eastern edge of an ugly cloud bank. Travis's rented Jeep was still where he had left it, on the street outside number 437, the house where Purity First was storing Rachel Bloom's furniture. Skottie dropped him off and then drove her Explorer around the block to the alley behind the church. Sheriff Goodman was around the corner in the other direction, waiting in his cruiser, and Deputy Griffith was armed with the Winchester and a scope, perched on a cell tower behind the long unbroken stretch of fence. Between Skottie and Goodman, they had scrounged four radios so they could keep in touch.

Much of their plan hinged on the lucky fact that Goodman had never returned his keys to the church. He would use his key to the main gate to sneak in and search the outbuildings while Travis let himself into 437 again and accessed the compound through the back door of the house. At the same time, Skottie would go through the alley and over the fence. She and Travis would approach the church building from different angles, and Quincy would cover them all with the rifle from the cell tower. He was ready to move in with his cruiser and get the others out of there as soon as they found Maddy and Ransom.

None of them was optimistic, but there wasn't time to come up with anything better and they had no idea who else they could trust.

With Bear at his heels, Travis bounded up the porch steps and used his bump key once again on the front lock. They entered the house, and Travis closed the door behind them. He moved quickly through to the kitchen, set his radio down on the counter, and took a look out the small window above the sink. Rose-hued sodium lights illuminated the entire compound, and there were already people out and about, moving in focused patterns, some of them carrying boxes back and forth between the church building and the sheds, others performing calisthenics on the basketball court, all of them wearing identical brown shirts. There were perhaps twenty of them, their pink skin scrubbed clean, their fair hair neatly parted, their bellies full of pancakes and orange juice.

He heard a click at the front door and felt a momentary gust of cold wind. He reached for his Eclipse, but Bear was already in motion. A few seconds later he heard a clatter and excited shouting from the living room.

"Doc! It's me, dammit!"

Sheriff Goodman had been chased halfway up the stairs to the second floor and Bear had him cornered. Goodman was holding a pair of bolt cutters, old and solid, its handles wrapped in friction tape, and he looked like he wanted to take a swing. Travis put his gun away and called the dog off. Bear backed off just far enough to let Goodman slide along the wall past him, then followed the sheriff down into the dark room.

"I don't think he likes me much," Goodman said.

"What makes you say that?" Travis said.

"He still wants to bite me," Goodman said.

"If he wanted to bite you, he would have done so."

Travis reached down and carefully ruffled Bear's mane, got a sloppy lick in return. Emmaline had bathed Bear and stitched up the wound across his shoulder, and a few hours of sleep seemed to have done the big dog a world of good.

"They changed the locks," Goodman said. "My key doesn't work anymore."

"Of course." Travis shook his head. "It was too much to hope for."

Goodman followed Travis to the kitchen window and squinted out at the activity in the yard. "Looks like they're gearing up for something," he said. He took a pouch from his jacket pocket and stuffed a wad of tobacco in his mouth. "If you could've got that driver to tell us where he was going, we'd have a better idea how much time we got."

"We did not have the luxury of time," Travis said.

"I could've made him talk pretty quick, if I was there," Goodman said. "Guy was stealing little girls."

Travis changed the subject. "Some of this activity may be for my benefit. They are expecting me later today. I surprised Heinrich with my visit to the church yesterday, but your brother invited me to return for the holiday meal." He glanced out the window at the activity in the yard. "No doubt they are setting a place at the table for me now."

"But why so early?"

"I think maybe this is their regular routine. Their brand of paranoia requires constant preparation." Travis glanced at his watch. "A little after seven o'clock now."

Goodman nodded and went to the back door. "Sun'll be up soon. Better get moving."

"Skottie will be anxious," Travis said.

He picked up his radio and called her.

# 5

"About time," she said. "I'm going in now."

Skottie took her thumb off the button and clipped the radio onto her belt next to her handcuffs, LED flashlight, and Taser. She shut off the Explorer and got out, checked her Glock and holstered it. She had considered wearing her uniform, thinking she might need the extra edge it would give her, the deference to authority it engendered, but had decided against it at the last minute. Instead she had on a comfortable old pair of jeans and a sweatshirt that fit over the top of her Kevlar vest. Her hair was fastened back under an old Cubs cap.

The fence was unbroken, but detoured down one side of the alley and back up the other, then continued along the rest of the block and around the corner. The alley was just wide enough for a garbage truck to back into, with thin grass strips running down both sides of a concrete driveway. At the other end was a gate built from the same tall cedar planks as the rest of the fence. The church had apparently recognized that the alley was a vulnerable spot and had accessorized with a few yards of barbed wire.

Skottie reached into the car and grabbed the blanket that covered the back seat. She shook out Bear's heavy black fur and rolled the blanket up, carried it into the alley. On the off chance someone had been careless the last time the trash was taken out, Skottie tried the gate's handle. It was secure. She went back and rolled one of the sturdy plastic garbage bins to the gate. She tipped it over on its side, then went back and got another bin. She used them as steps, folded the blanket in half and threw it over the wire, grabbed the top of the gate, and pulled herself up far enough to see into the compound.

There were more people moving about the grounds than she would have liked, but all the activity was concentrated away from the gate. She strained and pulled herself up a little farther and looked at the concrete below her. There was nothing there to cushion her landing, but there was nothing in her way, either.

She jumped down and paced along the alley to the street, breathing carefully and swinging her arms, aware that Maddy was depending on her, then she ran at the bins, took two steps up, grabbed the blanket-covered barbed wire, and vaulted over the gate.

She hit the ground hard on her good ankle and rolled, aiming for the shadows at the base of the church building. She stopped under a hedge and listened for alarms, then stretched out and raised herself to a crouching position. The ankle she had twisted jumping off the plane was still sore, and she had scraped some of the skin off the palm of her left hand, but she was otherwise unscathed.

She unclipped her Glock and stood, held the gun down at her side, and trotted along the outside of the stone wall, looking for a door.

# 6

"Where's that generator you saw?" Goodman kept his voice low and adjusted his grip on the heavy bolt cutters. "Maybe we should cut their power? Give us a little advantage."

"Up closer to the church," Travis said. "But I think it was just for backup."

Goodman nodded and they moved out along the inside perimeter of the fence. When they reached the first outbuilding, he wiped a window clean and looked inside.

"Somebody's bunking down here," he said. "You think it's that army they got? Or maybe this is where they keep the women and kids before they transport 'em out?"

"I had the feeling the women were already in the truck yesterday. The driver did not wait to load it; he hurried out of here as soon as Heinrich gave him the word."

"So they keep them in the truck? This just gets more awful. Dad's nutty as a Snickers, but Heinrich's always been the schemer. This has to be him. Gotta be about the money for him."

They moved on, looking inside each shed as they passed, but every building stood empty. With only two sheds left to check, Goodman stopped and held up his hand. When he had Travis's attention, he pointed past the outbuildings in the direction of the parking lot.

"You look in that garage?"

"No," Travis said.

"You said they were keeping that truck in the parking lot. Right out in the open. Why do that if you got a garage you can park it in?"

Travis raised his eyebrows.

They left the shadows of the fence and crossed an open area, watching men in brown shirts run through a calisthenics regimen just a few yards away. Bear stayed nearer the fence, weaving between the outbuildings while keeping Travis in sight. They reached the back of the garage without being seen and crept around to a door on the sheltered side. Goodman tried the handle and shook his head.

"Solid lock, solid door. Didn't come with the building when they bought it. No windows, either."

Travis produced his leather pouch and went to work again. The lock on the garage was several steps better than the one on the front gate. Heinrich had gone to some extra trouble to keep people out of his garage.

Goodman shuffled from one foot to the other. "Hurry up."

"This is difficult."

It took him three minutes before he heard the familiar sound of a dead bolt drawing back. He straightened up and put the pouch back in his pocket, traded it for the Eclipse.

"A lock like that," Goodman said, "building's probably alarmed."

"Maddy may be in there," Travis said.

"Or your dad."

Travis turned the handle and the door swung open. There was an immediate ear-piercing squeal, and they ducked down, entered the building low, and separated on either side of the door. Bear stayed close to Travis, breathing hard. Goodman straightened up and found a light switch. He flicked it and overhead fluorescents blinked to life. There was a plastic box mounted to the wall next to the switch that had a series of buttons and a red blinking light. Goodman gave Travis a thumbs-up and used his bolt cutters to chew through a thick cable that led up toward the rafters. The alarm continued to sound and he frowned at it, then raised the bolt cutters over his head and brought them down hard on the box. It broke in half and hung limp against the wall. Its lights blinked green and it went silent.

Travis shut the door and bolted it.

"Shit," Goodman said. "Somebody's gonna have a key to that door. We got maybe a minute before them goons are all over us."

Maddy was not in the garage, that was obvious at a glance. The double-wide building was filled with pallets, stacked with crates that stretched from the door to the back wall. An olive-green truck with a canvas top was parked, nose out, in the narrow space between crates.

Goodman went to the back of the truck and used his bolt cutters again to remove a padlocked chain, while Travis pried open the nearest crate.

"Guns," Travis said. "Rifles."

There was a commotion on the other side of the garage door and the handle rattled. Travis could hear men's voices. Bear looked back and forth between the door and his master, his brown eyes watery. Travis moved to the next crate and opened it.

"Kalashnikovs," he said.

"Machine guns?"

"A lot of them."

Goodman lowered the truck's gate and took a step back. "Come here, Doc."

Travis went around and looked inside. The cargo area contained an enormous object that was dominated by tall metal cylinders that had been welded together and spray-painted matte black.

"A bomb," Goodman said. "They're going to war?"

"I think Heinrich may be supplementing his slave trade by selling weapons."

"He's selling bombs?"

"I do not think this is a regular bomb." Travis pointed at a lever that protruded from a smooth panel that was welded to the right side of the device. "Unless I am wrong, this is an NNEMP."

"A what?"

"A non-nuclear electromagnetic pulse generator. If we were to push that lever and arm it, we could potentially kill every electronic device in the area. Everything would stop working."

"How big an area?"

"I could not say. Possibly the entire compound."

They stood contemplating the contents of the truck for a minute, listening to the people on the other side of the door.

"What have we got to lose?"

"Nothing, really," Travis said. "Shall we?"

"How's it work?"

"There should be a remote control somewhere."

Goodman went to the driver's-side door and opened it. He came back a moment later holding a small flat plastic box with a single red button on one side. He handed it to Travis.

"This all looks homemade."

"It is," Travis said. "We will not want to be near this when it explodes."

"You said it wasn't a bomb."

"It still has an explosive component."

"Keys are in the truck," Goodman said. "How 'bout we send it on a little trip?"

"Yes," Travis said. "Let us hope those people out there have the good sense to run."

Goodman went back to the cab and climbed in. Travis reached out to the device and flung the lever upward just as the truck started. There was a low whine that made Bear back away and snort. The truck rolled forward and Goodman jumped out.

"I rigged the gas pedal," he said.

He walked back to Travis and they stood side by side watching as the truck hit the garage door and kept going, crumpling the corrugated tin and pushing through it into the gray air outside. People in brown shirts scrambled in every direction and the truck rattled on, over the ruins of the door, through the brittle grass and away, finally bouncing to a stop at the far edge of the basketball court.

Travis pushed the red button on the remote control.

There was a muffled thump, the back end of the truck popped up and slammed back down, and the lights in the garage winked out.

# 7

Skottie's flashlight went dark, leaving her in the pitch black of the church hall. She checked the switch, pushing it in with her thumb three or four times, but it was dead. She clipped it to her belt and waited for her eyes to adjust.

What if Maddy wasn't even in the compound?

She pushed the thought out of her mind. She would scour the church for her daughter and, if Maddy wasn't there, she would move on to the next logical place and search it. She would keep looking until she found her.

The building appeared to be deserted. She had gained entrance through the unlocked front door and gone through the vestibule to a long hall with a red carpet, just as Travis had described. From there, it had been slow moving, stopping to check each empty office along one wall, then doubling back and checking the rooms along the other side of the passage.

She heard people yelling outside, and she hoped Travis and the sheriff hadn't been caught. She rolled her shoulders to loosen the tension in her neck, then adjusted her grip on the Glock and moved to the next office along the hall.

# 8

Goodman lifted a machine gun from one of the crates and hefted it. "I'm thinking if Maddy's alive, she's over there in the church," he said. "And these guys are gonna figure out we're still in here and come lookin' any old time now."

"I would prefer we not shoot our way out."

"You're not a real fun guy, Doc."

"I am a fun guy. This is not a fun situation."

"You go help Skottie look for her girl. I'm gonna create a distraction."

Travis considered arguing, but he agreed with Goodman's logic. Their phones and radios were dead. Skottie was cut off in the church. The longer they spent searching, the greater the odds they would be caught. Once that happened, the chance of finding Maddy alive would plummet.

"If I can get to that truck, will it still run?" Goodman said.

Travis shook his head. "It would have to be a Faraday cage. Clearly it is not."

"You ever get tired of me asking what you're talking about?"

"It would have to have been altered to withstand the pulse, but it has a canvas top. At this point it is as useful as your nephew."

"It might still make decent cover." He patted the stock of the machine gun. "You see any clips for this thing?"

They hunted quickly through the crates until they found ammunition for the Kalashnikov. Goodman slid the safety lever up and inserted a magazine into the weapon, then took three more clips and stuffed them in his pockets. The sound of voices outside the garage grew louder as Heinrich's men returned.

"Follow me as soon as you can," Travis said. "Try not to get killed."

"Beer's on me when this is over." Goodman flipped the gun's safety back down.

"I will hold you to that promise."

They flattened themselves against the wall on either side of the opening. Goodman took a deep breath, then ducked and launched himself out across the crumpled tin door. His hat fell off and tumbled down the corrugated slope. He fired off a burst from the Kalashnikov that sent up a spray of mud and ice, then scrambled to his feet and grabbed his hat before heading toward the basketball court.

Travis waited a minute for the brown shirts to give chase, then slipped out through the gaping hole in the wall and sprinted for the church. Bear loped ahead of him, then circled back and got ahead again, keeping pace. The sky was a deep silky purple at the edges of the cloud cover. Fat raindrops spattered on Travis's face. The world went silent for a split second as lightning flashed across the sky, and then came the rolling drumbeat of thunder.

Goodman was running in a zigzag pattern, going the opposite direction, using short bursts from the gun to tear up divots of grass. One of the brown shirts caught up and grabbed the end of Goodman's flapping shirttail, but the sheriff bashed him with the butt of his gun and the man went down in a heap, blood spurting from his nose. When Goodman reached the basketball court, he dove behind the truck, then clambered up on the hood, and fired another burst into the air. Everyone except Travis stopped in their tracks and looked up at him.

"You all know who I am," he said. "And you know I mean business, so drop your guns and raise your hands high."

Travis kept going. As he drew close to the church doors, he could hear the church's flags rippling above him and a rope banging against the solid metal flagpole. A tall woman, the skin of her face drawn tight against her skull, stepped around the corner and raised a handgun at him. Her fingernails were painted bright red. Bear leapt forward and Travis raised his Eclipse, but he knew they were reacting too late. An instant before the woman could pull the trigger, her head exploded in a soft plummy mess of gray and red. The woman toppled forward, her gun skittering away under a hedge.

Travis looked for Quincy up on the cell tower, but the rain was coming down harder. He waved in the right direction, knowing the deputy could see him through his rifle scope, then turned and ran to the church.

# 9

Skottie was coming out of the last office at the end of the passage when the door to the vestibule opened, a black rectangle in the deeper darkness. She raised her Glock and pointed it down the length of the hall. Something nudged her leg and she jumped, startled. She reached down and felt a familiar furry mane under her hand. Bear snorted into her palm.

"Skottie?" Travis said from somewhere. "Skottie, it is me."

She lowered her gun. "You didn't find her?"

Travis entered and let the door shut behind him. "No."

"None of the lights are working in here, and my flashlight's dead, too."

Travis filled her in on what they had found.

"So Maddy's not out there," Skottie said. "And she's not in any of these rooms here."

"That gives us only one direction in which to go."

They were little more than silhouettes moving through the murk, but as their eyes continued to adjust, they were able to pick out details. Travis pointed to the series of framed photos as they drew near the double doors that led to the nave.

"Pride goeth before a fall."

"Why isn't there anybody in here?"

"Too much going on out there," Travis said. "But Rudolph is here. I feel sure of it."

They stood sideways and pulled the doors open, keeping themselves close to the walls on either side, presenting minimal targets for anyone in the nave. Bear looked to Travis for a signal, and when Travis crooked his index finger at him, the dog charged silently through into the church. Travis and Skottie followed him. Tall candles lined the center aisle, flicking shadows at the stone walls around them. A man stood alone at the far end of the room, resting his hands on the edge of the podium as if about to give a homily.

"Welcome, friends," Heinrich said.

# 10

The hardest thing Ransom had ever done was to walk from the outbuilding, down around the swimming pool and the far corner of the church, and out to the parking lot. When he started, it was still dark.

There had been a few early risers in the compound, perimeter guards and cooks preparing breakfast, but no one had questioned him. They were used to Rudy's experiments, people like Kenny who showed up out of nowhere and disappeared as quickly as they had come. All of these poor creatures moved erratically and spoke slowly, if at all, so Ransom's presence there wasn't unusual.

By the time he had reached the green van with its bloodred spots, Ransom had lost what little control he had over himself. It was hard to remember how to move his arms and legs, and muscle memory was slipping away. He had rested for a while, sitting with his back against the van, and then spent another long while standing back up, working the key fob and opening the door. He fell with his upper body and head on the driver's seat, the door still open, and then drifted into sleep.

When he woke up, the sun was rising and he could hear shouting across the compound. A soft rain was coming down, pattering gently against the van's metal roof. Ransom grabbed the other side of the bucket seat and pulled himself up behind the wheel. He sat for a few minutes, getting his breath, mustering his energy, then maneuvered the key ring in his hand until he was holding the key by its base. Unable to bend down and look, he stabbed blindly out in the direction of the steering column and managed to insert the key in the ignition on his first try.

He took a moment to savor this small victory, then began the process of turning the key. The engine chugged, then died. He held his breath and worked the muscles in his shoulders, down his arm, clasped his fingers together. He turned the key again. The van made a sickly rasping sound, then chugged harder and shuddered to life.

Ransom smiled and began the painstaking process of putting the van in reverse.

# 11

"All we ever wanted was to be left alone," Heinrich said. The golden lightning bolt fastened to the altar loomed huge behind him. "All you had to do was let my father live out the rest of his days in peace."

"Bear," Travis growled. *"Ataku!"*

Bear leapt silently forward, moving fast and sure up the red carpet toward the altar.

"No!" Heinrich ducked behind the podium and came back up with a Kalashnikov identical to the guns being stored in his garage. "Call the dog off!"

But he didn't wait for Travis to obey. He fired off a burst that tore up the carpet and splintered the sides of several pews, but missed Bear by at least a foot.

"Bear, *haltu!*" Travis said. *"Preta."*

"'Preta'?" Heinrich said.

"Tell my friend where she can find her daughter, and tell me where my father is."

"Don't be ridiculous, Dr. Roan. You have no leverage here. Please put your pistol down. And you, lady, drop your gun and lay down those rifles you've got on your back."

Travis and Skottie glanced at each other, and Travis shook his head. Bear was still too far away from the podium. There was no chance. The two of them laid down their handguns, and Skottie unslung her rifles, set them on the floor.

"Kick them away from you."

"Why are you doing this?" Skottie said.

"Doing what? You came into my home."

"After you came to mine," Skottie said. "Give me my daughter back."

"I didn't take her."

"You ordered Deputy Puckett to do it," Travis said. "You are responsible for that and for countless other crimes, including slavery and weapons dealing."

"You want to know what I'm responsible for?" Heinrich said. "I turned a freak show into a profitable enterprise. Do you know how much this church made last year? How much we're predicted to make by the end of this year?"

"But at what cost?"

Heinrich moved the machine gun away from Bear, pointing it at Travis.

"I didn't make this place," he said. "But I took my father's demented hobby and made it work. Everything I've done is for the good of this town and this county. I provide jobs, I provide infrastructure. My father's not going to live forever, and I'm all these people have. They need me."

"Your brother was right about you," Travis said.

"Enough," Heinrich said. "I didn't want to kill you, because that's gonna cause a lot of problems, a lot of attention. But I don't really see that I have much choice at this point."

He pulled the trigger and fired another burst that went wide over their heads. Skottie and Travis both ducked and scrambled for cover behind a pew.

*"Ataku!"*

Heinrich raised the Kalashnikov again, but stopped and turned away as a sound like thunder rocked the church. An engine roared and tires squealed as the wall behind the altar bulged inward and broke, stones crumbling and wooden studs splintering. Heinrich backed away and fell against the podium. Through a new hole in the wall, they could see the chrome grille and bright green hood of a van. The window above them, with its depiction of an electrifying tempest, came out of its casing whole, plummeted to the floor, and shattered into a thousand glittering pieces. Rain arrowed in at them through the perfect round hole above, life imitating art. The van disappeared as the driver backed it up, then slammed forward at the wall again, smashing all the way through. It hung up on the shattered remains of the wall, its tires spinning three feet above the ground on a stony ledge. The engine ground as the driver tried to back away, and the van bucked up and down, but couldn't get enough traction to break free.

The iconic lightning bolt above the altar trembled.

"Heinrich!" Travis stood and waved his hands. He pointed at the altar. "Move!"

Heinrich looked up just as the bolt tore free from its base. It toppled over on him and continued down to the floor, where it broke apart. When the dust settled, Heinrich lay bleeding but conscious, grabbing feebly at the carpet.

Bear turned in a circle and sat down, craning his neck so that he could see Travis, looking for some kind of assurance.

Travis grabbed his Eclipse off the floor and ran past the dog, kicking the Kalashnikov under a pew. When he got to the wall, he jumped up on the front bumper of the van and scrambled over the hood and out into the compound. The engine was still grinding, the tires still spinning, kicking up wet sod and mud in a diminishing spray. Several parishioners were approaching the van from behind, but they were moving cautiously. The driver's-side door was swinging loose on its hinges, and crushed glass from the windshield littered the shrubbery.

Behind him, Travis could see Skottie inside the church, leaning over Heinrich. She stood up and shouted something, but he couldn't hear her over the sound of the engine.

"What?" Travis shouted.

"He said she's in the basement! They have her down there!"

*"Go. Take Bear."*

She nodded and disappeared from sight.

Travis pulled the van's door free and stuck his gun in at the driver, but the familiar figure hunched over the steering wheel didn't move. Travis stepped around to the back of the van where the doors were hanging open. Inside, drawers and cabinets installed around the walls of the van had come open, spilling medical supplies and tools. The windows had been covered on the inside with sheets of black metal, and there were manacles bolted to the floor. Whatever evil purposes the vehicle had once been used for, it had been altered in such a way that it had resisted the EMP effect.

Travis went back to the cab and pushed Ransom's head off the steering wheel. He got his father under the arms and pulled him out of the van. As soon as Ransom's foot came off the accelerator, the tires stopped spinning and the van went quiet. Travis gathered his father up like a sleeping child.

A man in a brown shirt came running at him across the grass. Travis saw him from the corner of his eye and pivoted, driving his elbow into the man's throat. Ransom's limp body threw Travis off and he adjusted his stance as the brown shirt went down on one knee, his hands coming up in an effort to ward off the next blow. Travis kicked him in the face. The man twitched once and went still, his chest rising and falling steadily. Travis could feel blood pounding against his skull, hear it throbbing behind his ears. He stepped backward, resisting the urge to keep going, to grind the unconscious man into the mud. He closed his eyes and concentrated on his breathing, on the cool raindrops sliding down his face.

When he could think clearly, he carried Ransom back inside the church, laid his father on a pew, and checked for a pulse. It was weak. Ransom's body was unnaturally still; it lacked the subtle signs of life, the tiny shudder of straining muscle, the rise and fall of the diaphragm, the flutter of eyelashes. Ransom had always been proud of his wardrobe: his bespoke suits, monk strap shoes, and the tiny martini-glass tie tack with its emerald olive that Arletta had given him on their fifth anniversary. Now he wore a University of Kansas sweatshirt and dirty track pants. White stubble had replaced Ransom's long silver hair.

Travis touched the odd crescent-shape wound on his father's temple. He recognized it as the same injury Margaret Weber had suffered before she had been put in the lake, and he realized that the first time he had spoken with Heinrich Goodman in the church nave, Ransom must have been nearby enduring pain and torture.

Travis put his hand on Ransom's chest and whispered, "I am sorry, Father. Perhaps Judah would have found you in time. *Mi malsukcesis.*"

There was a clatter of rock and metal. Deputy Griffith scrambled over the hood of the van and jumped down onto the wet red carpet.

"Hey, my radio died," he said. "I figured I better come in." He looked around. "Damn, this place is ruined."

Travis wiped his eyes and stood, broken glass crunching under his boots, the carpet squelching. The lightning bolt sculpture had ripped the altar apart and smashed the podium, but Heinrich was nowhere to be seen. The Kalashnikov no longer lay where Travis had kicked it.

He moved toward the open door next to the altar, his grief and anger forced aside by a jolt of adrenaline. At least, he thought, Skottie had Bear with her.

"Hey!" Quincy pointed at Ransom's unmoving body. "Who's that? Is he okay?"

Travis turned around. "That is my father. And, no, I do not think he is okay."

"Lemme take a look, amigo."

Quincy knelt on the floor in front of the pew and unbuttoned Ransom's shirt.

"Have you had training as a paramedic?" Travis said.

"A few basic courses the sheriff made us take." Quincy looked up at him, and Travis saw that the skin around his eyes was dark and swollen. "You know, I killed that lady out there."

"If you had not, she would have killed me."

"I know."

"Skottie needs my help."

"Go find her," Quincy said. "I got this."

"I will be right back."

The door was standing open and Travis went through in a hurry. He stepped out into empty air and almost fell down a staircase in the dark. He put a hand against the wall and moved down slowly, feeling ahead for each new step until he reached the bottom. His footfalls echoed, giving him the impression he was in a large unoccupied room with no furniture.

"Bear?"

A moment later, Travis heard the soft click of Bear's nails and felt the moist snuffling of a muzzle on the palm of his hand.

Skottie's voice floated out of the darkness. "Travis, move to your left. There's a partition and three steps. Be careful. I fell down them and just about broke my arm."

Travis grabbed Bear's mane to orient himself and followed Skottie's directions. Once he had descended the steps, he entered a larger area that had a series of small windows up near the ceiling that let a bit of light in. He could see Skottie outlined against the far wall.

"Heinrich has disappeared," Travis said.

"He didn't come this way," she said. "Unless he snuck past me in the dark. There's a kitchen over here. And a closet down there at the other end of what seems like a meeting hall. It's hard to tell, but I think it's just full of folding chairs and tables and Christmas pageant stuff. I can't find Maddy. But there's a door here. There's more steps and another door at the bottom. It's metal and I can't open it."

Travis reached for his lock picks.

# 12

"We got your weapons," Sheriff Goodman said. "All them guns you had stashed away? We took 'em." This was not technically true, since he and Travis had left the guns where they were on church property, but Goodman felt that having seen them was good enough. They were supposed to be a secret and were probably less valuable the more people knew about them.

He looked around at the men surrounding the truck. He was holding his gun loose in his hands, not aiming it at anyone, but ready to use it if he had to. Most of the crowd had obeyed him and dropped their weapons, and even those who hadn't seemed to have lost the will to fight. He was the son of Reverend Rudy, and even though he had been excommunicated, it was clear that no one knew how to treat him. They were confused and leaderless.

Behind them, the church wall was still settling in around the remains of the bright green van, but Goodman had seen Travis take someone out of the cab. Quincy had followed him inside the church, and Goodman knew he needed to buy them some time.

"We took your truck, too," he said. "The other one with all the people in it. Yeah, those folks are gonna tell everybody in the world what you been up to." He smacked the stock of the Kalashnikov with his palm for emphasis. "But there's a couple people missing. Maybe more than a couple. You got a little black girl somewheres. And an old guy. There's a nice lady, too, name of Rachel Bloom. Hell, just bring out everybody you got stashed here."

There was a low murmur at the back of the throng as people moved aside to make way for a huge man. His dirty brown shirt was too tight and rode high on his belly, the buttons straining to remain fastened. He had a single bushy eyebrow that hid his eyes and a heavy shadow on his jaw from five o'clock some previous day. He had a machete in one hand and a pistol in the other.

"Stanley Mayhew," Goodman said.

"You remember me?"

"You're kinda hard to forget, Stanley."

"I missed you round here," Stanley said. "You was always good to me."

"I'd sure hate to have to fight you, Stanley."

Stanley snorted.

A bony little man shook his fist. "Get him, Stan!"

"Stanley, I got snipers all around the fence there," Goodman said.

"I ain't gonna fight you, Kurt."

"Well, that's a relief," Goodman said. "I had a bad feeling about that."

"But they didn't have to kill Lou-Ellen."

Goodman glanced at the feet of the dead lady near the church doors. They were all he could see of the body. The rest of her had fallen into the hedge.

"That was Lou-Ellen? The years have not been kind."

"Me and her had a thing," Stanley said.

"Oh, sorry."

Stanley shrugged. "You're lookin' for the lady?"

Goodman nodded. "You got her?"

"Yeah, they had me put her stuff in one house and her in the house next door." He pointed to a back door at the other end of the pool. "I been watching her most nights."

"What about the others?"

"Only girls I seen are the ones they bring through end of every month. Wasn't no black kid with 'em."

"Every month? You know what kinda jail time you folks are lookin' at? Human trafficking is about as serious as it gets."

"Yeah, I don't know. I just do my job. Make sure things stay peaceful. Only one left here's the lady."

"You wouldn't be kiddin' me, would you, Stanley?"

"Man, who cares? I'm outta here. This place is done."

He shrugged again, then turned, loped away through the silent crowd toward the gate. Goodman raised his gun and pointed it at the giant's back. Then he shook his head and lowered it. Arresting Stanley was a problem for another day. Rachel Bloom wasn't a resident of Paradise Flats, but Goodman was still responsible for her safety, and she needed immediate help.

"Serve and protect," he said to himself. "Who knew it would come to this?"

The throng of parishioners had already begun to drift away. Their perimeter had been breached, their church had been ruined, and the scariest guy any of them knew had just turned tail and fled. A lot had changed in a short amount of time, and the realization that they were facing prison sentences had shattered their notions of superiority. Some were following Stanley out to the fence; others were wandering aimlessly. Robbed of their self-righteous anger, they seemed pathetic. Brown had been a poor choice of uniform color. They looked like scouts without a map. At some point they would gather their belongings and leave, but Goodman knew he would eventually have to find them all, starting with Stanley.

The house Stanley had pointed out was next to the one Goodman and Travis had come through to gain entrance to the churchyard. Goodman tried the knob and it turned. The door swung open, and he stepped into a kitchen identical to the one next door. He flicked a switch on the wall above the sink before remembering that the electricity was dead. There was enough ambient light through the windows that he was able to pick out shapes and shadows. He crept silently through to the living room, wishing he had Travis's big dog with him. There was a television against the wall and a couch opposite it, but no other furnishings. A pile of empty beer cans and a greasy pizza box littered the floor beside the couch. Goodman went to the bottom of the staircase and listened. There was no sound, but there was an undefinable sense of heaviness in the air, someone else breathing somewhere. He gripped his gun tight and took the steps two at a time, watching the landing above for movement.

There were four doors on the second floor. One was open and led to a bathroom. The other three were closed. Goodman moved down the hall, stopping outside each door to listen. Behind the last door he heard a soft noise, fabric shifting, tendons creaking, and he reached out, turned the knob, then pushed the door open and flattened himself against the wall beside it.

Nothing happened.

He counted to ten, braced the machine gun against his shoulder, and entered the room in a running crouch. The walls were painted flat white and were bare of decoration. New indoor/outdoor carpeting covered the floor. Three sets of metal bunk beds filled the space, one each against the side walls and the third in the center, leaving a double walkway between them. A pasteboard chest of drawers was shoved under a window on the wall across from him.

A woman lay on the bottom middle bunk, her wrists handcuffed to a chain that ran to the rail above her head. Her dark hair was bedraggled, her face pale, and her red sweater torn and dirty. A strip of duct tape covered her mouth, and she breathed loudly through her nose.

"Mrs. Bloom?"

She didn't react.

He knelt beside the bed, placed the gun on the floor next to him, reached out, and gently shook her.

"Rachel?"

There was still no response. He carefully peeled the tape off her face and stuck it to the side of the bed.

He sat back on his heels and watched Rachel's face, wondering who had drugged her. Stanley or Heinrich? Maybe Rudy himself? On the most basic level, there was no escaping the knowledge that his family was responsible for this. How many girls had been shipped through the compound every month? Taken through the middle of Burden County right under his nose? He thought of his friend's missing daughter, the case he had never solved and that now seemed unsolvable. He thought of his daughter, his mother, his sister who had never had the chance to know Magda, of all the women who were important to him—who had *shaped* him—any of whom might have taken Rachel Bloom's place, chained to a bed, or packed into a truck like cattle. He remembered that Heinrich had never married, never had children, and he realized what a blessing that was. How many times had Uncle Heinrich visited them when Angela was a child? What wriggling wormlike visions had gone through Heinrich's head at the dinner table? Goodman's stomach turned. He had never been comfortable with emotions other than anger, and now he felt himself translating his shame and confusion to something more easily understood, something he could act on.

He rattled the chain and cursed himself for his lack of foresight. He had left his bolt cutters in the garage after finding the EMP device. A trip back to the garage would take too long. He considered kicking the bed rails apart to free the chain, but he was afraid Rachel might be hurt in the process. His best hope was that her captor had stashed the key to the cuffs somewhere nearby.

A rolling suitcase sat next to an overstuffed black duffel bag beside the door. He had passed them on the way into the room without paying much attention. Now he unzipped the bag and saw toiletries, folded T-shirts, socks balled up in pairs. Nothing of interest. But the suitcase was packed with hundred-dollar bills. Goodman didn't even try to estimate how much money it might add up to.

He stood and went to the dresser, opened the top drawer. Inside was clutter, like a shoe box in a flea market or the souvenir collection of a madman: a tiny stuffed bear with a red heart sewn on its chest, a locket on a silver chain, a mood ring that wouldn't have fit his pinky finger, a pair of glasses with rose-tinted lenses and a broken temple bar, a satin ballet slipper, a pink plastic coin purse with a cartoon cat on the side . . . A jumble of heartbreaking keepsakes.

Goodman picked up the coin purse and unfastened the clasp. It held a tube of bubble gum–flavored lip gloss, a house key, and a photo strip from a carnival booth: three pictures showing a pair of little girls mugging for the camera.

A voice from the doorway startled him and he dropped the purse. "If you're looking for the key to the handcuffs, it's not in there."

"Already figured that." Goodman took a step backward.

"Leave your gun where it is, brother."

Goodman sighed and turned around. "I shoulda kept a better eye on you, Heinrich."

# 13

When Skottie pulled the door open, there was nothing on the other side. No light, no sound, a complete vacuum.

"I have matches here somewhere," Travis said.

A voice drifted out of the darkness. "Is that the hunter there? Did you bring your negress or have you come alone?"

"Rudolph Bormann," Travis said.

"Yes, Dr. Roan, I'm right here."

"Mr. Bormann, I'm placing you under arrest," Skottie said.

"Mom!"

"Maddy?" Skottie took a step forward over the threshold, her Glock held down at her side, trying to locate where Maddy's voice had come from. She had no idea how big the room ahead of her was or where Rudy was located.

"Please stay where you are," Rudy said. "My saw has stopped working, along with the lights, but I am holding a scalpel against your child's throat, Mrs. Foster."

"Maddy, has he hurt you?"

"Mom, I'm scared. I can't move."

"Let her go, Bormann."

"Why would I do that?"

The *scritch* of a match being dragged across a rough surface, the smell of sulfur, and Skottie could suddenly see Travis next to her in a small circle of flickering light, a furry shadow beside him. Ahead of her the room was visible for a short distance, fading into black at the edges. She could see vague shapes at the fringe of visibility, Rudy leaning on a cane, standing over a still form on a metal table. They were roughly four feet away from her. She took a step forward and raised her gun.

"Mrs. Foster, if you knew what I've done in the past, you would believe me when I tell you I will spill this girl's blood. There's a drain in my floor here that's very thirsty."

Skottie stopped where she was. Travis exclaimed as the match burned down to his fingertips and he dropped it. They were plunged back into darkness. But now Skottie knew where her target was.

"Put your gun away," Rudy said. He had moved, his voice coming from a point two feet away from where he had been a moment earlier. "Do it now or she dies."

Skottie holstered her Glock. "Maddy, stay calm, okay? I'm right here."

"He hasn't done anything to me, Mom. He just talks and talks."

"I think you must have used my son's device," Rudy said. "The machine that kills electricity."

"It shut everything down," Travis said. "Your church is in chaos."

"I'm surprised, I'll admit that," Rudy said. "Very surprised. If everything else has stopped working, why am I still standing?"

"We have your weapons, your people, we have your device. You will not be able to sell it to Joseph Odek now."

"The machine was never intended for Odek. That device was always for me. My grand exit."

"I do not understand."

"I'm very old, Dr. Roan. And I'm tired. But the lightning won't let me rest. I know it's looking for me again. So what choice did I have, really? I need to kill the lightning if I ever want to escape. I can't control the weather, but I can shut off whatever's left inside me. I can stop it here and force it to find someone else."

"I still fail to understand," Travis said. "You thought an EMP generator would stop the electrical field within your body?"

"Imagine my disappointment right now."

"Enough of this," Skottie said. "Bormann, get down on the ground and put your hands behind your back."

"I don't think so, Mrs. Foster. Say good-bye to—"

"Bear," Maddy said. "Bear, *ataku!*"

There was a sudden sound of clattering metal, objects falling to the floor. Rudy began to scream.

Skottie ran forward, her hands out in front of her, until she reached the table. She ran her fingers gently along the edge until she encountered warm fabric. She could feel her daughter breathing, feel a heartbeat under her thin T-shirt.

"Mom?"

"Maddy?"

"There's straps, Mom. On my wrists and ankles. They have buckles."

Skottie found Maddy's right arm, her wrist, a thick leather cuff.

"Bear," Travis said. *"Haltu."*

Rudy continued to howl in pain, but Skottie felt Bear's soft mane brush against her as she worked at the buckle on Maddy's wrist. The dog's tongue lapped at Maddy's hand and made the cuff slick with drool.

"Hi, boy," Maddy said. Her voice sounded chipper, but then she drew in a series of short panting breaths and Skottie could tell the adrenaline rush of being rescued had worn off. Maddy was close to hyperventilating.

"I have her feet," Travis said. "Maddy, my name is Travis. I am a friend of your mother's."

"Please, just get me out of here."

"Stay calm, baby," Skottie said. "You're almost free."

"Maddy," Travis said, "did you know that a flock of starlings is called a murmuration?"

There was a long silence before Maddy spoke. "Is that true?"

"Yes. I only recently found it out. Thank you for watching Bear for me, Maddy."

"You're . . . He's a good dog."

"He does not usually take commands from strangers. He must like you very much."

Maddy's breathing slowed a bit, and Skottie put her hand on her daughter's chest for a few seconds to help reassure her, then attacked the straps again. They were ancient and stiff. She finished with one buckle and moved on to Maddy's left wrist. She could hear Travis at the other end of the table. They worked together, freeing Maddy as Rudy's moans began to subside. At last, Maddy came loose and Skottie scooped her up, carried her away in the direction of the door. Up the stairs, into the big room with its tiny windows, just light enough that she could see the way ahead. Below her, she could hear the Nazi groan, then the scuffle of shoes on the concrete floor. With the metal door standing open, Rudy's subbasement room had lost its soundproof quality, and they could hear Travis talking to the Nazi.

"I hope you are able to walk, but I will carry you if necessary."

"Where's my cane? Your dog bit me. He'll be put down, you know."

"Mom! They can't!"

"Hush, baby. Nobody's gonna hurt Bear."

"Skottie," Travis said, his voice floating up at her from the pitch black nothingness of the dungeon. "May I borrow your handcuffs?"

Skottie set Maddy down and took her hand, gripped it too hard, and Maddy yelped.

"Stay right here," Skottie said. "Don't move."

She patted her waistline, found the cuffs clipped to her belt, and went back down the stairs, sliding her free hand along the wall until she felt solid ground beneath her feet. Another match was lit and Travis stood in a pool of light beside her. Behind him, Rudolph Goodman was moving up behind him, his cane raised above his head. Skottie dropped the cuffs, pulled her Glock, and fired past Travis in one fluid motion. The match went out, the cane dropped to the floor, and Rudy grunted.

"Travis? Are you okay?"

"Yes, and thank you. I do hope you have not killed him."

"Does it really matter?"

"Yes. It matters to a great many people."

# 14

Heinrich Goodman sat on a bunk across from Rachel Bloom. His right arm hung useless at his side, and the machine gun in his left hand was aimed at the floor. Kurt Goodman leaned against the chest of drawers and cast longing glances at the gun he had left on the floor.

"You knew what was going on," Heinrich said. "You had to."

"Not nearly, I didn't," Goodman said. "No, sir."

"What did you think?"

"I guess I tried *not* to think too much."

"You got paid very well for a sheriff."

"I figured you were fleecing people dumb enough to join your church. That was okay with me. And maybe you made a mistake and somebody got hurt every once in a while. But they chose to be here, so they got the short end of the stick they grabbed." He pointed to Rachel, who had begun to stir, moaning in her sleep and tugging at the handcuffs. "She didn't choose this."

Heinrich groaned and rubbed his forehead with the heel of his good hand, inadvertently shaking the machine gun at the ceiling.

"You're bleedin' pretty good there," Goodman said.

"I was never going to harm her," Heinrich said. He squinted and aimed his gun at Goodman. "Her husband's a lawyer with the firm we use."

"Too expensive to chain *him* to the bed?"

"This business with the old woman and the state trooper stirred things up. I needed him to do things, but he was asking a lot of questions."

"I got some questions, too."

"You're my brother," Heinrich said. "Whatever our disagreements, we're family." He used the Kalashnikov to point at the suitcase in the corner. "I have enough there you could come with me. We could start again somewhere."

"Another Purity First?" Goodman put his hands in his jacket pockets, felt the smooth bulk of his stun gun.

"That was Dad's thing. He never saw the potential in it, but I did."

"Funneling drugs and people and guns through here?"

"Never drugs."

"How much money you got?"

"Plenty for both of us," Heinrich said.

"A little R & R on a beach somewheres?"

"Pretty ladies and fine food. No more tornadoes or blizzards. I've got it all figured out."

Goodman nodded and looked out the window. He took out his pouch of tobacco and pinched a fresh wad into his cheek. On top of the dresser, the cartoon cat winked at him from the side of the little pink purse.

"Sounds like a pretty sweet deal," Goodman said. "You got so much money, why didn't you get outta here yesterday or last week? Why'd you wait?"

"I still had a shipment to send out, more cash coming in."

"Couldn't leave it behind, huh?"

"You were distracting the hunter. I thought I had time. I thought the holiday would slow everyone else down. I only needed till the end of the week."

"You shouldn't've took the girl."

"I see that now."

"And you shouldn't have brung my deputy into this."

"Christian's *my* nephew."

"He was *my* deputy."

"This is pointless. Do you have a car? We should go."

"Thing is, my car's not gonna work. Nothing's getting out of here except maybe that big juice-killer truck you got. Don't think we'll get too far in that."

Rachel moaned again and her eyes fluttered open. Goodman pushed away from the chest of drawers and looked down at her. He smiled and hoped he didn't look menacing.

"Ma'am, we're gonna get you out of here in just a minute, okay?"

She shook her head. The skin around her mouth looked sore where he'd pulled the tape off. She worked her jaw without speaking and rolled her shoulders.

"Leave her," Heinrich said. "We don't have much time."

"Where's my duffel of undies?"

"What?"

"You wanted me with you, so I guess you must've already got me a change of socks or something."

"I don't—"

"How'm I gonna go along if I don't got socks?"

He wheeled and pulled out the stun gun, reaching out toward his brother, already pressing the button with his thumb. But Heinrich was ready for him, raising the machine gun. He fired off a burst that splintered the floor and the box springs under Rachel. Goodman tried to dodge and smacked his head against the railing of the top bunk. As he fell back he brought his knee up against Heinrich's jaw and heard a loud pop. He ducked and lurched forward again, falling on top of his brother. The stun gun was pressed between them, and Goodman's thumb was trapped holding down the button so that the voltage was divided between them. They juddered and shook, the thin mattress bouncing under them.

Goodman accidentally swallowed his tobacco and gagged. He rolled sideways and dropped the stun gun, jammed his arms outward, unable to work his fingers, and knocked the Kalashnikov away from his brother.

He fell off the edge of the bed, still tingling, and pushed himself up off the floor, blinking hard and shaking his head back and forth, trying to bring the room into focus. He crawled around in a circle, scrabbling at the carpet until he found the warm stock of the Kalashnikov, and he grabbed it. He got to his knees and swung around as Heinrich sat up.

"Kurt—"

Goodman pulled the trigger and Heinrich's body danced down the edge of the bed and toppled to the floor. Goodman took his finger off the trigger and counted to ten again, watching Heinrich's body, then he dropped the gun and stood up.

As the echo of gunfire faded, he realized Rachel Bloom was screaming, and he turned toward her, held his hands out.

"Give me a second and we'll get you out of here," he said.

He went to Heinrich and bent over him, checked each of his pockets until he found a key ring. The smallest key on the ring was stamped with the brand name of the handcuff manufacturer. He held it out for Rachel to see and knelt by the bed.

"You know Doc Roan," he said. "I'm his good buddy. We been looking for you."

# 15

The stairs were easier going up than they had been coming down, except that they had the extra weight of Rudy Goodman supported between them, his cuffed hands swinging limp, blood trickling down his arms, dripping on their shoes. Maddy climbed the steps on her own, clinging to Bear. They emerged into the church nave and stood blinking for a moment at the sudden daylight, and at the damage that had been done to the old stone structure. The back wall had crumbled further and rifts had opened in the ceiling. Water trickled from above and splashed onto the remains of the intricate woodwork and the stained glass.

Quincy was sitting in a front pew, and he jumped up when they entered.

"Your dad's doing okay for now, amigo," he said, "but I think we better get out of here. This whole building's gonna fall apart."

"Let it," Skottie said.

# 16

They came out of the church into pouring rain. Lightning lit up the sky. Travis carried his father in his arms. Quincy had hoisted Rudy over his shoulder in a fireman carry, and Skottie carried Maddy, aware she was squeezing her too tight but not caring.

A handful of the men and women of Purity First were wandering in and out of the sheds carrying bags and boxes, their brown shirts hanging limp and wet. Sheriff Goodman came out of a house beside the church with his arm around a woman's shoulders, supporting her weight. Travis had to look hard to recognize Rachel Bloom.

"She'll be okay," Goodman said as they drew even with the others. "Probably not goin' to any church socials for a while."

"Good work, Sheriff."

Goodman flashed him something he must have thought was a smile and tipped his hat. Rainwater poured off the brim.

Quincy let go of Rudy's body and let him drop in the mud.

"Damn," Goodman said.

"I am sorry," Travis said. "It was not my intention to kill your father."

"It was me," Skottie said, raising her voice to be heard over the rain. "It's not his fault. I did it."

ALEX GRECIAN

Goodman shook his head. "Hell of a day I'm having."

Travis took a step toward the sheriff, but stopped when he felt the hair on the back of his neck stand up. His skin tingled with static electricity. He looked at Skottie, and her eyes were wide. She felt it, too. She turned back toward the shelter of the stone wall, shielding Maddy with her body, and at the same instant lightning slashed down, striking the flagpole. Every shadow in the compound disappeared, swallowed by the bright blaze of electricity. Travis jumped, and he heard Maddy scream. The flagpole sizzled with heat and the flags burst into flames, the wolf's head suddenly ablaze. A finger of lightning split off, flashed through the air, and touched Rudy Goodman. Rudy twitched and writhed in the mud as the lightning faded to an afterimage and a clap of thunder rocked the compound.

There was a moment of complete stillness, even the rain seemed to stop, frozen in midair, then life and motion returned again. The flags atop the pole crackled and sparked in defiance of the pelting rain, turning black at the edges.

"Quincy," Travis said, "are you all right?"

"I'm fine, amigo," he said. He let out a long sigh. "Just scared the hell out of me."

He dropped to one knee and held two fingers against Rudy's throat. He leaned down and listened, then looked back up at them, wide-eyed.

"You're not gonna believe this," Quincy said.

PART FOUR

THANKSGIVING

# CHAPTER TWELVE

## 1

There was no turkey dinner for any of them that day.

Four agents from the Kansas Bureau of Investigation arrived before nine o'clock that morning after having received a tip from the Comanche County sheriff that girls were being run out of Purity First. They brought the local police and Lieutenant Johnson of the Highway Patrol with them.

The presence of Sheriff Goodman and Deputy Griffith helped Skottie and Travis persuade the other authorities that they weren't vigilantes. The sheriff told a story that was at least partially true: He had been given reason to believe that a young girl was being held against her will in the church and was in imminent danger. He had deputized Officer Foster and Dr. Roan, and they had entered the compound without a warrant but with just cause.

KBI agents went through the churchyard and the outbuildings and seized the weapons cache. They found evidence that people had been chained to beds in many of the buildings. Rachel Bloom was led away to an ambulance and, along with Ransom Roan and Rudy Goodman, was taken to the Burden County Clinic.

Dr. Iversen was called in to deal with the corpses of Heinrich Goodman and Lou-Ellen Quinlan. The doctor greeted Skottie and gave Maddy a lollipop from his pocket.

"You are a very brave girl," he said.

When he left to examine Heinrich's body, Maddy put the lollipop in her pocket and shook her head. "A lollipop?"

"Hush," Skottie said.

"But a lollipop, Mom."

Skottie laughed. "Maddy!"

"What am I, five years old?"

All of them—Skottie, Maddy, Travis, Sheriff Goodman, and Quincy—were taken to the sheriff's office in Paradise Flats, where the KBI had set up a temporary base. A canine control officer was called in, but Travis persuaded the agent in charge to let him keep control of Bear. They put Bear in the enclosure behind the offices with the three German shepherds. The other dogs retreated to the far corner of their pen while Bear ate their food.

All Thanksgiving day, they sat in plastic chairs in the waiting room, were called into the back offices one at a time for questioning, then brought back out and left waiting until they were called back again to confirm answers they had already given. When they were finally released, they were too tired to talk.

Skottie took Maddy home, and Emmaline fed them soup and put them to bed.

# 2

Skottie slept until the following afternoon and woke with a splitting headache. She stumbled out into the living room, surprised to see Sheriff Goodman dozing on the couch in front of the television. Maddy sat on the floor in front of him, braiding Bear's mane. The house smelled like cranberries and roasting turkey.

Emmaline was in the kitchen, cooking a late Thanksgiving feast. Skottie tried to help, but Emmaline pushed her out of the kitchen.

"You just tell everybody to wash up," Emmaline said. "Five minutes till we eat."

Skottie delivered the message. Bear rolled his big mournful eyes up at Skottie as if asking to be rescued, but he didn't move from Maddy's side.

Goodman yawned and stood up. He grabbed his hat from the back of the couch.

"Just checkin' in on you today," he said. He looked like he had aged a decade since Skottie had first met him. "I don't mean to be underfoot."

"I'm sure my mom cooked way more than we can eat."

"Thanks, but I got plans to eat Thanksgiving leftovers with my girls and Quincy."

"Listen, I really am sorry about your dad."

"Don't be. I don't claim to be any relation to that monster. What they're finding in that place of his, the things he was doing . . . I had no idea, but this has been comin' for him since before I was born."

"Any word from the KBI?"

"They ain't gonna tell me anything. I'm not exactly their kinda lawman." He sighed. "I think I'm gonna hang up the badge. After I fire Puckett."

"Can I watch you do that?"

"Front-row seat," Goodman said. "Got a lot I wanna do. The church'll drift apart, now that my dad and brother are gone, but I wanna speed up the process some. I'm gonna tear down what's left of the fence, fix up the hole in the wall, and turn that place into something useful. Maybe serve lunches in there." He shrugged. "Enough harm got done to folks out there, be nice if the place was good for somebody."

"If Heinrich was selling weapons and . . . well, people . . ."

"Yeah, he had some money, but the KBI's gonna seize that. Too bad, too."

"You think it'll be easy to quit being sheriff?"

"You think I oughta stay? After everything goin' on under my nose?"

"You think you should take all the responsibility?"

Goodman grinned at her. "I was never much good at it anyway. My aim was running folks off if I thought they might be trouble. Turns out the trouble was already there. But this way I get to go out on a high note, a blaze of glory. I rescued the damsel in distress, you know?"

Skottie laughed.

"Anyway, I'm the only Goodman left, and it'd be nice if that name could stand for something."

"People are gonna need a sheriff."

"I got an idea one of my deputies can do the job better'n me." He winked. "Gonna talk to Quincy about running. Think he'll go for it?"

"He'd be good for it," Skottie said.

"I think so, too. And I'd be around if he needs advice."

"He shot that woman, though."

"It was a righteous kill," Goodman said.

"Doesn't matter. He shot a white woman at her church."

"Well, since his rifle disappeared, I don't see how anyone's gonna prove that ever happened."

"Where . . . ?"

"You see how many rifles them people had out there? Shotguns, machine guns, you name it. If somebody dropped one or two more in there, it'd be like needles in a haystack." He tipped his hat and winked.

Travis was on the front porch smoking a cigarette when they went out.

"I am only having one," he said. "Then I will throw the pack away."

"Hell, smoke 'em all, Doc," Goodman said. "We ain't gonna tell nobody."

"Happy Thanksgiving," Travis said.

They were quiet for a while after Goodman drove away. The rain had turned into a light snowfall that dusted the hedges and the porch railing. At last Skottie broke the silence.

"Any news about your dad?"

"No good news," Travis said. "But my mother is on her way. I will take her to the hospital when she arrives. My father has some motor control, and his mind appears to be his own."

"Must be frustrating for him."

"I imagine so."

Skottie realized Brandon was probably still in the hospital, too, still recovering from a concussion and worrying about their daughter. Skottie decided she would take him some turkey and pie later in the day.

"I think my father was on a suicide mission, ramming the church the way he did."

"What he did was heroic."

"Perhaps," Travis said. "I cannot decide whether he truly wanted to die after what was done to him, but I believe he thought his death would bring attention to the church and get the authorities to take a look at what was happening there." He didn't look at her, but stared out across the low rooftops, where snow was gathering along the gutters and eaves. The air smelled clean. "Either way, he will not be coming back to the Foundation."

Skottie touched his arm and he shook his head.

"It was time anyway," he said. "He can retire knowing he found Rudolph Bormann and helped bring him to some kind of justice." He ground his cigarette out against the railing. "You know, I have spent the past few days wondering why someone would choose to exile herself in this place. Kansas, at least this part of it, is so quiet."

They stood and listened to the patter of snow all around them and the muted sounds of Emmaline bustling about inside the house.

"But that is why you like it, am I right? I think I understand it now."

"You could stay here," Skottie said. "Real estate's cheap."

Travis smiled. "Perhaps when I am my father's age. I still have work to do. The Foundation always has work to do. But we will be shorthanded now. I spoke to my mother about you, and she trusts my judgment. Should you wish to move on from the Highway Patrol at some point, leave all this peace and quiet behind, you would be welcome to join us."

"I don't know anything about hunting Nazis."

"It is not an exact science. And hunting Nazis is not all we do. I told you when we met that I am kept busy ferreting out all manner of bad people. In fact, I plan to go after a different sort of evil man as soon as I can."

"Joseph Odek?"

Before he could reply, the screen door banged open and Maddy grabbed her by the hand, pulling her toward the house.

"C'mon," Maddy said. "Grandma's putting out the food."

"Turkey time?"

"Yup." Maddy cleared her throat and looked at Travis, then looked quickly away.

"Do you know what a flock of turkeys is called, Maddy?"

"No."

"Neither do they." He smiled.

Maddy grinned back at him. They went inside, where Emmaline was setting a huge bowl of potatoes in the middle of the table. The turkey was already there, plump and golden on a silver platter, waiting to be carved. Around it were dishes overflowing with pearl onions, greens, yams, soft white butter, tiny pickles and olives, a tray of cornbread, and a plate holding a rare steak for Bear. Emmaline wiped her hands on her apron and sat down at the head of the table, prompting everyone else to sit, too. Bear padded over and plunked down under the table at Travis's feet. Travis winced when he saw the colorful beads Maddy had put in the dog's mane.

"Skottie," Emmaline said, "why don't you say a few words to start us off?"

"Okay." Skottie looked around the table and cleared her throat. "I guess . . . well, I guess I have a lot to be thankful for," she began.

And she realized as she said it that it was true.

## DECEMBER 2018

He was released from the hospital and was transferred by bus to a federal prison camp in Minnesota. He had nothing with him but a small overnight bag and the clothes on his back.

He was issued a green one-piece uniform, a towel, and a washcloth, then escorted to an eight-by-eight-foot cubicle that contained a cot, a small table, and a shelf for books. He had arrived late in the day and was warned that he had only ten minutes before lights-out. Then he was left alone.

Other inmates milled about in the narrow walkway outside his cubicle. Some of them looked at him with open curiosity, but no one spoke to him. He folded his towel and set it on the bookshelf with his washcloth, changed into the green jumpsuit, and lay down on the cot. He did not think about anything at all, and soon he drifted to sleep.

The following morning he was taken to a large room filled with long cafeteria-style tables. Five minutes later he was joined by an attorney who introduced herself as Abbey Roth. She sat down across from him, opened her briefcase, and took out an iPad, which she glared at for a long moment, her eyes darting back and forth as she read. Finally she looked up at him.

"I'm here on behalf of Morrison, Ellis, and Moore," she said. "Your New York lawyers."

"They sent me a Jew?"

"I can leave, but I can't promise they'll send anybody else for you."

"How long do I have to stay here?"

She shook her head and looked back down at her tablet. "Probably quite a while."

"I entered this country illegally in 1951," he said. "I've done my research. The Justice Department will want to deport me, won't they?"

"Since 1951, sir, you have apparently murdered and mutilated several people. Engaged in human trafficking and sold weapons overseas, using your church as both a base and a cover. Allegedly."

"My son was responsible for the human trafficking. And for the guns."

"Is that Heinrich?"

"Yes," Rudy said.

"He's dead."

Rudy sighed and looked up at the big clock over the door. "Heinrich was always weaker than his brother."

"Well, it's not like he died of natural causes."

"They can't prove I did anything. The same is true for the murder charges."

"They're dragging the reservoir at Kirwin sanctuary," she said. "And they're finding bodies that have been there for . . . well, maybe for decades."

"Can those be traced back to me?"

"They're going to try. They're building a case. And while they do, you're going to have to wait in here."

"No bail?"

"No bail."

"They can't hold me indefinitely," he said. "I know my rights."

Abbey Roth stared at him. Then she stood without a word and put the iPad back in her briefcase. She latched it and picked it up by the handle and walked away. When she reached the door, she turned back toward him, motioning for the guard to wait.

"They can do whatever they want with you, sir. They're going to run down the clock, wait until you die in here. And, frankly, I have a lot of other cases to deal with. I don't think I'll be very helpful to you."

The guard opened the door for her, and she walked out.

He was led back to his cubicle. His towel and washcloth were gone, and he assumed they had been stolen by another inmate. He looked at his empty bookshelf, at the cot with its paper-thin mattress, then turned and left the cubicle. He walked through the maze of cubicles to the window, which was covered from top to bottom, side to side, with wire mesh.

Rudolph Bormann, formerly Rudy Goodman of Kansas, was ninety-four years old that winter. He looked out the window at a chain-link fence that surrounded the building, beyond it a broad empty field. Clouds were gathering at the horizon, and Rudy could hear distant thunder.

## ACKNOWLEDGMENTS

The fictions in this book are entirely mine.

I would like to thank the following people for the facts.

Trooper Ryan Kufahl and the Kansas Highway Patrol, Aaron Breitbart and the Simon Wiesenthal Center, Dr. Lyle Noordhoek, Tony Green, and Till and Alison Clayton.

I am also grateful to my agent, Seth Fishman, and everyone at the Gernert Company; my editor Mark Tavani, Helen Richard, Ashley Hewlett, and all the wonderful people at Putnam; my copy editor, Kate Hurley; Jane Ashkar; Lindsay Kufahl; Melanie Worsley and Kevin O'Leary; Philip Grecian; Roxane White; Ande Parks; and the Bad Karma crew.

And, of course, Christy and Graham.